JOHN B. OLSON

A NOVEL

PUBLISHING GROUP

WWW.BHPublishingGroup.com

Published by B&H Publishing Group
Nashville, Tennessee

Dewey Decimal Classification: F
Subject Heading: MYSTERY FICTION \
SUPERNATURAL—FICTION \ GYPSIES—FICTION

Scripture quotations are from the Holy Bible, New
International Version, copyright © 1973, 1978, 1984 by
International Bible Society.

To Amy,
The heart whose beat fills me with life.

I

$\backsim$ 1 $\sim$

Mariutza

SMOOTH MOONLIGHT, SOFT AND timid as a sleeping babe's breath, seeped through the forest canopy, painting Old Man Oak's mossy beard with twisting ribbons of silver and shadow. The swamp folks were full awake now. All stoked up with joy, singing hallelujah for the tolerable coolness of another summer night. Bachelor bullfrogs barked out their steady bass against a piercing cicada threnody. Crickets and peepers and creepers hollered their praises full on top of the other, singing out to the Lord for the blessings He hath made.

It was a glorious song, filled with deep magic and considerations of awesome wonder. It made a body thankful to be alive. Squish-squashing through soft cool mud. Hop-scotching dead wood and fresh fallen branches. Pausing to look out across dark star-dusted waters where the proud Cypress sisters, skirts hitched high above dark bony knees, waded through reflections of ringing light. Swaying and sighing to the night music. The sounds of blessed freedom and sweet never-ending joy.

MARIUTZA LET LOOSE WITH a wistful sigh and felt her way through the dark forest. Purodad would be getting home soon. He was going to be mad as a dirt dauber when he learned she'd run off again.

But she couldn't just sit there in the wagon and let him lock her up. She was a proper lady now, a full-grown woman—Miss Caralee said so herself. Proper ladies didn't hold to being locked up in diddlecars. Proper ladies had work to do. Washing and cooking. Tending to the nets.

Gradually, step by step, the forest opened out into a moonlit clearing. Mari tiptoed around a sun-burned vegetable patch and ran for the cover of a gnarled old oak tree. Miss Caralee would take her side. Purodad was getting superstitious in his old age. She'd said it herself. She wouldn't stand for any more of his nonsense. That's what she called it: utter nonsense.

"Yoo-hoo! Miss Caralee?" she called out from behind the old oak. "Don't shoot. It's me, Mariutza."

She peeked out at a ramshackle hut pieced together with drift-boards from the storm. "I'm coming out now. Just me alone." Stepping out from behind the tree, she hesitated. The cook fire wasn't burning and there weren't any candlelights shining through the windows. Caralee couldn't be off visiting. It was long time past dark. Had she already gone off to bed?

"Here I am. Walking to the door!"

A scrape sounded inside the shack. The clank of metal against metal.

"Don't shoot. It's me!" Mari put some wind behind her words. Miss Caralee's eyes were sharp as stickers, but her ears were starting to wear thin.

A strong voice, dry and weathered as sun-bleached driftwood, called out through the screen. "Lands, chile. What you doin' out

the door? Night's most black as soot. Don't just stand there gawping like a catfish. Come on up!"

Mari ran up to the shack and sat down on the smooth old
stump just outside the narrow door.

The screen flared bright as a match struck against the jamb
post. Hollow cheeks and soft dark eyes. The flame flickered and
steadied as it took hold of a tallow candle. Miss Caralee pressed it
against the screen and peeped outside, squinting into the darkness
like it was light.

"Your grandfather know you out this late?"

"He said he was going to lock me up. Keep me in the diddlecar
till I learned some sense."

"Mmm-hmm . . ." The ancient woman sighed. "That man!
What have you gone and did now?"

"I was just looking. Didn't nobody seen me. There haven't
been any hunters since spring."

"Lord have mercy. Spying on the road again. Don't you have
work to tend?"

"No, ma'am. I done finished it. But if Purodad locks me up, I
won't be getting nothing done. He thinks he can do it all himself, but
you know he can't. He's got town folk to visit. Healings to tend."

"Hush up, chile. Ain't nobody locking nobody up, but you
listen to me. You a grown woman now. Time is for you to be telling *him* what to do. If you want to go running your skirts through
the pluff mud, that's nobody's business but your own—so long's
your work's done—but laws . . . spying on the road? I told you that
myself. If Mr. Jonah say it ain't safe, it ain't safe."

"But if they don't see me—"

"You think your grandfather don't know what is? Folks all
around paying him good money for his sight, and you too good
to listen?"

"No, ma'am." Mari looked down at the ground and tried to put some respectful attitude in her voice. "But I was just—"

"Just say you're sorry and don't do it no more. That's all he want."

"But, if nobody seen me—"

"*If?* That's what that little white spot say? *If?*" Caralee jabbed a gnarled finger at the screen.

Mari caught her breath. She was pointing at her chest. Had Purodad told her? It was supposed to be a secret.

"That's right. That little white spot on your chest. You was the one what prayed a healing? That how you know so much more'n Mr. Jonah?"

"I wasn't saying . . ." Mari's throat tightened, choking off her words. "I didn't mean to . . ." Her eyes filled with tears. "I—"

"You a sweet girl. I know you don't mean nothing by it, but you got to listen to your grandfather. Mr. Jonah's got the sight. If he say it ain't safe, it ain't safe."

"Yes'm." Mari hung her head and blinked her tears onto the ground.

"That's right. Maybe he ought to lock you up. Running off in the middle of the night and scaring a body half to death. That how I taught you?"

"No, ma'am."

"That's right. Now get on to that fancy diddlecar wagon of yourn before he sets the hunters on you hisself."

Mari nodded and looked up at her teacher. The old woman's mouth was pressed firm, but her eyes still had the laugh in them. If she wasn't too angry, maybe she'd be willing to—

"Go on. Get going. And don't peep out of that wagon till Mr. Jonah say it's safe."

"Maybe if you come with me, he won't be so—"

A scream blasted through Mari's senses, sending her staggering into the screen. Another scream. Another. They were inside her head, dozens and dozens of them, clawing and scratching like possums in a wire cage.

"Lord have mercy. What's gotten in you, chile? What you going on?"

"Don't you *hear* them?" Mari swung around and searched the shrieking darkness. The whole forest echoed with ringing silence. The frogs and peepers and creepers, they were still as the deep waters. Even the mosquitoes had left off their buzzing.

"Lord have mercy." Caralee jangled with the latch and pushed open the screen. "Come in the door, chile! It's the Badness. It's the Badness for sure!"

A hand closed around her arm and tugged her back toward the door.

"No ma'am, please. I can't!" Mari twisted free of her teacher's grasp and jerked away from the doorway. She was being ornery and obstinate and desperately wicked, but she didn't have time to put on the respect. The Badness had found the woods. She was supposed to be making for the hiding place.

"Come on, chile. This ain't no house to fear. Get in the door!" Feeble hands pawed at Mari's back. "Get in the door now!"

Another scream rattled up her spine, filling her head with the rabble of a hurricane. She weren't a baby no more! Miss Caralee didn't know anything. A real Standing didn't go inside. A real Standing wasn't supposed to be afraid!

"Chile, please." Caralee whimpered in her ear. "Come in the door. Mr. Jonah'll understand. He just want you safe . . ."

Mari twisted away and pushed across the cook yard, leaning into the dark waves crashing against her mind. She had to get to the hiding place. It was in the training. She had to get to the hiding place now!

Pale blue moonlight appeared before Mari's eyes. A patchwork of branches, bobbing up and down. The soft glow of a distant lantern set in a shuttered window. Their diddlecar! The Badness had found it!

"Purodad!" Mari broke into an all-out run. Through the garden, across the clearing, dodging in and out between the shadows of phantom trees, she leaped and twisted and splashed through the roiling blackness. Jolting moonlight flashed inside her head. Cloaked figures, maddening screams, the slap of raking branches.

The Badness! The swamp was drowning in it. Suffocating, choking, soaking deep into her soul. A dim shadow swept past her, catching her arm and spinning her around. Tangles of grasping vines, sucking mud, splashing water.

"Purodad!" The forest shifted around her. "Purodad, I'm coming!"

The weight of a hundred staring eyes pressed into her brain. They knew where she was. They would destroy her, suck the marrow from her bones. She was theirs now. Helpless and alone. There could be no escape.

Clawing at her face and hair, she threw herself to the ground, rolling over and over across the bracken. It was in her head. Pouring out from deep inside her filthy heart.

A gunshot sounded against her screams. Distant shouts.

"No!" Mari fought to her feet and stumbled forward, ripping through clinging stickers, pushing through clacking reeds. She was running now, faster and faster toward the distant light. The diddlecar pounded and jolted into view. A light jumped and flared in the window. "Purodad?"

Throwing open the door, she dove inside and rolled. Onto her knees, grasping at the swinging door, she slammed it shut and yanked down on the bolt. She scoured the interior of the wagon with darting eyes. Her grandfather wasn't home yet? That meant he was still—

An exultant scream shook the wagon, sending Mari crashing into the floor. A chorus of answering howls jolted like lightning through her body. Purodad was out there. He was out there with *them*.

Holy One, please . . . I can't do it. A tremor shuddered up her spine, sucking the heat from her body. *I know I can't.* She climbed unsteadily onto her feet and slid back the door bolt.

Blackness pushed into the wagon, filling her mind with a muzzy haze. *Help me.* She tumbled out of the wagon and landed in a heap on the ground.

Another howl rattled into her brain. Mari's stomach seized up. She was on her hands and knees. Her stomach heaved, over and over. The Badness buzzed in her head like a swarm of cuckoo bees. Filling her, surrounding her, covering her skin with stinging pain.

Holy One, please . . . She pushed onto her feet and tottered forward. He was out there. Out there with the Badness. Her gentle, crinkly eyed grandfather! She broke into a run, faster and faster, charging through thickets, plunging through rending, tearing thorns.

Another gunshot rang out. Another and another. Flashes of sparking light.

A jolt slammed into her, knocking her onto the ground. Tongues of burning darkness licked at her skin, coiling around her arms, forcing their way into her mouth and nose. A scream convulsed her body, but the Badness wouldn't let it escape. She was drowning in it. Couldn't breathe.

A sudden explosion of blinding light ripped through the forest. Shining through her eyelids, into her skull, penetrating deep into her brain. The swamp shook beneath her, sending her skittering across the ground. The earth was moving, tilting onto its side. Mari grabbed at a sapling, clung to it with both hands as she was tipped out over the inky blackness of the night sky far below.

The light faded slowly and finally winked out. Suddenly the ground was beneath her again and the sky was back in its rightful place. Silence rang like a bell. Its throbbing echoes reverberated in her ears. Something had happened. Something deep and awesome in its all-consuming terror. She rolled onto her back and lay, panting and trembling, at the bottom of the deep moonlit night.

"Purodad?" Her whisper shouted against the silence.

A thud sounded in the distance. The crackle of dry leaves.

"Puro—" Her voice caught in her throat as a rustle shook the undergrowth nearby. Something was moving toward her. Something big.

Mari rolled over and tried to climb onto her feet, but her legs were heavy as wet shrimp nets. She couldn't move. Couldn't lift herself from the covering weeds.

A gurgling rasp sounded from the edge of a clump of trees. It was getting closer. Mari struggled onto her knees, but she could only stare. A low shadow was creeping through the foliage. Panting breaths. Sputtering gasps.

The figure broke through the leaves and collapsed at the base of the trees.

"Purodad!" Mari jumped up and stumbled toward her grandfather. "Purodad!" Her eyes filled with tears. She collapsed in a heap at his side and clutched at his hand.

A dark stain slowly spread across the old man's stomach. He was coughing now. Gasping for breath.

"No!" Mari pushed off the ground and knelt at his side. "Stay right here! Miss Caralee'll know what to do."

"Quiet!" her grandfather barked. "Listen to me!"

"But Miss Caralee . . ." Mari clasped his hand to her chest. "I'll be right back. She'll pray a healing. You'll see. Everything's going to be fine. I'll be—"

"Listen to me! This is my time. Nothing can stop it now."

"Grandfather, no! We'll pray—"

"You're no granddaughter of mine!" the old man rasped. "No relation at all. Hear?"

"I'm sorry, I didn't mean—" A sob wracked her body, sealing off her throat.

"No relation at all." The man's face tightened and his head lolled back onto the ground.

"I'm sorry," Mari blurted through her tears. "I tried to hide. I didn't think they seen me. I—"

A wheezing sigh cut her off. Her grandfather's eyes were still open. His lips were trembling. He was trying to talk.

Mari leaned closer and shook the tears from her eyes. His breath was coming in short gurgling gasps. Finally he took a hiccupping breath and let it out in a long sigh.

"Find him. I want you to promise me. Find him first. Then find the others."

"Find who? Miss Caralee?"

"Shhhh . . ." Purodad's face tightened into a grimace and gradually relaxed with another sigh. "Dig the grave yourself. Round. Two and a half feet wide. Hear?"

"No!" Mari shook her head. "You're not going to die. You can't. You're the prophet—"

"Hurry. They're gone now, but they'll be back soon." His eyelids fluttered and slowly drifted shut. "Bury me standing. I must be buried standing."

↶ 2 ↷

Jazz

JAZZ TOOK A DEEP breath, letting the smoke-laced air slide across the mic in a long, rasping sigh. E minor. He switched keys, blending the Steinway's plaintive tones to the sound of his breathing. A high-pitched buzz rang in his ears. The room was starting to spin again. He shut his eyes and pressed his chin against the microphone, a solid anchor against the gently swaying room. The murmur of distant voices lulled him. Gulf waves crashing against a distant shore. Soft, soothing. A balmy breeze on a warm winter afternoon.

A woman's tittering laugh shocked him back to the present. Had he quit playing? He glanced up at the manager of the club. Gerard was leaning over the bar, talking to a brunette in a neon pink top. The whole building could burn down and Gerard wouldn't notice. But the customers . . .

Jazz blinked the grit out of his eyes and upped the tempo, hammering at the old ivories, left hand battling the right in a discordant duel between majors and minors. One by one the murmuring voices died away, leaving the bar frozen in silent expectation. Jazz could feel their confusion, the building sense of anticipation.

He took another breath, filling his lungs with burning pain. His right hand hammered harder, faster, building to a last frenzied gasp before collapsing under the weight of the throbbing bass. C washed away by E minor. Hope swallowed up by despair.

"Washed, washed away with the waters . . ." Jazz's rasping voice slurred in and out through the tumbling notes. "Many lost . . . many more, many maybe . . . many more waiting to be found." The lyrics scraped past raw vocal chords. Two hours tops. It was all he had left. "Washed, washed away with the waters . . ." He flung the words into the room, letting them splash like a pounding tide against startled concrete faces.

"I remember, I remember, when I was young I remember most of the time . . ." Jazz pressed his face to the microphone, filling his senses with the cold taste of metal and stale beer. "The sun so shining-bright on your face . . . in the memory of moments we stole from this place, I can see that the ages will never erase . . . most of the time."

A natural blonde was on her feet. Stepping toward him. Flushed cheeks, deer-shined eyes. The cut of her dress screamed money.

Digging deep, he channeled even more intensity into his voice. Longing, yearning, unendurable pain, he sent it reverberating through the room, surrounding her, lifting her up, pounding into her swaying slender form.

"Washed, washed away with the waters . . ."

Her lips parted. She was gripping her purse in both hands. White-knuckled, trembling arms.

Almost . . . Just a little bit more. This could be his big score, but everything had to be just right.

He pulled suddenly back on the piano, letting his voice hang on the thin desolate air.

Her eyes locked onto his. He could feel the rise and fall of her swelling chest. He had her. It was going to be a huge score. Fifty dollars at least. Maybe even a hundred. He'd gotten bigger tips from women much less well-off than this one.

Flashing her a smile, he let his fingers drift across the keyboard in a tripping musical interlude, an invitation for her to approach the bench and pour out her heart, to exchange cold cash for the privilege of remembering what it meant to be alive.

She smiled back at him, but didn't move. Something was holding her back. What was it? The piano? He knew he should have switched to guitar. Too late now. Maybe a ballad would do it. Something soft and innocent. A ballad of friendship and faith and love. Quick, before she got away. She was already starting to—

A pulse of blinding white light erupted inside his head. Burning heat. Stabbing pain. He slumped forward, crashing through discordant notes into the depths of a dark and churning sea. The clamor of frightened voices rose up all around him and then receded like sea foam riding the surface of a spent Gulf-coast wave. Gentle hands buoyed him up. He was floating now, drifting. Riding the soft swells of inky black waters. Staring down into their shifting rippling depths.

Smooth moonlight suffused a dimly lit forest deep below the surface of the murky waters. Movement caught his eye. Dark figures wove in and out through the trees. The darkness closed around him and he fell. Swooping down in a long graceful arc, he hit the lead runner with a mind twisting jolt.

Dark branches slashed across his face. Panting breath rasped in his ears. He was running. Twisting and turning, dodging this way and that through shadowy bushes and moss-draped trees. They were gaining on him. Getting closer. He vaulted a dark thicket and ducked beneath a canopy of reaching limbs.

An unearthly howl sounded behind him, blasting through his body like an icy winter storm. What was going on? It was a dream; it had to be. If he could just stop and think, it would all go away.

But he couldn't stop. His muscles refused to respond. Something had taken over his body. He could feel its alien presence pulsing just beneath his consciousness. Exhausted, terrified, lashing out like a wounded beast.

A low growl rattled through his bones.

It came from inside him, behind him, through the darkness all around. The crash of massive bodies sounded to his right. More crashing to his left. They were spreading out, surrounding him. He had to go faster. Had to. Why wouldn't his body respond?

Mariutza!

The word reverberated through his frame. Was it a name? Why was it so important? The beasts were going to kill him. Was that what they were called?

The darkness rang like a snapped guitar string. The twang of bullets ripped past his ears.

Exhaustion pressed down on him. Suddenly he was weak and weary, unspeakably old. It was finished. They were going to kill him. The long fight was finally over. He ducked around one last tree and plodded out into a moonlit clearing.

Just ahead of him, backlit by an enormous pink-orange moon, an old oak tree rose up from a mound like a grasping, twisted hand.

The vision hit Jazz with the force of a wrecking ball. He dropped to his knees, reached out with tingling arms toward the moon as a million wildfires raged inside his brain.

Revelation.

Enlightenment.

Understanding.

The whole universe shifted around him. His skin was on fire. He was changing, metamorphosing into an alien being. The transformation burned through him in a blaze of heart-wrenching ecstasy.

"Yes!" He threw back his head and howled into the surrounding darkness. *"Yes!"*

He staggered to his feet and turned slowly to face his pursuers. He was invincible, unstoppable. Nothing could stand in his way!

A man-shaped shadow flickered against the sizzling darkness. It stepped forward into the clearing, growing darker and darker as the dim moonlight sputtered and distorted around it.

Another growl rattled through his bones.

Jazz swung around, heart pounding. Three more figures advanced across the clearing behind him. Two more on his right, even more on his left.

He was surrounded.

He turned as if in a daze, watching, waiting. Ten hooded figures stood around him, shrouded in fluttering black cloaks. The tallest stepped forward, raised a gun, and pointed it at Jazz's chest.

A spasm shook Jazz's frame. The image of a beautiful girl with thick dark curls blossomed before his eyes. He was gasping for breath now, laughing like a maniac.

It was true!

The realization washed through him, filling him with a sense of fiery power. *It was all true!* They couldn't hurt him. He was finally safe.

An explosion sounded. The shock of searing pain. Another explosion. Another.

And then silence. Jazz tumbled forward onto the ground as a blinding light filled the clearing.

Screams. White-hot flames blasted through him, burning the thoughts and images from his mind. The ground shook. Thunder roared in his ears.

And then . . . peace.

He was floating again. Up through the clouds, higher and higher, an air bubble rising up through a sparkling sun-filled sea.

Voices murmured around him. The light was fading. Something brushed his arm.

He opened his eyes with a gasp. A sea of bleary faces pressed around him. The familiar smell of cigarette smoke and stale beer. Pushing up onto one elbow, he looked around the room.

"Easy." A woman in some kind of uniform reached behind his head and eased him back to the floor. "I gotcha. Everything's fine. Just lay on back down."

Jazz pulled away from her and sat up. Gerard and a few of the staff were gathered around the piano, but most of the customers were looking on from their tables.

"Sir?" The woman tugged on his shoulder and pushed around to get in his face. What was she? Some kind of paramedic? "Sir, you passed out. Do you have any medical conditions we should know about?"

"I'm fine." Jazz leaned around her to search through the faces.

"What about medication? I need to know everything you're taking—prescription or, uh . . . not."

Jazz shook his head and looked over to Gerard. "There was a girl standing right over there. Black party dress—extremely well-heeled. You saw her, right?"

"Sir!" The woman grabbed hold of his head and forced him to look at her. "I need you to focus. You were having a seizure. According to these people, you've been out over twenty minutes. We need to—"

"I'm fine." He pulled away from her and pushed onto his feet. "It's okay, everybody. I'm good. Just needed a quick nap."

Drawn faces. Worried frowns.

He glanced at his watch and eased himself back down onto the piano bench. Two more hours. He could do it. He *had* to do it. He wasn't about to lose his mailing address now.

He raised his hands and tried to play, but his left arm flashed out in excruciating pain. Wasn't that . . . ? He'd been shot there. Jazz shook his head. No, it was just a dream. He must have hurt it when he fell. It was just a bruise. He was fine.

Closing his eyes, he tried to concentrate, but a lightning storm of images flashed through his mind. Running through the forest. The gnarled tree against a pink-orange moon. He could still feel it. The triumph of revelation. What did it mean? What was going on?

A hand clamped around his shoulder. "Hey, pal. Why are you still here?"

Jazz glanced up. Gerard was looking down at him with that paramedic woman hovering at his side.

"I still have two more hours." He forced his fingers to move across the keys. "That's what we agreed, right? One a.m."

"The doctor here says you should be in a hospital, getting some tests."

"I'm fine, really. It was just—"

"Mr. Rechabson." The woman pushed forward. "What you just experienced was a seizure. It could be very serious. Even if you feel okay now, you should still be tested."

"But I don't have to, right? You can't make me go if I don't want to."

"This is about your health. You need to be checked out, no matter what caused the seizure. Your test results will be kept strictly confidential."

"Hold on there." Gerard's eyes hardened and he glared at Jazz. *"That's* what this is about? You're using? We had an agreement. This club is strictly—"

"I'm not on drugs, and I'm not sick!"

"That's why you was jerking around on the floor like a slab of bacon? Cause you're so happy to be clean?"

"Look, I haven't been sleeping lately, okay? I fell asleep on the job and I'm sorry. It won't happen again."

Gerard shook his head. "I'm sorry too. I like you, Jazz. You know that. The customers like your music. But either you go to the hospital and get checked out, or you pack up your stuff and go home. It's one thing being undisclosed, but now that I know, I'm responsible. Know what I mean? The club don't bring in enough for me to be responsible. You know that."

The paramedic smiled at him and retrieved her medical box from the floor. "Ready to go?"

"Sorry." Jazz shook his head and slid off the piano bench. "I don't do drugs and I don't do hospitals. You want to get all federal about it, that's your business. But you're going to have to find yourself another act!" Shoving his guitar in his gig bag, he headed for the door.

ᑌᎧ 3 Ꮗᑌ

Mariutza

MARI LAY ON HER back at the bottom of the deep, dark night. Cold moonlight lapped at the edges of her mind. She was all hollowed out and wasted away, shriveled up and caved-in like the empty skin of a butternut squash. Everything that was good, everything that had any meaning had been scooped out and gobbled up. She was worthless and alone. Leftover table scraps fit only to be cast into the swamp.

No granddaughter of mine!

Her breath caught in another wrenching sob. Purodad's words tore deep into her soul. If only she'd listened. If only she hadn't gone to the road. He'd told her over and over. Why hadn't she listened?

And now he was gone. The weight of his absence pressed down on her, pinning her to the ground. She reached out with the *dikh* sight like he'd taught her, again and again probing the empty gap beside her.

But Purodad was gone. She was all alone. What was she supposed to do without him?

"Find him. I want you to promise me. Find him first. Then find the others."

A chill shuddered through her frame. Was he talking about—? No, Jaazaniah was once upon a time. *Darane svatura*—a Gypsy legend for campfires and scaring the little chaps at night. He didn't people daylight hours like ordinary folk.

But who else could he mean?

Her mind flashed to the faded painting hanging above the diddlecar window. Jaazaniah the Prophet. He couldn't be real. Real-world folk didn't have time to fight battles and rescue beautiful princesses. They dressed in fine clothes and worked away the daylight at stores and schools and smoking factories. They looked at television pictures and read about the news on wide papers and were afraid of the night air. Besides, nobody remembered the old powers. Purodad said so himself. Real-world folk didn't know anything about the *dook* magic.

A tremor rumbled through the forest, shushing the songs of the night folk. The Badness again? Mari leaped to her feet and reached out with the sight. Silence rang in the air like a plucked bowstring, but it was out there somewhere. Flitting at the edges of her mind, dark and feathery like the last wisps of a fading dream.

Mari took a reluctant step toward the diddlecar and stopped to cast one more glance at the still form stretched out on the ground. He'd been crawling through the thicket. What had happened on the other side?

The night mashed down on her as she wriggled her way through a hedge of stickers and twisters. Cool wet leaves licked at her skin. Darkness crowded in on her from all sides. She finally stepped out into a wide moonlit clearing. Dozens of uprooted tupelos lay crisscrossed on the ground.

What happened here? Whatever it was, Purodad said it was coming back. She needed to start digging. Mari leaped over a jagged stump and started out into the clearing, but a dark shadow appeared on the ground in front of her. She tried to turn, but her legs crumpled beneath her, sending her sprawling into a patch of silky black fabric.

A lump pressed into her ribs. She tried to stand, but something soft turned beneath her foot. A patch of reflected moonlight gradually resolved itself into the five fingers of an outstretched hand.

She screamed and leaped backwards. It was a man! Revulsion shuddered through her frame. She'd stepped on his arm. A man! Backing away she kept her eyes locked on the still figure. Cold sightless eyes peeped out from beneath a clothy black hood. She took a deep breath, let it out slowly. He was so still. Surely he wasn't—

Another shadow lay on the ground to her right, a bare white arm sprawled across its face. It held a gun!

Mari dropped into a defensive crouch and turned to survey the clearing. Another body. Another. They were everywhere. Ten in all, spaced evenly around the perimeter of a wide circle. All of them wore robes and all of them had guns.

A chill seeped into her body. She stumbled toward the center of the circle, pushed through a clump of knee-high shrubs. A patch of plants had been trampled flat. Splatters of inky darkness stained their leaves.

Her grandfather. She could see it so clearly, but it didn't make any sense. If the men shot her grandfather, what killed them?

A faint tremor tickled at the back of her mind. Whatever it was, it was coming back. If she was going to bury her grandfather, she was going to have to hurry.

Mari picked her way back through the undergrowth, sweeping the moonlit clearing with wide, darting eyes. The body to her right. Had it moved while she wasn't looking? She broke into a trot. Then she was running. Through the gap in the thicket, across the clearing, in and out through the trees, she raced back to the diddlecar and flung herself onto the ground by the door.

Wriggling beneath the old Gypsy wagon, she reached out a hand and felt her way through the darkness. They had an old broken signpost somewhere. One end was flat and pointed. She'd used it as a shovel before. And she could use the big peach can to carry dirt.

There it was. She grabbed the post and was just starting to back up when she saw it. Glowing faintly in the moonlight—a long smooth handle. The wood was almost white—like it had been cut down yesterday. She dropped the sign post and brushed a grimy hand over the polished surface of the wood. Smooth as candle wax. A small rectangular tag was stuck to its glossy surface. A price tag from a store?

Mari pulled the handle toward her, careful not to scrape it against a pile of jagged cans. It caught for a second and then turned loose with a metallic ping. It was a shovel! A beautiful store-bought shovel. Why hadn't Purodad told her?

She squirmed out from under the wagon and examined the new tool in the light of the moon. The blade was covered with thick gray mud. What kind of hole would have needed something so beautiful and new? The tool must have cost a fortune.

What else had he gotten? A weapon maybe? Something to battle the Badness? She dropped back onto her knees and searched beneath the diddlecar. A pile of lighter wood, their Mason jars, the cook pot filled with emergency water . . .

Then she noticed a patch of gray near the back wheel. Thick mud, it felt the same as what was on the shovel. She tugged it free and pulled out a heavy, mud-covered board. It was perfectly round, about two and a half feet across. She carried it out into the moonlight and scraped off some of the dirt to expose the wood underneath. Just as light as the shovel handle. It was store-bought too. Why did her grandfather buy a board and a shovel?

She rolled the wooden disc around to the front of the diddle-car and flopped it down next to the shovel. What did it mean? Was she supposed to use the board to measure the hole? It didn't make sense. There was a measuring string in the diddlecar. The string would be a whole lot easier to use. Was she missing something?

She climbed back under the diddlecar and searched back and forth through the limp white weeds, but she couldn't find anything else. Finally she gave up and crawled back out. Time was getting away. Even with a store-bought shovel it would take forever to dig a proper grave. She had to hurry.

Grabbing up the shovel and muddy board, she ran through the trees toward the spot Purodad called the mound. He'd always said it was the most beautiful part of the swamp, and the ground there was a good head higher than anything else in the area. It was the perfect spot for a grave.

When she finally reached the mound, she ran up its southern slope and searched out the clearing at the shady side of the turtle-shaped hill. Then, using the board as a guide, she started digging. The ground was crisscrossed with so many roots, she could barely cut through them. Even with the store-bought shovel, it took hours and hours to get through the biggest roots. And then, once she reached four feet, the ground was so hard it took all her strength just to scoop out a few crumbles of dirt. She chipped painstakingly away at the stubborn soil until her bruised and bleeding hands were too cramped to grip the shovel.

It was too much. She couldn't do it. Mari climbed out of the hole and rolled over onto her back to lie panting on the dew-drenched ground. She hadn't dug down five feet yet and Purodad was over six feet tall. She had to go deeper. Purodad deserved deeper. He was a prophet of the Standing. If anybody deserved a proper burying, it was him. But the Badness was on its way, and it was taking so long. . . . And she still had to burn the wagon and all Purodad's earthly goods.

What was wrong with her? She was being a Miss Lazy-bones.

A cool wind played the shivers across her muddy arms. Where had the night music gone? Mari groaned onto her feet and reached out with the *dikh* sight. Something was out there. Dark, at the edges of the night. Buzzing voices. It felt like—

An angry roar rattled through her bones. Hunger. Wave after wave of shuddering rage. A howl sounded from the direction of the diddlecar. The shouts of living men.

Mari took off running. *Holy One, hide me . . .* Dodging and leaping, weaving in and out through the trees, she tried to lose herself, but the shielding prayer didn't seem to be working. The Badness was getting closer, coming at her from every direction.

A snap sounded in front of her. The crunch of fallen leaves. Mari veered to her left and kept on running. More footsteps. They were everywhere. The whole mound was surrounded!

A growl rattled through the darkness. Hatred closed around her, lashing out with tendrils of blinding rage. Mari staggered back up the hill and ran for the hole. It was too late. They knew where she was.

Grabbing the shovel, she spun it around and dropped into ready position. Turning in a tight circle, she searched the darkness. They were getting closer. Any second and she'd see the tongues of fire.

She stepped back onto the muddy board and froze. It was her only hope. *Holy One, shield me. Help me, please . . .* She closed her eyes tight and pictured her grandfather's kindly face. The crinkle of his eyes when he smiled, the music of his voice when he recited the old legends, the tickle of his beard when he kissed her good night.

Without opening her eyes, she launched the shovel out into the woods. Purodad laughed like a braying donkey. He always fussed about being fat, but it never stopped him from taking one more piece.

Dropping onto her hands and knees, she grabbed the muddy board and felt her way to the hole. *Hide me in Thy almighty hands* . . . A body was shouting now. She could hear his thudding footsteps. More footsteps climbing up the mound.

Mari dropped into the hole and tried to pull the board down after her, but it was too wide. She wrestled with the slippery disk, tugging it this way and that until it sliced through the dirt and smacked into the side of her head.

No! She tried to cover for her mistake by imagining a low tree branch and the crush of scratchy weeds poking into her back.

Footsteps pounded toward the hole. *Good night, Purodad.* Mari curled into a tiny ball at the bottom of the hole and pulled the board down on top of her to lie flatwise across her body.

Happiness. Good thoughts. A thick warm quilt on a frosty winter night. Purodad's whispery voice as he told her the story of Jaazaniah and the princess. *Jaazaniah is a great warrior. His veins run thick with the dook powers of old—*

Suddenly a bright light glared down on her, lighting up the gaps between the board and the sides of the hole. She hadn't thought that they'd have torches.

Holy One, shield me . . . She squeezed her eyes shut and held her breath, waiting for the blast that would end her life.

↝ 4 ↜

Jazz

JAZZ PUSHED OUT INTO the thick night air and stalked across Bourbon Street. Gerard was a sog-brained idiot! He knew Jazz was clean. He was just being paranoid—projecting his own insecurities onto everybody else. He probably had one too many strikes on his record. That's what it was. The count was 0-and-2 and he was too gutless to even step up to the plate. The owners were going to hear about this. Jazz was the best thing that had ever happened to the Hookah Club. His music had tripled the crowds in less than two weeks. And this was how Gerard repaid him?

The melancholy tones of a brass quartet blasted him from the crowded entrance of the Maison Bourbon. Jazz stepped out into the street to circle around a gaggle of chattering chimney-heads. Behind him, the lead trumpet shrieked and wailed like a castrated banshee. It wasn't bad, really. Not if you liked that kind of thing. But it was way too dry. The stuff blew over the heads of an audience like a desert wind. The band wouldn't get a five-dollar tip the entire night.

Tips . . .

Jazz kicked at a loose handbill and pushed past a row of empty storefronts. He'd been so close. The rich girl had been reaching for her purse. A few more minutes and she would have pulled out the fattest wad he'd ever seen. What had happened? Had he really fallen asleep? It felt so real.

Maybe Gerard slipped something in his drink just to have an excuse to fire him. But why? Jazz had only been late twice, and both times he stayed longer to make it up. He'd been a picture-perfect model of suck-up exemplary behavior.

The click-clack of heels from across the street arrested his attention. A pair of hotter-than-thou party girls passed beneath a streetlight. The one closest to the street was a brunette in a trashy black dress; the other was blonde. Her dress seemed to be the right cut—and it certainly looked nice enough from this angle.

He started out across the street but caught himself and stepped back onto the sidewalk. He couldn't go chasing after her like a half-grown puppy. Her loser detector would pick him up before he was halfway across the street. A *meet-cute* would be even worse. He needed something direct and in your face. Sometimes the *no plan* was the best plan of all.

"Hey!" He jogged out onto the street.

The brunette glanced over her shoulder and increased her pace.

"Wait a second. Hold up! Weren't you at the Hookah Club?"

The blonde turned and regarded him, her frown shifting to recognition as her eyes settled on the guitar case. She stopped and offered a timid smile. "You're the piano player, right?"

"I'm better at guitar." He returned her smile and looked her straight in the eyes as he stepped up onto the sidewalk and held out his hand. "Jazz Rechabson." He took her hand and held it a few seconds longer than necessary. "You looked like you wanted to say something at the club, and I . . . well, I guess I owe you an apology."

"I'm sorry, an apology?" The girl took a half step backward, but her eyes were fixed on Jazz. So far so good. Intrigued and off-balance—just where he needed her.

"For fainting like a fangirl. I don't know what happened. I guess the exhaustion is finally catching up with me. I'm new in town and have been working three jobs just to make ends meet." He shrugged and flashed his best lopsided smile.

The blonde nodded and her smile warmed. Her eyes flicked back and forth across his face. She seemed to be locked in some kind of internal battle. Trust or disgust? Flirt or flight?

"I'm Madison. Madison Edwards." The brunette reached in front of the blonde and shook Jazz's hand. "Hollis was just telling me about your music. She says you're amazing." The girl stepped closer, pushing between him and her friend.

"Hi, Madison. Nice to meet you." He smiled and stepped to the side to keep his focus on the blonde. "It's nice to meet you too, Hollis. Most people don't get what I do. I think you were the only person in the room that really heard what I was playing."

"It was . . . beautiful," she breathed. "I've never heard anything like it. Never in my entire life."

He nodded and prompted her with an encouraging smile.

"It's like your voice was inside my head. Like I could feel it in my heart. It was so beautiful it hurt. It still hurts just thinking about it."

"I know what you mean." Jazz tightened his throat, and the effect was perfect. A husky, almost bluesy tone that quivered with swelling emotion. "But I don't think it's the music." He let his unblinking stare capture her, mesmerize . . . opening himself to the emotions he saw rippling across her features. Uncertainty, hope, fear. Someone had hurt her bad. He could see it written all over her face.

Don't be afraid. I'm a healer. I won't hurt you. He let the message flow from his eyes into her soul. His guitar was sharper than any scalpel. His voice penetrated deeper than any prescription drugs. He'd give her another song. A chance to cry and receive comfort. A chance to tear down the walls around her heart and give to an artist in need. She'd walk away happy and content and complete.

And he'd be able to pay his rent.

"Would you like to hear another song?" He let his voice tremble on the damp night air. "I have my guitar with me."

The blonde smiled again and gave a barely perceptible nod. Jazz set his guitar case on the sidewalk and started to open it, but the brunette cleared her throat.

"Would you . . . like to come back to our hotel?" The blonde's voice was almost a whisper. "We're at the Ritz-Carlton. It's not that far away."

Jazz glanced at the brunette before rising to face the blonde. "I'm not sure that, under the circumstances, that would be entirely appropriate." He searched the blonde's eyes and tried to reestablish the broken connection, but her brow puckered, signaling a gathering storm.

"Madison doesn't mind. Do you, Maddy?"

"Not at all," the brunette purred. "It'll be fun."

"I really want . . . what you want." Jazz kept his gaze fixed on the blonde. She was crying out for help. *Come on. Trust me. Trust yourself.* He reached further, pushed harder . . .

There was a wrenching snap and suddenly he was falling. The night splashed down on him like a giant wave. It lifted him up and spun him round and round. The girl's eyes expanded to fill his vision. A crescent of silver light peeked out from behind her head. The moon. Its blinding light stabbed into his brain. He could feel it coursing through his body, filling his limbs with fiery flames. Spasm after spasm shuddered through his body. Rivers of boiling blood surged through swollen muscles. He could feel them tightening, bulging beneath burning skin.

A roar blasted inside his head. He was running, leaping, bounding through a maze of twisted dark streets. White-hot power raged through his limbs. Shrieks and screams rang in his ears. He was all-powerful. Mighty. Let everyone cower and scrape at his feet. The world and all it contained was his.

The city lights shimmered and distorted and finally winked out as a pink-orange moon rose out of the darkness to backlight a gnarled old tree. Cloaked monsters were surrounding him. One of them had a gun! Blinding light flashed in his eyes, and then he was digging a hole—at the corner of a red doghouse in a cluttered, dug-up yard. A tall wooden fence surrounded him on all sides. He leaned against a mud-spattered shovel and turned toward a shadow, but there was another flash. A radiant young woman in a sparkling green dress walked toward him, freezing his heart in his chest. She smiled at him, brown eyes laughing. Glistening cascades of thick dark curls framed a pixie face. The sparkle of gold against rich caramel skin.

So beautiful . . .

The ache in his heart expanded to fill his entire body. He loved her so much, knew her so well. But how? He'd never seen her before in his life. How could he recognize someone he'd never met? How could he love someone who wasn't even real?

The vision gradually faded, leaving him floating in an eternity of black emptiness. His arms and legs ached. How long had he been running? When would it ever end?

The darkness flashed. Moonlight streamed like molten lava through his eyes. Water beaded on his skin, sparkling diamonds of soft twinkling light. He was so tired. So impossibly tired. He collapsed into a field of waving grasses. Rolled onto his back, stared up at the moon.

His body twitched and trembled. He could feel himself leaking out into the night. Fading away. Soon there wouldn't be anything left.

Slowly, calling up his last ounce of strength, he raised a hand to his face. His fingers felt hot and sticky against his skin. Too sticky. Lifting the hand toward the moon, he squinted into its pearlescent brightness.

A long jagged cut ran the length of his sleeve. Dark blotches stained the tattered white fabric.

His hand was covered with blood.

Daniel Groves

DANIEL GROVES PULLED OVER to the side of the road and killed the headlights of his van. A weathered two-story building stared down at him from across the narrow New Orleans street. Greasy moonlight reflected off narrow, dark windows. A shadowed door rose up from the sidewalk like a gaping mouth. It looked more like a haunted house than a voodoo temple. Where were the tiki torches and snake dancers? And shouldn't there be a zombie or two chained to the front walk?

Craziness . . .

Groves reached back and grabbed a notebook from the bureau-issued child's car seat—criminals never expect someone with a car seat to be law-enforcement—clogging the back seat of his ever-so-low-profile minivan. Chevalier was out of his paper-pushing bu-brain. Thanks to his boss's new Gypsy obsession, Groves had spent two weeks chasing after fairy tales when he could have been doing something useful like putting child predators behind bars. But no . . . Real criminals weren't sexy enough for the *new* bureau. The *new* bureau was too forward thinking to waste time on crimes that had actually been committed. They only cared about potential crimes—about catching bad guys who hadn't done anything wrong yet.

He pushed the door open and shoved out into the thick night air. The wail of distant trumpets assaulted his ears. The raucous voices of alcohol-crazed partiers. Once, just once before he left the city, he'd like to investigate an actual crime. Was that so much to ask?

He slammed the door of the van and stalked across the street. Stepping up to the shadowed building, he pounded on a door and waited. No movement, no lights, no blood-curdling screams . . . Maybe all the voodoo priestesses were still in their coffins.

"Hello? Anybody here?" Groves knocked once more and headed back to the bu-van. No terrorists here. He was officially finished with the assignment. The whackos and crazies of the city could breathe a collective sigh of relief.

Halfway back to the bu-van he heard a noise—a long, bone-chilling creak—just like in the movies. They'd probably been salting the door hinges for months.

Groves sighed and turned back. A shrouded figure stood in the open doorway. Floral scarves, colorful skirts, enough necklaces to turn a rapper green. This was going to be good.

"Priestess Zazou?" Groves tried to keep a straight face as he walked back across the street.

The woman inclined her head in a slow-motion bow.

"I'm Special Agent Daniel Groves of the FBI. Thanks for taking the time to answer my questions."

The priestess stepped back from the doorway, motioning him into the dark room beyond.

Groves followed her inside and waited as she struck a match and lit a long, tapered candle. "I, uh . . . don't usually schedule meetings so late at night. I take it your calendar for today was completely filled?"

The woman didn't respond. She floated across the cluttered room and started lighting one candle after another with slow, elaborate gestures.

Groves cleared his throat and studied the candlelit room. Carved wooden masks cast flickering shadows on water-stained walls. Cloth-draped tables were laden with all manner of trinkets: voodoo statues, voodoo dolls, voodoo spell kits . . . There were even gift sets of voodoo bath beads. All for fifty percent off the original price.

"Daniel Groves . . ." The woman's voice was low and resonant. "What information do you seek from Priestess Zazou?"

Groves flipped his notebook open and turned to the first question on Chevalier's list. "First, I'm supposed to ask if you've ever run into anyone with"—he slashed quote marks in the air with his free hand—"'mysterious and unexplainable powers'?"

The priestess inclined her head. "We all have access to such power. We need but a guide to help us unlock it."

"So have you ever run into someone who was particularly unlocked? Someone in their early twenties, maybe? Someone with a Gypsy background or heritage?"

The woman shook her head slowly. "The reputation of Gypsies has been greatly exaggerated. Race is irrelevant. We are all brothers and sisters in the eyes of the spirits. We need only a guide to help us find the path. Is this what you seek, Daniel Groves? You seek a spiritual guide?"

"Sorry. I'm just here for the questions."

"And the questions concern other practitioners of the Hoodoo faith?"

Groves shrugged.

"I normally answer such questions as part of our Voodoo city tour." The priestess extended her hand with a flourish. "The usual fee for a private tour is one hundred dollars."

"Just one more question, and I won't take any more of your time. Have you ever heard of Beng or Mariutza Glapion?"

"Marie Paris Glapion?" The woman's voice rang with genuine surprise.

"You know her?" Groves had started to think Chevalier had made the names up. "So . . . do you have an address or phone number where she can be reached?"

"Normally such information is covered on the private tour." She extended her hand again.

Groves swore under his breath. It was bad enough Chevalier's witch hunt was keeping him after hours, but a hundred bucks? Chevalier was going to pay for this. "This Marie Paris Glapion. She's a Gypsy girl, right? About twenty years old?"

The priestess inclined her head. "Or so she might appear to one such as yourself."

"What's that supposed to mean?"

The woman shoved her hand in his face, all pretense of subtlety abandoned now that she'd scented blood.

Groves sighed and pulled out his wallet. Twenty-three bucks was all he had left. "I don't suppose you'd take a credit card?"

"Of course!"

He handed over his bu-card and watched as the priestess carried it to a dark counter and swiped it through a credit card reader. Another chunk of the taxpayer's money flushed down the toilet.

"Okay, you've got your money. Would you mind explaining that crack about Glapion's age? How old is she really?"

The woman lifted a candle from the table and held it before her face. "The high priestess is not like other mortals," she intoned in a sing-song voice. "She might choose to appear as a woman in her prime or she might choose the form of one of the ancients, but she is beyond age and time."

Great . . . He'd just paid a hundred bucks for the fairy godmother. "So what's her address? Second star to the right and straight on till morning?"

A low growl emanated from deep inside the priestess's chest. She stepped forward and jabbed a crooked finger in Groves's face. "You will find the High Priestess in a hut at the end of a long dirt path. The middle of Bayou Road—just after the bend. I, Priestess Zazou, have already foreseen it. Turn from your path now or disbelief will be your ruin. You will cower before the High Priestess and beg for mercy, but she will not be appeased."

"Thanks. I'll keep that in mind." Groves crossed the room and stepped out into the sultry night air. Fantastic. Just what the witch doctor ordered.

He had one more wild goose to chase before he was done.

Mariutza

HOLY ONE, WE THANK YOU . . .

Mari breathed the words in and out, letting them fill the tiny space at the bottom of the hidey hole. Rivers of blessed gratitude flowed through her, surrounding her, shielding her from the eyes of her enemies.

Of the Badness.

They'd looked right at her, sure as night. Over and over they'd shined their beamy lights into the hole, but not one of them had seen her. The good Lord had blinded up their eyes. Just like the story of Jaazaniah and the Faeries! They'd walked straight through the lands of the darkness, and the darkness had comprehended them not.

Somewhere above her, a pulsing roar sounded above the tumult of distant shouts. Helicopters! The training said they'd come, but she'd never wanted to believe it.

Mari took a chestful of air and eased it back out. She could do this—just like Purodad had taught her. She focused on the roar and tried to separate out the beats. There were two of them at the least. Maybe as many as four. Either *thumpa-thumpas* or *thwumpa-thwumpas*. It wasn't likely to matter which. *Thumpas* and *thwumpas* both had the heat sensors. Her sheltering board, even with all its covering of mud, wasn't near thick enough to hide under. She'd have to run.

Tingling pins and needles stabbed through Mari's legs as she pushed up on the board and struggled to right herself in the narrow hole.

A shout sounded above the din of the approaching helicopters. It sounded like it was coming from the stream. Mari froze where she sat, balancing the board on the top of her head. She reached out with the *dikh* sight and immediately felt a burning sting. Something was off to her left. Something hideous and foul—about fifty yards away.

Slowly, inch by inch, she pushed the board up through the grabby roots. Almost there. She put some shoulder into it and the board sliced through the dirt to land with a *thunk* beside the hole.

Mari froze and reached out with the sight. Purodad would have had a fit if she'd done that in a training exercise, but the Badness didn't seem to be listening with its ears. It was still moving toward the stream. She peeped out above the edge of the hole and searched the dark forest for movement.

Nothing she could see. She climbed out of the hole and rolled across the loose soil. Hundreds of footprints crisscrossed the ground. What were these people? How could there be so many?

She bent low to examine the tracks, but a loud crash sent her scrambling for the cover of a large tree. There it was. Over to her right. Intense, mind-pummeling rage. Mari circled the tree and plunged into the deeper shadows of the forest. Weaving through the trees, keeping low to the ground, she climbed through the thickest parts of the undergrowth, twisting and turning like a fish swimming against the tide.

The Badness was heading away from her now. Had it lost her scent? It couldn't be running from the helicopters too. She turned and ran for the diddlecar. She and Purodad had stoked its roof full of dirt. It was more than enough to shield out the heat sensors. If she could just reach it before the helicopters found her.

A beam of light swept through the forest.

Mari dove to the ground and rolled to the base of a tree. Two shining lights bobbed across her path. She double-checked the area with the *dikh* sight but couldn't feel a thing. Something was wrong. The Badness couldn't shield itself. What were normal Gadje doing out in the middle of the Badness?

She peeked out from behind the tree as the two figures stalked past. Ceramic plate body armor, modified M-16s, night vision goggles . . . They were . . . soldiers? It didn't make sense. Purodad was dead. Why would soldiers be searching for *her*?

As soon as the men passed, she crept out onto the path and ran in the opposite direction. The helicopters were approaching low over the trees. Bright spotlights swept back and forth across the ground. They'd be on top of her soon. She had to get to the diddlecar. If they caught her on their sensors, they'd hold on tight and never let her go.

Another cluster of flashlights pushed her to the right, but she didn't stop running. She vaulted a fallen tree and sliced through a curtain of saplings. The helicopters were almost on top of her. It would be close.

A flash of white caught her eye. There in the trees . . . a sheet of paper was blowing in the wind. She slowed to a walk and stepped out into the clearing. The door of the diddlecar had been torn off its hinges. Purodad's books lay scattered across the ground.

The scene dissolved into a haze of liquid light as the helicopters appeared above the tree tops. Too late to run. Her body heat was lighting up their machines like a bonfire.

Pulling herself up to her full height, she marched toward the diddlecar. A miniature hurricane blasted down on her, whipping her hair into a frenzy. *Holy One, please . . . Don't let them use their eyes.* She squinted into the storm and kept on walking. Nice and calm. A trained soldier making a routine inspection.

The helicopter drifted past her, but another one was on its way. Its spotlight swept back and forth across the ground ahead of her. Another few seconds and—

Mari leaped into the diddlecar as a blinding light swept past the door. Collapsing in a heap on the floor, she looked back through the open door, waiting for the alarms to sound, for the hunters to close in around her and pump the diddlecar full of bullets.

A third helicopter roared overhead and followed after the others. As soon as it passed, she climbed to her feet and turned to inspect the damage.

The wagon was a wreck. Purodad's diddlecar—the only home she had ever known. The mattresses had been ripped to shreds. Pieces of torn foam were everywhere. She dug through a pile of clothes and papers, hugging a torn field guide to her chest.

They'd been after something. But what? She dug through the debris, but nothing seemed to be missing. The silver candlesticks, the teapot and tray, all the forks and knives . . . She climbed over the remains of the table and froze. The shelf was emptied out of books. She dropped onto her hands and knees and searched through the rubble. Her calculus book, Latin, the empty cover of *General Chemistry* . . . But where was Purodad's Bible? The ancient leather-bound tome was too big to miss.

She sorted through the debris, working her way from one side of the wagon to the other, but it just wasn't there. Purodad's Bible. The only one óf his possessions she wasn't supposed to burn. First they'd taken Purodad, then they'd taken his Bible. She had nothing left at all.

And it was all her fault.

If she'd burned everything like she was supposed to—right soon as he'd died—they never would have found it. She could have squirreled it away in the thick of the woods. Why hadn't she followed the rules? She knew how long it'd take to dig the hole. She should have tended her duties first.

Blinking back her tears, Mari stepped over a pile of foam and knelt down in front of Purodad's old wooden chest. Her hands trembled as she reached out and opened the lid. The contents of the box had been rifled through, but nothing seemed to be missing. Taking a deep breath, she pulled out a white store-bought blouse and a beautiful multicolored skirt. Tears welled in her eyes as she stripped off her rags and pulled on the stiff new clothes. Then, pushing up on the thin panel of wood at the back of the box, she reached into the hidden keep-safe and pulled out a long chain strung with ten sparkling gold coins.

Her traveling necklace and traveling clothes. How she'd loved to take them out and look at them when she was a little chap. She'd been half mad with the wanting to try them on, but Purodad wouldn't hold to it. Even when they'd traveled north to escape the big storm, he hadn't relented. They were meant for the special time—the special traveling time. She'd been so crazy for that time to arrive. And now it was on her . . .

What she wouldn't give to go back!

She dug through the pile of foam beneath the table and came up with a box of matches. The kerosene lamp still hung from its chain. She unhooked it and hefted it in both hands. The diddlecar was very dry. There would be more than enough fuel.

Unscrewing the chimney and langa piece from the lamp's base, she splashed kerosene onto the walls and floor. Then, looking out though the door, she pulled out a match and struck it against the box.

The match flared to life, lighting the wagon with wild flickering light. She held the match rigidly before her. She could do this. It was her birthright. The most ancient of Gypsy customs, her grandfather's last, most precious gift: freedom. It had been bought with a tremendous price. She must never allow herself to forget. The memory would stand forever as a reminder, a ward against the temptation to take up the yoke of slavery—to serve comfort and possessions and place.

"Stand firm, Purodad," she whispered and dropped the match onto a pile of kerosene-soaked rags.

↶ 5 ↷

Jazz

THE MOON STARED DOWN at Jazz, pounding into his upturned face with blue, ice-cold fury. Swaying blades of hissing grass rose up all around him. They were watching him. Waiting. He could feel their eyes burning jagged holes in his skull. Sinister voices tickled at the back of his mind.

Gritting his teeth, he struggled to sit up. What was happening now? He felt like he'd been hit by a truck. Jazz flexed his hands and tried to work the stiffness out of his joints. His shirt was stained and torn in half a dozen places. A long bloody gash ran the length of his right forearm.

Drugs?

It was the only thing that made sense. Somehow, someone in the club had slipped something into his drink. Gerard maybe. Or maybe a jealous boyfriend, an insecure pusher who hadn't liked the way his girlfriend responded to Jazz's music.

Whatever it was, he had to get out. Something bad was happening. The whole city felt wrong. Jazz climbed onto his feet and blinked into the darkness. Where was he anyway? Some kind of park? He took a step toward the nearest streetlight, and his right foot sank into a puddle of oozing mud. *Great.* Just what he needed. He pulled his foot out and froze.

Where was his guitar? He turned and searched through the weeds. He'd had it when he left the club. He was going to play the rich girl a song. What had happened to it? He wouldn't have left it on the sidewalk. Not even amped on drugs . . . would he?

Jazz took off running. Cold water splashed beneath him. Soft mud sucked at his feet. A distant streetlight danced and bobbed before his eyes. He passed it and kept on running, searching each intersection for a street name he recognized. Two blocks later he finally found it. Esplanade Avenue. He was in . . . City Park? That was halfway across the city. How had he gotten there?

Turning right onto the gravel-littered street, he crossed a bridge and ran back in the direction of the Hookah Club. Whatever had happened to him, the girls wouldn't have left his guitar out on the street. It was a Martin D-45. Surely they'd know enough to take it back to their room. It was one of a kind.

Jazz ran as long as he could, but he couldn't keep the pace for long. He slowed to a jog and then to a limping walk. By the time he got back to Bourbon Street, most of the clubs were closed. The streets were dead. He searched up and down the sidewalks, but it wasn't there. The rich girl had taken it back to her hotel. That's what happened. He'd established a connection with her. She wouldn't have left it out on the street. It was living it up at the Ritz-Carlton. He should be so lucky.

Jazz limped across the street and headed for the hotel. It wasn't too late. He could still make this work. The girl had to have his guitar. If he could just find her, he'd almost be expected to reward her with a private concert. She'd jump at the chance. If he played his cards right, he still might be able to pull a big tip. Maybe enough to pay off his rent.

The streetlights sputtered and suddenly went dim. A sudden chill tingled across his skin . . . something was behind him! He turned and searched the pulsing shadows. The street seemed to be deserted, but there was something . . .

The sidewalk jolted beneath his feet, knocking him against a wall. Jazz clung to the rough bricks as a low-pitched growl rumbled down the street. What was happening? Earthquake? He staggered out onto the street and collapsed onto his hands and knees. Another roar blasted through his brain. He pressed his palms to his ears, but it didn't make a difference. It was coming from inside his head. It was the drugs. It had to be. Whatever they had given him was still in his system. He closed his eyes and groped his way to the edge of the street. He had to get to his apartment. He had to get to his apartment before he passed out.

A shriek ripped through his head and suddenly the dizziness was gone. He eased onto his knees. So far so good. Lurching to his feet, he tottered down the sidewalk. He needed milk or water. Something to flush the drugs from his system. The thud of his footsteps pounded in his ears. Lots and lots of water, that would do it. Before he had another relapse. He couldn't afford a trip to the hospital. It would cost him his guitar.

He plodded up to his dilapidated apartment building and threw open the door. The stairs pounded and dimmed before his eyes. Three flights and then he could rest. He leaned against a bank of cold metal mail boxes and fought to catch his breath. Just three flights. He could do this. The dizziness was starting to come back.

He pushed off the wall, but a flash of white caught his eye. How could his mailbox be full? He'd just checked it last week. He fumbled through his keys and inserted the smallest into his box. They didn't seem to be bills. Two of them were hand addressed. He thumbed through the envelopes as he trudged up the creaking stairs. The address on the largest envelope was written in an elegant, old-fashioned script. *Jaazaniah Rechabson.* Nobody called him that—not even the government. A lump formed in his throat, but he swallowed it back down. His father was dead. He'd attended the funeral himself. It couldn't be him. But who else knew his full name?

He started to open the letter, but the embossed design on the back of the next envelope caught his attention. It looked like a coiled snake draped across a mystical-looking hand. The snake's eyes were almost hypnotic. They bored into his brain, stirring up vague memories in the dark recesses of his mind. Had he seen it somewhere before?

He flipped the envelope over and examined the embossed return address. Sabazios Vladu from San Francisco. Didn't ring any bells. A credit-card application? Health insurance? He stuffed the letters in to a pocket and tiptoed past Miss Alice's apartment. The building was quiet. Too quiet. His keys jangled like cymbals as he sorted through them and fitted one into the lock. Then, listening at the door, he opened it slowly and stepped inside.

His room was a total wreck! His clothes, sleeping bag, all his books and sheet music . . . everything he owned had been dumped in a big pile in the middle of the floor.

Jazz grabbed the metal guitar stand from beside his bed and tiptoed across the room. Heart pounding in his ears, he flattened himself against the wall outside the bathroom door. *One, two . . . three!*

He leaped into the tiny room and swung the guitar stand at the shower curtain. The curtain gave way with a plastic rip. He shouldered through the curtain and smashed into the back wall. The curtain bar clattered to the floor, draping him in slimy plastic.

A creak sounded in the bedroom.

Jazz fought free of the curtain and ran back out into the room, but nobody was there. The closet? He checked it top to bottom and swept the stand under his bed before probing the pile in the middle of the floor with a mud-coated foot.

He was being ridiculous. Elvis had already left the building. He tiptoed back to the door and slid the dead bolt shut with a snap. First someone tried to poison him and now . . . his room? Why? He didn't have anything worth stealing. His guitar wasn't even here. But it couldn't be a coincidence. The two were somehow connected.

He crouched down and started sorting though the pile of junk. His clothes, the sleeping bag . . . None of it seemed to be damaged. Nothing seemed to be missing either. He picked up a handful of papers and tossed them on the bed. Wait a second . . .

He pulled a blue envelope from the stack and ran a finger across its top. The envelope had been carefully slit open with a knife. It couldn't have been him. Even if he'd been desperate enough to read junk mail, he wouldn't have used a letter opener.

Carrying the envelope over to the window, he thumbed through its contents by the light of the moon. It was just a bunch of coupons. Salad dressing, baby wipes, and the like. Why would a thief go to the trouble of opening his junk mail?

A creak sounded behind him. Another creak followed by a wooden groan. Someone was coming up the stairs!

Jazz's brain buzzed like a beehive. He turned, searching the room for a place to hide. The thieves were coming back. He could feel the force of their presence inside his head. Festering like gangrene. Or was it the drugs? It felt so real.

He ran back to the window and yanked it open. His neighbor's metal balcony lay directly below his window. It was narrow and a good fifteen feet beneath him, but it looked solid enough. Maybe if he—

He was lifting a knee to the sill when he saw them. Three man-shaped shadows gliding across the fenced-in yard. Sputtering like the shadows of a dying flame, they stopped at the base of the wall and looked up at him with vacant shadow-cloaked faces.

Fiery rage exploded in Jazz's brain. He was hungry. Maddeningly, ravenously hungry.

The figures leaped onto the wall and climbed toward him like fluttering black spiders. He was theirs now.

There could be no escape.

Mariutza

BRIGHT FLAMES DANCED BEFORE Mari's eyes. A wave of hot smoke billowed past her face, sucking the life from her lungs. The wagon was starting to spin, but she couldn't leave. Not yet. The diddlecar was crowded up full with blessed memories. Purodad's tea service and all his books. The portrait of Jaazaniah the Prophet . . . How could she pull the cup from her lips while even the tiniest swallow of his presence still remained?

A shout cut through the roaring flames. More shouts. The soldiers had seen the fire. She was supposed to run now. The helicopters were turning back. She could feel them probing the forest all around her, brushing her mind with tendrils of hatred and twisted desire.

No! A pang stabbed through her chest, pinning her to the floor. Her stomach muscles clenched into a knot as she tried to shove her raging emotions aside.

Strength, discipline, control! Her grandfather's voice drilled into her head. *Fear fights faith. Get through the darkness first. The time for mourning is in the morning.*

Mari leaped from the burning wagon and raced across the clearing. A white flash lit up the sky. The helicopters were heading her way, sweeping the forest with blazing trails of electric light. She wasn't going to make it. Even if she managed to reach the trees, they'd still get her with the heat sensors. She'd waited too long.

A loud crash sounded from the brush just ahead of her. More crashes. A group of men was running through the woods. Mari dodged to the left and dove behind a tree as a cluster of bristling shadows burst into the clearing. Gleaming rifles, night vision goggles—the soldiers were heading straight toward her.

Mari tore her eyes from the approaching men and searched the floor of the forest. A fallen limb showed dark against a thick blanket of weeds. Snaking her way through the under-growth, she lunged for the limb and broke off a rifle-sized branch. Then, pausing to let the soldiers pass, she jumped up and fell into step behind them. If they looked with their eyes they'd see her, but the heat sensors wouldn't be able to tell the difference.

A pulsing storm beat down on the trees as the helicopter passed slowly overhead. Mari pulled the stick to her chest and followed even closer behind the men. They were circling the clear-ing. If she could stay close to them for a few more minutes, she'd be able to hightail it to Caralee's without being—

One of the men stopped and turned.

Mari didn't wait for his reaction. She took off running, zigzag-ging in and out through the trees. A gunshot rang out behind her. Two more shots. A blast near her ear sprayed the back of her neck with bark and slivers of wood.

A huge spotlight cut through the trees like the sun. The helicopter was on top of her now. Mari sprinted toward a stand of mature tupelo gums. The training said the foliage wouldn't block the heat sensors, but it was supposed to make her harder to shoot.

She wove in and out through the trees, gradually angling toward Miss Caralee's shack. If she could just get to the old alligator hole, she might have the tiniest spider-silk-thin strand of a chance.

The ground squish-squashed beneath her feet. The weeds were thicker now, taller. Mari bounded through the high grasses. A puddle splashed beneath her feet. She was going to make it. *Holy One, let the gator be in one of his stupors!*

Leaping high over a bank of swamp grass, she plunged face-first into a muddy dark pool. A powerful tail clipped her knee, twisting her onto her side. The water thrashed around her. Kicking and paddling with her last ounce of strength, Mari plowed through the water and scrambled up the bank on the other side.

She cut to the right and looped back around toward the swamp. The massive old oaks were thick with spreading branches. Curtains of Spanish moss brushed by her face. Rivulets of muddy water trailed down her skin and ran into her eyes. The water was cool, but her skin still felt warm. Surely they could see her. She was still within the range of their sensors.

The swamp opened out before her and she was suddenly on the path to Caralee's. She pounded up the path, ignoring the roar of the helicopter circling off to her left. Heat sensors couldn't tell one warm body from another. She had to warn Caralee. If the Badness flew over her hut, it wouldn't stop to check who was inside.

A low voice sounded just ahead of her. The squish-squash of footsteps across the muddy path. Mari dove to the ground and tried to duck behind the weeds, but they weren't tall enough. Fumbling with the drawstrings around her waist, she loosened her skirt and pulled the wet fabric over her head. They might still be able to see her heat signature, but at least it wouldn't have arms and legs.

She balled into a tiny ball as the footsteps approached.

"Too big for a rabbit." A loud voice shattered the silence.

"I don't know. Maybe it was a deer." The footsteps moved toward Mari and stopped.

She held her breath and willed her pounding heart to slow. It was too loud. Surely they could hear it. She had to strike now. There were only two of them. If she could disarm one of them, maybe the other would—

Something squish-squashed next to her head. The sound of rustling fabric. There was a metallic click and the smell of tobacco smoke. Finally the footsteps started moving again.

Mari gritted her teeth as they stepped further and further out of her strike zone. She waited for the explosion, the agony of bullets ripping through her body. But the men didn't stop. As soon as they were out of earshot, she peeked out from under her skirt and leaped to her feet.

The men had come from Caralee's shack. If they had—

No! Holy One, please . . . No!

Mari raced around the bend and plunged into the forest, leaping and ducking and weaving her way through the trees. As soon as she reached the garden clearing, she slowed to a walk and draped the skirt back over her head. She didn't feel anything, but that didn't mean much. Most of the soldiers weren't infected. And with their night vision goggles, they'd be able to see her long before she could see them.

She stepped, quiet as a whisper, out into the clearing. She was halfway to the big oak tree before she saw them. Two small patches of ghostly white against the dark ground. Mari dropped to a crouch and peered through the waist of her skirt. They were too small for humans. What were they?

Keeping low to the ground, she crept toward the first patch. It was small and rectangular with writing on it and . . . a picture? Saltine Crackers. It was a box of Caralee's Saltines!

Mari swallowed against the bile rising into her throat and tip-toed around the tree to peep out at Caralee's cook yard.

Stifling a cry, she collapsed onto her knees. Pieces of charred wood were scattered all over the ground. Papers, tatters of canvas, a clot of blood-stained cloth . . .

Caralee was gone.

A shadow moved on the other side of the clearing. The glint of diffused light on glass. Mari staggered to her feet and started running up the path, but the sound of approaching footsteps brought her up short.

Dodging to the left, she bounded across the garden and plunged into the thick of the forest. A shout sounded behind her. She leaped a low shadow and twisted in the air to avoid a dark blur.

Smack! Sparkling red clouds lit her eyes as a blow to the fore-head knocked her off her feet. She rolled and fought her way to her knees. The voices were still behind her. She pushed through the darkness, ripping through brambles, scraping into trees. She was on her feet, running, dodging, getting knocked back onto the ground.

A blast of light dazzled her eyes. She dropped to the ground, fought to untwist the skirt from around her neck. But it was only the moon. The helicopters were almost a mile away now, searching the area by the road.

The safest hiding spot is the last spot searched. That's what the training said. But how long would they stay put before moving on? Mari pulled the skirt back over her head and ran toward the roaring helicopters, pushing harder and harder until her breaths came in great ragged blasts. They were drifting off to the right so she angled to the left and pressed doggedly on. The soldiers didn't matter now. If they saw her, she'd fight—but she had to reach the road before the helicopters came back. It was her only chance.

The forest finally opened out into a narrow clearing. The road! It looked so different at night. Mari ducked behind a tree and searched the road up and down. The painted white lines glowed like streaks of magic in the soft moonlight. Its surface was black and impossibly smooth. Somewhere in the unknowable vastness of the Lord's green earth, the road was connected to towns and cities and entire states filled with millions and millions of people. Millions! Even the word sounded magical. She was a traveler now. She was going to see those people.

A strange light appeared at the end of the road. Mari ducked behind the tree, but it wasn't a helicopter. The ball of light slowly resolved itself into two bright spots—headlights. Purodad had taught her all about headlights, but she'd never expected to see them out so late. She watched as the lights grew brighter and brighter and then passed her by in a streak of glowing red.

Mari crept out from behind the tree and searched the forest until she found a large fallen limb. She pulled it through the trees and dragged it out onto the road. The left end of the road was supposed to be connected to New Orleans and the right end was supposed to be connected to the rest of the world. But which side was she supposed to search first? According to the legends, Jaazaniah lived mainly in the faerie world, but sometimes he fought in New Orleans and sometimes he fought in San Francisco. The question was: where was he fighting right now?

Mari dragged the branch across the street and angled it to block the far lane. Then, scampering up the bank, she settled in behind a stand of saplings and pulled the skirt back over her head. The night sky reverberated with the helicopters' distant roar. They seemed to be getting closer, and her clothes were getting too dry to do much good. If a car didn't wander up soon, she was going to have to start running.

She loosed up her arms and tried to do the relaxed breathing, but the roars were getting closer. She needed to go now. It was nigh unto too late.

Finally a point of light appeared on the horizon. Mari leaped to her feet as a car sped down the road. What if it didn't see the branch? Cars had people in them. Someone could get hurt! She ran for the road as red lights flashed out behind the car with a high-pitched squeal. The car swerved around the branch and roared up the road until it disappeared around the bend.

No . . . Mari glanced up at the approaching helicopters and started to run, but another light appeared on the horizon. She dropped to the ground and crouched under her skirt as a much bigger car slowed and swerved around the branch. Then, with another blast of red lights, it pulled over to the side of the road.

It was stopping!

Her pulse pounded like drums in her ears as a tall muscular man in a beautiful white shirt and loose short pants got out of the car and walked back toward the branch. Her mind raced. What was she supposed to say? After all those years of training, her mind was a complete blank. *Hello, my name is Mariutza,* that was the first part, but was she supposed to say the *pleased to meet you* part before or after he returned her greeting? And when was she supposed to ask to go inside his car? Begging was wrong. Was asking to be inside a car begging?

She watched as the man dragged the branch to the side of the road and sauntered over to his car. The helicopters were coming. She had to do something, but he was so pretty and clean and everything nice. He wouldn't want someone like her in his beautiful car. It was asking too much.

The car door slammed, breaking Mari out of her reverie. The hum of the engine was almost lost in the roar of the approaching helicopters. She was on her feet, sprinting toward the car. It was moving now, pulling out onto the road. Mari bounded over the tall grass and leaped for the metal rail that circled the edge of the roof. Her hands closed around the bar as she slammed into the side of the car.

A loud squeal sounded over the roar. The car stopped again. Had the man heard her? She froze as the driver opened the door and climbed out. The helicopter was almost on top of them. She didn't have time to spend on greetings! Her thoughts bubbled to a boil as heavy footsteps made their way toward her. Dropping onto the ground, she rolled under the car as the man walked around the back. He said something, a low, emphatic phrase in a language Mari didn't understand. Then he was walking back in the other direction. He stopped and paused outside his door.

Go! Move! What's taking so long? Panic clawed the roots of her hair as the helicopters got closer and closer. It was too late to run now. Why didn't he get in his car?

The door squeaked open and slammed shut.

Mari rolled across the pavement and swung herself onto the car's flat roof as the engine surged to life. Cold metal trembled beneath her. She was moving. She reached across the roof and grabbed both rails as the car picked up speed. Wind pounded into her face with the force of a hurricane. She closed her eyes and hung on as a loud roar filled her ears.

co 6 ov

Jazz

Jazz stood frozen at the window. This wasn't happening. Men didn't crawl up walls. It was a hallucination—a side effect of the drugs. His stomach twisted as glinting eyes looked up from beneath dark, fluttering cloaks. He could feel a dark venom oozing into his mind. Anger . . . bitterness. An unquenchable hunger. They were the hunters; he was the prey.

"No!" Jazz pushed away from the window and stumbled toward the door.

A floorboard out in the hallway groaned. Heavy footsteps. They were at the top of the stairs, walking toward the door with slow, deliberate steps. Thick shadows pushed into his mind, expanding to fill his mouth and nose. He couldn't breathe.

Jazz staggered back to the window. The shadow men had already reached the balcony. Nothing could stop them now. He was theirs. They would suck the marrow from his bones.

A blast of cold white light streamed into his eyes. He could feel it flowing through his veins, freezing the night around him with startling knife-edged clarity. The shadow men were just below the window. A few more seconds and they'd crush him like a bug.

A crash sounded behind him. The shriek of splintering wood.

Jazz vaulted onto the window sill and leaped out into the void.

A claw-like hand slashed out at him as he plummeted in a rush of streaking light. *Slam!* Pain stabbed through his legs. He hit the deck and rolled into a clot of plastic chairs. Untangling himself from the flimsy furniture, he pushed himself up onto throbbing feet and leaned over the railing to search the ground below.

It would be an easy jump, but it was too obvious. He turned to one of the large windows darkening the old brick wall and jabbed his fingers into the soft, dry-rotted wood. Lifting with all his might, he tried to open it, but it didn't budge. One more tug and the window gave way with the crash of shattering glass. He dove through the opening and rolled through a tangle of potted plants. Piercing screams filled the room. A woman danced in place with her back against the far wall. Hugging a wad of blankets to her chest, her screams rapidly degenerated into a series of hysterical shrieks.

"The police!" Jazz cried out. "Call the police now!"

He slammed into the door and yanked it open. Footsteps pounded above his head. A series of crashes sounded on the balcony just behind him.

Jazz swung out into the hallway and leaped down the stairs. He hit the landing with a thud, pounded down the remaining steps, and threw open the door.

Cool moonlight bathed his eyes, washing the shadows from his brain. The police! The shadow men were right behind him. He had to get to the police!

Crossing the empty street in an all-out sprint, he raced down a dark alley and vaulted a chain-link fence. Then, cutting across a vacant lot, he ran through a well-lit intersection and plunged into the shadows of a side street. He jogged down the rutted pavement, studying the boarded-up windows of the buildings lining the street. The wood was weathered, old. If he could pry one of the boards off a window, maybe he'd be able to get inside.

He thudded to a stop at a dark, unboarded window. It was a huge building. They'd never find him inside. He stepped toward the opening but stopped as the hairs rose on the back of his neck. A dark wave crashed over him, washing away his thoughts in a swirl of tangled confusion.

The city rushed past him in a blur of darkness and dancing lights. Turning left and right and left again. Dark buildings, flashing lights. Signs and windows and doors. He had to find the police. Had to rest, catch his breath, figure out what was happening. If the shadow men had cars, they'd find him eventually. He had to get off the streets.

A huge building rose up before him. Bright lights illuminated beautiful ornate walls. The Ritz-Carlton. The girl that had his guitar! They'd never think to search for him there. It was the last place someone like him would hide.

Out of breath, dizzy with fatigue, he plodded toward the well-lit entrance. A uniformed doorman tensed at his approach, but opened the door without a word and ushered him inside.

The lobby was a fairyland of brass and gleaming wood. Jazz strode across the polished marble floor and flashed a smile at the pretty Asian desk clerk.

"You have two guests named Hollis and Madison. Could you call up to their room? It's an emergency. I was just attacked, and I need to get something from them before I can call the police."

"Attacked as in . . ." The girl's eyes slid to Jazz's arm and went wide. "You want I should call the police?"

"I need to get something from them first. It's important. Life and death."

She reached toward the keyboard and then pulled suddenly away as if she'd been burned. "Yes, sir. What is the name again?"

"Hollis and Madison. I think Hollis's last name is Edwards."

The attendant tapped a few seconds at the keyboard and bit her lip. "I'm sorry, but I don't show any guests named Hollis Edwards."

"Then it's Edmund or Edwin. Something with an *e*."

"I'm sorry, but it's against our policy—"

"I know you found her. Please." Jazz glanced at her name tag. "Please, Mili. My life depends on it."

She glanced back at the area behind the counter. "My manager will be back in a few minutes. If you'd like to—"

"Mili, please." Jazz forced an edge of desperation into his voice. "I might not have a few minutes." He let his legs go wobbly and staggered forward to lean heavily against the desk. "Your manager wouldn't want me bleeding all over this nice desk. What would the police say?" He looked her in the eye and smiled his most pitiful puppy-dog smile.

She leaned over the counter and spoke in a low voice. "You say the guest is here with a friend whose name is . . . ?"

"Madison . . ."

The girl nodded encouragingly.

"Madison Edwards?"

"Yes." She flashed him a smile. "If you will be so kind as to pick up the courtesy telephone"—she pointed to a phone at the end of the counter—"I will call up. But only if you're sure she won't mind being woken up."

"You're calling Hollis, right? She won't be happy, but I promise you won't get in trouble."

"I better not." She lowered her eyes and glanced up at him through her thick lashes. "Because if I do, you owe me dinner."

"Be careful." He lowered his voice. "Now I have incentive to get you in trouble."

He picked up the indicated phone and leaned over the counter to watch as the girl punched a number onto a recessed keypad. It looked like five-three-four-one. Even if Hollis didn't answer, at least he had something.

The phone seemed to ring forever. Jazz was just about to hang up when a drowsy voice sounded over the phone.

"Hello."

"Hello, Hollis?"

A long pause. "Who is this?"

"Jazz Rechabson—the musician from the Hookah Club. Listen. Somebody tried to kill me—"

"The musician what?" The voice was suddenly wary. "How'd you get this number?"

"Hollis, please. . . . Listen. I know this is going to sound crazy, but I think someone drugged me. Five men just attacked me at my apartment. I think you may be in danger too."

"Danger? What are you talking about? What happened back there? If you're doing drugs—"

"I just need my guitar back, okay? If the men find out you have it, they'll come after you too. You do have it, right? Please tell me you didn't leave it on the street."

"What are you talking about? This is crazy. You call me at four in the morning—just to get a guitar?"

Jazz glanced up at the desk attendant. She was making a show of typing on the computer, but she was definitely listening. "Thanks, Hollis. Room 341. I'll be right up." He caught Mili's eye and shook his head. "That's okay. I can find it."

"What are you— How—"

"See you in a minute." He hung up the phone and turned back to Mili.

"Is everything all right? Should I call the police?" The clerk stepped toward him and paused.

"That depends. Where are the elevators?"

"It depends on the elevators?" The girl turned to the hallway at the corner of the lobby.

"No, it depends on whether or not I can think of a way to get you in trouble." He flashed her a parting smile and hurried across the lobby. She was still watching him as he rounded the corner. At least she wouldn't be a problem.

Now to deal with Hollis.

He rode up to the third floor and considered his strategy as he walked across the richly carpeted hallway toward room 341. His guitar was the number-one priority, but he needed money too. He couldn't risk going back to his apartment so he'd need to buy all new stuff. Plus he'd need a bus ticket out of town. The more money he could get out of Hollis, the further he'd be able to go.

But first he had to convince her to open the door. He stepped up to room 341 and hesitated. Now that he was inside the hotel, he was safe. Maybe he should just hide out in a stairwell until morning. If the girl freaked out and called security, he was dead.

Of course, if he didn't get any money, he was dead, too. The girl was his best shot. He couldn't afford to back away now.

Reaching up with his injured arm, he pressed it against the door jamb. Hot pain oozed into his arm as he smeared it across the wood to leave a trail of fresh blood. Then, slashing his arm across his face, he collapsed into the door and knocked.

Sudden movement sounded inside.

Jazz waited and knocked again.

A tight voice called through the door. "Who is it?"

"Hollis, please. Just give me the guitar and I'll leave you alone."

"Go away!" Her shout was laced with panic. "Leave now or I'll call the police."

"Then they'll kill me. Maybe you too. Please, you don't want my death on your hands. Just give me the guitar. That's all I ask. Don't make me tell them you stole it."

A light switched on inside the room. The sound of soft footsteps approaching the door. She'd look through the peephole first. This was his only chance.

Jazz swayed on his feet and backpedaled away from the door to give her a better view of his face. Then, teetering dangerously, he let his head roll back and collapsed with a groan onto the floor.

The door clanked open. A breathless gasp. Footsteps stuttered across the carpet and a shadow fell across his face. Then she was swearing, running back into the room.

"Please," he called after her in a feeble voice. "No doctors or police. They'd find me."

Did she hear him? Jazz lifted his head as the door clicked shut. "Hollis, please." He called out louder. "They stole all my money. I can't afford a hospital."

The door eased open. The girl peeked out into the hallway, panic rippling across her pale features. He'd served up more than she could handle. He needed to throw her a lifeline. Quick.

"I'm okay." He pushed himself up onto his left arm and shot her just the right dosage of smile. "Just help me up and I'll be fine."

"What happened?" Her eyes flitted between his arm and face. Finally, she stepped out into the hallway and crouched beside him to wrap an arm around his back.

"Someone drugged me and then attacked me." Jazz tried to stand up, but a real wave of dizziness tipped him back onto the floor. "Sorry." He fought his way back to a sitting position, but she put a restraining hand on his chest.

"It's okay." The softness of her voice told him he'd scored. "I've got you. Put more weight on me."

He had no choice. His arms and legs were suddenly so weak it was a battle to stand. The hallway tipped and lurched beneath him as she inserted the key into the lock and pulled back on the door.

"I don't do drugs, I swear." He blinked his eyes and tried to focus on her face. "You've got to believe me. I was attacked by a bunch of men. They were wearing . . ." He shook his head and let her lead him into a spacious antique-furnished room.

"What's wrong? What were they wearing?" She eased him onto a blue velvet couch and crouched down beside him. "Can you hear me? Want me to call a doctor?"

"No! I'm— I know it's going to sound ridiculous. The whole thing sounds crazy, but it's true. I swear."

"I believe you. Just tell me. What am I supposed to do?"

"The men were wearing black robes. I don't know if it was the drugs they gave me or what, but they were all hazy and shadowy— like flickering black ghosts."

"Is that why you ran away? Did you see them coming?"

"When?" Jazz blinked again to clear his eyes. "You mean back on the sidewalk—with you and your friend? All I remember was . . . it felt like I was suddenly being chased by a nightmare. I don't even know what happened."

"You just sort of changed. I don't know how to describe it. It was really creepy. Like someone else was suddenly inside your skin. It scared us half to death. Then you just, I don't know, screamed like a wild animal and ran away. I've never seen anything like it."

Jazz shook his head. "It was drugs. It had to be. Someone must have slipped them into my drink at the club. But why? It's not like I have anything anyone would want."

"What about the men?" She looked down at the blood staining his shirt. "When did they . . . do this to you?"

Jazz tried to come up with a convincing story, but the truth was just as good as anything he'd be able to make up. "I woke up halfway across the city. I was all beat up and lying out in the middle of the park. I got back to my apartment, but when I opened the door the whole place had been torn apart: my clothes, my music, everything. Even my mail had been opened. I was just about to call the police when I heard footsteps in the hallway. I ran to the window and saw three hooded men climbing up the wall. If I hadn't seen them and jumped before they got to the window, I wouldn't have gotten away. I almost didn't. I kept hallucinating and getting dizzy. I don't know how many of them there are, but I guarantee they're still searching for me. Whatever it is they want, they want it bad."

The girl nodded, but she didn't believe him. He could see it in her eyes.

"So you think they want your guitar?"

Jazz shrugged. "I don't have any money. No family or friends or social connections. Now I don't even have any clothes or a place to stay. The guitar is the only thing of value I own. It's the only thing that wasn't at my apartment."

"So what's in the envelope?"

"What envelope?" Jazz followed her eyes to the crumpled edge of the manila envelope poking out of his pants pocket.

"I thought you said they opened all your mail."

"They did. This wasn't—" He pulled the envelopes from his pocket and looked them over carefully. "I got them out of my box before going up to my room. They weren't . . ." Setting the junk mail aside, he unfolded the large envelope and ripped it open.

There was a single sheet of white paper inside bearing the same ornate handwriting that was on the envelope. It was a will— the last will and testament of . . . Jonah Rechabson?

His grandfather?

Jazz read through the document twice as the girl leaned in close to read over his shoulder.

I, Jonadab Rechabson, being of sound mind, do
hereby declare this instrument to be my first, last, and
only will and testament. I hereby leave my blessings
and full inheritance to Jaazaniah Rechabson, who is
my grandson and only surviving heir. To Jaazaniah
Rechabson and his family I also leave a shovel, the
contents of my blue plastic box, the Rechabson family
Bible, and the following instructions: Rth 116.

I hereby direct that all other worldly possessions
be burned in accordance with ancient traveler custom
and that my remains be buried standing.

I herewith affix my signature to this will on this
eleventh day of May.

Jonadab Rechabson

At the end of the page, written in a shaky scrawling hand, was
another message:

I saw Jonah write this paper. My name is Wilmer
Salley. Right now.

When Jazz finally looked up from the document, the girl was
watching him with a guarded expression.

"I have no idea." He shook his head and looked back down
at the date on the paper. "It says it was signed three days ago, but
that can't be right."

"Why not?"

Jazz shook his head and stared down at the paper. "Grandpa
Jonah was a crazy old coot who lived out in the swamps with alligators and mosquitoes. But he . . ."

"But?"

He took a deep breath and met her eyes. "My grandfather died
when I was a little boy."

7

Mariutza

MARI SQUINTED INTO THE blasting wind as the sleeping city sped by in a blur of shadows and flashing light. Impossibly tall buildings frowned down at her through hundreds of browsy, glassed-in windows. Signs big enough for a giant to read. Massive bridges leaping over roads and rivers and dry rocky ground.

And so many lights . . . They were everywhere! Flung out further than the eye could see. Lighting up windows and road-sides and beautiful green signs. Perched high on the tops of tall, limbless trees, beaming their sparkle down on nothing but plain old grass. It was all so big and stupendously wide. Like the town folk had mounted the stars of the heavens on pins and needles and stuck them to the ground. How could anybody make so many beautiful things? It pained her head to think on it. The Gadje had to be the wisest folk on earth. Why else would the Holy One have entrusted them with so much awesome power?

The headlights of an approaching car filled her eyes with star-bursts of streaking light. A loud horn blasted in her ears. The cars had been making with the horns all night. She knew they were just trying to be friendly, but she didn't like it one bit. It was too loud and brashy in her ears. It made the town folk seem angry and out of sorts, like they hadn't learned to hold onto their horses when they were young.

How did they talk when they weren't in cars? Were they louder than Purodad and Caralee? What did they talk about? She thought back on the strange words of the driver. Purodad never said anything about them speaking foreign languages. What if she couldn't understand them at all?

Her car eased to a stop behind a long line of smoking cars. Mari took a deep breath and blinked the film from her eyes. Her chest burned deep down to her lungs. It was like inhaling a campfire—a campfire that burned metal and grit instead of clean honest wood.

A loud squeal sounded behind her. She turned to see a huge truck shuddering to a stop. A man leaned forward and glowered at her through the window. His head was smooth and shiny, like a greased egg. He didn't seem to have any hair at all. He spoke something into the glass and greeted her with a loud honk of the horn. She smiled at him and waggled her hand in a greeting, but he yelled at her and sent out a louder, even longer blast.

The car jolted beneath her, and its door swung open. The man in the beautiful white shirt stepped outside and yelled back at the truck driver. It was the same language as before, but this time she could make out a few of the connecting words.

The truck driver stabbed a meaty finger straight at her, and the man in the white shirt turned. His face contorted into a scowl, and he let out another stream of words.

"H-h-hello." Mari's throat tightened. "My name is Mariutza. I am pleased to meet you." She flipped herself up and over the railing to land, catlike, on the road facing the man.

The man's mouth dropped open. He looked her up and down as a strange inward-focused kind of smile twisted his features.

"Do you understand my words?" She spoke slowly, fighting to keep her voice from shaking. "I'm sorry to ride on your roof without asking permission. It was wrong of me. I understand this now. But the Badness was trying to kill me. It was the only way I could think to escape."

"The badness what?" The man's eyes came suddenly into focus. "You're kidding, right? I mean . . ." He looked her up and down again. "You're serious? Someone tried to kill you. I can call the police if you want. If you're serious, I mean."

Mari stepped backward. The police were one of the strongest power centers. They couldn't all be trusted. Would the man know who was safe?

"It's okay. I don't have to call nobody." He lifted his hands, like a prophet at his prayers. "Just tell me what you want. Breakfast, maybe? Do you need a ride?" His eyes drifted down her body and back up to her necklace. Was she supposed to give him a coin? What was she supposed to say?

"Thank you. I'd like to ride in your car—if you don't mind. Do you know Jaazaniah the Prophet?"

The truck blasted them again. The man with no hair was shouting something, gesturing with his hands.

"Keep your pants on. We're moving!" The man turned back to Mari and spoke in a gentle voice. "I don't know about any prophets, but I've got an Internet connection in my apartment if you want to do a search. What do you think?"

"I think you're a generous, beautiful man, and I thank you for your help." Mari smiled at the man, letting all the gratitude and love she felt for him radiate through her expression.

The white-shirted man stepped toward her and put a warm hand on her shoulder. Mari glanced up at him as he led her around the car to the passenger door. His hand slid down her back, leaving a trail of tingling flame. So beautiful! *Holy One, thank You. Thank You for sending me a friend.*

She choked out a breathless "thank you" as he opened the door and helped her into the car.

The truck honked again, and the man turned to blast it with a torrent of angry words. Then, turning back to her with a smile, he closed the door and walked around the car.

The inside of the car was miraculously cold—like it had taken a bite of winter and stored it up in there all through the spring. Mari leaned forward on the seat, hugging her skirt to her knees to keep the muddy fabric from soiling the car's furniture. The air was filled with a heady perfume. Everything was so clean and new. She felt like the princess at the palace of the elf king. It was too wonderful for words!

The door opened and the man slid behind the steering wheel. He moved a lever and the car leaped to life. It rushed forward, silent as a dream. She couldn't believe it. She was actually riding inside a car!

"So . . . do you have a place to stay?" The man glanced at her and then looked back out the glass window.

Mari shook her head. "I'm a traveler, but this is my first time to leave the woods."

The man shook his head and blew a long blast of air at the window before turning on her with a soft smile. "If you want, you can crash at my place. I've got plenty of extra room."

Crash at my place? Mari looked down at her torn muddy clothes and tried to think. He was so modern and sophisticated. He probably thought she was some kind of cave woman. "Thank you. You're very kind." She glanced over at him to see if she'd gotten the answer right. His smile was wider than ever.

Mari forced her gaze to the glass window and tried to pay attention to the other cars, but the man's presence drew her back in. He was a real Gadje. There were so many things she could say to him. So many questions she could ask.

The man finally broke the silence. "Relax. With this traffic it's going to be a while."

Mari nodded and tried to put some gratitude behind her smile.

"Seriously." He shot her another look. "Sit back and put your seat belt on. It'll be another ten minutes at least."

"I . . ." Mari looked down at her lap as her face grew dangerously warm. "I don't know how."

The man laughed and fixed her with an indecipherable expression.

"I'm sorry." The heat was starting to burn in her eyes. "This is my first time in a car. I've never done it before."

Mari felt the man's eyes on her. He was staring. Probably wishing he'd never let such an ignorant person inside his car.

"Hey . . ." His voice was soft as a dove on a still day. "It's okay. I didn't mean nothing by it. Everybody has a first time."

Mari looked up at him and wiped a sleeve across her face.

"It's easy, see? Just sit back in your seat. Slide on back and relax."

"But my skirt's all full of mud."

"It's okay. The seats are leather. They'll wipe off." He gave her an encouraging nod as she eased back into the seat. It was so soft. The smooth cushions hugged her body like a fresh-stuffed tick. It felt wonderful.

"See that strap by your shoulder?" The man pointed and tugged on the cord wrapped around his waist. "Just pull the buckle out and stick it in this slot." He reached over and tapped a device by her hip. "That's it. Just pull it across."

Mari pulled on the shiny buckle, but it kept pulling back on itself. Finally, after pulling it out as far as it would go, she managed to stick it in the slot until it clicked in place. She looked up at the man and grinned.

"See there? You're an expert now." He grinned back at her. "A few more lessons and I'll have you driving."

"Thank you." Mari started to look away but forced her eyes back to his. "Is it permissible for me to ask for your name?"

"Heck, yeah. Name's Jack, Jack Baldassaro."

"Thank you, Jack. Thank you for everything."

The man—Jack—huffed and shook his head. He looked over at her and opened his mouth to say something, but then turned back to the glass window and went back to shaking his head.

Mari leaned back in her seat and watched as the trees sped past her. The sun was at her back. To anyone spying on the road, she'd appear as a dark featureless shadow. Try as they might, they'd never be able to guess the story of her life. They'd think she was a rich, sophisticated Gadje, riding in a shiny car with a beautiful new friend.

The car turned onto a smaller road which branched this way and that before it let out onto a narrow street lined with huge, many-windowed buildings.

"Okay, here we are." He pulled onto a wide rectangular road and stopped the car between two painted white lines. "It ain't much, but it's home."

Mari sat still as Jack opened his door and got out of the car. She leaned forward and looked through the glass windows at the cars standing around her. They were all empty. Where were all the people?

Her door opened and Jack reached across her lap to release the buckle from its slot. He was so close! Blazing eyes licked like fire at her skin. She could feel his breath on her lips. It smelled like peppermint tea. Even his skin gave off a pretty scent. It was sweet and fragrant—like rhododendron blossoms on a hot summer day.

"There you go . . ." He carefully removed the strap and then took her by the hand. His palm was soft and impossibly smooth—like the calluses had been scrubbed magically away. "Watch your head." A hand tingled on her shoulder as he helped her step out into the summer heat.

Mari took a deep breath. She felt light-headed and dizzy as if she were floating on a cloud. Still holding her hand, he led her across the hot pavement toward a massive gray building. It was immense—easily the biggest thing she'd ever seen. She followed a line of gleaming windows all the way to the top until she was bending over backwards.

"It's beautiful. Amazing."

"What? The building?"

Mari turned to study his face. He seemed confused. Had she said something wrong?

"Come on." He pulled her toward a door at the bottom of the building. "Let's get out of the heat. I've got some clean clothes you can put on while we wash your stuff."

"What?" Mari snapped suddenly out of her daze. "Inside? There?"

"It's okay. I'm not going to try nothing." He started to pull her toward the door, but she planted her feet and yanked her hand free.

"I can't. It's not allowed!"

"It's okay. I'm not like that." Jack stepped toward her and held out a hand. "You can call the police and maybe get cleaned up while I fix some breakfast. That's all. I'm just trying to help."

"In there?" Mari looked up the towering building and the strength suddenly drained out of her body. She felt shaky and quivery inside. "I'm Standing. To go inside a building is not allowed."

"It's all right," Jack cooed and eased toward her with outstretched arms. "You don't have to do anything you don't want to do. Just tell me what you want."

She looked up into his beautiful, smooth face. Kindness lived in those eyes. He just wanted to take care of her—like Purodad.

"Thank you." She stumbled forward and leaned into Jack's embrace. Strong arms circled around her. The warmth of his body soaked through her, filling her head with pounding thunder. Mari tensed.

Something bad was happening. She was shaking like a reed in a storm.

The man's hand slid up her back. Caressing fingers twined into her hair. What was he doing? She gasped and looked up into his down-turned eyes. Suddenly she couldn't breathe.

"Shhh . . ." His thumb hooked under her chin and lifted her gaze. Then he was leaning closer, pressing his lips against her open mouth.

An explosion went off inside Mari's head. Her arms swung up and around. She was twisting, spinning through the air. Up and around the man's flailing body until he smacked into the ground with her forearm in the soft of his neck.

Mari's ears rang with the sound of the thud. What had she done? He was her friend. He was trying to help her! She jumped to her feet and stood breathlessly over him as he gasped and sputtered and struggled to catch his breath.

"I'm so sorry! Jack, please. I . . . Please forgive me. I didn't know what I was doing."

The man let out a stream of words hot as coals as he struggled to his feet and glared down at her, eyes blazing. His face was a dark shade of purple-tinged red. He lunged toward her with clenched fists. Veins bulged at his neck.

"You sorry little—"

"I am." Mari hung her head and tried to match her expression to her heart. "I didn't mean to. It was the training. My grandfather made me practice all the time."

The man's eyes narrowed. "Hah!" He swung a fist at her face and pulled back halfway before impact.

Mari was sure her sorrowful expression didn't change, but her training had betrayed her. As soon as he'd started to move, her open hand came up and her weight shifted backward into a defensive stance.

The man let out a loud blast and stalked off toward the building.

"Jack, wait." Mari hurried after him. "I'm sorry. It's just the training. I didn't mean to hurt you."

"You didn't hurt me." He strode to the door and threw it open. "I just don't like being played with."

"But I'm not playing—"

"Right. Help me." His voice rose an octave. "People are trying to kill me—the sweet innocent girl who doesn't even know how to use a seat belt." He stepped through the door and slammed it shut.

Shouts and muffled thumps gradually faded to silence behind the heavy metal door. Mari collapsed onto the steps and buried her face in her hands. It was too much. She was an ignorant swamp girl. She didn't belong here. She didn't know the first thing about making town friends. She'd be better off with the Badness. At least there in the swamps she couldn't hurt anybody.

Except Purodad and Caralee.

Her stomach seized up and a loud sob escaped her lips. Jumping to her feet, she ran out into the sea of stopped cars and turned in a wide circle. Where was she supposed to go? It was all so big! She had no idea how to find Jaazaniah. She didn't even know how to find her way back to the swamp.

Eyes streaming with tears, she walked back to Jack's car and unclasped the necklace from around her neck.

"I'm sorry, Jack. Please forgive me." She pulled a thick gold coin from its hook and slipped it through the tiny crack above the glass in the car window. The coin bounced off the edge of the door and landed in the middle of Jack's beautiful leather seat.

Holy One, please return blessings on Jack Baldassaro.

She turned to face the rising sun. The roar of distant cars filled her ears. Buildings and roads and concrete as far as the eye could see. It was so big. Stretched out deep and wide as the night sky. How was she supposed to find Jaazaniah now? She didn't know the first thing about city folk. She couldn't even dig a grave right. She was just going to let Purodad down. Only one thing could help her now.

A miracle.

∽ 8 ∽

Jazz

JAZZ RAN FOR A stand of trees as hot, sulfurous air beat down on him. The ground crashed and buckled beneath his feet, pitching him onto his face. A deafening roar blasted him from behind. He rolled over and tried to scoot backward on his elbows. The monster was huge! As big as a dinosaur—no . . . a dragon. That was the word for it. Neck straining forward, clawed feet churning, it lumbered toward him like a charging rhino, shaking the forest with every step.

Throwing up his hands to shield his face, Jazz screamed and lunged to the side.

A sharp pain sliced into the side of his head, echoing with the sound of an urgent voice. "Shhh . . . It's okay." The touch of cold hands against hot skin. "Shhh . . . Wake up. It's just a dream."

Jazz opened his eyes and squinted up into a woman's face. Where was he?

"You're okay. It's just a bad dream."

Gritting his teeth against the pain, he turned his head and looked around the room. He was lying on the floor by a blue velvet sofa. The blonde—Hollis—was kneeling beside him cradling his face in deliciously cool hands.

"You have a fever. I think we should get you to a hospital."

Hospital. Jazz tried to focus on the word. No, not a hospital. The police. He needed to go to the police.

"Jazz, can you hear me?" Hollis's taut voice cut through his thoughts. "I need to call an ambulance. Nod if you understand what I'm saying."

Jazz shook his head and tried to sit up. "No hospitals. I'm fine."

"No, you're not. You're burning up with fever."

"Hollis, the men who were chasing me. They'll search the hospitals first. They're probably there right now."

The girl's eyes clouded. She looked like she was about to break down. "I'm sorry I didn't believe you. I just . . . I don't know. It sounded so crazy."

"It's okay. I—" Jazz caught his breath as pain lanced through his body. Taking a deep breath, he pushed himself up and leaned back against the base of the sofa. "It *is* crazy. If it's any consolation, I don't believe it either." He leaned his head back and closed his eyes. As soon at Hollis had seen the will, she'd been convinced the whole thing was a scam—a con job where she was supposed to give him money to help him follow some sort of crazy treasure map to his inheritance. It had taken an academy-award-level performance to keep her from kicking him to the street.

"What changed your mind?" he asked. "About me, I mean."

"Pretty much everything. Your story was too far-fetched—way too crazy to be a scam."

Jazz started to nod but the motion filled his head with throbbing pain.

"And last night, while you were asleep. Do you remember any of it?"

"Not really."

"You whimpered and cried the whole night. It was like post-traumatic stress or something. Sometimes you even talked, but it didn't make any sense."

"What did I say?"

"Something about shadow men and monsters. I think they were chasing you."

Jazz nodded and winced. "Anything else?"

"You kept talking about the moon. Once you said something about a shovel and a doghouse. And a butterfly man that wouldn't get out of your hair."

"Of course. Butterfly men. At last something that finally makes sense." He forced a smile and stretched out his stiff arms and legs. Hollis watched him beneath a furrowed brow. He couldn't blame her for being confused. How could she not?

He turned to the window. Bright sunlight glowed around the edges of the heavy drapes. "What time is it?"

"Almost eleven. Are you hungry? I think you should at least drink some water."

Jazz shook his head. "I should get going. I want to get to the police station before noon."

"I thought you wanted to get out of town."

"I do, but what if my inheritance is here in the city? If it's valuable enough to kill for . . . I can't just run away without trying."

Hollis's expression turned suddenly wary.

"Would you get over it? I'm not a con man. I'm not asking for any money."

"Not yet."

"Not . . ." He sucked in his breath and considered his options. "Okay. Here's the deal. I thought maybe I would ask for enough money to buy a change of clothes and a bus ride out of town. But that's all. It's not like I'd stage all this for the price of a bus ticket. I could get that much playing half a day at the station."

Hollis stared at him thoughtfully. "And what do I get out of the deal?"

"Now who's the con?"

"I'm just saying—"

"Look, I'm asking you a favor. You get the satisfaction of doing something nice for someone other than yourself."

"No deal." Hollis shook her head. "New clothes will run close to a thousand dollars. And who knows how much a bus ticket costs."

"A thousand dollars? Where do you think—"

"I'm not finished!" The girl raised a hand and glared at him. "If I'm going to drop that kind of money, I want in on the action."

"I don't even know what the treasure is. For all I know—"

"I didn't say treasure. I said *action*. I want to be at the police station when you talk to them. If they put you in protective custody, I want to go too. And if they find the treasure, I get to be there when it's opened."

Jazz waited for her to continue. "That's it? No treasure? You just want your share in the joy of having hit men trying to kill you?"

She nodded and held out a hand.

She really meant it. The girl was crazy. Stark-raving bored out of her spoiled little mind.

"Okay, deal." He shook her hand and groaned his way onto his feet. "And if you throw in a toothbrush and some toothpaste, I'll even let you drive me to the police station."

Daniel Groves

"FOR THE LOVE OF—" Daniel Groves pulled his foot out of a puddle of avocado-colored goo and stamped it on a tuft of dry grass. "Great . . . just great!" So much for his brand new pair of Clarks. Ninety bucks flushed down the stinking toilet. And for what? The drug-induced ravings of a mail-order voodoo queen? He was out of his mind. The whole bureau was out of its mind. He'd interviewed toasters with more credibility than Zazou.

Groves leaped over the patch of mud and shouldered his way through a wall of whispering leaves. What was wrong with him? All he had to do was leave the Zazou interview out of his report and he'd be done. It wasn't withholding information. The woman's voodoo doll had one too many pins in its head.

He should be at the office sipping a double latte and doing something useful like playing FreeCell on his computer, but no. . . . He had to slog through malaria-infested swampland to chat up another Gypsy crackpot who thought she was the direct descendant of a teaspoon. What was she going to do? Blow up the world with a crystal ball of mass destruction?

He stepped into the shade of a massive old oak tree and a sudden hush settled over the forest. It was as if someone had tripped a breaker and all the birds and chirruping insects had lost power at the same time. Even the buzzing swarm of bloodsuckers that had been harassing him since he stepped out of his car was gone.

Searching both sides of the muddy path, he crept through the gloom. Something was wrong. He could feel the weight of it hanging on the still morning air. The stench of death and destruction and decay. A cold chill tickled up his spine. He was walking into the lair of some predator. He could feel the beast's eyes. Watching him. Waiting for its chance to pounce.

Groves pulled the gun from his shoulder holster and flipped off the safety. Maybe Little Miss Voodoo Doll wasn't so crazy after all. Mariutza Glapion . . . The crazy priestess at the temple said Glapion lived out here all by herself. Voodoo queen or not, people didn't choose to live out in the middle of a swamp because they were fond of mosquitoes. She was definitely hiding something, but he'd eat his shoes—swamp goo and all—if it was a WMD.

The shadows closed in, hemming him in on all sides. Whatever it was, he was getting closer to it. The forest seemed to be holding its breath, waiting, watching . . . He spun and pointed his gun into the darkening gloom. The hairs on the back of his neck stood at attention in stiff military formation. His heart was doing disco fever in his chest. He had to get a grip. Glapion wasn't a terrorist. Period. End of discussion.

He turned in a slow three-sixty, staring deep into the shadows. The woods were completely still. No birds, no squirrels, no voodoo terrorist ninja assassins. He was being ridiculous. There wasn't anybody out here. He was in the middle of a mosquito-infested cesspool. He swept the area again and crept forward at a low crouch as the path opened into a grove of ancient live oaks.

Great sheets of Spanish moss hung low to the ground all around him. Great way to reduce visibility. He stepped around the curtains of green-tinted gray, careful not to trigger any sensors that might lie hidden within their lacy networks.

A blast of ice-cold dread hit him in the chest.

Just ahead. It was there. An invisible cloud of darkness, sick and twisted. The stench of a rotting corpse . . .

He could feel it in his bones, feel it screaming through every cell in his body.

Groves stepped around a blanket of moss and froze. There, nestled in the shadow of five enormous trees, sat a dilapidated old hut. His stomach convulsed as he stepped toward the festering

pile of unpainted boards. The stench of death clung to the shadows like some deep-rooted disease. He swallowed back his nausea
and forced himself toward the rough-hewn plank door.

"Hello?" His voice came out as a hollow whine. "This is
Daniel Groves, FBI. I'm looking for Mariutza Glapion. I need to
ask her a few questions."

Something inside the shack stirred. A choking scent wafted
through the air. His stomach convulsed again. A primal revulsion
filled his being. He raised his gun and aimed it at the door. Sweat
streamed down his forehead and trickled into his eyes. He was
going to shoot it. Hostile action or not, he was going to shoot it
until it was dead.

"Come out with your hands where I can see them! You have
three seconds!"

"That won't be necessary." A woman's smooth voice flowed
out into the shadowy yard. "I don't know this Mariutza of whom
you speak. I am Marie Paris Glapion, high priestess of Nzambi
Mpungu."

Suddenly the forest was spinning. Groves's legs buckled as he
doubled and retched, over and over, onto the ground. A shuddering wave passed through his body. Chills crawled up his back like
some venomous snake. He could feel it chewing its way through
his head, slithering deeper and deeper into his brain.

The high-pitched squawk of rusty hinges assaulted him.
Fighting the numbness in his muscles, Groves managed to raise
his head. The door was opening, spilling wave upon wave of heaping shadows out onto the ground.

Smooth shapely legs. A belt of hair and bone woven together
with tiny strips of curling leather. Groves's heart pounded in his
throat as he looked up into a woman's horribly disfigured face. Her
eyes shown like black suns, drilling into his head, filling him with
darkness and longing and despair.

"Where's Mariutza Glapion?" He managed to croak out the words. "Tell me now or I . . ." Fighting with all his strength, he raised his trembling gun to the woman's face.

"Or you'll what?" Laughter rang in his ears. "You think to threaten . . . *me?*" She was laughing again. The sound ripped through his brain like a ricocheting bullet.

Groves blinked his eyes back into focus. His gun rested, muzzle down, on the black dirt. He tried to raise it, but it was too heavy. He tugged on it with all his might. Grabbing it with both hands, he forced it from the ground.

"Step away from the hut . . . or I'll . . . shoot." Groves hoisted the barrel upward.

"Of course." The woman cackled. "By all means. Go ahead. Shoot the gun if it makes you happy."

Groves started to pull back on the trigger, but something wasn't right.

He blinked twice and the world melted before his eyes. The gun was pointed at his stomach, his chest, his neck . . . He tried to fight it, but he couldn't make it stop. It was too strong. It angled higher and higher until he was staring down its dark barrel. Slowly the gun moved closer and pressed itself against his forehead. The sound of distant drums pounded in his ears as the woman's black eyes bored into his brain.

Slowly, though everything in his being screamed against it, his finger tightened around the trigger.

ᴄꙅ 9 ᴄꙅ

Jazz

Jᴀᴢᴢ ꙅʟᴏᴜᴄʜᴇᴅ ɪɴ ᴛʜᴇ back of the rattling, shimmying rental car. The longer he rode, the worse his head throbbed. By the time Hollis pulled up to the police station, his brain felt like it was crawling with a thousand angry bees.

"Are you all right?" Hollis's distorted face pushed into his vision. "Jazz?"

"Fine." He nodded and stepped shakily from the car. "I think I'm a little hung over, that's all. Whatever they poisoned me with isn't out of my system yet."

"I can take you to the hospital. We don't have to do the police first."

"I'm okay." He checked up and down the street and then stumbled toward the station steps. "I don't think I'd survive another trip in your car. I've ridden jack hammers with better shocks."

"There's a convention in town. It was the last car on the lot." Hollis appeared at his side and pulled his arm over her shoulder. He grimaced at the thought of what his shirt was doing to her clothes. But that's what she was paying for—the chance to experience real danger and discomfort. How many other rich girls were out there just like her? Maybe he could open up a franchise.

He pushed through a glass door and stepped into a claustrophobic lobby. A line of people stood in front of a glass-faced counter. The sign said *Traffic*. Where was the *People are Trying to Kill Me* window? He stepped up to the spot labeled *Information* and waited while a uniformed woman sat typing at the cubicle behind the glass. The area behind her swarmed with activity. Two uniformed officers appeared behind a line of cubicles and yelled something at a cluster of white-shirted men. A man in a rumpled suit charged through the room, shouting orders like a drill sergeant—something about helicopters and search parties and grid patterns. Jazz tried to pay attention, but his head pounded so hard his vision went all blurry and hazy. The buzzing in his ears was worse than ever. He felt like he was going to throw up. Was it possible to be so hungry it made you sick?

"Jazz?" Hollis was looking into his eyes. She reached up, touched his forehead, and frowned. "I don't like this. Let's get you to the hospital. We can call the police from there."

"I'm fine." Jazz forced a grin. "Besides, we don't want to lose our place in line."

"I don't think they're set up for this sort of thing. We'd get their attention sooner if we called."

Jazz nodded and watched as another group of men strode through the office. One of them, a tall thin man with a nose like the curved beak of a hawk, was yelling so loud Jazz could feel the words echoing in his head.

"Excuse me. Miss?" Hollis knocked on the glass. "My friend here is sick. He needs to get to a hospital. Miss?"

The woman looked up from her computer and wheeled her chair up to the window. "Can I help you?"

"My friend was attacked late last night." Hollis was suddenly all business. "First they drugged him, and now they're trying to kill him. He needs to get to a hospital, but he won't go without the police making sure it's okay."

"I'm sorry? You say someone tried to kill him?"

"Not *tried*. Is *trying*. Someone's still trying to kill him."

"Cedric!" The woman turned in her seat and called over to a gray-haired officer reclining at one of the cubicles. "Come help this nice couple. They got a situation."

The officer rose slowly to his feet and sauntered over to an unlit hallway. A few seconds later he appeared at a door at the corner of the lobby and smiled. "There something I can help you with?"

"It's about time!" Hollis guided Jazz over to where the officer stood holding open a paneled wooden door. "He shouldn't be here. He needs to get to a hospital."

"I'm sorry, ma'am, but things are a bit crazy here these days. We got us an FBI infestation. If someone don't swat the queen bee real soon, they'll have us all working out of the parking lot." The old man shuffled down a short hallway and led them into the busy office. He motioned for Hollis to sit down at the only chair in the narrow cubicle and then leaned back against the desk. "All right, . . . what can I do you for?"

A jolt passed through Jazz's body. The heaviness in his stomach expanded. He could feel it pushing through his body, soaking into his mind. The room dimmed and went blurry. Hollis's distorted face filled his vision. She was saying something. The officer was talking too. Both of them were staring at him, talking at the same time.

A hazy image appeared in front of their faces. The backs of three ghostly, white-shirted men. They were walking down a hallway, stepping through an open doorway into a crowded room.

The buzzing in his head stopped as everything slammed into focus. The tall, hawk-nosed man was staring at him from across the room. His black eyes narrowed, burning into Jazz's brain.

The man stretched out his arm to point a finger at Jazz. "Stop that man!"

Jazz spun. A heavyset black man stood frozen in the doorway behind him.

"Gun! He's got a gun!" Jazz pointed at the man by the door and dove onto the floor. Three officers converged on the heavyset man as Jazz scrambled across the aisle. Under a desk, around a low cubicle, he leaped to his feet and darted through an open door.

Shouts sounded behind him as he sprinted down a long hallway and burst through a pair of swinging doors. Blazing sunlight hit him in the face. Police cars in a small lot. A row of trees. A wall of older office buildings just across the street.

Jazz leaped down the steps and cut across the parking lot. Swinging out into the street, he zigzagged through a clot of cars and charged down the next street. The police were working with the shadow men? It was too much. How had they found out about the treasure?

A siren wailed just ahead of him. A whole chorus of sirens was chasing him from behind. Skidding to a stop, he turned and darted back down the sidewalk. One of the buildings was a dentist's office. Surely they wouldn't lock the doors during lunch.

He ambled up to the door, pulled it open, and stepped inside as a police car raced down the street. Then, taking a deep breath, he walked up to the window and glanced casually around the office area beyond. Voices sounded on the other side of a partition, but nobody was at the desk. Hurrying across the waiting area, he eased open a door and stepped into a dimly lit hallway. *Perfect!* A low appointment counter separated him from the office area.

Sitting on a desk on the other side of the counter was an orange-handled pair of scissors.

Jazz climbed over the counter and tiptoed over to the desk. Scooping up the scissors, he was about to vault back over the counter when he noticed the coffee maker. Perfect! Just what he needed. He crept over to the machine and eased the coffeepot out of its bay. Over half a pot left. If he was careful—

The door to the outside swung open with a bang.

"Excuse me?" A man's voice called out. "Hello?"

Covering the open pot with his hand, Jazz vaulted the counter and dropped to the floor as clacking footsteps entered the office.

"Excuse me, ma'am. We're looking for a twenty-year-old, brown-haired, brown-eyed Caucasian male, about six feet tall, wearing jeans and a white blood-stained long-sleeved shirt. Have you seen anyone close to that description?"

Jazz held his breath. *Had* she seen him? Why was she taking so long to answer?

"Last night I was at this party. There was a guy there wearing a white shirt, but he—"

"No ma'am. Just now. Within the last fifteen minutes."

"I've been working here all morning."

"Thank you, ma'am." The door swung open with a whoosh. "If you see him call 9-1-1 immediately." Scraping footsteps. The clank of the closing door.

Jazz let his breath out slowly. The police were searching the streets for him. Had they been in on the scheme to poison him? This probably wasn't the best time to find out. He needed a better hiding place.

Pushing onto his hands and knees, he crawled down the hallway, pushing the coffeepot ahead of him. An unlabeled door stood ajar to his right. Maybe . . . No. The next door was a bathroom. It would be risky, but at least it would have a lock. He climbed onto his feet and slipped into the bathroom, pulling the door closed behind him.

The light clicked on with the soft whir of a fan. Jazz locked the door and moved to stand in front of the mirror. His face was deathly pale. Great beads of sweat dotted his skin. With his blood-stained sleeve and disheveled curly hair, he looked like some kind of undead zombie.

He unbuttoned his shirt and spread it flat across the sink. Using the borrowed scissors, he cut off the blood-stained sleeves and threw them into the trash can. Then, wadding the shirt into a compact ball, he fed it through the narrow neck of the coffee pot and tamped it down until it was completely submerged. It would be disgusting and he'd smell like a coffee addict, but better nasty than dead. He pulled the shirt out and wrung it out into the sink. Thin brown stains ran down his arms and streaked the white porcelain.

The bathroom reeked, but at least his shirt wasn't white anymore. It was actually a pleasant shade of beige. He spread it out to dry and shucked off his jeans to turn them into cutoffs. It wasn't much of a disguise, but it was as good as he could do given the circumstances.

A loud knock sounded at the door.

"Just a second." Jazz jammed a foot into his freshly cut pants and had to hop to keep from falling on his face. It wasn't going to work. What could he say? The receptionist knew about the manhunt. She'd call the police for sure. And then . . .

He'd be dead.

Mariutza

MARI DODGED AROUND A parked car and raced up a busy street. Buildings towered over her. They were everywhere, reaching to the skies, hemming her in at every turn. They stared down at her with invisible eyes, mocking her weakness and ignorance. She was an interloper in the lofty affairs of Gadje more powerful than kings.

She stopped at a coming-together of streets and reached out with the *dikh* sight. The Badness buzzed all around her, filling the polluted air with its fetid stench. Where was the voice? It rang so clear a few minutes ago. Pure and lyrical and sweet. Like her grandfather's voice. A fresh presence against the decay and corruption eddying all around her.

She jogged up a hard, gray path, searching for a passage that would take her further to the right. The cry came from this direction, but it stopped—like it had been silenced or cut short. If it was the prophet, maybe he'd been forced to shield himself from the enemy. Maybe he was in trouble and needed her help!

A cluster of trees broke the wall of buildings to her right. An oasis of green in the midst of a desert of stone and grit. Mari ran for the trees and lost herself in their cool embrace. The clamor started to fade as she walked down a smooth stone path. The chirp of birds soothed her tortured ears like a balm. Cutting across a carpet of short green weeds, she stepped toward a beautiful many-colored structure and froze.

A woman stood beside the structure as a fair-haired child slid down a shiny blue slope. *Beautiful!* Mari's legs wobbled and gave out. She collapsed onto the ground and stared at the child. Wispy blond hair, fat dimpled cheeks. It was so beautiful! Mari had seen children in pictures, but never one so beautiful as this. And its voice!

A tiny laugh rang through the park. The sweetness of the sound took Mari's breath away. It was soft, like the quack of a duck, but ever so much more beautiful! It made her heart ache. She felt like she was breaking in two.

Mari watched as the child pranced across the ground and stooped over to pick up a tiny fistful of sand. Its face crinkled as it held the sand up to a Gadje woman and squealed. The woman squatted down next to it, reached out a hand, and took some of the sand—

"Are you crying?" A soft voice sounded at her ear.

Mari turned with a gasp. A tiny brown boy stood next to her, looking into her face with wide, cherubic eyes.

"Why are you crying?" The boy stepped closer to her and reached out with a chubby little hand. "Are you sad? Is that why you're crying?"

Mari blinked her eyes and wiped an arm across her face. He was so beautiful. So absolutely perfect. An ache rose inside her. She wanted to reach out and touch him. To pick him up and squeeze him to her chest.

"My name is Mariutza." Her voice came soft, barely controlled. "I'm pleased to meet you."

"Why are you crying?"

"Because you're so beautiful. I used to live in the swamp and we didn't have children there."

"But why are you crying?"

"Because I'm so happy." Careful not to make any sudden moves, Mari raised a hand to her neck and fumbled with her necklace to unclasp a shiny gold coin.

The boy pressed his hands together and watched her with wondering eyes.

"May I give you a present?" Mari reached out slowly and opened her hand with the coin resting on her palm.

The boy stepped forward and bent over to study the coin. "What is it?"

"It's a gold coin. This one is Spanish. It was part of a pirate's treasure."

The boy reached out for the coin. Mari lifted her hand gently and her fingertips slid across the smooth soft skin of his arm.

"Mommy!" The boy spun and danced up and down with the coin raised high in the air. "Mommy, look! Pirate treasure. Real gold pirate treasure!"

Mari looked past the boy at a tall, brown woman in a beautiful green and gold dress. She strode toward them. "Is he bothering you? Jarod, leave that lady alone!"

"I'm s-sorry." Mari backed away from the boy and turned to look around the park. The woman with the little girl was staring at her. A man in a white hat jogged up the path behind her. He was staring at her too.

Something hard rolled beneath her feet. Mari stumbled backward, turned, and ran. The shouts of the boy rang out behind her as she weaved in and out between the trees. For a heartbeat she wanted to turn, go back to him . . .

But an inhuman wail filled the air. It crescendoed. Approached at an incredible speed!

A jagged-edged chill shuddered through her body as she ran. The Badness. It was almost on her. Mari leaped a wide wooden chair and darted out into the street. Blue flashing lights bore down on her from the right. She spun around and dove between two stopped cars as a black and white car roared past her in a flash of wailing blue light. Climbing onto her feet, she stared after the screaming car. More of them were coming. She could feel the Badness closing in on her. It was getting closer. She could hear it screaming through the streets.

Mari darted across the road and made for a narrow gap between two buildings. A short dirty street ended at a bank of giant metal boxes. Keeping to the shadow of the building on her right, she followed the narrow street to its end. Something smelled dreadful—like the rotting carcass of a dead swamp rat.

Stepping around the metal boxes, she stopped and sucked in her breath.

Standing against the wall were three plastic bins. Trash cans! That's what they had to be. Purodad had told her all about them, but she'd never believed him.

Heart pounding in her throat, she crept toward the first can and carefully lifted its lid. A gleaming white plastic bag sat just inside. Mari untied the bag and pulled it open. Paper and bottles and even food! Her heart leaped as she dug through the materials. Just what she needed—a plastic jug for her water supply! A can with a sharp lid to make a knife!

She set the treasures aside and dug deeper into the bag. So much paper! It was enough to last her a whole year! She pulled the paper out and started sorting it into piles on the ground. There was even a piece of string! And a coil of wire she could use to tie her water supply around her waist!

"Excuse me, ma'am?" A loud voice sent Mari spinning around.

Two men in tight, navy-blue uniforms walked toward her. One of them, a tall white-skinned man with thin reddish hair, was looking back and forth between her and the black notebook he held out in front of him.

She reached out with her mind, groping for some trace of the Badness, but they didn't seem to be infected. Breathing her relief, she smiled at the men and stepped out from behind the trash cans.

"Ma'am, I'm going to have to ask you for some ID." The other man was shorter and light brown. He returned her smile and stepped forward.

"I'm sorry," Mari was careful to enunciate every word. "But I do not understand."

"I need to see a photo ID—a driver's license or identification card." The man looked at her and frowned. He thought she was stupid—an uneducated girl from the swamps. Say *something. Don't just stand there gawping like a caught fish.*

"I'm sorry, but I don't know where to find a photo ID. I just came to the city. Perhaps you should ask someone else."

The short man glanced back at the tall man, who stepped forward and placed a heavy hand on her arm. "Ma'am, we're going to have to ask you to come with us. There are some men at the station who'd like to ask you a few questions."

✐ 10 ✐

Jazz

ANOTHER KNOCK SOUNDED ON the bathroom door. Louder. Sharper.

"Just a second!" Jazz buttoned his shirt and tried to smooth the wrinkles out of the wet fabric. He reeked of coffee, but that couldn't be helped. He turned off the lights and stepped away from the door before pulling it open.

"Oh!" An older woman with dark-rimmed glasses and dyed red hair stood in the doorway. "I'm sorry. I wasn't expecting . . ."

"Sorry. It was an emergency." Jazz stepped forward into the light and grinned. It wasn't the woman the police officer had talked to. Her voice was deeper and scratchier. "Can the dentist take me now? My appointment isn't until 1:30, but I'm happy to go earlier."

"No, 1:30 is fine. I just needed to . . . get in."

Jazz nodded and glanced at her name tag. "Thanks, Sally." He spoke loud enough to be heard at the end of the hall and stepped quickly around her to hurry past the front desk. A woman was sitting behind the counter. She looked up as he opened the door and slipped back into the waiting room. So far so good. He sank into the furthest chair from the office window and glanced down at his shirt. It was wrinkled and ragged as an old dust cloth, but it definitely looked beige. If the receptionist would just leave the room for a few seconds, he'd be able to—

An interior door bumped open and a haggard-looking woman stepped into the waiting room carrying an infant and leading a young boy by the hand. Just what the dentist ordered!

Jazz jumped to his feet and hurried over to the front door. "Please . . . allow me." He held it open and, as soon as they were through, stepped out after them onto the sidewalk. "Wow, is it ever hot!" He followed them down the walk and turned right at the street.

The woman didn't respond. Maybe following them would be enough. It's not like they had to become best friends.

A police car turned onto the street a block ahead of them and approached them at a crawl.

"Excuse me, ma'am?" Jazz dug in his pocket and pulled out his keys. "Ma'am?" He stepped around the boy and came up alongside her. "Did you drop your keys? I just found them on the sidewalk."

The woman looked at the keys and shook her head.

"Are you sure? I thought I heard them fall." He flashed her a casual smile as the police car drove slowly past.

"I—" The woman looked up and her face seemed to soften. "Yes, I think I would know my own keys. Thank you though."

"No problem. My pleasure." He smiled again and fell into step beside her. "Tough day at the dentist?"

"Tough day." She nodded and walked over to a white minivan parked by the curb.

Jazz glanced back down the street. The police car had disappeared. "Hope it gets better." He flashed her a parting smile and hurried up the sidewalk. He turned right at the next intersection and scanned up and down the street. A tiny park stood across the way. Cutting through the park would minimize the risk of meeting up with police cars, but if they were searching the streets on foot, the park was one of the first places they would look. He should just—

A tremulous whisper tickled at his ear, fresh and clean as an early spring breeze. It felt like . . . a woman's voice? He turned and searched the street around him. The soft lilt of her words lingered like a sweet aftertaste in his brain. Beautiful, scintillating, deliciously enticing.

Jazz checked once again for police cars and then jogged out onto the street. Whatever it was, it was coming from the alley. He stepped onto the curb and hurried toward the narrow street. There it was again—like a cloud of heady perfume. Was it a smell or a voice? A flashback from the drugs?

He slowed to a walk and searched the area one more time. This was ridiculous. There wasn't anything there. His brain was on overload. Short-circuiting like a beer-soaked amp.

But it didn't hurt to look. It wasn't like figments carried guns. He stepped out into the street and stopped dead in his tracks. Two cops were standing at the end of the alley. Their backs were to him, and they seemed to be talking to someone. Maybe if he—

Then he saw her. Thick dark curls, flashing eyes, creamy caramel skin . . . It was the girl from his dreams!

Her eyes slid past the men and went suddenly wide. "Jaazaniah!" she cried out and the road jolted beneath Jazz's feet. She knew his name? He stumbled forward to keep from falling. The alley blurred and spun around him. The girl from his dreams knew his name. What was happening?

"Police. Don't move!" A cop's voice cut through the haze like a knife. They were running toward him, pointing their guns at his face!

Jazz raised his hands above his head. He wasn't armed. They had to know he wasn't dangerous.

They yelled something at him, and he lifted his hands higher. The girl was right behind them, staring through him like he was a ghost. Did he know her from somewhere? How did she know his name?

"Up against the wall!" One of the cops grabbed him by the arm and swung him against the building. Jazz's arms buckled and his forehead slammed into the bricks with a sickening crack. His vision dimmed. Rough hands patted him down. The girl's voice screamed in his head as his left arm was yanked behind his back.

"Jaazaniah, I don't understand." The woman was wailing now. "What are you waiting on? They aren't the enemy?"

The enemy? Did she know what was happening? A steel cuff clamped tight around his wrist. "What's the charge?" Jazz demanded. "I haven't done anything wrong. Why are you doing this?"

Jazz's right arm was pulled down and his hands were cuffed together behind his back.

"Are they the enemy or no?" The girl's voice stabbed into his pounding head, setting off another wave of dizziness.

"Do they *look* like they're my friends?"

A loud smack sounded behind him. Another smack, followed by a groan. Jazz pressed his face to the bricks as the world spun around him. He was all right. It'd be okay, the words repeated like background vocals in his head. Everything was going to be just fine . . .

The world vibrated to a sudden stop as a warm hand pressed against his shoulder. "Jaazaniah, you're hurt." The voice eased through his mind like a sigh. "What am I supposed to do?"

He rolled across the rough bricks until he was leaning back against the wall. Two doe-soft eyes stared up at him with the eagerness of a little girl. He leaned forward, felt himself falling into their depths. Trembling arms closed around him. He was floating. So beautiful and young. How could he look so young after all these years?

He blinked his eyes and looked up from the ground. The two cops lay on the street next to him. They weren't moving.

"What happened?" He blinked to clear his eyes. The girl crouched down beside him. Intense eyes licked at his face, devouring him like a starving lion. So beautiful . . . How could he be so young? Was he one of the immortals?

His vision blurred and doubled. Suddenly he was staring at his own face, lolling on the asphalt with the crazed eyes of a madman. Fresh blood oozed from an angry-looking welt on his forehead.

Jazz clamped his eyes shut and tried to focus. He'd hit his head too hard. It was a concussion; that's what it had to be. A hallucination. He had to get a grip. The police would be there any minute.

He opened his eyes and turned away from the staring girl. The cops were still on the ground. "What happened? Why aren't they moving?"

"I'm sorry." The girl's voice sent a stab of fresh pain pulsing through his chest. "I thought they was the enemy. You're not pleased?"

"Pleased?" Jazz glanced back at the girl. Her eyes were starting to cloud over. It didn't make sense. "You . . . did this?"

The girl looked down at the ground. "They hurt your head. And the metal bands were so tight . . . I figured you didn't want to fight, but I was scared they'd hurt you even more."

"I . . ." Jazz's eyes drifted back to the two motionless men. "Are they dead?"

"No! I would never!" Tears flowed down her cheeks now. "I never meant—"

"No harm done. It's all good." Jazz's eyes were starting to blur again. He squinted up into the girl's face as a sob washed like a gentle wave through his body. He felt as if he were drowning.

"The cops," Jazz finally managed to choke out. "Whoever hired them will be coming for me. I need to get out of these cuffs." He rolled onto his stomach and tried to focus on the pavement swimming before his eyes.

A hand slid across his arm. The cuffs rattled and dug into his wrists.

"Ow! What are you doing? Get the keys. They have to have the keys on them somewhere."

The sounds of scuffling and heavy breathing. A few minutes later, keys jangled behind his back. He gritted his teeth as she tried one key after another on the cuffs.

Finally there was a click and the cuffs let loose. He shook his wrists free and rolled over to face the girl. She was standing at a crouch now, balanced on the balls of her feet. Watching him. Waiting . . . Something in her expression reminded him of a wild deer. One false move and she'd bolt.

"It's okay." He spoke in a low voice. "I won't hurt you. I know what that looked like, but I didn't do anything wrong. I swear."

The girl gasped and her eyes narrowed. She cast a quick look toward the street and turned back to stare at him even harder. Her eyes burned into his forehead. He could feel her questions boiling in his brain.

"It's okay." He forced his expression into a gentle smile. "You saved my life. Thank you."

The girl nodded up at him with the eagerness of a hungry puppy. She took a faltering step forward and dipped her head in what looked like an old-fashioned curtsey. "M-my name is Mariutza." Her voice quavered. "I am very pleased to meet you."

"Mariutza?" Jazz tried to sit up, but a wave of dizziness forced him back down.

"Your head!" The girl sprang forward. She knelt at his side and reached toward his face with a trembling hand. "What should I do? I'm not a healer. I don't have the gift."

"The gift—what?" Jazz shut his eyes and tried to concentrate. "I'm fine. Just a little dizzy, that's all. Could you give me a hand up? I've got to get out of here!"

He pushed himself up onto his elbows and waited for his head to clear. The girl reached out a hand but pulled it suddenly back.

"It's okay. It's only a bump on the head. I'm fine." He sat up and took a couple of deep breaths. The alley was swirling around him like a whirlwind.

Holy One, heal him. Holy One, please . . .

The words echoed in his head. What did it mean? It was just a bump on the head. He wasn't hurt that bad. Was he?

He climbed onto his feet and stumbled across the cement to lean against the weathered brick wall. A low moan sounded at his feet. The cops would be waking up soon. He had to move!

Jazz turned toward the girl. She was watching him with wide expectant eyes—like a baby bird watching its mother. What did she want? Money? If she did, she was in for a big disappointment.

"Look, I appreciate the help, but I've got to run." Trailing a hand along the rough wall, he shuffled toward the entrance into the alley. If the police found him now, he was cop kibble. They'd never believe the girl had taken their buddies out. He didn't believe it himself.

Turning left at the main road, he broke into a shuffling jog. Headache or not, he had to put some distance between him and the cops. He needed to get to the bus station before they started circulating his description. But first he needed to get his guitar from Hollis—and a little bus money wouldn't be such a bad thing either.

"Where are we going?"

Jazz gasped and almost fell on his face. The girl was right beside him. Her face distorted and blurred in his eyes. He could almost feel her presence leaking out into the air. He was running through her, breathing her in. He veered to the right and bumped her shoulder. She felt solid enough. It was all in his head. He shouldn't be running, but what choice did he have?

The girl's head cocked to the side and her eyes drifted suddenly out of focus. Then they went wide and locked onto him with an almost audible click. "We're going to fight them? That's what we're running for?"

"Fight who? The police?" Jazz couldn't take much more of this. It was like coming in at the end of the movie. How had *he* suddenly become a *we*?

"The Badness . . ." Her words came out in a breathy sigh. "We're fixin' to fight them, right? That's why we're chasing after them?"

"The what?" Jazz backpedaled to a stop. "What are you talking about? Who's wanting to fight? What's going on?"

The girl swung around him and dropped into a low crouch. She scanned the street ahead of them, testing the air like a bloodhound. She straightened and turned on him. A firestorm of emotions bombarded his brain as wild eyes raked at his face.

Great, she was a head case! That explained everything. Something in his innermost being rebelled against the idea, but it was the only explanation. Beauty wasn't proof against mental problems. All gorgeous girls were at least a little off-balance.

"What do you think is going on?" Jazz spoke the words slowly and clearly.

"I don't understand." Her voice had a hysterical edge to it. "The Badness is getting closer. Why do we wait? Are we fighting or not?"

"Okay, slow down. Take it easy. Tell me what this Badness is you're so worried about. Maybe I can help you. Are you talking about the police?"

"The Badness, the . . ." The girl cast a wide-eyed glance over her shoulder. "It's either the mulani or their shimulo. I'm only an apprentice; I can't tell them apart. They're the strongest I've ever felt."

"Okay . . ." Jazz gritted his teeth. Why was he so angry? It wasn't her fault she was like this. He had to get a grip. "I'm sorry . . . Mariutza. I want to help. I really do, but I have to get going." He stepped around the girl and jogged up the sidewalk.

"Is it shimulo or mulani? How do you tell?"

"Stop following me!" A geyser of fury boiled up inside his brain. "Get out of here. Leave me alone!" He broke into an all-out run, pushing himself harder and harder. His arms and legs burned. Streams of molten lava boiled in his veins. Through his heart, his throat. Seeping into his brain. Suddenly he was hungry. Starving to death. He needed something, everything . . . Food, music, women, pain!

Two hands clamped around his wrist and dragged him to a stop. He swung around and glared at the girl. So puny and weak. Infuriating in her maddening beauty. He'd fix her! He'd rip her to bloody shreds with his bare hands.

A deep rumbling growl rattled through his bones. Raw unquenchable power. He could feel it exploding through his veins. Swollen muscles knotted beneath rippling skin. He was invincible. Immortal!

"The Badness. It's getting inside! We gotta get done of it!" The girl flung a stream of empty words at him, but he was beyond her control.

He stepped toward her, swung a massive steel fist at those infuriating eyes.

The girl blurred and disappeared. A thump beneath his arm. Sharp pain between his shoulder blades and he was stumbling forward. She was pushing him. The maddening pixie was shoving him back toward the police.

"No!" He spun around and swung another fist at her face, but a tiny hand came up and pulled him off balance. An arm wrapped around his waist. A shoulder in the back. She was pushing him again, running him out into the street.

A horn blared in his ears. The screech of squealing brakes.

A gray car and a black car. Shouting voices pounding against his ringing head. A blow to his shoulder, his side. She was still shoving. She wouldn't let go.

Holy One, hide us. Holy One, be our shield . . .

He tripped over a raised curb, stumbled into the warmth of her embrace. He was okay, now. She had him. Everything was going to be okay.

Jazz wrapped an arm around her and staggered down the sidewalk. Fresh air burned in his lungs, clearing his head. Everything was going to be okay. He'd feel better soon. He could feel the madness lifting, evaporating like a wet sidewalk on a hot summer day.

"You feeling any better?" Her voice rang like tinkling bells in his ears. He nodded and looked down into her straining face. Her eyes were tense, almost frantic. Was she worried, freaked out, afraid?

"I'm sorry. I don't know what happened. When I hit my head . . . All of a sudden everything's gotten all . . . weird. I think maybe I have a concussion."

The girl's mouth dropped open. "Your head. I should have knowed. You're not set to fight. The wall knocked the sense out of you. That's why you forgot the signs."

"What signs?" Jazz blinked and tried to get his eyes to focus. "What are you talking about? Who am I supposed to fight?"

"We should go faster." The girl grabbed his arm and pulled him across another street. "I know you're not scared, but you can't fight 'til your head's set straight. If you don't remember—"

"I haven't lost my memory. I'm just a little dizzy. Who are we running from?"

She shook her head and pulled him up the street. Her entire body seemed charged with tension. He wouldn't be surprised if she flew to pieces any second.

"Could you please answer just one of my questions?" Jazz tugged on his arm and tried to force her to slow down.

"What question?"

"First of all, who are you? I know I've seen you before."

"When I was a little baby?" She looked back at him with shining eyes. If she had a tail, it would be wagging.

"Recently. I know I've seen you before." Jazz studied her face and compared it to the image from his dreams. The luminescent skin, soft eyes, thick curly hair . . . It had to be her. He must have seen her at one of his gigs. There was no way he'd forget a face like that—not if he'd met her in person. "Your hair was up and you weren't so dirty, and I . . . think you were wearing a green dress. Were you at the Hookah Club last night? What about Atlanta? Have you ever been to Churchill Grounds?"

"I don't understand." Her eyes flickered and fluttered like someone in the middle of a dream. She looked like she was having some kind of seizure.

"This way!" She crossed the street at a quick run. "It's getting closer."

"Wait a second!" Jazz took off after her. He didn't manage to catch up until she was halfway down the next street. "Wait up! Who's getting closer? What's going on?"

"The enemy. They want to kill us."

"But why?"

The girl turned and stared. "Because that's what the enemy does."

Jazz reached out and caught her by the hand. She slowed to a walk and waited as he huffed and puffed to catch his breath. She was playing him like an accordion. He could see it in her eyes. She knew the police were after him and wanted a piece of the action.

"You're mad at me?" Her voice was suddenly tight. "I don't understand."

"I'm not mad. Just frustrated. When you saw me back with the police, you called out my name. How do you know me?"

"My grandfather. He had a painting of you on the wall of our wagon."

"He had a painting . . . of *me*?" Jazz tried to wrap his mind around it. "So how does *he* know me?"

"He's been telling the stories since I was a little girl. I thought everybody knew."

"What stories?"

"Jaazaniah and the Princess, Jaazaniah and the Elf King, Jaazaniah and the Dragon . . . He told them every night, just as soon as we was snuggled under the quilts."

"Fairy tales? He told you fairy tales about a hero named Jaazaniah?"

"Not fairy tales. Stories. The history of your adventures."

"My adventures . . ." Jazz studied her face. She seemed to believe every word she spoke. "So you heard someone calling me Jazz and assumed my name was Jaazaniah?"

"No!" The girl shot him a dark look. "I know you from the painting. My grandfather sent me to find you when he died. Have you forgotten everything?"

She stopped, capturing his gaze. Holding it.

"You are Jaazaniah the Prophet. The Mighty Warrior of the Lost Dimension."

II

Such I created all the ethereal Powers
And Spirits, both them who stood, and them who fail'd;
Freely they stood who stood, and fell who fell.

—John Milton
Paradise Lost

ꭎ 11 ꮎ

Mariutza

JAAZANIAH THE PROPHET! SHE'D actually found him! Mari snuck another peek at the man walking beside her on the narrow stone path. So beautiful . . . He was even prettier than the painting. And he looked so young! Purodad's painting had been hanging in the diddlecar most long as she could remember. It was twenty-five years old at the least—maybe even forty. And he still looked exactly the same. It was a miracle. He had to be one of the immortals. It was the only explanation. No wonder there were so many stories. He could be hundreds of years old. Maybe even thousands!

The prophet laid eyes on her, and his smile nearly sucked the breath right out of her chest. She tried to look away, but his look was too strong. His gaze surrounded her, drew her deeper. She was falling. Losing control.

He was making with the mind reading. She tried to focus on the path, but her mind kept jumping back to her grandfather. The blood seeping through his shirt. The agony of betrayal creasing his face. *You're no granddaughter of mine. No relation at all!* It was her fault he was dead. She'd played the harlot with the road. Led the Badness straight back to him.

"So where do you live?" The prophet's deep voice rang in her head.

She gasped for breath and blinked to clear her eyes. He was still looking at her. Sifting her thoughts like bread flour.

"I . . . don't know. I . . ." Her voice caught in her throat. Why was he asking? Surely he already knew. Was he testing her?

"You don't know where you live?" His tone brought the heat coursing into her face. It wasn't a question; it was a scolding. She must never try to hide the truth.

"It was my fault . . ." Her voice broke as tears started to fill her eyes. "He told me over and over not to spy on the road, but I wouldn't listen. I led them to him. If it wasn't for me, he wouldn't have died."

The prophet's forehead crumpled up like an accordion. She could see the shock in his eyes. Why hadn't she listened? Would it have been so hard?

"Who died?" The gentleness in his voice only increased her shame. "I don't understand."

"You don't have to stay with me. I'll leave if you want. I just wanted to . . . I never meant—"

"Who died? Can you talk about it? Tell me what happened."

"My grandfather. The Badness found him and . . ." A sob choked off Mari's voice. "I tried to help, but he was too far away. By the time I got there he was—"

"What Badness? Is it a person? What's his name?"

"It was too . . . I don't know. I think it was shimulo. There were ten of them—all dressed in black cloaks. But there could have been mulani too. I haven't finished the training yet. I don't know how to tell them apart."

"You say they were wearing black cloaks?" The prophet's features shifted. Tensed. "Are you sure? Who are they? What do you mean by shimulo?"

Mari stared up at him. Was he testing her or . . . Her eyes drifted to the gash on his forehead. "You don't remember . . . anything? Not even the shimulo?"

"I've never heard of *shimulo*. I'm almost positive."

"But . . ." She checked his eyes, but they didn't have the laugh in them. He was a prophet. How could he have forgotten so much?

"What are shimulo? Do they have a thing about climbing walls? Why do they wear black cloaks?"

"They're . . ." Mari turned and searched the road behind them. If he didn't remember the shimulo, he wouldn't be able to fight. "We've got to get going! Lickety click!" Mari started to run, but the prophet grabbed her by the arm and swung her around.

"What's going on? Why won't you answer my questions?" His eyes flashed. She could feel his anger burning into her skin. "I'm not taking another step until I get some answers."

"But the Badness. It's getting closer. If you don't remember how to fight, you'll be killed!"

"What do you mean by the Badness? What are shimulo?"

Mari reached out with the *dikh* sight and tried to draw a bead on the Badness, but there was too much of it. The whole city was infected with it. Like it had taken root and sprouted up into a jungle of concrete and metal and glass.

"You have three seconds, and then I'm out of here. One. Two."

"I'll answer!" Mari lunged forward and grabbed him by the arm, astonished she'd be so brazen—and that he'd let her. "Please. I'll answer anything; just don't go. You're injured. You shouldn't be—"

"Three!" The prophet turned and stalked away.

"The shimulo are the walking dead. Very powerful enemies. The undead, but eternally dying." Mari trotted to keep up with him. "They were created by the mulani—the great powers, the rulers of this present age. They're our—"

"Do they wear black cloaks with hoods?"

"The ones that killed my grandfather did. I found their carcasses in a buzzard circle around the place he was shot. There were ten of them and they all had palm guns."

He turned and fixed her with a burning stare. "Were they in a clearing? In the middle of the woods? A clearing filled with stumps and fallen trees?"

"Yes, sir . . ." Mari's response was a breathless whisper. He knew. The prophet already knew.

"And why were they trying to kill him?"

"They . . . They're the enemy."

"And they're trying to kill me too?"

"Of course. They—"

"Why?" Jaazaniah's voice rattled inside her head. She could feel his impatience gathering in on itself. If she didn't do a better job answering his questions, it was going to crash down on her like a storm wave.

"Because you're a child of the Standing, a great prophet." She searched his eyes for some sign of recognition but there was none. "The mulani are our ancient enemies. They wish to kill us, because only we can stand against them. They—"

"Look at me. Quick!" He wrapped an arm around her and pulled her into a tight embrace. Mari knew she should do something, but her body refused to respond. She stared helplessly up at him, unable to look away. His face was so close. She could feel the heat prickling at her skin. And his eyes . . .

Holy One, help me. Please!

"Hold still," he hissed and held her even closer. "Keep walking. They can see us through their rearview mirror."

Mari's thoughts churned like the waters of a tossing stormy sea. "I can't breathe. Please . . ."

"Shhh . . . It's okay. Just a few more seconds."

Seconds? Mari's heart was pounding in her ears. She didn't have seconds. She was slipping into his eyes again. She didn't have any time at all!

"There. Almost gone now. I don't think they saw us."

Mari swayed on her feet as the grip around her shoulder loosened. She took a deep breath and closed her eyes.

"You okay?"

"No, sir." Mari took another breath and tried to step away. "What was—why did you do that?"

"You didn't see the police car?"

"No, sir." Mari stumbled after him. "But why . . . even with a police car, why do . . . that?"

"They're expecting a lone guy on the run, not a couple." He looked into her eyes—and his smile was most unprophet-like.

"A couple . . ." Suddenly her words were gone. Her head felt like it was filled with winter water. "By walking close together we look more like two people than if we walk far apart?"

"What are you talking about?" The prophet stepped even closer to her. She felt a light touch at the small of her back. His hand?

"No more police!" She gasped and pulled away from his grasp. "Please. You make me feel all funny inside."

"Funny inside?" Jaazaniah laughed and stared down at her with a twinkling smile. "This is a bad thing?"

Mari felt her ears glowing again. How was she supposed to answer his questions if she couldn't understand a word he said?

"So you were saying something about standing?" All of a sudden he looked amused—like he was almost pleased with her. What had she done? She hadn't even answered his question.

"The mulani have sought to kill the Standing for thousands of years. They—"

A soft fluttering chill brushed against her mind. The Badness! How had it gotten so close? "This way!" She grabbed the prophet's hand and pulled him across the street. "They're right behind us. Coming up fast!"

The beat of a helicopter sounded in the distance. The Badness was riding inside one of the thumpa-thumpas!

"Hunt us up a place to hide. Quick!" Mari called out behind her as she raced down the street. "They're inside the helicopters. Searching for us with the sensors."

"Searching for you or me?" His footsteps were gaining on her. "What's going on? What do they want with us?"

"We're the *Standing.*" Mari searched both sides of the street as she ran. There were more trash cans, but the lids were too thin. She needed a tunnel or a bridge or a deep and murky swamp.

The prophet shouted between breaths. "What do they want . . . with the Standing?"

"To kill us. You're a great prophet. They want you most of all." The roar was getting louder. It sounded like three of them. The same three from the swamp.

"I'm not your stinking prophet!"

The helicopters were close enough now that she could hear the space between them. Two of them were off to the right, but one was coming up right behind.

She dodged around a wooden pole and swung left across the next crossing of roads. Jaazaniah's footsteps pounded behind her. Maybe if they split up—

"Quick, in here!" He grabbed her by the hand and pulled her to the left.

Mari followed, searching frantically to her left and right. A small metal box stood by the wall of the building. Did he know a way to crawl under it? It looked so small.

He ran past the box and pulled her up a low flight of stairs. Toward a door!

She tried to stop, but the prophet pulled her stumbling forward.

"Come on," he hissed. "Get inside!"

"No!" Mari ripped her hand out of his grasp and backed away from the door. The helicopter was almost on top of them now. What had he done!

He shouted something but his words were swallowed up by the rush of whipping wind. Turning back to face the building, he dove through the doors and ran inside.

The helicopter passed over the street and then drifted back to hover just above her head. They had found her.

There could be no escape.

Jazz

JAZZ TWISTED AROUND AN old lady and plowed through a rack of shimmering dresses. Sequin barbs slashed at his face. A whirlwind of pelting sand and choking grit. Pushing through the debris, he charged for the back of the store. They were chasing the girl, swooping down on her, smothering her under the weight of their fury.

He pushed through the blasting wind and staggered into an empty dressing room. Jolting streets, swerving cars, flashing poles . . . He reached up, tried to lock the door . . .

A ragged scream tore through his body, doubling him over in an agony of gut-wrenching pain. Fear burned through his senses like an army of stinging ants. How could this be happening?

He could see the helicopter. Feel it beating down on her, harrying her as she raced down a deserted street.

A loud knock sounded at the door. A woman's insistent voice.

"Just a second." Jazz climbed onto his feet and leaned heavily against the wall. The girl was in trouble. He couldn't just stand by and let it happen. He took a lurching step toward the door and fumbled with the latch.

A large, red-faced woman stood in the doorway. Her face distorted as purple-tinted lips formed around a rush of garbled words. He nodded and tried to form a response, but the helicopter was too loud. It was sinking lower. Soon it would crush her to the ground!

"No!" Jazz pushed past the woman and stumbled out into the chaos of a jolting, careening shop. He ran for the exit and burst through the door.

The sun beat down on him, sparkling like diamonds through tear-distorted lenses. He leaped out onto the sidewalk, searched up and down the street. The din of wailing sirens almost drowned out the sound of the helicopter. He was too late. He'd never be able to get there before the police. There was nothing more he could do.

Stumbling out into the street, he veered to the left and took off at an all-out run. Idiot! He was such an idiot! The police would catch him for sure. For all he knew, they were working for the shadow men. What if the girl was right? He could end up getting killed.

He turned at the next intersection and pounded toward the distant roar. The image of streaking cars and blurred telephone poles jolted through his head. A riverboat loomed large in the distance and then disappeared. The girl was running toward the river. Maybe she still had a chance!

Jazz swerved around a parked truck and sprinted across the street. There it was, the helicopter! It was turning to the side, hovering motionless in the air. Was it giving up? She was almost to the river. Why were they giving up now?

A volley of explosions rang out. Red-hot pain seared through his hip. Jazz hit the sidewalk hard and scraped to a stop. Wave upon wave of agonizing pain crashed over him. He pressed his hand to his hip and pulled it back. No blood. How?

The world tilted suddenly around him and he was falling. A wall of sparkling water slammed into him. Starbursts of white-hot pain in a sea of icy blackness. She was sinking! Jazz kicked out with his legs and paddled with his arms, but a tangle of clinging wire was dragging him down. Thrashing and twisting and tugging. Crusty metal biting into his skin. Hot throbbing pain radiated from his hip. His lungs were on fire. He had to break loose. Had to breathe.

A burst of bubbles and a last choking gasp.

Slowly the pain receded until he could feel nothing at all. Jazz lay on his back, gulping in the thick hot air. Clacking footsteps approached him and then circled around. He opened his eyes and watched as a shopping-bag-toting woman retreated slowly down the sidewalk. The tap of her heels echoed loud and lonely in the empty recesses of his mind.

He was on his own now. The girl was gone.

He had to find a place to hide or he'd be next.

∽ 12 ∽

Daniel Groves

A SHARP PAIN JABBED into Groves's shoulder blade, cutting through the muddy images swirling in his brain. What happened? He'd been out in the woods. There'd been a woman in a hut . . .

His gun!

He tried to sit up, but a throbbing headache knocked him back onto the ground. His gun—it had tried to shoot him! It had possessed his hand, forced him to point it at his own head!

He squinted up into the light of a full moon and tried to remember. Had the whole thing been a dream? None of it made any sense. It had to be a dream. Either that or he'd been drugged. He sat up slowly and reached for his holster. Empty.

Please no . . . Not his creds! An icy fist tightened around his chest as he reached into his breast pocket and pulled out the thin wallet containing his credentials. He flipped it open and sighed. His badge was still there.

Groaning from the effort, he climbed onto his feet and turned to survey the dark trees hemming him in on all sides. The dilapidated hut was nowhere in sight. He seemed to be alone—somewhere out in the middle of a swamp if his nose was right. What was going on? Had the woman drugged him and dumped his body out in the woods? Maybe she'd had an accomplice. Someone could have snuck up behind him and clubbed him on the head while he was freaking out about his gun.

He reached up to check the back of his head and froze. His arms and hands were covered with patches of glistening black. The patches were sticky and hot to the touch. It smelled like . . . blood? He patted himself down and checked his arms and legs by the dim moonlight. His clothes were ripped to shreds, and he had a few cuts and bruises, but nothing to account for so much blood. What had they done to him? Blasted him with some kind of voodoo paint gun?

A low hum reverberated through the trees to his left. It sounded like some kind of gasoline generator. Groves dropped to the ground and ran his hands through the dead leaves littering the ground. Nothing. Like Glapion would have left his gun. She knew he was FBI. She and the gun were probably halfway to Canada by now.

He climbed back onto his feet and picked his way gingerly through the trees. Every step wrung stabs of pain from his feet. It felt like he'd hiked barefoot across a field of broken glass. He shut his eyes and sorted through his memories, but he couldn't remember having walked anywhere. The past day was completely gone.

Off in the distance, a strange orange glow lit the woods. A shadow passed in front of the light, painting the intervening trees with a host of fluttering phantoms. The murmur of voices sounded above the hum of the motor. It sounded like two men, but there could be more. Groves bent low to the ground and made his way from tree to tree as fast as his tender feet would allow.

The light was coming from a small clearing. He worked his way closer until he could make out its source. Three banks of halogen lights mounted on tripods. They were all angled toward the center of the clearing, but nothing was there. No people, no generators—just a jumble of fallen logs.

Groves ducked behind a vine-choked sapling and turned to check the shadows behind him. Something wasn't right. Why would anyone set up work lights out in the middle of the forest? It was too early for the marijuana harvest. Drug smugglers maybe?

A muffled squawk turned Groves's attention back to the clearing. Two bluish blobs with enormous doughboy heads lumbered toward the clearing. The shiny material of their suits reflected light in eerie ripples.

Hazmat suits—biosafety level four! The men lumbered toward the center of the clearing. He could just make out the hoses running from their masks to the packs strapped to their backs. Air tanks—not filters. Whatever they were afraid of, it had to be pretty nasty. And he was right in the middle of it. Without a suit.

He looked down at the dried blood covering his hands and arms. Not good. Not good at all. Were these good guys or bad guys? He watched as they shuffled across the clearing and bent over to examine a log on the ground. No—not a log . . . It was a body! The victim was partially covered by some kind of cape. There was another one—not more than ten feet away. And another one . . . They were all over the place! Groves circled the clearing and came up behind a large tree.

The men were walking away now. Their backs were turned. This was his chance to get away.

He peered out once more from behind the tree and stared at the bodies littering the ground. There were nine of them in all—arranged in an uneven circle. What was this? Some kind of cultic ritual? Glapion had to be involved. Why else would she drag him all the way out there? But why? It didn't make any sense. Nothing made any sense. Unless . . .

He stared down at the blood covering his hands and then back up at the ring of bodies. As soon as the men disappeared from view, Groves ran out into the clearing and crouched next to the closest victim. Good. There wasn't a trace of blood anywhere. Whatever killed him hadn't done it the messy way. That meant . . .

A wave of nausea passed through him, turning his legs to rubber. He ran back across the clearing and plunged back into the shadows of the trees. He felt light-headed, dizzy—like he was going to hurl any second. This couldn't be happening to him. It didn't make sense. It was all just a horrible dream.

A high-pitched buzz jolted like an electric shock through his body. He turned this way and that, searching the shadows with darting eyes. The buzz sounded again. It was coming from his pocket!

Pressing his hands to his pocket to muffle the sound of his cellphone, he raced back through the forest. Sticks stabbed into his feet, thorns tore at his skin, but he didn't care. He had to get away—away from the lights and bodies, from the memory of the dark shack. He ran twisting and turning and leaping through the tangled undergrowth until finally, when he'd almost given up hope of ever seeing civilization again, he heard the blessed roar of a speeding car.

He staggered toward the noise until the trees finally spit him out onto the shoulder of a narrow two-lane highway. Collapsing into a trash-strewn ditch, he rolled onto his back and gulped down breath after breath of fresh air. If he could just find his bu-van, everything would be okay. He'd check himself into the hospital and have them run a whole battery of tests. They'd figure it out. He'd be fine. There was a perfectly reasonable explanation for all of this. He just needed to pull himself together.

His pocket buzzed again, sending him leaping to his feet. He pulled out his bu-phone and squinted into the glowing display. Great . . . his boss. Just what he needed. He flipped the phone open and took a deep breath.

"Hello? Groves?" Chevalier's voice blasted in his ear. "Where the blazes have you been? You were supposed to check in five hours ago. Why weren't you at the meeting?"

"Sorry about that. I was running down a lead and—"

"About the girl? Please tell me you found her."

"Maybe. One of those freaky voodoo priestesses in the city put me onto a Marie Paris Glapion."

"Forget about Paris. She's a dead end. The girl we want is still in the city. I need you to—"

"What do you mean dead end? Are we talking about the same person? This woman lives in a shack out in the middle of a swamp. She drugged me and took away my gun and—"

"I told you to forget Paris!" Chevalier's bellow rattled through the receiver. "You're supposed to be covering the city! Do I have to engrave it on your hide? Abandon your post one more time, and I'll have you reassigned to the Mexican border with a bu-mule for transportation. Do I make myself clear?"

"Yes sir, but—"

"No excuses! I need you here five hours ago, got that? If you're not plugging the hole in your desk by the time I get there, don't bother coming in at all, because you're fired."

"Yes, sir. It will take me a few minutes to—"

"Ten minutes! There's been an event, and I need all hands on deck. Our terrorist cell has just detonated a weapon of mass destruction."

Mariutza

HOLY ONE, WE THANK *Thee. Holy One, hide us in Thy almighty hand.*

Mari bobbed to the surface of the river and gulped down a quick breath before sinking back into the inky water. The night was dark as it was likely to get. She had to keep moving. It was time for another change of directions. They wouldn't expect her to double back to the big boat now.

She pushed away from a slimy piling and swam through the darkness. Every kick brought fresh throbs of pain from her hip, but she forced herself to keep paddling. Where was the next piling? Had she overshot the dock?

Her left hand brushed a rough surface, and she wriggled toward it. Pulling herself up the algae-coated pole, she crested the surface of the water and took another breath. *Holy One, hide me . . .* She ducked back down and clung to the slimy post as a large motorboat cruised past her position.

Hunger mingled with rage. She could feel it crawling like maggots through her brain. The boat was full of shimulo. A dozen more of them were patrolling the shore. So much for Purodad's brilliant plan.

After jumping into the water she had tried to project the sensations of drowning, but the Badness hadn't been fooled. Either her act hadn't been good enough, or she'd let her shield wear too thin. The pain in her hip made it almost impossible to concentrate. It wouldn't have taken much of a slip to bring the enemy swarming back to her.

Mari came up for another breath and peered out from around the piling. It was too dark to see clearly, but the boat seemed to be heading away from her. She dove deep and started to swim in the opposite direction, but a jolt of pain stabbed through her hip. *Holy One, shield me . . .* She fought against the pain, tried to shush it from her mind. *Holy One, please . . .*

It was no use. She swam back to the pier and came up behind a piling. The shimulo on the shore were moving back toward the paddleboat. The ones in the motorboat were moving in the opposite direction. Maybe if she stayed really low, they wouldn't be able to see her. The moon wasn't out. If she moved fast . . .

Mari pushed away from the pole and reached up to grab an angled cross-brace. Gritting her teeth, she climbed up the brace and pulled herself onto the uneven dock. Then, rolling into the shadow of a squared-off ledge, she reached out with the sight. The boat was turning around. Had they seen her? She forced her body to go limp and tried to control her breathing.

The boat crept closer until it was almost even with her position. A scuffle sounded on deck. They'd seen her. She had to run. They were watching her through the night-vision scopes of their guns.

Cease striving and know! Purodad's voice beat against her rising panic. Where was her faith? Even if she were able to run, she wouldn't make it more than five steps. She had to trust and know. *Trust and know* . . . She took a deep breath and closed her eyes, focusing on the rumble of the boat engine as it drifted further and further away.

Holy One, thank You . . .

If they didn't have night vision she might still have a chance. Just a few more minutes. As soon as they were further out of sight—

A gunshot rang out. It came from the direction of the paddleboat. Had they found Jaazaniah? She should have known he'd come looking for her. But why couldn't she feel him? If he was hurt, she'd feel it for miles.

Struggling onto her feet, Mari hurled herself over the wall and rolled across the gravel-strewn path beyond. She pushed herself up and tried to crawl, but her hip wouldn't bend so she climbed onto her feet and hobbled toward a line of low trees. Her hip screamed with each step, but she managed a slow run. Past the trees, past a line of parked cars, she limped toward the shielding buildings.

A line of bright lights shined down from the tops of a half dozen poles. The whole street was lit up like daytime. Mari slowed to a walk as she entered the lit area. She was a normal Gadje woman who belonged in the city. She was rich and drove inside a car and went inside buildings all the time. The city was full of strangers, but she wasn't afraid of any of them.

She crossed the street and hobbled down one of the narrow gray paths that ran deeper into the forest of buildings. As soon as she reached the next coming together of streets, she turned and started running. Across the road, through a line of stopped cars, past giant buildings and painted signs and huge wooden poles. She ran for what seemed like hours, but no matter where she went, she couldn't find any place dark enough to hide. The lights were everywhere. Behind glass windows, coming up from the ground, hanging on wires . . .

So many lights, but where were all the people? During the daytime, the paths had been piled up with them. Jaazaniah had had to teach her how to *blend in* as one with the crowd. But now the streets were empty. The city folk couldn't all be sleeping. But what else was there to do? Sitting on chairs inside their buildings?

Mari turned onto a brightly lit road and paused to listen. The sound of music drifted up the street. She limped toward the strange sound. It wasn't a fiddle or a buzuq. It was something else, some strange city instrument that made city-sounding music. The further she walked, the louder the music got. Beneath its pounding beat, she could just make out the murmur of voices. That's where the people were. They were listening to the city music.

She reached out with the *dikh* sight, but the Badness didn't seem to be coming from inside the building. She crept toward a window flashing with colorful lights. Up close the music was almost deafening. She could feel it throbbing inside her chest like a second heart beat.

The music blared even louder as a door swung open. A strange man stepped out onto the sidewalk. Mari smiled at him and started to speak the greeting, but a woman stepped out from behind him and grabbed him by the arm.

Mari gasped and took a step backward. The woman was wearing only her underwear! A silky black bra with long, skirt-like red panties. Before Mari could avert her eyes, the man put an arm around the woman's shoulders and kissed her. Right on the mouth!

Mari turned and started running. She shouldn't be here. She never should have come to the city in the first place. It was chock full of free-falling people. It wasn't safe! The Holy One would destroy it like Sodom and Gomorrah.

She plunged down street after street, searching the dark corners for a place to hide. Under a big car or inside a trash can, maybe. She wasn't going to find any wild trees. The city had sunk too low for any of Eden's children to take root. She was alone in a wilderness full of corruption and rebellion and death.

A soft whisper blew like a sigh through Mari's mind. Warm and familiar, so much like her grandfather. Jaazaniah? Would he still feel so clean after going inside a building? It wasn't possible.

She turned toward the sensation and limped out onto the street. Past the stopped cars, through a row of naked palms, left down one road, right down the next. His presence was getting stronger. She could feel his hunger gnawing at her stomach, feel the shadows of fear and despair. Black loneliness prickled beneath her skin like seed pods roasting on hot coals. He was searching for her. Risking the open places—for her.

A low roar sounded in the distance. Mari cast a glance behind her. The helicopters! How had they managed to get so close without her hearing them? She tried to run, but crumpled to the ground as a flash of pain turned her leg to tallow. The roar was getting louder. Mari struggled onto her feet and hobbled up the street. She had to go faster. The helicopters were right on top of her. She gritted her teeth and broke into a shuffling jog.

There! About a block ahead of her. A small tree grew up through a narrow strip of weeds. She jogged toward the tree, but its foliage was too thin. They'd be able to see her though the leaves—even without the night vision. Further down the street, a car was stopped by the side of the street. She could hide under it if only she could—

A flash of light painted the building across the street. Mari glanced back and started running. The helicopter was right on top of her. If it shifted just a few feet to the left, it would be able to see her. She hugged the wall of a huge open-faced building. If she could just—

A shadow appeared directly in front of her. Mari tried to leap away, but her leg gave out. Two strong arms closed around her. Jaazaniah!

The prophet hissed in her ear. "Quick! Inside!"

"No!" She twisted her body around and struck out with her hands, but he grabbed her even tighter. He was dragging her toward the open building!

"Please. I can't!"

A dark doorway loomed over her. Closer and closer, it yawned open wider. The roar of the helicopter pounded through her brain. He was dragging her toward the opening. It would swallow her whole!

"I won't!" She kicked out with both legs and screamed. Her vision dimmed as agonizing pain filled her head. He was carrying her now, through the doorway and into its throat!

Shadows closed around her. Icy darkness clamped like a fist around her heart. She was in a building now. After having done everything to stand, she had finally been brought low.

Her last flicker of hope had been snuffed out.

She was fallen.

⌒ 13 ⌒

Jazz

"SHHH!" JAZZ HISSED. "STOP squirming!" He wrenched the girl's body to the side and tried to pull her deeper into the parking garage, but she twisted free and lunged for the street.

Jazz pounded after her, grabbed her around the waist, and lifted her off her feet.

A piercing scream sliced through the helicopter's roar. Unbridled terror, agonizing pain. It tore through his mind, ripping his sanity to shreds. Shriek after shriek reverberated in his head. What was wrong with her? Did she *want* to be captured?

He wrapped both arms around her waist and dragged her deeper into the shadows. An elbow connected with his ribs, a kick to the thigh, a fist to his jaw, but still he held on. Something besides the helicopter was out there. He could feel it clawing at his senses. Ravenous hunger. Hatred as black as death.

"Quiet! Something's out there. Do you want to get us killed?"

The girl's body convulsed and then melted into a puddle of gasping sobs.

"Shhh . . . It's okay. I've got you." Jazz eased her head onto his shoulder and hooked an arm under her legs to support her weight. "There, that's it. We'll be—"

Her body flipped up and out of his arms. There was a loud smack, a spinning blur. Blows to his face, his chest, the back of his knees. Then he was sailing backward, crashing with a thud against the side of a dark sedan.

Jazz slid to the ground and lay there in a daze. She was running—to the helicopter? Had she made a deal with the police? He climbed onto his feet and stumbled after her. The helicopter sounded like it was a couple of blocks away. If he hurried maybe he could catch her before—

A shadow shifted at the base of a low wall. Jazz slid to a stop and pressed himself against a large concrete pillar. What was it? One of the shadow men? He peered around the pillar as the shadow twitched once again. It looked like . . . a body.

Jazz ran across the intervening parking spaces and collapsed onto his knees beside the girl's still form. "Hey, what's wrong? Are you okay?"

She whimpered and started shaking.

"It's okay. I'm not going to hurt you." He placed a hand on her shoulder. Her skin was cold as ice. Something was wrong. "Shhh . . . It's okay." He touched her face, smoothed the hair out of her eyes.

Then he saw the blood. The right side of her skirt was covered with it. Two jagged holes perforated the material at her hip. She'd been shot—

His heart double-thumped. She'd been shot in the exact same spot he'd felt pain. He hadn't imagined it. It had been real.

It had been her!

"How? How can this be happening?"

The girl's eyes cracked open and her face contorted into a mask of pain. "Let me be!" She jerked her head away and pressed her face into the concrete floor.

"You're hurt." Jazz reached for her arm and then hesitated. "You need a doctor."

"Go away!"

"But I . . ." He turned and looked around the garage. The weird feelings were fading; the helicopter was moving on. "I'm not going anywhere—not until you tell me what's going on."

The girl brought her hands up over her face and curled into a ball. "Just go. Please . . ." She gasped between sobs. "It's over now. I'd be better off dead."

"Who did this to you? What do they want?"

Silence.

"The men in the helicopter . . . why were they shooting at you?" Jazz lifted her head up and slid an arm around her shoulders. "You can trust me. I won't go to the police; I promise. But I have to know. Who are they? This isn't some mumbo-jumbo superstition. This is the police we're talking about. Real men with real guns!"

The girl didn't move. Tears overflowed her eyes and ran down her cheeks. She looked like she was about to pass out. Going into shock maybe? He had to get her out of there.

"I'll get you to a doctor, okay?" He slid an arm under her knees and hoisted her into his arms. She gasped and her body went rigid. She was heavier than she looked. How could someone so tiny be so hard to carry?

Staggering under her weight, he carried her around the wall and stepped out onto the street. He couldn't carry her all the way to the hospital. He didn't even know where it was. But what else could he do? He couldn't just leave her.

"Why?"

Jazz looked down at the girl. Tears filled her eyes and spilled down both cheeks.

"Why did you do this?"

"You need a doctor. I couldn't just leave you there."

"Why did you make me go . . . inside?"

"What? The parking garage? The guys in the helicopter were trying to kill you. I was trying to save your life."

"By despoiling my virtue? By defiling the one hope I had left?"

"What?" Jazz's head was starting to spin again. "No, I wouldn't—"

The girl's eyes clamped shut and a low sob escaped her lips. Finally she sighed and her body went limp.

"Is it some kind of phobia? Is that why you didn't follow me into the store? Because you're afraid of enclosed spaces?"

"You don't remember?" Her eyes fluttered open and she looked up at him with a strange expression.

"I'm not . . ." He took in her pain-etched face and quickened his pace. "It doesn't matter what I remember. Is there anything else I should know? Drug allergies? Other phobias? Streets or businesses we should avoid?"

"We are the Standing." Her voice was a faint whisper. "To go inside a building is forbidden. It's one of our most sacred responsibilities."

"Okay. No more buildings. I got it." So much for the hospital.

"You mustn't go inside either. Please . . . The mulani are searching for you. You must guard your purity."

"Don't worry about me. I'm fine." Jazz shifted the girl in his arms. "I don't share your religion. I've lived in—"

"Not religion. It's who you are. Part of your heritage as Standing, as a great prophet and warrior." She lifted her head, desperate eyes seeking his.

"Shhh . . . Calm down. It's okay." Jazz pulled her onto his chest and readjusted his grip. "There's been a huge mistake. I'm not who you think I am. My name isn't Jaazaniah, it's Jazz. I'm not a prophet or a warrior. I'm not even religious. And I definitely haven't lost my memory."

The girl arched her back and twisted away from him. He grabbed her around the waist and tried to set her on her feet gently, but she pulled out of his grasp and turned to face him.

"You *are* Standing. I could feel your presence for miles. You are stronger even than my grandfather, and of all the Standing, he stood the tallest."

"Your grandfather . . . The one with the painting that looks like me. The one who . . ."

Her face creased with pain. Fresh tears streamed down her face. He stepped toward her, but she pulled away and started limping down the street.

"This is ridiculous! At least let me help you." He trotted up to her and fell into step beside her.

"I prefer to walk." She didn't turn to look at him, but he could see she was still crying.

"Come on. You've been shot." Jazz held out his hand and smiled. "Don't you think you should at least take it a little easy?"

"The wound isn't deep."

"That's why there's blood all over your dress, right?"

"They killed him. Because of me. It . . ." Her shoulders shook, and her whole body started to sway.

Jazz reached out and caught her up in his arms. "It's okay. We'll find a doctor. Everything will be fine."

"It was my fault. I spied on the road. I led them to him." Her body went tense and then relaxed with a hiccoughing sigh.

"It was the cloaked men, right? They're the ones who killed him. It wasn't your fault." He turned her toward him and adjusted his grip. Fresh blood oozed from the wound at her hip. This was crazy. The police were looking for both of them. What was he supposed to do with that? He had to get out of town. He didn't have time to mess with doctors. It wasn't safe.

The murmur of a distant helicopter cut through his thoughts. It was moving their way. He had to find a place to hide.

"Jaazaniah?" Pain tightened the girl's features, but her lips were turned up in a determined smile.

"Jazz." He swallowed and tried to force an upbeat tone. "My friends call me Jazz."

"Just like the music." The smile touched her eyes. "My family name is Mari. I'm Mariutza only when I'm bad."

"Are you doing okay, Mari? Are you going to make it?" He leaned back and walked even faster. The helicopters had drifted further to the left, but they seemed to be getting closer now.

"Thank you for rescuing me." Something in her voice sent shivers through his frame. It felt like she was talking inside his head. "I realize now you meant everything for good. I was wrong to be angry. Will you forgive me?"

"Of course. There's nothing to forgive."

"I was very angry. I'm sorry." She looked up at him and her eyes seemed to swallow him whole. So trusting and innocent and mind-numbingly beautiful.

Her features faded into a haze of swirling light. The darkness spun around him. A shadow-drenched face against a halo of streaking light. Beautiful and noble and brave. Was it . . . *his* face?

The night opened out around him, and his vision slowly cleared. He was looking at the girl again, staring into brown, bedazzling eyes.

"What was that?" Jazz swallowed hard and tore his eyes away from her face.

"Do you feel them? Put me down. You have to get away!"

"I'm not leaving you." He hitched her up in his arms and staggered forward at a shuffling run. "I know someone who can help us. She has a car and money for a doctor."

"You can move faster without me. Please . . ."

"Would you stop squirming! I've got it, okay? Just give me a chance to think." The girl wrapped her arms around his neck and suddenly she was light as a feather. Her eyes clung to him, pulled him down. He was falling again. The world was starting to spin.

No. He tore his eyes from her face and focused on the lights ahead. Just one block at a time. He could do this.

"Jaazaniah." The girl's voice sounded against the rush of his breathing. "Jazz, you must leave the city."

He shook his head and kept on going. The next intersection was Canal Street. He was almost there.

"Please. I have a traveling necklace with eight more coins. Use them to get away." She reached a hand to the chain around her neck and pulled it over her head. A cluster of large golden coins glinted in the streetlights. "When your memory returns, you can return to defeat the Badness. I'll wait for you in the swamps."

"Are those . . ." Jazz slowed to a stop and lowered her to the ground. He examined the coins under a streetlight. They were too heavy to be Mardi Gras replicas. They looked ancient. "These aren't . . . They can't be real."

"Yes. It's my traveling necklace."

"What's a traveling necklace?" Jazz held one of the coins up to the light. It looked like an old antique Spanish doubloon. He'd seen an exhibit once in a treasure store—a whole slab of coins just like these. They were corroded and fused together after being under the water for hundreds of years. He'd asked how much they were, but the guy said they were way too valuable to sell. These were in much better condition. They could be priceless. Was that what everyone was after?

"Where did you get this?" He handed the necklace back to the girl and swung her into his arms.

"My grandfather. I think he meant it to help your escape."

"My escape? Why would he . . ." He sucked in his breath as something finally connected. His grandfather's will mentioned a shovel and the contents of a blue plastic box.

He'd buried a treasure.

"Mari"—Jazz could barely control his voice—"what was your grandfather's name?"

"What's wrong? Are they coming? I can't feel anything. I can't feel anything at all!"

"Mari, calm down. I need you to focus." He looked her in the eyes and willed her to stop struggling. "Everything's okay. I just need to know your grandfather's name."

"Purodad. That is, I called him Purodad. But his outside name was Jonadab. Jonadab Rechabson."

Jonadab Rechabson . . .

Jazz slowed to a stop. Was it possible? His father told him his grandfather died twenty years ago. Why would he lie?

"Jaazaniah, what's wrong? Do you feel something?"

"What?" Jazz turned back to the girl. Her features were soft and delicate. He couldn't see his father in her face at all. But it couldn't be a coincidence. He'd felt the connection the instant he saw her.

"What do you feel? Can you tell the direction?"

"No, I just . . ." Jazz shook his head and started running. "My full name is Jaazaniah Rechabson. Jonadab was my grandfather too." He held her astonished gaze.

"Mari, I think we might be related."

Daniel Groves

GROVES PUSHED THROUGH THE stairwell doors and ran up the steps two at a time. Clipped voices sounded above his head.

The clatter of slapping feet. He hugged the wall as a small platoon of harried agents stampeded down the stairs and burst out onto the ground floor. Who were these guys? More rent-a-goons? It was almost 3:00 a.m. and the building was crawling with new faces. You'd think the bureau didn't have anything better to do than shuffle agents from one office to the next.

He pushed out onto the third floor and pounded down the hallway. Running wouldn't make a lick of difference as far as Chevalier's deadline was concerned. It had taken him almost an hour to find his bu-van, and then he'd had to drop by his house to change clothes. Terrorists or no terrorists, he couldn't go into the office looking like an axe murderer. Who knew what had happened while he was passed out in the woods? If somebody turned up dead and the blood on his clothes ended up being a match, what was he going to say? A swamp witch put a voodoo hex on him? Besides, he could have been exposed to some serious nastiness out in the woods. To come in without a shower and a change of clothes would be a serious shirking of responsibility.

He slowed to a walk and stepped into the special ops office. The place was a madhouse. A half dozen agents were scattered about the outer office, barking orders into bureau-issued cell phones. Three empty suits he'd never seen before stopped talking and glared at him. Was it his imagination, or had everyone's voices suddenly become more guarded?

Mills, the one agent he actually knew, turned and motioned him across the crowded room. "Where have you been? Chevalier's been screaming his head off for you. We need intel on the Gypsy girl. I hope for your sake you've got something really good."

"Which Gypsy girl? Glapion? What's going on?" Groves sidled up to Mills and lowered his voice. "Chevalier said there's been some sort of attack?"

"Where have you been?" Mills stared at him like he was some new form of extraterrestrial life. "A command post was stood up twelve hours ago!"

"So it's true? There was an explosion?"

Mills shook his head and guided Groves toward Chevalier's door. "Whatever you do, don't breathe a word about any of the other task force agencies, okay? And don't question anybody's intel. No matter what it—"

The door swung open, and Chevalier stepped out of his office. "Ah, Groves." The man glowered down at him like a bird of prey. "So nice of you to finally join us." His mouth contorted into a cold smile. "I trust you enjoyed your vacation?"

"I was forcibly detained." Groves stepped forward and squared his shoulders. "Everything will be explained in my report."

"I look forward to reading it then. Please." He stepped back and swept a hand toward his office.

Groves took a deep breath and stepped inside. He tried to keep his stance open and casual as Chevalier strode across the office and turned to lean back against his desk. "Before we get to your report, I need to know what you found out about the girl. Does she have friends or acquaintances in the city? Any places she might hole up?" His boss flashed him a saccharine smile and scooted a couple of feet to his left.

Was he trying to block Groves's view of the papers on his desk?

"None of the people I questioned had ever heard of a Mariutza Glapion. The only lead I got was to a Marie Paris Glapion, who was supposed to be much older. I thought she might be a relative so I drove out to the swamps, where she reportedly lives."

Chevalier's smile widened. "Based on your absence, I have a very good idea how that meeting must have gone. If you had bothered to follow procedure and report your intentions, I could have saved you a great deal of trouble. Better yet"—his features went suddenly rigid—"if you had followed orders and kept the command post apprised of your activities, none of this ever would have happened! What were you thinking? Give me one good reason why I shouldn't four-bag your butt right now and throw you in front of a firing squad?"

"Sir, while I was questioning Glapion I—"

"Let me guess." The man's mocking tone put Groves' teeth on edge. "She sprayed you with a hallucinogenic drug cocktail, and you spent the rest of the day swinging from tree to tree like Tarzan of the trippin' apes!"

"How did—" Groves could only stare. "You knew?"

"About Glapion? Of course we know. But she's not our headache, is she? We're after a twenty-year-old Gypsy girl who has the means to wipe out everyone in the entire state!"

"Sir, while I was gone . . . What happened? You said there's been an event?"

"Nine people dead! That's what happened!" Chevalier's skin pulled back from his eyes. His face darkened to an almost purple shade. "Nine of my best agents were killed—almost instantly by a new virulent form of biologics."

His gut lurched. "Killed instantly? What about incubation periods? I thought that stuff took time."

"Biologics, neurotoxins, neutron bombs . . . something! The CDC is still investigating. All we know for sure is that it killed nine agents without leaving a trace. And the terrorists who did it are holed up somewhere in the city!"

"You say terrorists, as in a whole cell or—"

The office door squawked open, and a bearded man poked his head into the room. "Sir, I have a call from a Mrs. Adelaide Calder." He nodded and arched an eyebrow.

Chevalier's expression remained blank.

"The wife of the police officer who died of a heart attack?" The agent nodded again. "I think you should take the call. She *specifically* asked to speak to you."

"By name?" Chevalier jumped up and hurried across the office. "She asked for me by name?"

"Yes, sir."

"One second." Chevalier shot a look at Groves and then stepped out of the room.

Groves shuffled his feet and watched the door. *Calder . . . Adelaide Calder . . .* Was he supposed to know that name? Why would Chevalier drop a situation to talk a uniform's widow?

He took a few steps toward Chevalier's desk and glanced at the thick stack of papers cluttering its surface. The topmost document was a blueprint of a multistoried building. A hotel, maybe? Did Chevalier already have a lead on where the cell was holed up? He leaned over to get a better look. The address was printed across the bottom in large block letters. Haight Street . . .

Was there a Haight Street in New Orleans?

"Is there a problem, Groves?" Chevalier's growl jerked him away from the desk. "You've decided you're ready to leave the bureau permanently. That's why you're still here?"

Groves shook his head and backed away from the desk.

"Then get out there and find the girl! If you don't bring me something by tomorrow morning, don't bother coming in, because I never want to see your sorry face again!"

⌒ 14 ⌒

Mariutza

MARI COULDN'T BELIEVE IT. Jaazaniah was Purodad's grandson? That meant Jeremy was Jaazaniah's father. But Jeremy had gone over to the enemy before she was even a baby. Had he married a Standing after he had fallen? He must have. Jaazaniah had to be full-blooded. He was as strong as Purodad—even stronger.

"Are you okay?"

Mari nodded and tried to put the happy back in her face. The prophet was looking down at her, but his eyes didn't match the line with hers. He looked like Miss Caralee the time Mari caught her in a lie.

"So do you think we're . . . you know, cousins or . . ." The frowns shadowed over his eyes. Like he was fair disgraced to be talking to her. "You don't think we're . . . We're not . . . closer than cousins?"

"No, sir . . ." Mari pushed down on the sadness rising up inside her, but it was like plugging a leaky boat with mud. Everything kept seeping around the edges. "You're a great warrior. I'm just . . ." She traced a finger along the scar beneath her necklace. "Purodad . . . I called him my grandfather, but I don't suppose he really was. Purodad said he wasn't any relation at all. He rescued me from my mother when I was a little baby."

"Your mother died when you were little?"

"She's fallen, not dead. Not in the body."

"So we're not . . ." His features relaxed into a half smile. "My mother died right after I was born, so we couldn't be . . . you know."

"Family?"

"Right. Just like you said. No relation at all."

Mari turned her face away. The happys were boiling up inside him again. She could feel it in his head. He was a great prophet. He didn't want to be kin to an ignorant swamp girl.

"I should walk now. Please put me down."

"But your hip . . ."

"I should walk." She pulled away from him and swung her feet onto the ground. A sharp pain stabbed up through her hip, but she didn't let out a peep. She took a step, two more steps. She could do this. Would do this. The prophet's safety was all that mattered now. Purodad sent her to help him—not to be a burden. The prophet wasn't in any condition to fight the Badness, and her hip would only slow him down. He needed to leave the city.

"What are you doing? This is stupid." Jaazaniah's arm circled her waist. "Your hip's going to start bleeding again."

"Take this." She thrust her traveling necklace into his hand. "Use it to get far away from this place. Always keep moving. They'll find you quick if you settle in one place."

"I'm not going anywhere—not until we get you to a doctor."

"Purodad gave me the training. I know how to bind wounds. You should go!"

"I can't believe this." Jaazaniah cut in front of her and fixed her with blazing eyes. "What kind of a jerk do you think I am? You think I'm just going to leave you out on the street to bleed to death?"

"You don't understand." Mari took a step and had to bite down on her lip to keep the pain from showing on her face. "This isn't time for the chivalries. If you stay with me, we'll both perish. But if you go now, you can use the coins to reach a safety haven."

"Is that what this is about? The treasure? You want me to have the necklace so you can keep it for yourself?"

"What treasure? I don't understand." Mari's mind reeled at the intensity of his emotions. Why couldn't prophets just say what they meant?

Jaazaniah reached into his pocket and brought out a folded, brown envelope. He pulled out a crinkled sheet of paper and smoothed it out across his chest. It was a message—

Mari's heart skipped, and her mouth fell open. A letter written in Purodad's beautiful hand! Her eyes devoured the familiar script.

I, Jonadab Rechabson, being of sound mind, do hereby declare this instrument to be my first, last, and only will and testament . . .

"I don't understand. When did Purodad give this to you?"

"It came in the mail. Last night. Right after all this stuff started happening."

"Last night?" Mari studied Jaazaniah's expression. "That's when they killed him. That means he wrote it . . ."

"He must have known they were after him. That's why he sent it when he did."

"But he's Standing. The enemy has been trying to kill him all his life."

"Maybe they suddenly had more of a reason. What's in the blue plastic box? Do you know where he kept it?"

"The blue box?" Mari took the letter from Jaazaniah and read it through to the end. Blinking the tears from her eyes, she read it two more times until she knew it all by heart.

Purodad had left him the family Bible.

Well, of course he had. The prophet was Purodad's only sur-viving heir—his kin. And she . . . What had she been to Purodad? He hadn't even mentioned her. Had he known then that she'd been spying on the road? Was that why he hadn't written her name?

"Do you know what's in the blue box? And Rth 116, what's that supposed to mean?"

Mari turned away from Jaazaniah's voice and limped up the street, gritting teeth against the paining in her hip—and her heart. Purodad mailed Jaazaniah a letter. She'd been right there, and he hadn't said one word.

"Hey . . ." A gentle hand closed around her shoulder. "I know this wasn't fair. I'm sorry. I'm totally cool with sharing the treasure, but we have to find it first. Whoever these guys are, they want it bad enough to kill. We have to find the treasure before they do. It's our only shot at making it out of this alive."

Mari wiped her eyes and kept on walking. "Purodad didn't have any treasure. He was a prophet—just like you. That's why they killed him."

"But what about these?" Jaazaniah held up her traveling neck-lace. "Do you know where he got these coins? They're ancient—the kind of ancient you find in museums. The kind you might find in a treasure chest buried underground."

What was the prophet jibber-jabbering about? It made no sense. "He didn't have a treasure chest. He didn't even have a plastic box. I don't know what he was talking about in that letter."

"What about Rth 116? Do you have any idea what it means?"

Mari glanced up at him out of the corner of her eye. Was he testing her, or did he really think she was stupid?

He grabbed her arm and turned her to face him. "You know what it means, don't you?"

Mari nodded.

"Please, I give you my word. Help me find it, and we'll split it straight down the middle. What does it mean? Where'd he hide the box?"

"I already told you. He doesn't have a box. It's a Bible verse. Ruth, chapter one, verse sixteen. I know you're a warrior, but I think he wants you to follow in his footsteps. To be a healer, just like him."

"Ruth 1:16. That's got to be it! Or maybe it's Ruth 11:6. The way he wrote it, it could be either one. Maybe he wants us to look up both verses."

Mari studied his face. "This is a test?"

The prophet's frown stabbed the daggers into her. Why did she keep questioning him? Miss Caralee was right—she was brassy as a pushpin. Straight questions called for straight answers. "Ruth only has four chapters. There can't be any other meaning."

"Yes!"

The prophet's excitement crashed through her like a wave. She'd given the right answer! He was happy with her again.

Jaazaniah folded the letter and slid it back in the envelope. "He mentioned a shovel. That was a clue too. He wanted us to know we'd have to dig to find the treasure. Come on." He took her by the hand and pulled her forward. "Are you sure you can walk? I can carry you. It's not that far."

Mari looked down and tried to focus on the markings criss-crossing the path. Emotions swirled around her like a storm. He was too excited. The Badness would swarm to him like bees to honeysuckle. "You must calm yourself or they'll hear you. Focus on the next step. Where are you going? How are you going to leave the city?"

"A hotel. It's just up the street. I know a girl who's staying there."

"Inside a building?" Mari pulled out of his grasp. "I mustn't. *You* mustn't."

"It's fine. You can wait for me outside. It'll only take a minute. The girl—her name is Hollis—she has money and a car. And there should be a Bible in the hotel room! We'll be able to look up the Ruth verse and follow it to the treasure. Hollis can—"

"But the Ruth passage says nothing about a treasure."

"Maybe not directly, but it could give us a clue where to look."

"But it's . . ." She covered her mouth and lowered her eyes. He was the prophet. If she didn't mind her place, she was going to get a wallop.

"It's what?" His voice was low and firm—not exactly a command, but it wouldn't do to step around the truth.

"I'm sorry. It's not my place, but I . . ."

He nodded for her to continue.

"I just thought the verse was about Purodad's wish for you to follow in his footsteps."

"And what makes you say that? Did he tell you that's what he wanted?"

"No, it's just the verse. What it says. 'And Ruth said, entreat me not to leave thee, or to return from following after thee: for whither thou goest, I will go; and where thou lodgest, I will lodge: thy people shall be my people, and thy God my God.'"

"That's the verse? Ruth 1:16?" Jaazaniah looked the wide eyes at her. "How did you know? Did your . . . *my* grandfather teach it to you?"

"Of course. He was a prophet. He taught me all the Scriptures."

"You mean . . . the whole Bible?" He looked down at the ground and shook his head. Questions swirled in his mind—she could feel them. He still thought it was a puzzle. He was trying to solve a mystery that didn't exist.

"I know you want for there to be a treasure"—she spoke in her softest after-bedtime voice—"but it doesn't exist. Purodad didn't have a plastic box. Our boxes were made of either wood or cardboard. There were only four of them. I would know if he had a plastic box. It would have been very useful."

"What if he buried it? You might not have known about it. He mentioned a shovel. It has to be a clue."

Mari shrugged. "I found a store-bought shovel under the wagon right after he died. A new one with a light wood handle. It still had the price tag on it."

"See? That proves it! He knew his enemies were getting closer. Why risk going out to buy a shovel unless he had to? It had to be the treasure. It's the only thing that makes sense!" He stopped in his tracks and stared off into space.

Mari stood off to the side and bowed her head.

Suddenly he spun around. "The family Bible! Don't you get it? We're supposed to look up Ruth in the family Bible. That's where the instructions will be. There'll be a note beside the verse. I guarantee it."

"But . . ." Mari looked up at the prophet. The Badness had stolen the Bible. Had it known about the treasure? No. Jaazaniah was wrong about that. Purodad stored up treasures in heaven, not earthly gold. Why put so much effort into hiding something that had no value?

"What? What's wrong?"

"The Badness stole it—the family Bible. I searched for it everywhere, but it was gone. They turned the whole wagon over looking for it."

"The wagon? That's where he kept it hidden?"

Mari shook her head. "Not hidden—sitting on the bookshelf."

"Was anything else stolen?"

"Not that I made notice of. But the whole wagon was torn up. They might have snuck something else without me noticing."

"See? That just proves my point."

"I don't understand."

"If the Bible was out in the open on a bookshelf, why tear the whole place up? He knew they were coming so he hid the Bible too. This whole thing is a treasure hunt. And you can't have a treasure hunt without a treasure."

Mari shook her head. "I would have known . . ."

"You said he didn't have a plastic box, but the will says he did. Maybe he was keeping it a secret."

"But why?" She looked down at the path. Jaazaniah didn't know Purodad. He'd said so himself. Purodad was a prophet. He didn't store up treasures on earth. He didn't. But the necklace and her traveling clothes . . . Weren't those treasures? What if the treasure was for something special? What if Jaazaniah needed it to fight the enemy?

She followed Jaazaniah across a dark coming together of streets. Her hip was still seeping, but it seemed to be getting less stiff. Maybe the heat meant it was healing. Maybe it was a sign it would get better on its own.

"So you'll help me?" His voice swept her thoughts aside like a gust of wind.

"Escape the city?"

"Find the treasure. I promise I'll split it with you. Fifty-fifty. Just help me find it and half of it is yours." He took her by the shoulders and looked down into her eyes.

Mari's heart felt like it was going to explode. "Of course . . . I'll do everything I can to help. But first we have to escape the city."

"Deal." He released her shoulders and stretched a hand out toward her. What did he want her to do? Was it the signal for the shaking of hands or was it something else?

She reached out slowly and took hold of his hand the way
Miss Caralee had taught her. His hand was soft—like the man's
in the white shirt. But so much bigger! It was like being ten all
over again.

"What's wrong?"

"What?" Mari dropped his hand as the heat rushed to her face.

"What were you thinking? Just now."

"That I . . . like your hand?" Mari watched his eyes to see if
she'd gotten the answer right. It didn't seem like what he was looking for. "I think it's big and warm and feels like a pool of loveli-
ness?"

He stared at her for what seemed an eternity. "Where are you
from, Mari?"

"I used to live in the swamp with Purodad, but now . . ."

"And this is your first visit to the city?"

"It's my first visit anywhere." She looked up at him and waited.
Had she done something wrong? His eyes were crinkled up like
oyster shells.

A slow smile spread out from his mouth until it smoothed his
eyes straight again. "Come on. Let's get you fixed up." He reached
out his hand and Mari shook it again. Only this time he didn't let
go. He walked slowly by her side while she limped up the path,
his hand tightening around hers every time she felt a twinge of
pain.

"Just one more block." He pointed at a huge building all lit up
like the morning sun. "My friend's staying at the Ritz Carlton, if you
can believe it. She'll have no problem paying for a doctor. I wouldn't
be surprised if she could even get one to make a house call."

Mari nodded and tried to pay attention to his words. How could
he be so calm? The Badness was getting closer and closer. The air
around them reeked of it. Was it coming from the glowing building? She reached out with the *dikh* sight and searched the massive

structure looming over her. The inside of the building didn't feel any different than the outside. Where was it all coming from?

"Okay, here we are."

Mari tensed as Jaazaniah pulled her toward a large covered door.

"It's okay. It's really spacious inside. High ceilings, huge rooms. You won't even know you're inside."

"But it's not allowed." Mari pulled her hand out of his and backed away from the door. "You shouldn't—" She covered her mouth and looked away. "Please forgive me. I didn't mean to presume . . . If it's like meat offered to idols, I just don't have enough faith. I'm only a swamp girl." She backed slowly away from the building. Jaazaniah didn't seem angry, just . . . concerned?

"I'll only be inside a few minutes, okay?" His voice was soft. He seemed to be asking, not telling. "Just a few minutes. Are you going to be okay?"

Mari nodded and reached out to search the building one more time. It felt clean enough. Most of the Badness was behind her. The helicopters were over a mile away. He'd be fine. Their instruments wouldn't be able to see him inside a building. Even if she weren't injured, he'd be much better off without her. They had her scent. Her presence would lead them right to him.

"You're okay, right?" He stepped toward the door and hesitated. "I'll be right out. Just a few minutes."

Mari nodded. A few minutes head start was all she'd need. He probably wouldn't even search for her. He was only helping her because his honor demanded it.

Jaazaniah turned and pushed through the sparkling glass doors. She waited until he was out of sight and then crossed the street to retrace their steps.

"Fare thee well, Jaazaniah. I will pray for you, always."

⤳ 15 ⤶

Jazz

JAZZ LEAPED OUT OF the elevator and ran down the hotel's third floor hallway. 337, 339 . . . There it was, 341. He stopped outside the door and checked his watch. 3:17 a.m. If she was here, she was going to kill him.

He pounded on the door and leaned in close to listen.

Nothing. Either she was a sound sleeper or she'd already left town. Or she was still out partying. He should have checked at the desk. Even if they had orders to keep him from going up, they still would have let him call. It was an emergency. He had fresh blood on his shirt to prove it.

He pounded on the door again, this time harder. "Come on, Hollis. Open up. It's an emergency!"

"I don't know who you are, but I want you to leave right now." Hollis's voice called out from the other side of the door.

"It's Jazz Rechabson, the musician from this morning. Open the door, and I promise—"

"Go away! I've already punched in 9-1-1, and my finger is on the send button."

"Hollis, there's a woman outside who's been shot. I need to get her to a doctor."

"Call an ambulance."

"It's . . . complicated. If you'd just open the door I could explain. I promise. I won't try—"

"Why should I? Give me one good reason why I shouldn't call the police right now."

Jazz raked a hand through his hair and turned to check the hallway. What could he say? The whole thing was crazy. He didn't believe it himself, and he'd seen it happening.

"Five seconds . . . Three, two—"

"Look, I know this sounds crazy, but I think the cops are in on whatever it is that's going on. They shot a girl who wasn't carrying a weapon or anything. Shot her from a helicopter. They've got just about every cop in the state searching for me, and I haven't done anything wrong. I promise. Do you seriously think I'd walk into the police station if I was hiding something? I have no idea what they think I did, but I promise I didn't do it."

"They say you're a terrorist. That you killed an entire unit of government agents."

"And you seriously believed them?" Jazz stepped toward the door and rattled the handle. "Come on. People are going to start complaining. At least give me my guitar back."

"Who's Sabazios Vladu?"

"Excuse me?"

"Sabazios Vladu. What's he have to do with this?"

"What are you talking about?"

"No more games! You knew I'd read the letter."

"What letter? What are you talking about?"

"The letter you left on my sofa. I know it's a setup. I may be blonde, but I'm not blonde!"

Jazz banged his forehead against the door and yanked on the handle. She wasn't going to help him. He was wasting his time. He turned and strode back up the hallway. What was he thinking? Leaving the girl on the curb like a leaky bag of trash . . . He should have called an ambulance the second he found her. If the ambulance workers called the police, then so be it. They were going to catch him eventually. Why prolong the inevitable?

A clank sounded behind him. The swish of an opening door. "Jazz, wait!"

He cast a look back over his shoulder and kept walking. Hollis was hopping down the hallway, trying to pull a pair of jeans over a fuzzy-slippered foot.

"I don't have time for games! If you're willing to help, help. Otherwise I'm taking my chances with an ambulance."

"Okay, I'll help. But first you have to tell me what's going on." Hollis skipped over the carpeted floor and fell into a prancing step beside him. Her baby-doll nightgown puffed and billowed with every step. It was like walking with a designer jellyfish.

"I already told you. I don't know what's going on. But a girl is hurt. We've got to get her to a doctor."

"What happened back at the police station? That detective took one look at your face and went ballistic. What did you do? Assassinate the president? Or was it personal? Did you con his wife like you're trying to con me?"

Jazz stopped at the elevators and swatted the down arrow. A faint *ding* sounded far below them. Stairs would be faster. Where was the door to the stairway?

"Know what I did all day?" Hollis stepped into his space and got up in his face. "I spent the entire day locked in a room with a mob of angry police officers. They threatened me, insulted me, yelled at me . . . It was nonstop questions for five hours. The same question over and over and over again. What was our relationship?

Why did you come to me? Who would you turn to for help? They didn't even break for lunch. The head detective guy was so mad I thought he was going to ship me off to Guantanamo."

"Did they say why?"

"Besides that little bit about you being a terrorist and killing nine men?"

"I thought it was a unit." Jazz grabbed her by the shoulders and forced her to look him in the eye. "Which was it? Nine or a unit? Think!"

"What difference does it make? If they weren't . . ." Hollis pulled out of his grip and took a faltering step backwards. Her eyes were wide and staring—like she was looking at a monster.

"Hollis, this is crazy! I didn't kill anyone. Not nine, not three, not one."

"So why does it matter?"

"Last night, when I passed out at the piano, I had this dream . . ." The elevator opened with a musical chime. Jazz stepped in and reached for the control panel. Hollis was still in the hallway. She stood frozen, wide eyed. She wasn't going to help. He'd been crazy even to ask her.

He punched the button for the lobby and stood back as the door started to close.

"Wait!" Hollis's arm shoved in the door and forced it back open. "What's a dream have to do with this?" She stepped into the elevator and moved to the side to stand well away from Jazz.

"Nothing. There were a bunch of cloaked figures chasing me. I don't know why, but it seemed like there were ten of them. Something in my head just kind of triggered when you said nine."

"And that's it? You think they're after you because of a dream?"

"No, I just . . . It's nothing. Just a stray thought."

Hollis's eyes narrowed. Her lips formed around a word and then relaxed back into a frown.

"What else did they ask?" Jazz coaxed. "Did they say anything about my apartment being ransacked?"

"No. They just asked questions: Why were you at the police station? What were you wearing? What were you carrying?"

"Did you tell them about the will?"

"I wasn't going to lie to them."

The elevator door dinged open. Jazz held the door for Hollis and followed her out into the lobby. He kept his head down and stayed close behind her, scanning the room for lurkers. The desk clerk from the night before flashed him a smile before turning her attention back to her computer. Everything seemed normal enough—so far. If the police knew about his guitar, why hadn't they stationed a watch at the hotel?

"Did you tell them you still had my guitar?" He took Hollis by the arm and guided her to the left, well away from the front doors.

"I told them everything. Your music, you passing out, the will . . . everything but the letter. I didn't find that until I got home."

"What letter?" Jazz demanded.

"The letter from Sabazios Vladu."

"Hollis, look at me." Jazz rounded on her and waited until he had her attention. "I have no idea what you're talking about. What letter?"

"The letter . . . you pulled it out of your pocket with the will. You know . . . your life is in danger. Get out of town and meet him in Butte La Rose so he can explain what all the fuss is about?"

"Wait a minute!" Jazz thought back to the night before when he'd come home to his trashed apartment. He'd gotten something else in the mail, something besides the will. "Was it in a fancy engraved envelope with a San Francisco address?"

She nodded warily, her eyes never leaving his face.

"I never got a chance to read it. What did it say? My life is in danger and I have to get out of town?"

Another nod.

"Did it say why? Did it give any explanations at all?"

"Just that he'd explain in Butte La Rose. It was written all mysterious, like some kind of a gang-cult ritual kind of thing. He wanted to meet you out in the middle of the woods."

"But why send a letter? It doesn't make any sense." Jazz scanned the lobby one more time and crossed over to one of the front windows. No cars or loiterers. Nobody walking or driving at all. The sidewalks and streets were completely deserted. He made for the entrance and pushed through the door. The night opened out around him like a waking dream.

Where was Mari? The sidewalk was completely empty.

He ran up the street, searched behind a parked car, the steps of the next building, a row of spot-lit palms . . .

Where was she? Had the helicopters come while he was in the building? He would have heard them. Wouldn't he?

"So where's this wounded girl you were talking about?"

Jazz turned at Hollis's voice.

"You're going to tell me the police kidnapped her, right?" Hollis jellyfished up behind him and fixed him with a look. "Or is this the part where you give me something valuable to ingratiate your way into my confidence?"

"Just shut up, okay?" Jazz pushed past her and ran back to the hotel entrance. The sidewalk was clean enough. No bloody trails or signs of a struggle . . .

"So you're telling me you left a dying girl on the front steps of the hotel?" Hollis stepped up behind him. "Unbelievable. Totally and completely unbelievable."

"Okay, I get it!" Jazz turned and glared at the girl. "Would you just get out of my face? Go back to your stinking five-star room and leave me alone." He stomped out into the street, pressed his hands to his temples. *Think!* He had to think. If the police had found her, they would have searched the building. Unless she managed to get away . . . No! They had to know where Hollis was staying. If they saw Mari anywhere near the hotel, they would have searched the building. They couldn't have found her.

What if the helicopters had flown overhead and she'd been forced to take cover? What would she have done?

He jogged out into the center of the palm-tree-lined median and turned in a slow three-sixty. There was a covered porch across the street, an even bigger porch to the right—part of the McDonald's. Would she have considered walking under a balcony being inside a building? He ran across the street and searched the shadows at the base of the building. She wasn't there, but it would have been the perfect cover if a helicopter had flown by. He jogged up the sidewalk and searched for more hiding places, the Walgreens marquis, a thick hedge of shrubs in the median of the street . . .

"Jazz, wait!" Hollis shouting from across the street. She ran to intercept him.

"Would you be quiet?" He hissed and started running faster. If she didn't shut up, someone was going to call the cops.

Her voice rose in an ear-grating shriek. "Wait up or I'll call the police!"

"What do you *want?*" Jazz stopped and took a deep breath as the girl caught up with him.

"Okay . . ." She thudded up to him and bent over to rest with her hands on her knees. The way she was huffing and puffing you'd have thought she'd just finished a thousand meter sprint. "Assuming there really is a girl, and she really has been shot. What then? Do we just drop her off at the hospital?"

"I thought you didn't believe me." Jazz turned away from her and started walking toward the hedges.

"I don't, but assuming I did, what would you want me to do?"

"Nothing. It was a bad idea." Jazz leaned over and searched the shadows beneath the hedges. The plants were too thick to hide under, but she could have burrowed down into them from the top.

"But what did you want me to do before? It was more than just drive her to the hospital. Wasn't it?"

Jazz jogged over to the next hedge and started to rattle the bushes, but his eyes didn't want to focus. A strange sensation fluttered at the back of his mind. Pain . . . All of a sudden his right hip ached. No, not *his* hip . . . He took a couple of experimental steps. Everything seemed to be okay. Was it her? Could he really feel what was going on in her head?

"What's wrong?" Hollis's hushed voice came from the haze beside him. "Are you okay? What is it?"

"I don't know." Jazz turned and walked in a wide circle. Was it possible? Whatever he was feeling . . . sensing . . . came from the next street. Off to the right, just beyond the Walgreens.

He jogged over to the intersection and peered down the narrow avenue. There weren't any obvious hiding places, but the feelings seemed stronger. Or did they? What if the whole thing was in his head?

Muffled footsteps padded up behind him and stopped. Jazz took a deep breath and waited for Hollis to start. There was a long pause. He could hear her fidgeting with her hair.

"Why are you still here? I thought you didn't believe me."

"Once I start a book I have a hard time putting it down."

"That's good. Real good. I'm glad this is so entertaining for you."

"It's not yet. If you're going to find your shooting victim, go ahead already. This is starting to get old."

Jazz let out a sigh and took off down the street at a fast walk. What was he doing? The whole thing was a figment of his imagination. He sniffed the night air and took a deep breath, but he couldn't get the feelings back. This was ridiculous. What did he think he was, a bloodhound?

Another stab of pain pierced his right side. It was the same dizzy-headed thing he'd felt before. It was Mari. She was here somewhere. Somewhere close!

He ran up to a construction dumpster and looked inside. A streetlight close by lit up the area like a spotlight. It didn't seem like the kind of place a fugitive would chose for a hiding place, but there was something about it . . .

A whimpering sob sounded inside his head. He spun around and searched behind him. Hollis froze and looked at him like he was going crazy—which maybe he was.

"You heard that, right?"

"Heard what?"

He studied her expression. She seemed just as confused as he was, but he *had* heard something. Hadn't he?

He stepped toward a narrow alleyway that was blocked off by temporary fence. Would she have gone through there? It looked like a dead end.

Jazz lifted the fence and set it aside. Glass cracked like eggshells under his feet as he crept through the dark alley. The lights mounted on the walls of the buildings had all been shattered. Some of the damage seemed fairly recent, but other—

The scrape of metal against stone sounded at the end of the alley. It seemed to be coming from a massive shadow. Whatever it was, it was big as a grizzly bear. He stared at the hulking shape. Was it his imagination or was it moving? He glanced back at

Hollis who was staring into the darkness from the safety of the fence.

Another noise emanated from the alley. This time it sounded like a moan. Jazz took a deep breath and crept forward. Another moan. He could hear it moving. He walked faster. The shadow was even bigger up close. Gradually it resolved itself into not one, but a whole pile of objects, a heaping dumpster surrounded by bags of trash.

Jazz jogged up to the pile and started digging through the bags. She had to be here. It was the perfect hiding place. But why couldn't he feel her?

Circling around to the far end of the pile, he tossed aside bag after bag after bag. She wasn't there. This was stupid. There were hundreds of trash piles in the city. The only reason he'd thought she was here, was because he'd thought he could feel her. If the feelings had been real, wouldn't they be even stronger?

He pulled the last bag free and tossed it back against the wall. What was he supposed to do now? Hollis probably thought he was nuts. He should have asked for bus money while he'd had the chance.

He turned back toward the entrance and started to make his way through the scattered bags, but his legs didn't want to move. He turned slowly and stared into the alley. There was something at the base of the back wall. Something still and round—smaller than a bag of trash. He stumbled forward and collapsed onto his knees.

Mari was curled into a little ball at the base of the wall.

She wasn't moving.

⌒ 16 ⌒

Mariutza

A GENTLE TOUCH, SOFT and light as a downy feather, brushed across Mari's face. So soft and cool. It was like floating on a cloud. Being borne up into the heavens on the whisper-soft wings of a thousand tiny angels. She sighed and cracked her eyes open, squinting into the blearing brightness. So bright. Where was she? How could it be bright and cool at the same time?

"She's waking up." A man's voice sounded close to her ear.

"Purodad?" She croaked out the word and tried to sit up. A blurry figure leaned over her. But it couldn't be Purodad. Could it?

"You should take it easy. Lie back down and rest." Cool hands eased her back into the cloud. "You lost much blood. Very dehydrated."

Mari repeated the words over and over in her head, trying to find the sense of them. It didn't sound like her grandfather's voice. No, it couldn't be. That would be impossible.

She blinked her eyes and forced them to focus on the figure leaning over her. It was a man. A strange man she'd never seen before.

She rolled onto her feet and leaped toward the light. A crash sounded behind her as she hit the ground and crumpled to the springy turf. A woman's voice, high and shrill, sounded in her ears. The man shouted something. He was creeping toward her. Reaching out to grab her.

Fighting a wave of dizziness, Mari climbed onto her feet and backed away from the stranger. A beautiful, golden-haired woman stood behind him. "It's okay. He's a doctor. We aren't going to hurt you. It's okay . . ." She had the voice of an angel.

"Stay back. My grandfather gave me the training. If you come closer, I might be forced to hurt you." Mari's eyes darted to the right and left, searching for a way of escape. She was in a large enclosed area. She looked up and screamed. The area was covered by a ceiling. She was completely inside!

She lunged away from the man, but the room spun circles around her, tipping her off balance. She fell backwards and a loud thunk vibrated into her brain. She was inside. She had to get out!

Gentle hands rolled her onto her back. The man was looking down at her, shining a bright light into her eyes. She tried to sit up, but he pressed her back onto the ground. No, not the ground— onto the floor! The floor of a stationary building. She was fallen, a prisoner of the Badness. Any second and it would completely corrupt her. Or had it corrupted her already? Would she be able to tell the difference?

Blinking against her tears, she reached out tentatively with her mind. If she was truly fallen, wouldn't she have lost the sight? The doctor seemed just fine. She pushed harder, reaching out in all directions. A flicker of delicious warmth lit a remote corner of her mind. Maybe it was just her imagination. It felt like it was coming from deep inside the earth.

"—hurt? Tell me what it is you feel. You are experiencing dizziness?" The man was talking in a loud voice.

Mari blinked him back into focus and tried to calm on back down. "What do you want with me? Why couldn't you just . . ."

Her throat choked shut as a spasm convulsed her body. She was fallen. It was impossible to recover what she'd lost.

"Mari? That *is* your name, isn't it?"

Mari opened her eyes and looked up into the golden girl's beautiful face. She wasn't the Badness; she couldn't be. Something didn't fit.

"Mari . . ." The girl's voice was buffed and polished, like a sparkling gold coin. "Nod your head if you can understand me."

Mari nodded her head and stared up at the vision.

"Jazz said you wouldn't like being inside my room. Is that what's bothering you?"

"Jaazaniah?" Mari tried to sit up but the strange man pushed her back down. "Where is he? What have you done to him?"

"Jazz—aniah's fine." The golden girl smiled and the room seemed to brighten. "He went to get some supplies, but he'll be right back."

"Your wound was infected, but mostly superficial. I put in stitches the best that I could, but you must take it easy on it." The man leaned over to interpose himself between Mari and the girl. "You lost much blood and are seriously dehydrated. You should drink lots of water and take two of these"—he held up a fistful of tiny silver and white packages—"every day until they are all gone. Do you understand?"

"Jaazaniah is unharmed?" Mari leaned forward to see the girl. "He knows you trapped me inside a stationary building?"

"He'll be here in just a few minutes. We—"

"Inside this building. No! He mustn't!" Mari twisted out of the man's grip and pushed herself up into a sitting position. Her vision dimmed and her head pounded like a woodpecker, but it seemed to get better as she sat still and focused on a point on the far wall.

"Shhh . . . It's okay, sweetie. Jazz told me about your religion, but I don't think they'll hold it against you, do you? You were hurt.

We couldn't very well leave you outside in a pile of trash. It was hard enough getting a doctor to make a house call to a hotel."

A tiny spark of hope flared up inside Mari's mind, but she quickly stamped it out. It wasn't for her to say what was acceptable or not. Her place was to obey. "I should go . . ." She looked around the room, searching for a way out. So many doors and tapestries and mirrors . . . Everywhere she looked. How would she ever find her way out?

She climbed shakily onto her feet and took a tiny step. Her hip was much better. It hardly hurt at all. She took another step as the room shimmered and rang in her ears.

"Careful. I've got you." The golden girl wrapped an arm around her and helped her across the floor. They were heading toward what looked like an enormous bed. "Please, could you just lie down for a few minutes?" The girl cooed in her ear. "For me?"

Mari shook her head but found herself being lowered onto the beautiful bed. So delicious and soft. Softer than the clouds she'd been lying on before. "Just a few minutes . . ." Mari nodded and let the girl ease her head onto a pile of giant-sized pillows. She smiled up at the girl to show her appreciation. She wasn't doing it for herself, she was doing it for the girl. Surely that had to count for something.

"Here, let me get you something to drink." The girl smiled at her and skipped across the room to a small wooden cabinet. A few seconds later and she was back with a crystal-clear glass with a beautiful many-colored stick poking out over the top. The glass was filled with boiling water. How did the girl hold it without it burning her hands?

"Here . . ." She set the glass down on a polished table. "Let me get you another pillow." She helped Mari sit up and added two more pillows to the pile behind her back.

"Thank you." Mari eased back down into the cloudy softness. "I'm so . . . Thank you very much for your kindness."

The girl held the glass close to Mari's face. The water was popping and spitting out the top of the glass, but she couldn't feel any heat. "I don't understand. What am I supposed to do?"

"The doctor says you should drink." The girl touched the colorful stick to her lips. "Is Sprite okay? I could get something else."

Mari sniffed at the glass. It smelled a little like honeysuckle. Sweet and fresh and unbelievably delicious. Was she supposed to drink it now or wait for it to cool?

The girl moved the glass closer to her face. Mari shifted backwards and reached out a hand to touch the glass. "Ow!" She drew back her hand as soon as her finger touched it.

"What's wrong? Is it your hip?"

"It burned me." Mari rubbed her fingers together. The glass was so hot, it almost felt cold. She reached out and touched the glass again. "It *is* cold. How is this possible?"

"I just got it out of the refrigerator. Do you want some ice? The machine's right down the hall."

"How can it boil and still be cold?"

"Excuse me?"

Mari took the glass from the girl and wrapped both hands around it. It was cold as winter. She sniffed it again and looked up at the girl. "I can really drink it?"

The girl nodded and glanced over at the man who was standing beside her now. Had she said something wrong? They both had the smiles going something terrible.

"My name is Mariutza. I am very pleased to meet you."

"Hi, Mariutza. I'm Hollis." The girl smiled to reveal teeth even brighter than her hair and skin. "And this is Dr. Khatun. He was nice enough to drive all this way—even after working in the emergency room all night."

"Fourteen straight hours, and I won't even charge." The doctor grinned and looked over at Hollis before turning back to Mari. "You should drink. All the Sprite and some water besides. You were very dehydrated. You should drink as much as possible—until the pee-pee is clear."

Mari looked over at Hollis for confirmation. She nodded and leaned closer. "It's all right, sweetie. Jazz will be right back. Drink your Sprite."

Raising the glass to her lips, Mari took a tentative sip. It was cold and deliciously sweet. It almost seemed alive the way it fizzled and stung the insides of her mouth. But it didn't hurt at all, not really. It tasted good! She smiled up at Hollis and Khatun and took another sip. "It's . . . amazing! You wish to try it? It stings the inside of your mouth, but in a good way. It doesn't hurt at all." She held the glass out to Khatun, but he shook his head and pushed the glass back to her.

"You must drink. All of the Sprite and a glass of water besides."

Mari offered the glass to Hollis, but she shook her head too. "I have five more cans in the fridge. Drink as much as you like."

"Really?" She smiled again to show her gratitude. "You're very kind." She raised the glass to her lips and took another sip. Delicious . . . Another smile and another sip. Another. Her two new friends knelt beside the bed and watched her in silence. Every time she thanked them, they looked at each other and made the smiles. She knew she was doing something wrong, but she didn't care. The drink was so delicious and the bed so soft; she wanted it to last a million years.

When she finally finished the whole glass and had licked out the last drop, Hollis took the glass from her and set it on the table. "Want some more?" Her smile was almost a laugh. She could hear it quivering in her voice.

"I shouldn't." Mari looked from the girl to the doctor and back again. "You've already done so much. I couldn't possibly . . ." She scooted over and flung her arms around Hollis's neck. "Thank you," she whispered in the girl's ear and kissed her on the cheek. "Thank you for helping. I don't know all the right things to say, but I think you're the most beautiful woman I've ever seen. You're kind and educated and smart, and I love you very much."

Hollis's body went rigid. Her shoulders shook. She pulled suddenly away from Mari, and dabbed at her eyes. "Well . . ." She grabbed the glass from the table and turned away to walk stiffly across the room. "Let's get you some more Sprite. I . . ." She wiped her eyes again. She was crying. Mari hadn't meant to hurt her.

"I'm sorry. I . . ." Mari watched helplessly as the girl made a click with a green and blue can and poured more juice into the glass. "I've never been to a city. I don't know the right things to say. I'm sorry if I said it wrong."

"It's okay, sweetie. You didn't say anything wrong." Hollis bustled across the room and knelt beside the bed. "Just the opposite. I . . . it's just too sweet. It's way more than I deserve." She handed the glass to Mari and dabbed her eyes with her sleeve.

"Well . . ." Khatun stood up and looked around the room. "I must be getting some sleep now. You have my card. Call me if there are any problems, and I'll be right over." He helped Hollis to her feet and walked with her across the room. "I'll come back tonight maybe? To check on our patient and maybe . . . go out for a nice dinner?"

Hollis cast a quick glance at Mari and turned back to the doctor. "Dinner would be lovely. Around eight o'clock?" She opened a door and ushered the doctor out into a brightly lit room. They stood talking in low voices at the doorway for several minutes before the doctor finally left and Hollis stepped back inside.

Inside . . .

Mari winced. She was inside. Fallen. She could never go back. The enemy was still out there, searching for the prophet, and she would be powerless to stand.

"How are you feeling?" Hollis walked across the room and sat down on the edge of the bed. "Dr. Khatun said to make sure you took one of these twice a day." She tore open a shiny packet and shook a white tablet into her hand. "He also said to drink plenty of liquids. As soon as you finish that, I'll get you some more."

Mari took the offered tablet and held it on the palm of her hand. The juice was delicious, but Miss Caralee would fuss at her for being greedy. Hollis was playing the hostess and she was playing the guest. She was supposed to act the politeness. "No, ma'am. Thank you very much. It's magnanimously delicious, but this is more than enough."

A loud knock sounded at the door. Mari sat up as Hollis ran across the room and flung open the door.

Jaazaniah entered the room and set a brace of bulging store bags on the table against the wall. "How is she?"

"She's fine." Hollis hurried over to the table and started pulling out small boxes of store-bought stuff. "The doctor just left. He stayed until she woke up."

"I'm sure he did." Jaazaniah made a funny face at Hollis and then walked up to Mari's bed. "How are you feeling?" He smiled and reached out a hand like he was going to touch her face.

Mari caught her breath and watched as his hand hovered above her forehead and then withdrew. "Hollis and the doctor healed my leg. It feels almost perfectly fine."

He glanced over at Hollis who nodded and sat down on the edge of the bed near Mari's feet. "He says she lost a lot of blood and needs to drink plenty of liquids, but as long as she takes the antibiotics, she should be fine. He even left two weeks worth of free samples."

"Your doctor is quite the hero."

"*Her* doctor is a very generous man."

"I'll bet he is." He shot another look at Hollis and turned back to Mari. "The helicopters are back again. They've been criss-crossing the city for the past hour and a half."

"You must escape the city quickly. If you stay here, they will find you."

"Not necessarily. Hollis checked us into the hotel under the name Adler. She paid cash, so we should be good for a while. And she still has her rooms at the Ritz-Carlton so even if the cops check up on her, they won't have any reason to be suspicious."

"These things will shield you from the Badness?" Mari looked from Jazz to Hollis and back again. "It can sense your presence from a great distance—through walls and trees and even water. How can names and hotels be any protection?"

"What do you mean *sense your presence?*"

"Just as we can sense each other—as one Standing feels the presence of another, so the Badness senses us. This was how I was able to find you."

"I don't get it." Hollis's voice was high and shrill, like Miss Caralee when a fish stole her worm. "You're saying they have some kind of an electronic see-through-walls device? How can they find us? I didn't use a credit card."

"We are the Standing. We resonate with the first dimension. No one knows why . . ."

Jaazaniah turned to Hollis. "Remember how I found her out in the alley?"

"But you already knew where she was."

"Actually, I didn't. I know this sounds crazy, but I could feel her in my head. It's like we have some kind of wonder twin mind-reading thing going."

"Not twins!" Mari shook her head emphatically. "It is the way of *all* Standing—whether they are family or not. We are no relation at all."

A half smile touched Hollis's lips. She was looking at Jaazaniah like they shared a funny secret. Had she said something wrong again?

Jazz didn't seem to notice. He was still talking about the Badness. "If they can see us through walls and buildings, how are we supposed to hide? Is there a shield or something we can use? Lead-lined walls, kryptonite?"

"There is prayer. But it will be best for us to leave right away. If the helicopters get close, they will find us."

"And what will they do if they catch us?"

"They do not wish to catch us. They will shoot us with guns until we are dead. That's what they did to my . . . your grandfather."

Jaazaniah turned to Hollis and spoke in a soft voice. "You've done so much already, I'd hate to ask for more."

Her forehead puckered. She looked frightened and fragile and pale. She wasn't a Standing. What help could she possibly offer? Their presence only put her in danger.

When she finally looked up, her eyes had grown determination-hard. "You actually think I'd put the book down now? I don't for a second believe any of this, but you *have* piqued my curiosity. I'm not about to let you two out of my sight. I'm still trying to figure out what your angle is."

"There aren't any angles, but if you could give us a ride to Butte La Rose, I'd really appreciate it."

"What's Butte La Rose?" Mari asked. "Is it a place outside the city?"

Jaazaniah nodded and searched her face for several seconds. "Do you know a man by the name of Sabazios Vladu?"

"I know a man named Jack Baldassaro and a healer named Khatun and of course Miss Caralee and Purodad, but they're—"

"But you've never heard the name Sabazios Vladu?"

"I don't think so. Is he Standing? Purodad used to talk of other Standing, but he never named them by name. They were all numbers. There was the man he met in '57 and the woman he met in '73 and my mother and a boy he met in '91 and '97 and '98."

"Did any of them live in San Francisco?"

"They don't like cities. It's too dangerous."

"How about California? Did he ever mention California?"

Mari shook her head. "Does Sabazios Vladu live in California? Why are we going to Butte La Rose?"

"Before all this started—the night your grandfather was killed—I got a letter from a man named Sabazios Vladu. He said my life was in danger, and that if I met him in the woods to the south of Butte La Rose, he would explain everything. He said he couldn't tell me in the letter, because I wouldn't believe him."

"So you think he's Standing? What if he's one of the Fallen? He could be on the side of the enemy."

"The letter was postmarked four days before the attacks. If he worked for the enemy, why would he warn me about the attacks? I think we have to consider the possibility he's a friend."

Mari opened her mouth to argue but caught herself just in time. She was being bigger than her britches again. Even if he had forgotten, he was still Jaazaniah the Prophet. His wisdom and power were legendary. Her place was to listen and obey.

She put some humble back into her eyes and looked down at the juice still boiling away in Hollis's glass. "What do you want me to do?"

Jaazaniah glanced over at Hollis and then back down at her. "I want you to help me find Sabazios Vladu."

⮷ 17 ⮶

Jazz

"QUICK, GET THE GUITAR. I'm starting to lose my grip." Jazz hefted Mari in his arms and turned to face Hollis in the cramped stairwell.

"I told you I can walk." Mari squirmed and raised her injured leg. "See? My leg is very good. The doctor healed it fine."

"Ow! Hold still." Hollis ducked beneath Mari's feet and grabbed the guitar. She reached back around Jazz, pulled her suitcase across his foot, and sent it tumbling down the stairs where it crashed into the dented metal door below.

Jazz clambered after Hollis and fumbled with the door while she struggled to wrestle the ridiculously large suitcase back onto its wheels. He'd tried to talk her out of packing it, but she refused to give them a ride if he didn't let her pack a few things for Mari. *A few things* . . . It was more than Jazz had ever owned in his life.

He shouldered the door open and held it for Hollis as she dragged the clack-clacking case out into the parking garage. Something had definitely happened between the two girls while he was gone. The way Hollis was treating Mari, you'd think she was her long lost sister. Or her long lost poodle more like.

A shudder trembled down Jazz's spine. He felt suddenly sick, like the polenta from room service had been too rich. No, it wasn't the polenta. Maybe it was—

"Hurry! They come again for another pass!" Mari looked up at Jazz. "Please. Let me run myself."

Jazz nodded and she twisted out of his arms like a frightened cat. Hitting the ground running, she caught up with Hollis and helped her pull the suitcase over to the rental car. He caught up with them and hoisted the suitcase and guitar into the trunk. Then, slamming it shut, he ran around to the passenger seat and jumped in while Hollis helped Mari into the backseat.

"I still don't get what we're running from." Hollis slid behind the wheel and started up the car. "Who's chasing you and why do you think they're coming now?"

"The bad guys." Jazz said. "Mari says she can feel them."

"And you believe her?" Hollis turned and backed the car haltingly out of the parking slot. She was driving like a sixteen-year-old on her first driving test. What had he been thinking? He should have insisted on driving. She was going to get them all killed.

"Yes, I believe her! Move! We've gotta get out of here!"

"You never answered my question. Who are we running from? Is it the police or not? How does a person feel the police?"

"It's the Badness." Mari leaned forward between the two seats. "They're getting closer. We need to pray the shielding prayers."

"Go ahead and pray," Jazz called back as the car jerked to a stop at the gate. "And put your seat belt on. This could get rough."

"You must pray too. I can't shield us both."

"I'm not your religion. If you want to pray, that's fine. But . . ." Jazz turned to Hollis and shouted, "What are you waiting for? Go! *Go!*" He stomped on the floorboards and braced himself against the dash to keep from grabbing the wheel. Hollis had stopped at the end of the drive and was sitting there with her blinkers on—as if they had all the time in the world. "They're not going to let you out. You've got to pull forward. Force your way in!"

"If you want to drive, be my guest." Hollis shifted the car into neutral and switched off the engine.

"No! No! I'm sorry, okay? I shouldn't have yelled. Just drive!" Jazz leaned over the dash and looked up into the sky. Two helicopters were approaching from over the river. They were less than a mile away! "Go! That's them! We've got to get out into traffic!"

Hollis just sat there, staring up at the approaching helicopters. "You're serious. You seriously think they're searching for you?"

"Yes!" Mari and Jazz shouted the word as one.

"Now please . . . just drive." Jazz squirmed in his seat as the helicopters drifted closer. "I promise I won't yell again. Just go!"

Hollis started the engine and slammed the car into gear. A horn blared and brakes squealed as they lurched out into traffic with a halting jerk. Then, tugging on the wheel in a flurry of fluttering hands, she swerved the car back into her lane and stepped on the gas.

"You must calm yourself. They can feel you!" Mari's voice sounded at his ear. "Please. Pray the shielding prayers. I can't shield us both."

"You don't understand! God and I aren't on speaking terms anymore. It's not my thing. I'm not religious."

"It's not religion. It's the Lord. Talk to Him. Ask Him to calm your mind. Say it any way you like, just say it!"

Jazz leaned forward to look out through Hollis's window. The helicopters had veered to the right. They were still heading toward them. "Step on it. Move!" He tried to keep his voice down, but it still came out like a shout. "Go around this guy. He's going way too slow!"

"I offered to let you drive, but you—" Hollis slammed on the brakes as the idiot in front of her slammed on his. "Shut up and let me concentrate! I'm doing the best I can!"

"Jaazaniah." A hand clamped around his shoulder, and a strange tingle spread out from her touch. Soothing warmth. His heart quickened. It was pounding in his ears.

"Jaazaniah. You must pray now."

"I can't. I don't believe in God."

"God believes in you. It will be enough."

"But I—"

"Please. They sense our presence. Repeat these words: Holy One, hide us in Thy almighty hands."

This was crazy. Jazz looked at Hollis, but she was too focused on the road to be any help.

"Say it after me." The grip on his shoulder tightened. "Holy One, hide us in Thy almighty hands."

"Okay . . ." Jazz leaned forward and jerked his shoulder out of her grasp. "Holy One, hide us in your hands. Are you happy? Does that make the bogeyman go away?"

"You are our shield and deliverer."

"The Spanish Inquisition ended three hundred years ago. You can't force me to convert. That's not the way it works."

"Just talk to Him. Ask Him to shield your thoughts from the Badness."

"You're not listening to me. I don't believe . . . in any of this."

"You don't have to. Just open yourself to the possibility. If He's not there, what harm comes from trying? But if He grants your petition . . . how can you disbelieve if you've never given Him a chance to prove Himself strong?"

Red-hot anger blossomed to flame deep inside his mind. Balling his hands into trembling fists, he swiveled in his seat

and cocked back an arm to strike. Frightened eyes shimmered
and distorted behind a wall of flickering fire. Her slender frame,
the trusting innocence of her face—it filled him to bursting with
maddening, sickening rage. He could feel the storm tides rising,
pounding at his self-restraint. He had to fight back. To fall on her,
rip her to shreds with tooth and nail.

A low rumbling growl erupted from his chest. The slumber-
ing beast was finally awakening. How long had it lay dormant?
This was his destiny. What he was always meant to be. Muscles
tense and straining, he reached toward the girl's horror-filled
face. The beast was going to kill her. He didn't have a choice.

God, help me! Please, no. Please . . . He pressed his face
into the back of the seat as a wrenching sob shuddered through
his body. *Please, no. Help me. Please . . . Don't let me be my
father. . . .* Torrents of roiling emotion drained through him, spilling out through the soles of his feet. He crumpled into the seat,
focused on the rhythm of his breathing. In and out and in . . .
The pounding in his ears was starting to subside. He felt empty
and hollow, too weak to struggle. He had to focus on his burning
lungs. In and out. If he didn't focus, he would stop breathing.
That was all that mattered now. In and out and in . . .

A fluttering roar sounded in his ears, remote and ethereal.
The murmur of distant voices. He squeezed his eyes shut and
focused on his breathing. For an hour, two hours, ten? Time had
no meaning. He was a cork on a stormy sea. The wind and the
waves raged all around him, but he would stay afloat. As long as
he remembered to breathe, he would be safe and secure and . . .
cherished.

A steady drone sounded against the static filling his mind.
Squeak and whir, squeak and whir, the noises beat out a steady
rhythm in his brain, soft and soothing, lulling him back into the
gentle embrace of slumber.

A pounding roar suddenly rattled him awake. "Wha—?!" He jumped and looked around the car. Hollis was sitting rigid as a sun-bleached post behind the driver's wheel as a torrent of rain pounded against the windshield. "What happened? Where are we?"

"I need you to drive." Hollis's voice sounded scratchy and raw. "I never asked to be a part of this. I need you to drive right now."

"What happened? Is Mari okay?" He turned and looked behind him. Mari was stretched out on the back seat, sound asleep.

"I can't do this anymore. She said not to wake you. If you woke up, you were supposed to go back to sleep, but I can't do this. I want out. Just drop me off someplace safe, and you can have the car. I don't care anymore."

Jazz turned to Hollis. Her eyes were puffy and her mascara was smeared. She looked like she was going to lose it any second now.

"Did anything . . ." He checked the windows and the doors. Everything looked normal enough. "What happened? I think I fell asleep."

"I *felt* it!" She spat the words out, and a fresh trail of tears began to trickle down her cheeks. "It was like . . . I don't know. It was just horrible. And you fell asleep and Mari said you were praying, and then she said I had to pray too, and it got worse and worse until I thought I was going to lose my mind."

"That's all? It was just a feeling?"

"More than a feeling! All the cars stopped. All around us. The helicopters were flying back and forth, and people were getting out and starting to fight . . . It was terrible. A woman . . . she tried to . . ."

"But you're okay, right? Nobody tried to hurt you?"

"No, I'm not all right," Hollis shrieked. "It was real! I'm not making this up! They were . . . some kind of monsters. Real live monsters!"

"Shhh . . . Calm down. It's okay now, right? The helicopters got chased away by the storm."

"What storm? There wasn't a storm. They just flew back through the city. I was about to jump out and try to make a run for it, but all of a sudden they just flew off. Mari said it was because you were shielded. She says you're some kind of prophet warrior— that you're more powerful than all the monsters combined."

"Mari's a nice girl, but she's confused about a lot of things. She was raised out in the swamps by a crazy old coot who filled her head with cotton candy."

"She said she was raised by your grandfather."

"She was. He was a nutcase all his life. My father told me he died when I was little, but it was probably just to protect me. Either that, or something happened and he managed to survive. Or the person raising Mari was only pretending to be my grandfather. Either way, she's been subjected to more than her fair share of whacko."

Hollis nodded without taking her eyes off the road. The rain had slackened to a light drizzle, but it was still dark. Jazz leaned forward in his seat and searched the overcast horizon. The sun would be setting soon. It would have been nice to get to Butte La Rose with enough time to search for Vladu, but perhaps it was just as well that they had a chance to rest up first. Something about Vladu's letter gave him the jeebies.

"You like her, don't you?" Hollis fixed him with an obnoxious smirk.

"Who, Mari? I just met her yesterday. And most of that time has been running from the police."

"But you think she's hot, right? You'd have to be blind not to notice how much she likes you."

"She thinks I'm some fairy-tale hero from my grandfather's bedtime stories. You heard her. I'm supposed to be some kind of a holy man kung-fu-fighting prophet. That's hardly the basis for a stable relationship."

"So you *do* like her!"

"No! I'm just saying . . . She doesn't have a clue who I am. She doesn't have a clue about anything."

"So you're afraid if she got to know you, she wouldn't like you anymore?"

"I'm not going there. End of story. It hadn't even crossed my mind until you brought it up."

"So why are you so worked up?"

"Why do you even care? I thought you were going to abandon us the first chance you got."

"Well, excuse me for not wanting to get killed. I'm not the one wanted by the police. I'm not the one your helicopters are trying to kill. But who paid for the hotel? Who flirted up a free doctor even though his hair was greasy and he hadn't taken a shower in a week?"

"Hollis, I'm not saying you haven't been a saint through all this. We really appreciate everything you've—"

"And when the helicopters finally catch up to us, what do you do? Just when things start getting really freaky? You fall asleep. You fall asleep and leave all the decisions to me. All the decisions and all the driving. Well, sorry to disappoint you, but I didn't sign up for this. I thought you were a nickel-and-dime con artist with the world's stupidest scam."

"Well excuse me for telling the truth."

"You knew I wouldn't believe the truth. Admit it. You purposely tried to mislead me."

"Hollis?" Mari's whisper-soft voice sounded from the back seat. "It's not his fault. I'm the one that got shot. He was just trying to help."

"Sweetie, it's okay. I'm not mad. I just . . . This whole monster thing is freaking me out."

"Then you must leave us. The Badness isn't hunting after you. It'll let you be once we're . . . once *I'm* gone."

Jazz turned at the tremor in Mari's voice. A feeble smile touched her lips, but her gaze didn't quite meet his eyes. "How long have you been awake?"

"Not long." She glanced down at her hands and a veil of curls cut him off from her eyes. "I didn't mean to listen in."

Great. Jazz shot a look at Hollis. If Mari had heard that bit about her being hot, things were going to take a turn for the complicated. As if they weren't complicated enough already.

"I just woke up a few minutes ago myself. What happened back there? One minute I was fine and the next minute—"

"Here it is. Butte La Rose!" Hollis announced. "Where are we supposed to go now?"

"All it said was south. I guess we keep going on Bayou Road." Jazz pulled out the directions he'd copied off the Internet and studied Hollis's crude sketch. "Look for Addley Wyatt Drive on the right. After that it's all wilderness for miles."

"And this is where we'll meet this man?" Mari leaned over the back of the seat. "In the woods of this wilderness?"

"All it said was to meet him in the woods to the south of town."

"What kind of psycho sets up a meeting in the middle of the woods?" Hollis eased up on the accelerator as the road narrowed at a turn. "He didn't even give any landmarks."

Mari leaned forward. "The forest is much safer for a Standing. Fewer people for the Badness to hide among. Only a true Standing could find us in the woods. He must be a Standing!"

"But why would he think I was like him? He couldn't have known about my ESP thing. I didn't know about it myself until yesterday."

Mari's eyes were shining. "He's not planning on us finding him. *He'll* find *us*. And the woods hold hiding places in case we're followed. Trees and bushes and water to confuse the heat sensors."

"But what if it's a setup?" Hollis's worried gaze shifted from him to Mari. "What if he's one of them? You'll be walking right into his trap."

"There it is." Jazz pointed to a narrow, dark turn-off. "We're at the south end of town."

"That was it?" Hollis hit the brakes and slowed to a crawl. "That was the whole town? I didn't think we'd reached the outskirts yet."

Jazz nodded and searched both sides of the narrow country road. Except for the glow of their headlights, it was pitch dark. Remote, isolated, wild . . .

The perfect place for an ambush.

He stared out the window as dark trees flashed past on both sides of the road. "I don't think it's a trap. This Sabazios sent the letter way before the shadow men showed up at my apartment. If he was working with them, he wouldn't have tried to warn me."

"But who knows how long the letter was in your box?" Hollis's voice was a high-pitched squeak. "What if he was trying to trap you—to get you to come out here to the woods where there weren't any witnesses? What if he only sent the men after his first plan didn't work?"

"It's not a trap." Mari's voice rang with confidence. "There are too many places to hide in the woods. He's a Standing. If he were a Gadje, he would have wanted to meet in a city."

Jazz wasn't so sure, but what else could they do? They couldn't run forever. Sabazios Vladu was the best lead they had. "If he sent the letter four days ago, he might not be here anymore."

"Well, I'm not waiting around to find out." Hollis's chin was set. "I'm happy to drop you off at a hotel, and I'm even happy to give you a little money to help you on your way, but I'm not going anywhere near the woods. Especially after dark."

"A hotel?" Mari turned to Jazz. "You promised. No more buildings. The meeting's in the woods."

"It's okay. Calm down." Jazz reached back and put a hand on her arm. "You don't have to go inside if you don't want, but we have to spend the night somewhere. I'm not going to sleep outside."

"What if the man has a diddlecar? Or a tent? Someplace we can all sleep?"

"You're saying you want to go looking for him in the dark? Are you crazy?"

"Of course in the dark. It won't be safe when the sun comes up. It's too easy to be seen from the air."

"But . . ." He turned to Hollis, but she didn't seem to be paying attention. "We won't be able to see, either. How do you expect to be able to find him at night? It will be hard enough in the day time. Not to mention the swamps and alligators and—"

"Stop the car!" Mari's shout rang in Jazz's ears. "Make it stop. *Now!*"

"What's wrong? Are you okay?" Hollis stomped on the brake and pulled over to the side of the road. Mari was sitting rigid as a statue. Her eyes were closed and a frown puckered her brow. She looked like she was in pain.

"Mari, are you okay?" Jazz reached over and put a hand on her shoulder. "It's okay. We won't make you go to a hotel. Just tell us what you need."

"They're here." Her voice was a tense whisper. "Do you feel them? Two Standing, with three more besides. It's very strange. I've never felt anything like it." She scooted across the seat, pushed the door open, and jumped.

"Mari!" Jazz hissed and swung his door open. "Mari, get back here!" He stepped outside—and froze. She was standing on the shoulder, staring into a band of dark trees. He took a step toward her and the high-pitched trill of insect noises suddenly stopped. Perfect, absolute silence. He could feel it pressing down on him, reaching out to hold him in an icy grip.

"Out there. Do you feel it?" Mari pointed toward the trees and took a couple of steps down the overgrown bank. "It feels like Standing, but they're so . . . different. So faint. Like they're close and far away at the same time."

"Mari, this isn't the time. Let's find a place to stay and come back tomorrow, okay?"

"Y'all?" Hollis called out from the car. "This isn't funny anymore. Either get back inside, or I'm leaving. I'm not staying out here another second."

"Come on." Jazz started toward Mari, but she was already wading through the long grasses. He stepped down into the ditch and his shoe filled with cold water. "Mari, come on! You're freaking Hollis out. You're freaking *me* out."

"They're not that far away." Her voice drifted back to him. "I think I can find them!"

"Mari!" Jazz shouted and the darkness seemed to gather around him. Strange, alien sensations slithered through his mind. Twisting and untwisting like a pit of snakes.

"I mean it, y'all! I'm leaving!" Hollis's shout pierced the storm of his thoughts. Dark shadows flashed in his mind. The silhouettes of jouncing trees and reaching branches. Something was running.

"Mari, come back here!" He sloshed into the ditch and ran after her. She was almost to the trees. If she got too far ahead, he'd never find her.

A car door slammed behind him, followed by Hollis's frantic voice. "I'm leaving! Do you hear me? I said I was leaving, and I'm leaving!"

"Hollis, wait!" Jazz called out and started to run faster. "Mari, wait. Hollis'll leave us. She's not kidding!"

Another door slammed. The sound of a revving engine.

"Hollis, stop!" He turned and raced back to the road—just in time to see the car pull forward and disappear around the bend. With a muttered oath, he spun back to the woods. "Mari!"

He stopped on the side of the road and looked back out over the shadow-drenched fields.

Mari was gone.

ᥱᥩ 18 ᥩᥱ

Mariutza

THE TREES CLOSED IN around Mari, welcoming her. The forest seemed timid and shy, but not afraid. Not exactly. The sensation was something new. As exotic as the confused emotions swirling in her head.

A jolt of anger stabbed through her, sending her skidding into a mound of matted leaves. Jaazaniah? She leaped to her feet and searched the darkness.

"Jaazaniah!" She paused to listen. Something was wrong. Anger, frustration, fear . . .

Jaazaniah was in trouble!

Plunging through a wall of tender saplings, she dodged and twisted and leaped through the crowding shadows. Puddles of dappled blue light painted the trees. The moon was peeping out through the clouds. She had to go faster. If the Badness caught them in full moonlight, they'd never be able to hide.

Mari sped through the thinning trees and burst out into the moonlit marsh. A shadow shifted at the top of the rise. Jaazaniah stood alone by the road, his profile streaked with shifting moonlight. Where was Hollis? The Badness couldn't have carted her off. Mari would have felt it.

Jaazaniah turned as she bounded across the marshy field. A wave of ragged anger hit her in the face. She had to stop him. The Badness would read it for miles. She slogged through a pool of standing water and climbed up the shallow slope. The prophet's emotions beat down on her, stealing away her breath. She gritted her teeth and forced her eyes to his face. Something terrible had happened. His grief was thick as pluff mud.

"Do you realize what you've done?" His voice cut into her mind like a burning blade.

"Please, I'm sorry. I don't understand."

"Hollis left us. You wouldn't come back, so she left us!"

"But why? There's Standing in the woods. I can feel them. Isn't that what we came to find?"

"You scared her to death!" He turned his back on her and faced the road. "We'll have to hitch a ride now. Who knows when a car will come by."

"But why are you afraid? I don't understand. Did the Badness come while I was tracking? Why couldn't I feel it?"

"It's dark and we're in the middle of nowhere and we left her all alone. What part don't you understand?"

"But we're finally safe. Isn't that what she wanted? I thought she would be happy." Mari's voice was trembling now. She was dangerously close to disrespectful. "We're out of the city and away from all the people that want to hurt us. And it's dark and quiet and . . ."

Jazz swung around and stared her in the eye. Finally he broke the silence. "This feels *safe* to you?"

Mari nodded. "I'm sorry I ran, but after the city with all its enemies and lights. . . . It was just such a relief. And when I felt the Standing . . . I thought you'd be happy. I thought they were the ones we'd come to find."

The prophet shook his head and stared at her from beneath a furrowed brow. "It doesn't bother you we're out here in the middle of the night? With no flashlights or transportation?"

Mari frowned. She was missing something, but what? Why did she always have to be such a thick-headed *dilo*? "You think the Badness followed us here? You wish for lights to create a false trail?"

His brow gathered into a bunch. Finally his expression softened. "You're serious, aren't you? You really think we're safe."

"Not safe . . ." Mari lowered her eyes and assumed the proper listening position. "I understand there are still risks, but—"

"But?"

"But after everything we faced in the city"—she snuck a peek at his face—"it's just such a relief. My feelings carted me off before the horse. It was very wrong of me. I won't let it happen again."

"And now that you're not being carted off"—his voice had a touch of the laugh in it—"what do you think we should do now?"

Mari looked up. Had she heard him aright? "What do *I* think?" She studied his expression. "I'm like to be a Miss Scatterbrains, but I'd feel a whole lot better if we weren't so close to the road."

"So you want to go back into the woods?"

Mari nodded.

"Even though it's dark?"

"This isn't the right answer?"

"Fine with me." He shrugged and started walking down the bank. "Lead the way, girl scout. If you're selling Thin Mints, I guess I'm buying."

Mari breathed out a sigh of relief as they waded out across the swampy waters and stepped into the cover of trees. The Standing were even closer than before. With some of them it was hard to tell how far, but one of them was less than a mile away. She zigzagged in and out through the trees, making her way toward the powerful presence ahead.

"Hold up a second!" Jaazaniah came crashing up behind her. "Ow!" He pushed through a thicket and almost ran into her.

"What's wrong? Do you feel something?"

"Yeah, a branch smacking me in the face. How do you do it? It's black as midnight in here."

"I . . ." Mari glanced around at the trees and turned back to Jaazaniah. "Something has damaged your eyes?"

His sigh came out deep and harsh. She'd said something else wrong. She should apologize, but every time she opened her mouth the wrong words plopped out.

Jaazaniah stepped closer and a light touch tingled across her elbow. She stiffened as the touch traced down her arm and a large hand engulfed her own. Mari stood frozen to the spot. A thousand thoughts swirled in her head at once, but she couldn't hear any of them over the pounding of her heart.

The hand tightened around hers. The prophet's thumb caressed the back of her fingers. He was saying something, asking her a question. She had to catch hold of her wilding senses. If she didn't give the right answer, he might turn her loose.

"Mari?" A gentle voice sounded close to her ear. "Are you okay?"

She opened her mouth, but the words didn't want to come. What was she supposed to say? He had taken her by the hand. Willingly, of his own accord.

"I know you think I'm some sort of superhero, but I'm not. I need you to know that. I'm not trying to con you. I can't see in

the dark and I can't read minds. I can reduce a hardened soldier
to tears with my music, but I'm not a warrior. I couldn't fight my
way out of a wet paper bag. Do you understand?"

Mari managed a stiff nod. This was where she was supposed to
say something. He had taken her by the hand. She was supposed
to say something pretty and ladylike, like Miss Caralee when
Purodad gave her the compliments.

"Okay . . ." He took another step forward but didn't let her
hand loose. "Lead the way, but remember, I'm depending on you.
Don't run me into any trees."

She guided the prophet forward, gentle-like, picking the
path that kept him the furthest away from any branches or
vines. Every time she paused or changed direction, his hand
tightened around hers, filling her head with choking mud.
Cascades of warmth coursed up her arm, giving her heart
the flutters. She had to say something. He'd think she hadn't
learned her manners.

"I like your hand." She finally managed to squeak out the
words. "I think it's . . ." Knife-edged panic stabbed through
her brain. What was the word? He'd think she was dim as a
faerie. "I think it's very . . . nice." Warmth rushed into her face
and ears. She could feel the heat radiating into the night. She
swallowed back the gibberish threatening to bubble out of her
mouth. He was displeased. She was supposed to say something
pretty.

"Thank you." Was that a laugh riding on his voice? "I think
your hand is nice too."

Mari's throat tightened. Her smile fountain was bubbling up
to overflowing. Toe-stepping through the underbrush, she fought
the urge to turn and sneak a peek at the prophet's face. She was
supposed to be watching out for branches. He'd put his trust in
her. She wouldn't let him down again.

"Do you still feel it?" Jaazaniah finally broke the silence. "The people you've been tracking, do you still think you know where they are?"

She pointed with her free hand. "Yonder ways. Close to half a mile. I think he's tracking us as well."

"I thought you said there were five of them."

Mari slowed to a stop and reached out further with the *dikh* sight. "There were four or five of them before. But now I only feel two. One close, the other far away."

"Are you sure? Where'd the others go? Are they out of range or did they just disappear?"

"They were right here a few minutes ago. I would have felt it if they—" A faint tremor touched her mind, strange and unnatural as the taste of city air. It was—right behind them!

Mari spun around and swept the darkness with her eyes. There were two of them. Maybe three. Circling 'round them. Coming in fast!

"Quick, shield yourself. They're coming!" She pulled Jaazaniah off to the right where the shadows were thickest. Branches slashed at her face, but she kept on running. The prophet would have to understand.

"What's going on?" He hissed in her ear as they circled around a clearing and plunged into a tangle of vines.

"They're behind us. Strange voices. They're hunting after us, and they're catching up quick." Mari grabbed his arm and pulled him deeper into the forest, but it was no use. The voices were moving too fast. They had to find a place to hide.

"What's behind us? What's going on?"

"We must shield ourselves. Pray!" She pushed the prophet under a branch and jerked him to the right toward a stand of new growth saplings. She cleared her mind and tried to lose herself in the maze of springy branches.

A crash sounded behind them. A rustle off to their right.

"Keep going. Straight ahead!" Mari guided him around a gnarled old tree and turned to face their pursuers. A dark shadow was moving less than thirty feet away. She could feel it reaching out for her. Probing tendrils twisted and turned in her mind. Cold and inhuman and wrong.

It stepped out from behind a tree and glided toward her. Thin and willowy, only about four feet tall. It looked like—a little boy! Mari tried to look away, but its hold was too strong. She had to see it. Had to know for sure.

"What is it?" Jaazaniah's whisper cut through her besieged thoughts. "A kid?"

"Go!" Mari tore away from the creature's mind and stumbled forward. "Find the other Standing and warn them. Run!"

Another tiny figure stepped out of the trees to her left. She dropped into ready position and waited for its charge. Fury and indignation rose up all around her. She could feel its power tingling through her feet.

"Get down!" Jaazaniah shouted as a fluttering shadow flew at her face. A high-pitched cry rang out as it snapped and flapped five feet away from her and then doubled back on itself to fly back through the trees.

Mari spun around as a loud crack sounded behind her. The sound of pounding footsteps, crashing trees. A wall of raw power hit her in the back, echoing in her brain like the roar of a thousand storms. Was it a Standing? It was so strong!

The night shifted around her and all of a sudden the tiny figures were gone. Mari blinked into the empty shadows. Where had they gone? They couldn't just vanish.

Another wave of power pounded through her. Shaking her head to clear her mind, she turned and braced herself to face this new, more potent threat.

A huge, shadowy figure churned through a sea of shivering trees. It was enormous—almost seven feet tall. It pushed through the forest, plowing its way with a tree-sized wooden staff. She stepped in front of Jaazaniah and dropped into a defensive crouch. Swirling power swelled to an almost unendurable intensity as the dark shadow approached.

It was a man. A huge man cloaked in a long, tattered black coat. He stopped a half dozen yards away from them and regarded them with an exultant smile.

Jaazaniah stepped forward with his right hand extended and spoke in a hushed voice, "Sabazios Vladu?"

The man nodded and his face twisted into a frown. "That's my legal name, but my friends call me Melchi."

III

O myriads of immortal Spirits! O Powers
Matchless, but with th' Almighty!—and that strife
Was not inglorious, though th' event was dire,
As this place testifies, and this dire change,
Hateful to utter. But what power of mind,
Foreseeing or presaging, from the depth
Of knowledge past or present, could have feared
How such united force of gods, how such
As stood like these, could ever know repulse?

—John Milton
Paradise Lost

⌒〇 19 〇⌒

Jazz

"YOU ARE JAZZ RECHABSON?" The giant wrapped a mammoth paw around Jazz's hand and shook it vigorously. "I am glad to meet you. We feared the Mulo had caught up with you before you got my letter."

"We?" Jazz extricated his hand from the giant's grip and backed up a few steps to clear his head. The guy was more than just huge. There was something unsettling about him . . . like his personality was too big to fit inside his skin. "Who's we?" Jazz glanced behind him and back again to watch the giant. "Are you here with the two children?"

A surge of warmth suffused the clearing. An image flashed in his mind. The face of a tall beautiful brunette.

"No," the giant's voice sounded strained. "I came here with a good friend. We aren't . . . married."

"Sir?" Mari's voice sounded at Jazz's side. "Just now, right before you got here, two children were chasing us. They felt like Standing—only they weren't. They aren't like anything I've ever felt."

"The other presences. They aren't with you?" The giant's eyes turned to Mari and locked onto her. A surge of irritation flowed through Jazz. Which only increased when Mari's mouth dropped open and her eyes seemed to lose focus. She just stood there, staring at the giant like a teeny at a rock concert.

"This is my friend, Mari," Jazz stepped forward, but they didn't seem to notice. They were still staring at each other. Like close-ups from one of those cheesy black-and-white movies from the twenties. "Okay, this is starting to weird me out. What's going on? Mari?"

She didn't move. She didn't even seem to be breathing.

"Okay, enough's enough." He stepped in front of Mari and turned to face the big man. "Thanks for the letter, but Mari and I can manage things on our own. Your warning came a bit too late."

The giant shook his head as if he were coming out of some kind of trance. He stood blinking and looking around the clearing before turning back to Jazz. "I am sorry. But your friend. Mari . . . She has received the training?"

"Ask her yourself." Jazz backed slowly away from the giant and took Mari by the arm. "Out loud. So I can hear you."

"I am sorry." The man looked down at the ground like a whipped puppy dog. "I meant no disrespect. But I . . . I've never met anyone with the training. My master died when I was a young boy."

"Your master?" Jazz turned to Mari. "What's he talking about? And what's the deal with the zombie staring contest?"

"The children aren't with Melchi," Mari whispered. "He thought they were with us."

"They're getting closer. We must hurry." The giant—Melchi—turned, and with a backward glance at Mari, started walking through the trees.

"Who? The children?" Jazz turned to Mari but she was already following the giant. "Mari, wait!" He trotted after her. "Will somebody tell me what's going on?"

He followed them in and out through the moonlit saplings. The giant stopped suddenly and glanced behind them. He cut to the left and set off at a more rapid pace. Jazz had to jog to keep up.

"You said you came here to warn me." Jazz spoke in a loud whisper. "Warn me about what? Who's after me?"

"You are Standing," Melchi said. "It's not safe for you to advertise your presence in the world of men—especially on the Internet where your enemies can easily search you out."

"But what enemies? Who are they?"

"An enemy called the Mulo was searching for you. I inherited its papers and found records of your performances in New York City and Atlanta, Georgia."

"What do you mean by Mulo?" Mari's voice sounded at Jazz's side. "Are you talking about a shimulo or the mulani?"

"It's . . ." Melchi glanced back at her with an apologetic shrug. "I don't know about such things. I was never trained. It's just . . . the Mulo."

"Can you see it? Is it more like a ghost or a man?"

"It takes the bodies of men when it can. They walk and talk just like living men."

"Then it's shimulo—the walking dead."

The walking dead? Jazz studied the giant's face, waiting for a response. The ESP thing he could handle, but zombies? The weird was getting thicker by the minute.

"Do you know what it wants with Jaazaniah?"

Melchi shrugged and pushed through a thick clump of saplings. "The Mulo hunts the Standing—either to kill them or to take them as its own. It has been tracking him for many years. For every record I found of Jazz's performances, I found a matching record of the Mulo flying to that city. Either it's a fan of his music, or it's been hunting him. Until we saw the announcement of him playing at the Hookah Club, we thought it had already found him."

Jazz tried to make sense of what he was hearing. "So you're saying this Mulo . . . is *hunting* me?"

"You are Standing. It's the only possible explanation."

"And you know this because you inherited its *papers*?"

"It's difficult to explain, but I now have the Mulo's papers in my possession. To decipher them has been very difficult. It had dealings with companies in Eastern Europe and Asia and all sorts of officials in the American government, but I found among the financial records several pages focusing on five people who live in this area. You were one of them."

"Who were the others?"

"Jonah Rechabson, whom we guessed to be your father?"

Jazz nodded. "My grandfather, actually."

"Also there was Marie Paris Glapion?" He shot a look at Mari.

"Her name is Mariutza," Jazz cut in before Mari could respond. "Mariutza *Rechabson*."

The giant nodded and stepped around a clump of dark vines. "What about Beng Glapion and Jean Baptiste Wedo. You know these people as well?"

Jazz looked over at Mari who shook her head. "Never heard of them. But you still haven't told us anything about this Mulo guy. Who's he working with? What's his connection to the military?"

Melchi shook his head. "The Mulo is very powerful. It doesn't work with soldiers."

"Well, somebody's got military connections. Military helicopters have been chasing us for days. The police are in on it too."

Melchi looked to Mari—for what? Verification? Since when did he need a signed note from home?

She nodded—a little guiltily, Jazz thought—and trotted up beside the giant. "Our enemies work most often through the powers and rulers of this world. My grandfather trained me to stand against military soldiers and the power centers of the police."

"Did he teach you the prophecies?" Melchi asked. "How about the history of the Standing? My training was very incomplete."

Mari shook her head. "He said these things were for later. I asked him time and again—especially about the prophets and warriors—but it was never later enough. Now he's gone, I'm like to never know."

"Shhh . . ." Melchi stopped and raised a hand. He and Mari stood frozen in the icy moonlight, staring out into the darkness. Jazz held his breath and tried to listen, but he couldn't hear anything. The night was perfectly still.

"This way!" Melchi hissed and plunged through the trees at an all-out run. Mari was right behind him.

"Wait! Where are you going?" Jazz tried to catch up, but they were already gone. "Mari!" he called out louder and kept on running. Branches slashed at his face, sending him careening in all directions. He zigzagged blindly through the maze until he was hopelessly lost. What was the point? For all he knew he was going in the completely opposite direction. "Mari!" He plodded to a stop and slumped back against a scratchy tree.

A rustle sounded behind him. He pushed off the tree and started running. Was that a flicker of light? He veered to his right, cut back to his left, wove in and out through the trees. This was crazy. They knew he'd get lost. Why had they run off and left him?

"Jaazaniah?"

Jazz spun around at Mari's voice.

"Why didn't you follow us?" Mari jogged up beside him. "You don't trust Melchi?"

"Why did you run off and leave me? I told you I'm no good in the dark."

"But the moon . . ." She reached out haltingly and took him by the hand. "I'm sorry. I left off thinking again. Purodad said I'm distractful as yellow jackets on a stew."

"What happened? Why did you run off like that?"

"It was the children. They were headed toward Melchi's friend."

"Did they—"

"She's fine. They run off again soon as we got close." Mari tugged on his hand and led him on a twisting course through the crowding trees. A few minutes later and he could see a bright light shining in the distance.

A dark figure passed in front of the light. The murmur of soft voices.

Jazz shielded his eyes as Mari led him into a tiny campsite consisting of two small tents, a dining fly, and a bed of dusty coals surrounded by a ring of half-burned logs.

"Jaazaniah!" Melchi stepped forward, leading a tall brunette who looked like she'd stepped off the cover of an Eddie Bauer catalog. "This is my good friend Hailey Maniates. Hailey, this is Jaazaniah Rechabson."

"Hi, Jaazaniah." The brunette brushed the hair out of her face and smiled. Jazz just stared. Her eyes sparkled in the moonlight, burning into his brain with blinding light. Her features distorted and blurred. He was falling, reaching out with flailing arms. A sea of moonlight closed around him, cool and calming, buoying him up. He was floating face-down in a foamy sea of soft, pearlescent waves. A grid of rooftops and trees flowed beneath him. A tall wooden fence surrounding a torn-up backyard.

Jazz drifted to the ground and stood facing the corner of a weathered old doghouse. It was so strange. He'd seen it all before. The doghouse, the holes in the yard, the fence . . .

A scrape sounded. He was stomping a shovel into the ground. He lifted a scoop of loose dirt and tossed it to the side. Something in his head screamed. This was important. Why was digging a hole so important?

He jabbed the blade of the shovel deeper into the ground, and the hole opened up around him. Reaching shadows, scratching limbs. He was in a dark forest. A teenager was running right at him. Caramel-colored skin, curly black hair. The guy didn't seem to see him.

Jazz tried to get out of his way, but his body wouldn't respond. He watched as two small figures appeared behind the teenager. It was the children from the forest. They were gaining on him. He couldn't possibly get away. The guy ran through him and there was a horrible tearing sound. One of the children, a disturbing looking boy with huge black eyes, looked directly at him. He stepped closer and his mouth twisted into a hungry-looking grin. He could see him!

"No!" Jazz screamed and pulled away with all his might. A shriek echoed through the forest, more sounds of ripping fabric. "No!" He squinted up into the blearing light. Faces crowded in around him. The crush of grasping hands. He swung his fists, but strong hands pinned his arms by his sides.

"Jaazaniah!" Mari's voice pounded into his brain. "Jaazaniah! Say something. Tell us what's wrong!"

Jazz turned at her voice and blinked until the shadow finally resolved itself into Mari's concerned face.

"Are you well? Jaazaniah? Tell us what's wrong. How can we help?"

"What?" He turned and squinted up at the other faces. The giant—Melchi—and his friend . . . What was her name? Hailey? He shut his eyes and turned away as soon as he remembered her eyes.

"Jaazaniah? Can you hear me?"

"I hear you. You can let go of my arms. I'm fine."

The grip around his arms loosened but didn't let go.

"I'm okay. It was just . . . I don't know. I guess it was a fainting spell or something."

"What did you see?" Mari's eyes danced like he was a package under her Christmas tree.

"What do you mean, what did I see? I fainted, passed out. It must have been all the running around. I don't know. Fumes from the campfire or something."

"But you saw something, didn't you?" Mari prompted him with a nod. "A vision that made you cry out."

"It was just a bad dream," Jazz growled. "I've been having a lot of bad dreams lately. It's what comes of having half the world trying to kill you."

"I'm not trying to kill you." Mari sounded stung.

He sighed as a tiny hand reached out and gently touched his shoulder. "Okay, maybe it was a little vision-like, but it was really stupid. I was just digging a hole next to a dirty old doghouse."

"Digging a hole with a shovel?" Mari asked in a hushed voice. "What did it look like?"

"What do you mean what did it look like? It looked like a shovel."

"A store-bought shovel from a store?"

"Of course."

"And where were you digging?" She leaned in closer, watching him with those soft, beautiful eyes.

"What does it matter? It was just a dream." He turned to look at Melchi but saw Hailey instead. His chest tightened a little, but no flashes of moonlight or melting faces.

"Have you had other . . . dreams lately? What else have you seen?"

"Nothing." Jazz focused on Mari's face to keep the jumble of pressing images out of his head. What was wrong with him? Was he going crazy?

"A hazy pink moon behind a dead oak tree." Melchi leaned forward and looked Jazz in the eyes. "Why does this frighten you so much?"

"What did you say?" Jazz stared right back at him.

"A moon behind a dead oak tree. It just came into my mind. This was part of your vision?"

Jazz pulled out of the giant's grip and pushed himself off the ground. He pressed the heels of his hands into his eyes and tried to make it all stop. It was crazy. None of this was happening. Visions weren't real, and people didn't read each other's minds.

"What does it mean?" Mari's voice sounded close to his ear. "The moon and the tree. It is a bad omen?"

"I don't *know* what it means," Jazz snapped. "I saw it the night all this started. One second I'm playing the piano, and the next thing I know I'm running through the forest from a bunch of men in black cloaks. There was this tree with the moon shining behind it. It knocked me to my knees like it was the most important thing in the world. For a second I felt like I understood the secrets of the universe, and then the feeling was gone. I got up and the men in black cloaks surrounded me."

A soft gasp sounded behind him. Mari's hand tightened around his shoulder.

"One of them pulled out a gun, and I think he shot me, but I didn't even care. I just shouted and all of a sudden there was a bright light. Then, next thing I know, I'm waking up on the floor of the club."

"When did you—" Mari's voice choked off. "When did you see this? Please . . . I need to know."

"Late Friday night. I don't know. It must have been close to midnight."

Mari nodded and blinked the tears from her eyes. "What you saw wasn't a vision. It was real. It happened to my . . . It happened to *your* grandfather. I think you were looking through Purodad's eyes."

"But what about the doghouse? You don't seriously think he's in heaven right now digging a hole?"

"No, but he may have dug a hole before he died. Please, you must think. Picture the handle of the shovel in your mind. What does it look like? What is the color?"

Jazz closed his eyes and tried to think. Did he really want to be channeling the thoughts of a crazy old man? It was so Syfy Channel. It didn't make a shred of rational sense.

"Do you see it? What does it look like?"

He sighed and opened his eyes. "It's just a regular shovel. A regular shovel with a handle made of really light-colored wood."

Mari's face lit with a triumphant smile. "It's the same shovel Purodad bought before he died! You saw where he was digging. Did you see anything else?"

"No, I was just digging. Or he was digging. I don't know. It was like I was in someone else's head."

"Do you think he was burying your inheritance?"

"I don't know. Maybe . . . Or maybe it was just a bad dream. The side-effect of too many people poking around in my brain." Jazz climbed to his feet and looked around the campsite. Melchi and Hailey were busy stuffing equipment into two enormous packs. They looked like they were about to bug out.

"So what happens now?" He nodded to Melchi. "You guys warned us about the Mulo. Was that it? You're just going to pack your bags and take off?"

"Of course not." Melchi looked hurt. "We came to offer you sanctuary in California. We have nice tents with water-tight floors and warm sleeping bags to keep out the cold. We have plenty. You can have as many as you like. And we have food and water and electric lights as bright as daylight. It's all very nice."

"What if I don't want to go to California?"

"The Mulo knows you are here, so you must go somewhere. If you don't want to go to California, we will go someplace else. Just name a place, and that's where we'll take you."

"Right . . . You'll give up your home and turn your back on your family and friends just for the pleasure of my company?"

"Yes, of course. To save your life, we will do anything."

"Nope. Not even tempted. Sorry, but I've got unfinished business to tend to."

"Jaazaniah, wait!" Mari stepped toward him. "It's not safe here. The mulani will send more soldiers. They'll keep searching until they find us."

"If you want to go with him, fine. Nobody's forcing you to stay. But I've got a treasure to find. You read the will. My grandfather left me something, and nobody's taking it away."

"Then I'll help you find it."

Jazz shook his head. "My mind's made up. You're not talking me out of it."

"I can help." Her voice was soft and thin as a whisper. "Remember the verse in Ruth? You'll want to go whither Purodad went and lodge whither he lodged. I can help you follow in his steps. I know I can."

"And what happens if we find it?"

"I don't understand," she said. "I thought that's what you wanted."

"You know what I'm talking about. How much of a share do you want?"

"A share?"

"Of the treasure. I'll go thirty-seventy, but that's it. Take it or leave it."

"But the inheritance is yours. Purodad wanted *you* to have it, not me."

"And you're okay with that?" He forced a laugh. "You lived with the guy all your life, and then he goes and gives his money to a total stranger and that doesn't bother you?"

"It's . . . what he wanted."

Jazz let out a sigh and combed his fingers through his hair. Something wasn't right. The whole thing wasn't right. He was being played like a fiddle. He should walk away now while he still had a chance. Every instinct in his body screamed for him to cut and run.

The giant leaned forward and a beam of moonlight lit the right side of his face. "This treasure you seek, it is important enough to risk capture by the Mulo?"

"You want a cut, too?" Jazz stabbed him with a look and tried to read his cool, expressionless face.

"If it is important, then I will help you find it. Then perhaps you will come with us to California?"

"Help me find the treasure, and I'll go wherever you want."

"I have just one question before I agree."

Jazz kept a wary eye on the giant's face. This is where he finally got to see what these people were made of.

"What is the treasure that you would risk so much?"

Jazz paused to give the silence a little more weight and then, keeping his expression neutral, he said, "I'm not entirely sure, but I think it may be my grandfather's papers. Mari said he was a prophet. Maybe they're some kind of prophecies?"

The giant's eyes went wide. For a minute Jazz thought he was going to call his bluff. Finally he nodded and spoke. "Of course I will help you find it. Even if it takes the rest of my life."

ᥬ 20 ᥬ

Mariutza

MARI POPPED ONE LAST morsel of bread into her mouth and sighed with blessed contentment. She leaned back into luxurious nylon fabric and listened to the campfire popping and sizzling at her feet. It was all so nice. So decadent. Soft delicate bread, spicy mustard sauce mixed with sweet tomato catsup, bite-sized cuts of tender roasted meat that didn't have any bones at all!

She shifted her hand a half inch and lifted a miniature jug of fresh, clean water from the special hole built into the arm of her chair. Even the water was delicious. It was so bright and clear. She couldn't see any color to it at all.

Mari took a long sip of the water, swishing it in her mouth to make it last. Hailey said she could have as much as she wanted. She said they had dozens and dozens of the little jugs, and plenty of money to buy more. She blinked her eyes and two streams tickled down her cheeks. Hailey and Melchi had both been so generous. Letting her sleep in Hailey's tent, giving her a pad and a sleeping bag and a pillow as soft as thistle down . . . The whole night had been a wondrous dream. It was like waking up after a nightmare and discovering she was the beautiful princess from the histories of Jaazaniah.

"Mari?" Jaazaniah's sleepy-time voice sounded from the other side of the fire. "Are you all right?"

Mari wiped her face and sat up straight in Melchi's chair. "I'm sorry. The Lord's given us so much blessedness. I feel like I'm living inside a dream."

"A dream or a nightmare?" His voice grated resentful-like, but the smile twinkled in his eyes. "Melchi says we should get moving. Our little friends are starting to get bolder."

Mari turned to look back at Melchi, who was rolling up the sleeping bags and belting them onto the packs.

He nodded and walked over to crouch by the fire. "I don't know what they are, but they're not Standing. It's possible they're working for the Mulo."

"Then we should go." Mari jumped to her feet. "I'm sorry. I'm slowing you down. I was wrong to sleep last night. We should have left then."

"You were tired and needed rest." Melchi's smile was soft. "I didn't feel a single trace of the Mulo's presence all night. Still we should go soon. It's not wise to stay long in any one place."

"The question is: where do we go?" Hailey looked up from the wrinkled sheet of paper spread across her lap. "The will suggests the treasure was buried in a blue plastic box, but where? It only makes sense that he would bury it someplace near Mari's swamp, but there aren't any doghouses in the swamp. If Jazz's vision was real, if he really was seeing through his grandfather's eyes, then shouldn't we search first in the city?"

"The city gets my vote," Jaazaniah said. "I'm almost positive it's in New Orleans. All we have to do is drive through neighborhoods until I recognize something."

"But you said it's in someone's backyard. Do you have any idea how long it would take to search every backyard in the city?" Hailey looked from Mari to Melchi and back again.

"I'm not a prophet." Mari looked to Jaazaniah. "But perhaps the passage from Ruth is meant to be a hint. If we follow Purodad whither he went, maybe we'll see the doghouse and Jaazaniah will know where to dig."

"When was the last time your grandfather visited New Orleans?" Hailey asked.

Mari shook her head. "I don't think he ever went—not after I was a baby. He said the city was wicked and full to the gills with perversion. And it's so far away. It would have taken him weeks to get there."

"So maybe one of the nearby towns?" Melchi suggested. "We could search the closest towns first and move out from there."

"I know what I saw," Jaazaniah said. "In the dream I was floating over a city—not a dinky little town."

"Did you see his face?" Melchi asked. "What if it wasn't your grandfather digging? What if you were seeing through the eyes of someone else? Another Standing who's still trapped in the city."

"There are an infinite number of maybes. What we need is a starting point. Listen to this." Hailey held up the paper and started reading. "*To Jaazaniah Rechabson and his family I also leave a shovel, the contents of my blue plastic box, the Rechabson family Bible, and the following instructions: R-t-h 1-1-6.*" She lowered the will and looked around the fire. "Does that strike anyone else as odd?"

Jazz shrugged. "The whole thing is odd. The man's brain was permanently off-key."

"I'm talking about the shovel. Why mention a shovel in a will?"

"We've already been through this." Jaazaniah stood up. "It's a clue to let us know he buried the treasure."

"But what if it's more than that? What if the shovel *is* the clue?" She turned to Mari. "Didn't you say the shovel was covered in gray mud? Maybe if we searched for an area with gray mud . . . ?"

Mari humbled her eyes. "The whole swamp is gray mud. It could be anywhere."

"But you said there was also a board. It was covered with mud too, right?"

Mari nodded.

"Well, what if we're supposed to put the two together? What if the board *and* the shovel are a clue?"

"But Purodad sent the will to Jaazaniah. He wouldn't have known about the board."

"I totally would have known," Jaazaniah said. "If the police and half the world's armies weren't breathing down my back, I would have had to visit his home to look through his stuff. And I would have met you . . . the granddaughter who isn't his—"

"I've got it!" Hailey jumped up and waved the will in the air. "The mud on the shovel! You said the board and the shovel were brand new, but they were covered with mud, right?"

Mari nodded.

"So did you clean the mud off to see what was underneath?"

Mari turned and locked eyes with Jaazaniah. Something was written underneath? Of course it was. She'd been too simple to look.

"Your grandfather knew his enemies were closing in on him, right?" Hailey got up and carried the will over to Jaazaniah. "Whatever's buried in the box, he definitely didn't want his enemies to find it, so he left you a clue he knew they were sure to ignore!"

"Mari," Melchi spoke in a low urgent voice. "Where are the board and shovel now?"

"Back at the swamp. I was digging a hole to bury my grandfather."

"And do you know how to get there?"

She shook her head and looked down at her feet. "It was dark and there were so many roads. I was running from the Badness and didn't think."

The fire crackled and popped in the heavy silence.

"Do you remember anything at all? Any landmarks that might be on a map?"

"Just swamps and trees. And there's a road, but Purodad said there's lots of roads . . ." She stared down at the fire, warming under the weight of everybody's gaze. Why was she so stupid? "Unless . . . Could this help? Purodad made me memorize a number. I had to recite it every morning before training started. *LA404*. I was supposed to say it to a stranger if I ever got lost."

Everybody just stared. Then, like some magic spell went off in their heads at the same time, they all jumped up on their feet and started running hither and thither around the camp.

"Is it a clue? Does it help?" Mari trailed after Jaazaniah and watched as he stuffed a rolled-up tent into a shiny slick bag.

He turned and stared at her for a long minute. "This really isn't a con, is it?" The muscles clenched and twitched beneath his skin.

Mari didn't know what to say. She just shrugged and tried to put more humble into her eyes.

A smile tightened Jaazaniah's face. Then he was laughing. He laughed and laughed, long and hard until he was moaning and gasping for breath.

Mari shook her head to let her hair fall in front of her burning face. Then, with a stiff-legged curtsey, she turned and walked out of the camp.

Jazz

JAZZ STOPPED NEXT TO the rotting shell of what had once been an enormous old oak and mopped the sweat from his brow. They'd been walking over an hour and still no end in sight. Melchi turned and shot him an impatient look, but Jazz touched his zipper and waved him on. He stepped behind the tree and waited for them to start walking. The sound of crunching footsteps. It was about time. He slumped against the tree and swiped an arm across his forehead. If he had to listen to one more word of Melchi and Mari's religious mumbo jumbo, he was going to puke.

Ooh, do you think there are three different gateway guardians or just one? Is a shimulo the same as a mulo? How many zombies can dance on the head of a needle?

The whole thing was insane. He felt like he'd fallen in with a band of runaway loonies. The more they talked, the more he wanted to run screaming back to the police and turn himself in. It wasn't so much what they were saying that bothered him. He could handle religious fanatics. But the more they talked, the more their voices seeped into his head. It was like driving down the highway and having talk radio bleed into his music. He could hear them even when they weren't talking. It was driving him crazy.

Assuming, of course, he wasn't already there.

Maybe that was his problem. He was a nutcase. That's why the police were after him. Maybe they were all crazy.

He hitched up his pack and trudged out from behind the tree. Crazy or not, they seemed to know where they were going. The last thing he needed was to get lost out in the middle of this bug-infested sauna. The mosquitoes would drink him dry within twenty-four hours.

How could anybody stand to live out here? He wouldn't last
a single day, much less twenty years. Mari had to be lying. She
said she'd come from the swamps, but she didn't have a single
mosquito bite on her. But why would she lie about something like
that? It couldn't be a hoax. It was way too elaborate. The helicopters and her wounded hip . . . And what was the point? He
could understand someone trying to con Hollis, but him? What
could anyone possibly hope to gain? Besides his grandfather's
treasure . . .

The gold coins around Mari's neck flashed into his mind. If
it *was* the treasure, why did they still need him? They'd already
seen the will. They knew just as much as he did. Probably a lot
more.

He waded into a mound of flowering vines. The perfume of
the flowers clashed violently with the stench of stagnant water.
He stomped through the flowers, high-stepping his way to the
edge of the mound. The others were getting further and further
ahead of him. He broke into a half-hearted jog. The pack on his
shoulders clanked at every step. It hadn't seemed that heavy at
first, but now that the sun was up, the extra weight was almost
unbearable. He should have let Melchi carry it—Mr. I'm-so-
macho-I-can-carry-two-packs. That wouldn't have lasted very
long. Mr. Macho would have been begging for help within fifteen minutes.

Jazz stopped at a tangle of fallen trees and searched right and
left to find a way around the overgrown mess. Which way had they
gone? Melchi and Mari were just disappearing into a thicket on
the other side, but he couldn't see Hailey anywhere. Had she gone
on ahead? He ducked under a thorny branch and pushed his way
through a jumble of clinging vines, but a wall of thorns blocked
him at every turn.

Footsteps sounded behind him. "It'll be easier to climb over the trees."

"Now you tell me." Jazz turned to see Hailey pulling herself up onto a swaying limb. "What's the matter? Tired of listening to all that Standing gobbledygook?"

"It kind of grows on you after a while." She shot him a grin and turned to focus on the quivering branches. "After a long, long while."

"If you don't mind my saying so, you don't really seem the type." He climbed up after her and threaded his way through the tangle of jagged limbs, stepping from trunk to swaying trunk. "How'd you get mixed up in all this?"

"All what? Coming out here to Louisiana?"

"The cult thing. I thought you were a scientist."

"I am . . . or at least I was. But this isn't a cult. As far as I can tell, it's some kind of genetic thing. I'm part of it whether I want to be or not. Because I happen to have Standing genes."

"You mean the mind-reading thing? You've got that too?" Jazz leaped through a gap in the limbs and landed with a rattling thud on the ground beyond.

"I wouldn't exactly call it mind-reading. It's more like . . . sensitivity to a plane most people don't experience. But yeah, I've got it too."

"So even though you're a scientist, you still believe in all this stuff?"

"It's hard to argue with something you've actually experienced—no matter how hard it is to explain."

"Tell me about it." Jazz waited for her to climb down from the trees and fell into step beside her. "So what's the deal with you and Melchi? Are you dating? Engaged?"

Hailey sighed and shook her head. "It's complicated. Melchi's convinced he's a prophet—just like you."

"That was Mari, not me. I never claimed to be a prophet. I never claimed to be anything at all. I don't even believe in God—at least not any more. I don't know what I believe."

"Melchi believes he's the object of an old prophecy. I'm not saying he's wrong, but sometimes I wish he were. He thinks his future is too dangerous for us to be close."

"Too dangerous? And camping out in an alien-infested swamp isn't dangerous?"

"I only got to come because he couldn't get here any other way. He doesn't have a driver's license."

"And he's never heard of airplanes?"

"No birth certificate or ID."

"So why not take a bus?"

Hailey looked down at the leafy trail. He'd definitely hit a nerve. Finally she looked back up. "He didn't take a bus because I haven't told him about busses yet."

"I see." Jazz tried to make it fit. "So why come out here at all? He's risking your life to help a total stranger? It doesn't add up."

"It does to Melchi. Where most people see shades of gray, he sees only black and white. If someone's in trouble or has any kind of need at all, he'll do everything in his power to help them."

"Noble guy."

"You have no idea." Hailey sighed. "He's getting better, but he puts such a huge burden on himself. If I ever let him read the newspaper or watch the news, it would kill him."

"So who's protecting who?"

Hailey shrugged and stepped into a pool of boggy water. Jazz slogged after her. When she reached the other side she turned and waited for him. "What about you and Mari? What's the story there?"

"I've only known her two days."

"Well, she's certainly a big fan."

"What?" He turned to take in her expression. "You don't see her back here talking to me, do you?"

"But she sure talks *about* you. Did you tell her all those stories or did she really get them from your grandfather?"

"The fairy tales? My grandfather didn't know dragons from dragonflies. The crazy old Gypsy filled her head with cotton candy and signed my name to it just to spite me. No wonder he kept her locked away out in the swamps. He was probably hiding from child protective services."

"What about the portrait? She said it looked exactly like you."

Jazz's throat tightened. His chest felt he'd snorted a pound of buckshot.

"Are you okay?"

"I'm fine!" Jazz spat out the words and looked away. "The picture was of my father. Being a child-abusing, whore-mongering drug addict took its toll on him, but even so, people said we looked a lot alike."

"Jazz, I'm sorry."

"No big deal. I just wish your friend wouldn't encourage her. It's not exactly helping. She wants me to be some kind of mythic superhero, but the higher she builds me up, the further she's going to fall."

"I'll talk to Melchi, but I don't know if it'll do any good. I don't think he'll understand." Hailey held a branch back for him and followed him into a thick copse of trees. "If it's any consolation, I know how you feel. It's not easy being Lois Lane to Melchi's Superman. Sometimes I wish I could be the one with the super powers. But instead I have to settle for being worshipped because I have a college degree and know how to drive a car."

"At least you got to go to school." Jazz didn't even bother to disguise the bitterness in his voice. "Me, all I know is how to sing people into giving me tips. That's my super power. I'm one step short of being a musical gigolo."

"But now you've got the whole vision thing going. Seeing through other people's eyes is very cool. Melchi was so excited I thought he was going to wet his pants."

"Right. I can't wait to write that one down on my next job application. That and a GED could probably get me a job as a stock boy."

"But your gift marks you as a prophet. If you give God half a chance, He'll—"

"Look. I don't really want to talk about this, okay? I'm not a prophet. End of story. Just because my grandfather was a Gypsy, it doesn't mean I'm going to buy a crystal ball and start cheating gullible old ladies out of their money."

"To Melchi and Mari—people like us—that's not what being a prophet means. Mari says your grandfather was a healer. People would come from miles around just to get him to pray for them. That's why he was considered a prophet. It didn't have anything to do with telling fortunes. And you, with your visions—"

"I don't want to talk about it." Jazz ducked under a mossy branch and ran to catch up with Mari and Melchi. He splashed through another pool of standing water and fell into step a few paces behind them.

They walked for a sun-drenched eternity. Mud and water up to their knees, thorn bushes higher than their heads, mosquitoes and gnats and no-see-ums feasting on their flesh. Only the coins around Mari's neck kept him going. Age-crusted gold against glowing caramel skin. Haunting dark eyes framed by exotic per-fection. He could feel them burning into his brain like a fever. But it wasn't real. It couldn't be. Any minute he'd wake up and find out it was all a bad, bad dream.

The undergrowth eventually thinned and their progress became easier. It was several minutes before Jazz realized they were walking along an old, washed-out dirt road. He hitched his pack higher and leaned forward to stretch the muscles of his burning lower back. Soon it would all be over.

A huge black car stood off to the side of the road under a spray of spreading branches. It looked like a limousine. What was a limo doing out in the middle of the woods?

He trudged over to the car and shrugged out of his pack, letting it hit the ground with a rattling smack. "What are you doing with a limousine?" He collapsed on the ground and rolled onto his back. "Is Jeeves sleeping in the back or did you give him the day off?"

Melchi's face darkened. He opened his mouth and stared. Finally, he turned to Hailey with a pleading expression.

"It was the only thing big enough to carry our gear. If you'd rather walk, I'll understand."

"Don't worry about me. I'm not proud. I can handle being chauffeured in a limousine for a few hours." Jazz climbed painfully back onto his feet. "I just wouldn't want to make a habit of it, that's all."

Melchi nodded solemnly and grabbed up the packs. Eyes still lowered, he hauled them over to the car and popped open the trunk. Whatever Jazz had stepped in, it had definitely touched a nerve. Something was seriously askew.

"So this is yours?" He flung the question at Melchi. "You drive a limousine?"

"I already told you. I'm the driver." Hailey stepped to the car and opened the back door with a flourish. "It's one of my most impressive super powers. You and Mari can ride in the back. Melchi will ride up front with me."

"Very good, Jeeves." Jazz shot her a smart salute and sauntered over to the car. Mari stood at the door, dusting the swamp debris from her skirt. Aside from a few twigs and leaves sticking out of her hair, she looked as clean and fresh as when they'd started. No bug bites, no scratches . . . She hadn't even broken a sweat.

Jazz raised an arm and took a surreptitious sniff. Great . . . Wouldn't you know it. His first ride in a limo and he'd have to keep his distance from the babe. Life was so not fair.

He walked around to the other side of the car and climbed into the backseat. The black leather burned through his clothes like a frying pan through wet oven mitts, but he was too exhausted to care. He leaned forward and waited while Hailey started the car and cranked up the AC.

Mari poked her head inside the other door. "I . . ." His eyes met hers and she looked away. "If you don't wish my presence, I could sit up front with the others."

"What?" He ran back through the morning and tried to figure out what he'd done now. "Because I got in through this door? It has nothing to do with you. I reek, that's all. If you can stand the smell, you're welcome to sit here, but I warn you. The car's pretty hot. It's only going to get worse."

She nodded and slipped uncertainly into the car. Melchi closed the door behind her and climbed into the front. Hailey eased the car forward. They bumped over the rutted trail in exhausted silence before finally turning onto a paved road.

Even after the car had cooled down, Mari remained perched on the edge of her seat. She radiated tension like a dental drill.

"What were you and Melchi talking about out there?" Jazz finally asked.

"I was telling him about Purodad's training . . ." Mari looked out the window and frowned. A black car swept past on the opposite side of the road. It almost looked like—

"Stop the car!" Jazz called out and leaned forward to bang on the window separating them from the front seat. "Turn around. We've got to go back!"

The window opened with a whir.

"What's wrong? Did you forget something?" Hailey called back and stepped on the brakes.

"There was a car on the side of the road. I think we know the driver." He eyed the parked car as Hailey navigated a clumsy twenty-three-point turn and pulled the limo in behind it.

Jazz got out and walked cautiously over to the rental car. It looked like Hollis's car, but where was she? She wouldn't have gone into the woods after them. That wasn't her at all.

He leaned over and looked through the driver's window as Melchi and Mari came walking up behind him.

"Jazz!" A voice called out from the side of the road. Hollis was picking her way through a cluster of small trees. "I've been looking all over for you. Where have you been?"

"What are you doing here? I thought you left." He waited as she picked her way through the weeds and climbed up the bank.

"I know, and I feel terrible, but you have to understand. It was dark, and I was still freaking out about the helicopters and all the . . . you know." Her eyes went suddenly wide. Uncertainty rippled across her features as she stared past him and took a faltering step backward.

"It's okay. These are the people we came to meet. They're friends."

She stepped closer to Jazz and whispered in a low voice. "Are you sure?"

"As much as I am about anything else."

She tensed and took another step backward as Melchi approached.

"Hi, I'm Melchi." He stopped fifteen feet away from where they stood and lifted his hands palms facing out. "This is my friend Hailey. Mari says you saved her life?"

Hollis nodded and cast another look at Jazz.

"It's okay." He smiled to reassure her. "Why'd you come back? I thought you'd be back in the city packing your bags."

"At the hotel . . . there were these emergency alerts on the television. I—" Another frightened glance at Melchi.

"What?" Jazz stepped toward her, but she took another couple of steps back. "It's okay," he soothed. "You can trust us. We're the good guys, remember? This isn't a con."

"Last night on the news"—her eyes darted back and forth between Jazz and Melchi—"they were showing your picture every five minutes. And a blurry video of Mari taken from the sky. She was running down the street . . . toward one of those big riverboats."

"What did they say? Did they say why they're looking for us?"

"They said . . ." She fell silent and her eyes seemed to glaze over.

"They said what?" Jazz coaxed in a smooth calm voice. "What did they say, Hollis? Did they say why the police are after us?"

"They said you're part of a terrorist cell." Her voice was a faint whisper. "That you've smuggled a weapon of mass destruction into the country."

Jazz shook his head. "You know that's not true."

She gave an almost imperceptible nod, but her eyes kept wandering back to Melchi.

"Did they say anything else? Like how we'd gotten our hands on a nuclear weapon? Or why we'd do such a thing in the first place?"

"Just that you were . . . a group of religious extremists." A wide-eyed glance at Mari. "And it wasn't a nuke. It's a disease.

Some new super-fast, super-fatal disease that can kill people in a matter of seconds. The CB . . . something. A disease detective group flew out here from Atlanta and is trying to isolate it right now." Her fearful gaze settled on him.

"They say you've already killed twelve people, and if they don't catch you soon, you'll kill a lot more."

⌒ 21 ⌒

Mariutza

MARI CROSSED ONE ANKLE over the other and eased on back into the slick seat cushions. Nice and loose—just like Jaazaniah. Like she'd ridden in a car dozens and dozens of times.

A strong wind blasted her in the face, sending the tingles all over her skin. She breathed the cold air deep inside, felt its lovely coolness soaking into her chest. It was heavenly glorious. And it didn't have to end at the swamp either. Melchi and Hailey said she could ride in the car all the way to California! With hotdogs and water jugs and everything unimaginably nice.

She snuck a quick peek at the prophet and grinned out her excitement. He nodded and turned to drape his arm casual-like across the back of the seat. So calm he almost looked bored— like the Badness didn't scare him at all. He wasn't even looking out the windows!

Mari twisted to the side like Jaazaniah and lifted her knee onto the seat, but she couldn't drape her arm. Her seat belt slot was missing, so she'd been holding the metal thing against the seat with her hand. Jaazaniah had gotten his right away. She should have asked for help, but it was too late now. He'd think she was putting on the airs.

"She's still back there." Mari jumped at Melchi's voice. He was looking back through the little window behind his seat. "You are sure we shouldn't be worried?"

"Positive." Jaazaniah didn't even move. "I guarantee she's not working for the police. I doubt she's worked a day in her life."

"Don't you think we should at least try to lose her? What if she calls the police?"

"She probably will—eventually. But there's nothing we can do about it. The best thing to do is find the treasure and be long gone before she makes up her mind."

Mari looked back at Hollis's car. "I don't understand. You told her it was too dangerous, and she said she'd go back. Is this the direction of her home? Does she live in the swamps too?"

The prophet shook his head. "She's just bored—too freaked out to stay and too freaked out to go."

"But she said she'd go home."

"People *say* lots of things." Jaazaniah shot her a strange look. "What matters is what they do."

"What matters—" Mari clamped her mouth shut and turned to face the window. He knew! He didn't say it outright, but he'd meant it for a rebuke. The metal thing burned in her hand. The heat crawled up her arm and crept out into her cheeks. He knew she was pretending with the seat belt. That's why he didn't want to be near her. She was telling the lie with her actions—just like she'd done with Purodad. He told her to stop spying on the road, but she'd done it anyway. She was worse than a liar, and he knew it. He'd seen it in his visions.

Mari felt the weight of Jaazaniah's eyes pressing into her back. Purodad was his grandfather—his *real* grandfather. No wonder he was mad. Ever since his vision, he'd been putting out anger like a fire. The window blurred and twisted in her eyes. Her chest tightened so much she could barely breathe.

"Keep going! *Drive!*"

Melchi's shout cut through her thoughts. Mari wiped her eyes and turned to face the front.

"Those are government trucks!" Jaazaniah yelled at Hailey.

Mari leaned forward in her seat and the seat belt slipped from her hand. "What's happening?" She followed their eyes to the front window. A score of trucks and cars were stopped by the side of the road. It was her woods!

"Get down!" Jaazaniah pulled her onto the seat. She tried to sit up but he was lying on top of her, pinning her to the seat with an arm around her waist.

"Shhh! Be quiet!" His voice hissed in her ear. "As long as they don't see us, we should be okay."

Mari tried to reach out with her mind, but Jaazaniah was too close. His arm pressed tight against her waist. His fingers lay only inches from her belly.

She sucked in her breath and tried not to move. He didn't mean anything by it. He was just trying to keep her safe. She reached out again with the sight, but all she could feel was the warmth of his presence.

His arm shifted and a light touch tingled against her skin. Her muscles went rigid. She bit her lip and tried not to squirm.

"Can you still see them?" Jaazaniah's breath tickled at the small of her back. "Pull over as soon as we're out of sight."

Mari couldn't stand it anymore. "No!" She rolled onto the floor and twisted around to sit up. "It's the Badness. They're hunting us. I've been to the road before, and there were never any cars!"

"They're looking for the treasure," Jaazaniah said. "Pull over. We need to get the shovel."

"I don't feel any Mulo." Melchi's words were almost a question. "I think they're just normal Gadzé."

Mari shook her head. "But they work for the mulani. It's too dangerous. We must keep going."

"And leave them the treasure?" Jaazaniah turned to face her. "What if it's prophecies or something? Your grandfather went to a lot of effort to hide it. Do you honestly think he'd want us to leave it for his enemies?"

Mari's face burned beneath the intensity of his gaze. He already knew. He knew what her grandfather wanted, and she didn't have the foggies. He'd never given her the slightest hint.

"I know you're afraid, but don't you think we should at least try?"

"I'm not afraid!" How could the prophet believe that of her? "I just—"

"There's a dirt road coming up," Hailey called back through the window. "Should I stop or not?"

"If there aren't any shimulo . . ." Mari turned to Jaazaniah. "Turn!"

The car swung around in a skidding turn. It bounced and bucked and rattled beneath them before coming to a stop on a narrow, overgrown trail. A squeal sounded as Hollis stopped her car right behind them.

"I'll go with Mari." Jaazaniah threw the door open and leaped outside. "Melchi, you and Hailey turn the car around. Be ready to fly the second we get back."

"But there will be soldiers." Mari climbed out into the heat and waited for Melchi and Hailey. "If the soldiers see us, they'll call for the mulani. We may have to fight."

"Then I'll go with you." Melchi turned to face the prophet. "Jazz, tell your friend it's not safe to be here. She must either go home or back up her car to let us out."

"I appreciate the offer, but I'm the one going with Mari." Jaazaniah moved to square off in front of Melchi. "My grandfather left the treasure to me. It's my responsibility."

"But Melchi's had more training," Mari said. "This could be dangerous. If the mulani come, we'll have to fight."

"What happened to the Jaazaniah the warrior prophet thing?" Jaazaniah shot her a look. "Or was that just a con to manipulate me into helping you?"

"No, it's true. It has to be, but . . ." Mari turned to Melchi, but he didn't seem to be paying any attention. "In this situation, I just think it would be safer if Melchi—"

"So you're saying you'd rather be with Melchi?"

"There will be many soldiers. The mulani could come—"

"Fine. Whatever you want. I was just offering to help." Jaazaniah stalked over to Hollis's car and whispered something through her window. Hollis glanced at Mari and started laughing. He'd said something about her. About the seat belt or the sleeping bag or those metal tube matches that shoot fire out of the wrong end.

"He'll be okay." Hailey came up behind Mari and put her arms around her shoulders. "He's just overwhelmed."

Mari nodded and tried to speak when spoken to, but her voice didn't want to work any more. Hailey's arms tightened around her, pulling her into a warm embrace. "This is hard on him. His whole world has been turned upside down. Everything he thought he knew was true has suddenly been thrown into question. Fantasy and reality are starting to switch places. It's not an easy transition to make."

Mari nodded. Transitions were . . . terrible. A tremor passed through her body. All of a sudden she was crying. She turned and leaned into Hailey as rattling tears shook her to the core.

"It's okay. Let it all out . . ." Soothing words washed through her. The stroke of fingers running through the tangles of her hair. Mari buried her face in Hailey's shoulder and held on tighter. "It's okay. I've got you. We're not going anywhere."

Time seemed to stop as she hung there, watering up Hailey's neck. Finally, when the storm of her emotions started to recede, a heavy hand pressed down on her shoulder.

"We should go now." Melchi's voice tensed. "I've searched the area and there aren't any mulo—mulani—yet, but we should hurry. If we're not gone before they get here, we'll all be in grave danger."

Mari nodded and pulled reluctantly away from Hailey. "Thank you, I . . ." She wiped her face and tried to find a safe way through the storm clouds swirling in her head. "I don't know what to say. I love you. I love you both. If it weren't for you, I . . ." She wiped her eyes again and let Melchi lead her into the woods.

"Can you run?"

Mari nodded and eased into a rolling jog. Her hip felt a little tight, but running wouldn't be a problem. Dr. Khatun's healing was working just fine. Could the Gadje be prophets too? What if Jaazaniah were like Dr. Khatun?

Melchi fell into step beside her, following her lead through the tangle of mossy trees. "Jazz will be fine. He's just afraid."

"But he was right." Mari dodged around an uprooted tree. "I should have more faith in him. I should have given him the apology."

"He'll understand."

"But how? I don't even understand. I thought he was a prophet, but he doesn't even believe in God."

"He had a vision. Maybe he believes more than you know."

"Maybe." Mari repeated the word, but she wasn't sure she could believe it. He'd said he didn't believe God. How could a prophet not believe God? Was he right? Had his father been a prophet before he'd fallen? Was this the tragedy that had broken Purodad's heart?

"He likes you, you know." Melchi accelerated and launched himself over a wide creek.

Mari stepped wrong and barely made the leap. She had to sprint several dozen yards before she could catch up with the longer-legged giant. "Who?" She gasped between breaths. "Who likes me?"

"How many men do we both know?"

"Jaazaniah doesn't like me at all. That's the problem. He doesn't even like to be near me."

Melchi laughed. "Which explains why he wanted so much to go with you to find the shovel."

"He wants to find his inheritance."

"He *wants* to spend time with you."

"You saw this in his mind?" Mari couldn't believe they were even speaking of such things. Miss Caralee would say she was being too big for her britches.

"I saw it in his eyes. And in his words and actions. And how he feels about me."

"But . . ." Mari shook her head furiously. Melchi had seen wrong. It was wicked to even countenance the notion. "Jaazaniah said he didn't like me. I heard him say it to Hollis."

"That's what he *said*." Melchi slowed to let Mari take the lead.

"Yes." Mari circled away from the road so they could approach the mound from the deep woods side. They ran for several minutes in silence. Too much silence. The swamp folk were all a-jitter about something. Even this far back off the road. Something wasn't right.

Mari raised a hand and slowed to a stop. Melchi was right behind her. She could feel his questions spilling out into the still afternoon air. She dropped to her knees and scanned the area. A robin sat rigid on the ground—not more than thirty yards away. No scratching. No digging. The threat was much closer than she'd thought. But where? Somewhere off to the right?

She shifted to the right a half inch at a time. There he was. A sliver of camouflaged uniform showed through a gap in the trees. She motioned Melchi over and pointed at the soldier until he nodded.

That was one. Where were the others? The training said they'd be stationed in a wide circle, standing guard at the perimeter of the site. She dropped onto her hands and knees and inched her way to the left. She hadn't gone more than twenty feet before she saw another one about a hundred yards away from the first. A tuft of shoulder-length red hair showed like a bonfire through the trees. This one was a woman.

Mari pointed at the two soldiers and then slashed a line with her hand between them.

Melchi nodded and crawled closer to whisper in her ear. "You do understand that when Gadzé say *like*, they don't mean *like*."

Mari frowned. What was he going on about now?

"It's very complicated. Hailey could explain it better than I, but sometimes *like* means romantic love, even though *love* almost always means *like*—unless spoken directly to the transitive object. Do you understand what I'm saying?"

Mari paused to show her respect for his knowledge—and then shook her head.

"If Jazz told Hollis he doesn't *like* you, he meant that he doesn't have romantic love feelings for you—not that he doesn't like you as a friend. But the only reason he would say that was if he does have romantic love feelings for you. See? It still fits with what I'm saying."

Mari shook her head. "I do not see, and I don't want to see. We shouldn't talk of such things." She knee-hopped onto her feet and wove her way through the trees at a low crouch. Purodad said the Gadje had been so twisted by the world that they believed up was down and right was wrong. She'd thought he'd been making an exaggeration to show his point, but now she wasn't so sure. Had Melchi been twisted too? He said his master died when he was a young boy. That left plenty of time for Gadje teachings to twist his mind.

She made for a thicket midway between the two soldiers and dropped onto the ground behind it. Creeping beneath a low canopy of spreading limbs, she searched the forest ahead. If the training was right, there should be tiny plastic boxes stuck to the trees.

Melchi crawled up beside her and whispered in her ear. "What are you looking for?"

"The brown and gray boxes."

"What?"

"The training says they'll be attached to the bases of trees, between one and three feet up. Little boxes that use magic to tell the enemy when someone walks past."

"Do you see any?"

Mari nodded. "Only one, but they're very hard to see. Did your master teach you the climbing training?"

"I think so. Do you have rope?"

She turned to him to make sure he'd understood. "You used rope in *climbing* training?"

Melchi shrugged. "Lead the way, and I'll try to follow. Just tell me if I'm doing it wrong."

"Okay. Quietly." Mari climbed onto her feet and leaped into the air. Catching an outstretched branch, she swung up and over the limb and scampered her way through the branches until she was a safe distance from the ground.

She looked down and watched as Melchi climbed up through the thick foliage. He was much heavier, so the leaves rattled a little as he climbed through the smaller branches, but a little noise was okay. Purodad said the Gadje had eyes and ears like hawks when they were in the cities, but out here in the swamps they were blind and deaf as earthworms.

She signaled for Melchi to wait where he was and then climbed up to what Purodad called the wobble point. Keeping her weight centered, she looked out across the tree tops and worked out a green route through the youngest and springiest trees. Then, circling around the trunk to the direction she wanted to go, she climbed higher up and leaned back until the tree bent under her weight. She hung from the tree top and climbed out hand over hand until she was able to grab the neighboring tree. There! She waited for a gentle breeze to mask the sound and then let the first tree swish back into place.

The noise was louder than she would have liked. She pressed herself to the tree trunk and listened for the Gadje soldiers, but apparently they really were deaf as earthworms. Melchi clambered up the tree with the stealth of a buck in mating season, but the Gadje didn't seem to hear him either. This would be easier than she thought. As long as they didn't shake the branches, they'd be able to make all the rustles they wanted.

Mari crossed easily from tree to tree, and Melchi followed right behind. Even moving like a snail, it only took a few jiffies to cross the perimeter line. Mari made a few more crossings and chose a thick sweet gum tree for their descent. She climbed down slowly, checking the area for soldiers. They all seemed to be stationed at the perimeter. It was going to be easy as pie. A quick run to the mound and a quick run back. They'd be back with Jaazaniah and Hailey before they knew they were gone!

Melchi dropped onto the ground beside her, and they set off through the woods at a slow jog. The undergrowth was thicker in this part of the swamp so they didn't have to worry about cover. Besides, the soldiers wouldn't be expecting them inside their perimeter. Even if they ran into one of the soldiers, they'd be fine. Purodad always said the element of surprise was worth five men. Twenty if the other men were Gadje.

They twisted and turned and leaped their way through the trees until they reached the edge of Purodad's mound. Pressing herself to the ground, Mari squirmed her way up the slope and snaked around to the hole. The ground was dug up with muddy footprints. She crawled back and forth across the area, but the shovel and board weren't where she'd left them.

"What's this?" Melchi crawled up beside her and motioned toward the hole.

"It's where I started digging Purodad's grave. But someone's dug it even deeper, and the shovel and board are gone."

"You think they took them?"

"They're probably at their camp." Mari crawled across the top of the mound and crept down the opposite bank. The hum of a gasoline generator sounded in the distance. It sounded like it was coming from the diddlecar clearing.

She signaled for Melchi to follow and then circled around to the thickest part of the forest. It would take some time to squirm through all the stickers, but it would be safest. And they'd be able to come right up on the clearing without being seen.

Just as she was about to make it through the first patch of stickers, a high-pitched beep sounded right in front of her. Mari pushed through the stickers and ran across a stretch of leafy ground.

Muffled voices were coming from the other side of a tall thicket. Beeps and clicks and strange goings on like a *mijwiz* double clarinet. She reached out with the *dikh* sight and plunged into the sticker-choked reeds. Crawling on her knees and elbows, she worked her way forward until she could see out into the storm-cleared field beyond. It was the place her grandfather had been shot.

A clicking noise sounded to her right. Mari turned as a man in a strange, hooded blue suit stepped over the trunk of a fallen tree. His face was covered entirely with a clear plastic sheet. A large black tube protruded from his mouth like an elephant's trunk and disappeared under his arm.

Another blue man appeared from behind a clump of cedars. He was sweeping a strange black box back and forth across the ground. The box was clicking. What did it all mean? Was it part of the Gadje burial ceremony? Why were they wearing such strange suits?

A rustle sounded behind her. Mari lifted her hand for Melchi to stop, but the weeds kept on rattling. It was enough noise to wake a sleeping earthworm! She inched away from the clearing and turned. Even an untrained Gadje could move quieter than—

"Don't move! Put your face down on the ground and keep your hands where I can see them!" Five soldiers stood over her, aiming their rifles at the base of her neck.

Mari turned slowly and let her head drop back onto the ground. Melchi was lying right beside her.

He'd been even quieter than she'd thought.

∽ 22 ∾

Jazz

"I'M STARTING TO GET an image . . ." Jazz intoned in his best entranced Gypsy voice. "Closer . . . It's getting closer . . . I see a round blob with a long pipe coming out of it—Hey! Ease up!" He grabbed Hollis's fingers and moved them so that they weren't pressing into his eyeballs. "So where was I? Ah, yes . . . It's an elephant sitting on a red-and-white speckled egg."

"No way! You cheated." Hollis shoved him back against the seat of the car. "I never said the color of the egg so this one doesn't count."

Hailey grinned at Jazz, then shot a look at Hollis. "You didn't specify a color so I had to picture something. I just wanted to see if he could mind-read in color. It's supposed to be a sign of intelligence."

"Seriously." Hollis's plaintive voice had taken on a note of urgency. "I know it's a trick. Tell me how y'all are doing it."

"But it's not." Jazz leaned forward in the seat. How could he make her understand? "That's what we're trying to tell you. This is as weird for me as it is for you."

"Okay, but this time I'm taking you back to my car. Hailey has to stay here and lie face down on the seat." Hollis slid across the seat of the limo and opened the door. "And no rocking the car or signaling with your feet. I'll be watching."

Jazz arched a brow at Hailey. "Does it work from that far away?"

"I don't see why not." Her features relaxed and her eyes took on a far-away look. "I can feel Melchi for miles. If a pretty girl so much as walks past him, I know about it."

"So is a pretty girl walking past him now?"

Hailey shook her head. "I'm not saying she's not gorgeous, but he really doesn't see her that way. All he can think about is the training she's received. When it comes to his mission, he has a one-track—" She sucked in her breath and her eyes went suddenly wide.

"What?" Jazz spun and looked out the windows. "Is it Mari? What's happening?"

"He's hurt!" Hailey slid across the seat and pushed through the door. "Something just happened!"

Jazz climbed out of the limo and ran to catch up with her. She was shuffling through the trees like a zombie, blinking her eyes as if to hold back tears.

"Hey. Wait a second!" He grabbed her by the shoulder, but she shrugged him off and kept on going. "What's going on?" He circled around to get in front of her.

"I already told you! Melchi's hurt. He . . ." She shook her head, and her eyes seemed to come back into focus. "First he was surprised, and then he . . . it was just pain. Lots and lots of pain."

"And you think getting yourself lost in the woods is going to help?"

She looked around—as if seeing the forest for the first time. "We have to do something."

"We will. But let's think about it. If they've captured Mari and Melchi, they'll have to get them to the road. Right?" Jazz put an arm around Hailey and guided her back to the limo. "Right?"

She nodded, but she didn't look good. It probably wasn't the time to mention the helicopters. If the police airlifted Mari and Melchi out, he'd have to come up with another plan. And quick.

He hurried over to Hollis, who was hovering, keys in hand, beside the rental car. "Could you give us a ride back to where all those cars were parked?"

Hollis jammed her fists into her hips. "First tell me what happened. Are y'all serious, or is this part of the trick?"

"It's not a trick!" Hailey's harsh tone brought a flare of color to Hollis's cheeks. "Melchi's hurt and we need to find him. Just drop us off and go for help. That's all we're asking. Call the police, firefighters, reporters, your congressman . . . anybody who'll listen. Tell them it's life and death."

"But how . . .?" Hollis looked to Jazz.

"Please. Hailey felt Melchi's pain. I know it sounds crazy, but it's an elephant-sitting-on-an-Easter-egg kind of thing. You have to believe us."

"Okay . . ." She stumbled forward and opened the door. "Get in. But when I get back, you two are doing the test in two separate cars. Lying down on the floors so neither of you can see."

They climbed into the car and drove back down the highway. Three vans and four cars were parked by the side of the road. They seemed empty enough, but one of those vans could hold an awful lot of men.

Jazz took a deep breath and let it out slowly. "Please tell me you know how to do that ninja fighting stuff."

Hailey shook her head. "I'm Lois Lane, remember?" She turned to Hollis. "Get out of here quick. Call as many people as you can and tell them what's going on. You can even tell them about the Standing. Just make sure they come."

"Okay, but . . ." She looked back at Jazz. "You have my cell number, right?"

Jazz nodded.

"The second everything's okay, you're going to call me, right? Remember, you still owe me another test. Don't even think of trying to squirm out of it."

"Thanks, Hollis. I . . ." Jazz shook his head and looked away. "Thanks for everything." He got out of the car and waited on the shoulder as Hollis pulled back onto the road and sped off.

"Think she'll actually do it?" Hailey watched the car disappear around the bend. "Think anyone will even believe her?"

"They'll believe her, all right." Jazz turned and crossed the highway. "And if they don't believe her, I guarantee they'll believe her congressmen. I wouldn't be surprised if she has a senator or two on speed dial."

Hailey fell into step beside him. Rivers of churning emotion flowed through his head. Was it coming from him or her? Did it even matter?

He strode up to the first van and knocked on the side of the door. Looking around at the other cars, he tugged on the handle, but it was locked.

So much for plan A. He moved on to the next van and then the next. All of them were locked. Hailey better have a plan B, because he was fresh—

"Jazz!" Hailey waved from the side of a long, brown car.

Jazz ran over to Hailey and watched as she snaked her arm through a crack in the window and popped open the lock.

"What are you looking for? Identification?"

"Whatever we can find." He pulled the door open and a wave of heat hit him in the face. The car was hot as an oven.

He used a dry corner of his shirt to open the glove compartment and rifled through its contents. No badges or radios . . . He carefully replaced the contents and closed it back up before checking beneath the seats. "Here we go!" He pulled out a clipboard filled with bureaucratic-looking forms and handed it to Hailey.

"What's this for?"

"Looking official. Check the trunk." He reached across the steering wheel and popped it open. Then, climbing over the seat, he retrieved a prize from the back window—a black baseball cap with a Homeland Security patch on the front.

Jazz loosened the adjustable band and pulled the hat low over his eyes. Now all he needed was an official jacket. He twisted around and spotted an old nylon duffle bag poking out from under the seat. *Come on! God, if You're there, let it be a uniform!* He grabbed the bag and ripped back on the zipper.

The whole thing was filled with golf balls. Dozens and dozens of dirty, grass-stained golf balls. He zipped it back up and flung it back down on the floor. "Find anything?" He circled to the back of the car where Hailey was digging through a cluttered trunk.

"Not much. What are we looking for?" She glanced back at Jazz and grinned. "Nice hat. I don't suppose you found one for me?"

"Your face isn't on the wanted posters."

"Not yet."

"Find any jackets or uniform shirts?"

Hailey shook her head. "A tackle box filled with lures and a couple of old fishing poles."

"What about these?" Jazz reached into the trunk and pulled out a pair of floppy fishing boots.

"Waders? They're not exactly inconspicuous."

"Who wants to be inconspicuous?" He climbed into the boots and hooked the suspenders over his shoulders. "Open up that case of water. We'll need as many bottles as we can carry."

"Okay . . ." Hailey grabbed an armful of water bottles and watched skeptically as he started stuffing them into the boots. "What are you trying to be? A fisherman from Homeland Security?"

"Anything but me." He slammed the trunk and waddled toward the trees. "Come on. Let's get out of here before someone comes back."

"But what about *my* disguise?" She plodded up behind him and started flipping through the clipboard.

"If you see any soldiers, just scribble on the clipboard and frown a lot. These military types are well-trained. As long as you're in a foul mood, they'll know enough to keep their distance."

Jazz tramped back through the trees, searching the forest floor for an opening in the weeds. They hadn't walked more than a few hundred yards before Jazz found what he was looking for—a bare spot beneath an old fallen pine tree. "Here we go. Time for mud pies."

"Excuse me?"

He cleared off a thick layer of dead leaves. The soil beneath them was pasty gray and hard as a rock. "I'm the grunt and you're the overpaid boss who doesn't want to get her hands dirty." He opened the bottles and dumped the water into a depression on the ground. "If anybody asks any questions, just tell them you need some help. They'll take one look at me and magically have something better to do."

"What if it doesn't work? What if they ask for ID?"

Jazz stirred the water with his hands, working it into the thirsty soil. "You've got a better idea?"

"Not to be seen in the first place?" Hailey crouched beside him and reached for the mud, but Jazz swatted her hand away.

"You're the boss. You're paid to be mean and clean. It's in your contract." He scooped up some mud and slavered it onto his arms until they were coated to his shirt sleeves. Then, wiping a muddy hand across his face, he coated the boots with the mud and stood up to let Hailey inspect the results. "How do I look?"

"A little over the top, but I doubt anyone will recognize you. They'll be too busy laughing."

"Works for me." Jazz grabbed a couple of waters and clomped back through the undergrowth. The trees went on forever. The vegetation was so thick they could walk within a hundred feet of Bill Gates's house and never even notice it. He pictured Mari in his mind and tried to focus on her thoughts, but he couldn't feel a thing. No tingles, no images, not even the vaguest wisp of emotion. Nothing.

"I don't suppose you could do that little mind thing and get us a direction?"

Hailey was silent for several minutes and then shook her head. "I've been trying, but it's like he . . ." Her voice grew husky and choked off.

"It's okay. They're just doing that prayer thing. You know . . . Kumbaya and pass the plates."

"But I'm not a Mulo. Why can't I feel him?"

"Maybe he's not near any pretty girls."

"But what if they—"

Voices sounded just ahead of them. Hailey started to duck, but Jazz grabbed her by the arm. "We already searched that one and we didn't find anything"—he spoke in a loud, clear voice—"Why can't we search the others first and *then* go back?"

"Because you botched the job!" The vehemence of Hailey's voice surprised him. She pulled a pen off the clipboard and started scribbling on one of the forms as two rifle-toting soldiers broke into view about twenty yards ahead of them. "If you'd gridded the area like I told you, we'd be done by now. And I wouldn't be out here in this cesspool teaching you how to do your stinking job!"

"But it's a small area. There couldn't possibly be—"

"You're not serious. *You're* telling *me* how to do *my* job? You couldn't even lay down a simple search grid!"

"I'm just saying—" Jazz broke off his speech and glared up at the intruding soldiers. He jutted his chin and added a little swagger to his step. He was fuming mad. Mad at his condescending boss. Mad that anybody was there to witness her condescension. He didn't take anything from anybody. He might not have a gun in his hands, but he could out-swagger them all.

The soldiers exchanged glances and kept on walking. He could feel the weight of their eyes on his back. Had they turned around? He plunged forward, stomping through the thick undergrowth at an angry, stiff-legged gait. There were only two of them, but they had rifles. What could he and Hailey do against rifles? The whole boot thing had been a stupid idea. They should have gone with Hollis to get the police. What had he been thinking?

Distant laughter sounded behind him. Far behind him! Jazz sighed and almost tripped over his oversized feet.

Clashing footsteps. Hailey bounded through the weeds and fell into step beside him. "Nice job," she whispered. "If I'd known you were such a good actor, I wouldn't have been so nervous."

"Nervous?" Jazz rounded on her. "You were nervous? I was terrified. This whole thing is crazy. It's not going to work! I can't believe you ever went along with it."

"But it *is* working. All we have to do is locate their search zone and we'll find Melchi."

"And then what? Those guys had guns! Machine guns!"

"Shhh . . . Tone it down. We'll think of something. We're fine."

"It's not going to work. Even if we find them, there's sure to be a guard. What are we supposed to do with armed guards? The balcony scene from *Romeo and Juliet*? This is crazy. We'd be better off going to the police. Or better yet, the newspapers! They'll believe us. All we have to do is get them to come out here to see all the hardware." Jazz turned and clomped back toward the road.

"Jazz, wait!" Hailey hissed. "We're okay. We should at least find out where they're keeping them." Footsteps padded up behind him. "Once we know where they are, then, if they're guarded, we'll go for the police. But we can't go now. They could pack up and leave before we get back."

Jazz kept walking. If they could make it back to the limo, they'd be able to get to a town with a newspaper or radio station. Then, if they did their little Easter egg trick, the reporters would have to believe them. They'd have to—

"At least hear me out!" Hailey grabbed his arm, but he shrugged her off and kept on walking. "We don't know what happened. Melchi and Mari could be fine. By calling the police we might make things even worse!"

"And getting ourselves captured will make things better? How about talking so loud every soldier in the woods knows where we are? Maybe that will help too."

"Okay . . . I'm whispering." Hailey jogged around him to block his way. "Couldn't we at least talk?"

"Fine. When we get to the limo, we'll talk. But right now—"

The sound of crashing footsteps sounded behind them. Jazz froze and tried to assume his wounded ego stance, but there were too many of them. They were coming too fast.

"One more stunt like that, and I'll have you up to your armpits in *Leptospira* for a month!" Hailey snapped at him and raised her clipboard to jot down a note, but Jazz could already tell it wasn't going to work. Too little too late. It was the story of his life.

"I said I'm sorry!" He caught her eye and nodded toward the highway. "What more do you want me to do?"

"Sir? Ma'am?" A clipped military-sounding voice sounded behind Jazz's back. "Could I see some ID?"

Jazz turned slowly, sweeping his eyes across the forest. Four soldiers were jogging toward them. Two with rifles drawn. "Do I look like I'm carrying ID?" Jazz spread his arms palms outward and looked down at his boots.

"I can vouch for him." Hailey stepped forward and handed the soldier a fistful of cards. "I'm Dr. Hailey Maniates, UCSF. I'm here to rule out another *Leptospira* outbreak. This is my assistant, Joe Knoll."

The soldier stared at what looked to be a California driver license. Finally he handed it back to Hailey. "If you'll just stay right here, I'll check this out and have you on your way."

He stepped back a few yards and started talking on his radio in a low voice. Jazz slouched and tried to look bored, but it wasn't easy with three automatic weapons pointing across his body. Under the circumstances, maybe tense and jittery wasn't such a bad idea.

The lead soldier mumbled something into the radio and glanced over at Jazz. A slight nod and he mumbled something else. His eyes narrowed slightly and he stared at Jazz several seconds before turning his back and speaking in a low urgent voice.

Not good. Jazz looked to Hailey, who gave a slight nod. The soldiers seemed more alert now. Was it his imagination or had the barrels shifted to point more directly at his chest?

"Ma'am?" The lead soldier stepped toward Hailey, his rifle gripped tightly in his hands. "I'm going to have to ask you to come with us. There seems to be a slight problem with your authorization." He nodded at his men, and they spread out behind Jazz and

Hailey. This time there was no doubt about the direction their guns were pointing.

"What kind of problem?" Hailey asked. "Do you need to see another form of identification?" She reached for her pocket, and a steel barrel jabbed Jazz between the shoulder blades.

Jazz raised his hands and turned to Hailey. "Maybe you can wait and show them when we get there?"

Hailey nodded and stumbled as one of the soldiers shoved her forward. No more pretense. No more kid gloves. He and Hailey were prisoners now. If Mari and Melchi were still alive, they'd be joining them soon.

They marched through an endless, sweltering jungle. Rivers of sweat flowed down Jazz's face and into his boots, weighing them down with squishing, squelching moisture. All of a sudden he didn't feel so good. He felt dizzy, like he was about to pass out.

A burning sensation tingled at the base of his neck as the forest twisted around him in a haze of shifting green. A veneer of trembling leaves parted before his eyes.

"I need to rest," Jazz gasped between breaths. "These boots are too hot. If I don't get out of them soon, I'm going to pass out." He stopped and gritted his teeth, waiting for another jab to his already bruised backbone.

The lead soldier turned and nodded. "Keep your hands up where I can see—"

A crash sounded overhead and a dark shape dropped through the branches. Mari! She landed with a thud in the middle of the soldiers and spun in a blur of fluid motion. Ripping one soldier's rifle from his hands, she kicked another in the face and smashed the rifle into the forehead of the third. The two soldiers hit the ground with a double *thunk* as Melchi came up behind the leader and sent him sailing through the trees.

Mari lunged forward, spun the rifle around, and raised it above her head to freeze, mid-strike, above the fallen men.

The disarmed guard stared wide-eyed at Mari's rigid back. Then, dropping suddenly to the ground, he came up with one of the fallen soldiers' rifles. Before Jazz could even shout, Mari jerked the rifle down without looking and swung it back into the side of the soldier's head, dropping him without a sound.

"How the—?" Jazz looked up as Mari dropped the rifle and turned slowly to face him. Her shoulders were shaking. Tears glistened in her eyes. She stumbled forward and collapsed into his arms. "I'm so sorry. I didn't mean to—"

"Sorry?" He brought a hand up and stroked her thick, dark curls. "Sorry for what? You saved our lives."

"But I forgot he was there." Her voice broke and her shoulders started shaking. "I didn't even see him."

"You heard him though. Just in time. You were amazing."

"But I didn't. It was the training. It was so like the three-from-above kata. It just took over. I dropped my wits and forgot he was even there." Mari looked up at him with glistening, tear-stained eyes. "Please, forgive me. I could have got you killed."

Jazz swallowed and pressed his lips to the top of her head. "There's nothing to forgive. Not now, not ever. We thought you'd been captured. I was worried sick."

A giant hand clamped down on Jazz's shoulder. "We must go now." Melchi's urgent tone spoke volumes. "More soldiers will come soon. They might call the Mulo."

Mari nodded and pulled away. "I'll get the shovel and—"

"I'll get them," Melchi said. "You take them back to the cars." With a last lingering look at Hailey, he turned and ran deeper into the forest.

"This way." Mari started jogging in the opposite direction. "Melchi will catch up. We've got to get a hurry on."

"What happened?" Hailey asked in a hushed voice. "Melchi wouldn't say. About an hour after you left we felt something—like Melchi was in pain. We thought you'd been captured."

"Jaazaniah felt Melchi's pain?" Mari turned to him. "You saw this through his eyes?"

Jazz shook his head and clomped through a tangle of tall bushes. "Hailey felt it. What happened? Was it real?"

Mari turned back to Hailey. Was it his imagination or did she seem disappointed? "A group of soldiers found us out, and Melchi had to fight. He's a very good warrior, but he didn't have much time. He had to hurt them more than he liked."

Hailey ducked under a low branch and jogged to catch up. "So what I felt—it was his regret. His pain over causing others pain?"

"He hasn't had the training." Mari reached back and took Hailey by the hand. "It hurt him very much."

Jazz hung back and followed the pair in and out through the heavier, thicker trees. He'd done it again. No matter how he tried, he always ended up disappointing people. His father, his music teachers, Mari . . . If he lived long enough, he'd disappoint Hailey and Melchi too. It was inevitable. Melchi the *very good warrior*. A few more hours and he'd be Melchi the Prophet. Mari's grandfather probably had a portrait of him on his wall too.

Branches slashed him in the face and weeds caught at his boots, but he staggered forward. Finally, when his head felt like it was going to explode, he called ahead to the girls, "Wait up! . . . Just a second while I . . ." He plopped back onto the ground and started shucking off the waders.

Clashing footsteps sounded behind him. He motioned to Mari and rolled beneath a vine-covered sapling as the footsteps pounded past him. It was Melchi, leaping like a deer, a shovel and a round, muddy board tucked under his arm.

"Wait!" Jazz climbed to his feet and ran after them. They zigzagged through the forest for an eternity of smoldering heat, ripping thorns, and swarming bugs. Finally they emerged onto the overgrown road and followed it back to the limo.

"Open the trunk!" Jazz ran to the back of the limo and leaned over to catch his breath while the others scampered around the car. "They're looking for me and Mari. We should hide in the back of the trunk."

"But what if they stop us and search the car?" Hailey threw open the trunk and started rearranging the camping equipment.

"Don't worry about the trunk; just refuse to open the back door." Jazz pulled out a grocery bag and tossed it aside. "Tell them your boss doesn't want to be disturbed. The more you make them focus on the back seat, the more likely they'll forget about the trunk."

"Okay . . ." Hailey pulled a wad of clothes out of a pack and thrust it aside. "Get in! The faster we move, the less likely we'll be stopped."

Jazz climbed inside the trunk and twisted around to help Mari tuck herself into the space beside him. "Careful. It's hot." He flopped over and lay down on his side as Melchi slammed the lid on top of them.

Everything went black. The only light came from a few small cracks near the brake lights. Jazz breathed in and out, trying to catch his breath, but the air was too hot. It felt like it was burning his lungs.

The engine rumbled to life, and then he and Mari were bouncing up and down against the burning-hot steel above him. He kicked out with his legs, but he couldn't move. The equipment was shifting around them. Pressing down to bury them alive.

The car stopped and reversed directions. The ride was smoother now, but he still couldn't breathe. If they didn't stop the car soon and let them out, they were going to suffocate. He kicked his feet against the back of the trunk, but it didn't seem to be doing any good. He kicked his feet harder. Harder still.

Finally the car slowed to a stop. Footsteps tapped toward the trunk. He gulped down the burning air, forcing it into his protesting lungs. Just a few more seconds and he'd be fine. A few more seconds and he'd never complain about the New Orleans heat again.

A strange voice barked out an order. The soldiers had stopped the car! The plan wasn't going to work. They'd taken down her license number. They'd already radioed back to their headquarters with her name!

A metallic knock sounded against the body of the car. A man's impatient voice. "Sorry, ma'am, but I'm going to have to ask you to open it. Now!"

ᥱᔐ 23 ᔐᥲ

Mariutza

MARI BUNCHED HER LEGS up against her chest and tried to twist around. If she could just get her feet up under her, she'd be able to jump out when they opened the trunk lid. She slowed her breathing and listened as the footsteps tapped on the pavement right outside the car. It was two people at the least. It could be four or five. They only moved one at a time. Like shimulo trying to hide their numbers.

The footsteps scraped across the surface of the road, and the left passenger door opened with a squawk.

"Good afternoon, officer. How can I help you?" Melchi's voice sounded cheerful. "If my driver exceeded the speed limit, I'm happy to pay the fine."

The reply was too muffled to make out clearly, but it sounded like he was describing Jaazaniah.

"Who do I call if I see them? Should I call the local police or is there some kind of hotline?"

Another muffled reply.

"Of course. I'll let you know the second I see anything suspicious."

Finally, the footsteps retreated and the limo started moving again.

Mari took a slow cleansing breath and stretched her legs out until her feet were touching the back of the trunk.

"That was close." Jaazaniah's voice tickled the back of her neck. "I thought it was out of the oven and into the fire."

"They did just what you said." Mari squirmed around and tried to face him. "Did you see it in a vision?"

"I'm just good at reading people. Especially macho types like soldiers and the police. They're all pretty much the same."

"It is a very special gift. Purodad taught me about it in lessons, but I thought he was exaggerating."

"Excuse me?"

"Exaggerating. Using bigger than life language to make a story lesson. Purodad loved stories about the true Gypsies. Embellishment, he said, was essential to the tone."

"What are you talking about? What gift? And what does it have to do with Gypsies?"

"He said the true Gypsies—not to be mixed up with the nowaday Tinkers—were very people intuitive. Some was so good at reading folks, it seemed they were looking into the future. That's where their fortune-tellers came from. They looked at the Standing living among them and fooled themselves into thinking they had the same gifts. Healings weren't so easy to imitate, but with their people intuition they got certain good at imitating blessings and fortune-telling."

"I wasn't faking. I never said I was telling the future."

"Course not. That trick is other nonsense. Purodad said it was only a cheap imitation of the true gifting."

There was a long silence. Mari could feel the bitterness and hurt swirling in his head. Her words had wounded him. She shouldn't have compared him to a Gypsy. He was a Standing. A true prophet—one of the most powerful prophets of all time.

"I'm sorry. I wasn't thinking. Miss Caralee says my mouth runs up and down like a squirrel in heat. I don't think what I'm saying before it's already out of my mouth."

"Is that what happened back in the woods? You have the gift for knowing what people are doing behind your back?"

"I left off thinking, let my emotions jumble my head into a knot. If the Lord hadn't been merciful, I would have got us all killed."

"But you were perfect. Better than a kung fu movie."

"I meant to wallop the soldier behind you, but when I hit the ground the training just took over. The two men were in the same place as one of my old training exercises—Purodad called them katas—and my body just started moving. I forgot all about the behind soldier. I'm very sorry. I've never been in a real battle before. Purodad said I don't have the warrior's gift."

"*You* don't have the gift . . ."

"Not like you and Melchi."

"Me and Melchi?"

She could feel the emotions stirring again. Confusion, bitterness, and anger. So much anger. She'd said the wrong thing again. Every time she opened her mouth, a heap of foolishness gushed out.

"I'm sorry. I . . ." She pressed her forehead into a hot canvas bag. "I'm too stupid to even know how to apologize. I don't have Gypsy people smarts. I don't even understand myself."

The bag rattled into her head, stirring her thoughts into porridge. She lay there a long time, but Jaazaniah didn't respond. He wasn't going to accept her apology. Whatever she'd said, she'd hurt him too deep to ever forgive.

Tears leaked out the sides of her eyes to mix with the sweat pouring down her face. The prophet's feelings churned around her like a raging storm. Melchi was so big and fierce. He was the true warrior. Was he going to reject her and choose Melchi instead? She'd told him she didn't have the gift. Of course he'd choose Melchi. It was the only choice that made sense.

The car turned suddenly and a great roar came up from the tires. The bags bumped and rattled beneath her like bouncing on Purodad's knee. *You're no granddaughter of mine. No relation at all!* Everything she touched turned to disaster.

The car rolled to a stop and the roar of the engine suddenly died down. There was a rattle and a snap and the overhead door lifted, filling the trunk with bright light.

"Are you guys okay?" Hailey's voice was a breath of fresh air. "We tried to stop sooner, but we couldn't find any place to pull over."

"Where are we?" Jaazaniah climbed out of the trunk with a groan. "Mari?" A hand settled on her shoulder. "Are you okay?" His voice was suddenly soft. All the emotions were gone. Had he decided to forgive her after all?

"I . . . will get out." She crawled to her hands and knees and let Melchi and the prophet help her out of the trunk.

Her legs felt like wet shrimp nets. She couldn't seem to get her balance.

"I'll get some water." Hailey ran to the front of the car and brought back two jugs of the same colorless water she'd had before. "Don't drink them too fast. You're probably dehydrated."

Mari nodded and gulped down the cool clear water. So deliciously fresh. She could feel the coolness seeping into her body. It was like being dead and coming back to life.

"So are we ready to take a look at the map?" Jaazaniah pulled the shovel out of the trunk and limped over to a pool of swampy water.

Melchi walked Mari over to the pool. She crouched down and watched as Jaazaniah washed the mud off the shovel. The gray steel was smooth and clean. No messages there.

"That's okay." Jaazaniah tossed the shovel aside and moved back to the trunk of the car. "I didn't expect anything to be on the shovel. Hailey's right. The board's the most logical place. Why cover a new board in mud unless it's to hide some kind of a message?" He pulled the board out of the trunk and brought it back to the puddle.

Holding it under the murky water, he and Melchi scrubbed it front and back with their hands. Finally, they pulled it out of the water and held it up to the afternoon sun. Nothing on the front, nothing on the back, nothing on the edges . . .

The board was spanking clean.

Jazz

JAZZ TOOK THE BOARD from Melchi and flipped it over. They were missing something—some secret compartment or hidden message . . . "Maybe it's written in invisible ink. Maybe if we heated it or coated it with lemon juice or did a rubbing with crayons on a white sheet of paper. There has to be something."

"Maybe . . ." Mari looked up at Melchi. For what? His imperious edict? When had he become the boss? Jazz didn't remember holding any elections.

Jazz carried the board and shovel back to the limo and tossed them back into the trunk. "We'll figure it out. We just need to keep on looking. If we can figure out where my grandfather went before he died, we'll have the missing puzzle piece."

He turned to check behind him, but the others were still down by the water. Hailey and Mari were watching Melchi. Apparently they weren't allowed to move unless his lordship granted them permission.

"I think"—Melchi finally deigned to speak—"the most important problem to solve right now is how we're going to escape. The area is no longer safe. Not with the Mulo controlling the military."

"And the police," Mari added. "During an offensive, one must consider all power centers corrupt."

"Wait a second. Slow down." Jazz walked back to the group. "This isn't a war. Nobody's talking about launching any offensives. Once we find the treasure, we're out of here. We just have to keep a low profile while we figure out the clues."

"The treasure may have to wait," Melchi said. "I am sorry, but it is too dangerous. If we leave now, perhaps we will be able to continue the search in a few months after the Mulo and their men have moved on."

"And what if they find it first?" Jazz asked. "What if it contains some sort of vital information that gives them even more power? Have you ever thought of that? What if it's enough gold to pay for even more weapons and equipment?"

"There is always a risk, but your grandfather was a prophet of the Standing. We have no choice but to trust his ingenuity."

"Yes, we do." Jazz stepped toward Melchi. "We can find it now. The longer we stand around talking, the more likely they'll find it. We've got to move!" He stepped toward the limo, but they still didn't follow. "If you're afraid, then give me the keys. I'll find it myself!"

"Where would you even look?" Melchi followed him to the car. "The board and shovel were our only clues."

"I don't know. Is there a town nearby? Maybe we'll find someone who remembers seeing him. The point is to keep moving. We're not going to accomplish anything sitting still."

Hailey and Mari drifted after Melchi. They seemed almost deliberate in their lack of enthusiasm.

Hailey finally broke the silence. "Hollis said your picture was being broadcast over the television. If anyone sees you, they'll call the police."

"So we don't let anyone see me. I can stay in the limo while you go out and search."

"The limo . . ." Hailey looked down and kicked at a leafy twig. "The limo isn't safe either. The highway patrolmen took down my license number when they stopped us."

"So?"

"So remember the soldier in the woods? He gave my name to his superiors. Once they compare notes, they'll start searching for the limo. It doesn't exactly blend in."

"So you're saying . . ." Jazz couldn't believe he was hearing this. They were going to abandon him just because they were afraid their precious limousine might be searched?

"I am sorry." The big man hung his head. "But it's not that far to walk. There's a town less than two miles away."

Jazz's face burned. His gut ached like he'd been punched. "Okay, fine! But I'm taking the clues." He pulled the board and shovel out of the trunk and stalked away from the car. Searching for the limo, indeed. They'd been planning this from the beginning, from the second they'd laid eyes on his will.

A blast of emotion hit him in the back. The sound of light footsteps.

"Jaazaniah, what happened?" Mari's tearful voice. "Why are you angry?"

Jazz stopped midstride. He wouldn't look back. Wouldn't give them the satisfaction.

"Did I do something wrong?" A light touch on his arm. "I'm very sorry."

Jazz's throat tightened. He turned and forced his eyes to Mari's face. The fear in her eyes clamped down on his chest. "It's not you. It's your new friends. They don't want me around any more."

"What are you saying?" Melchi stepped forward. "Why are you doing this?"

"Why am I . . .?" Jazz clamped his mouth shut and stalked out into the trees. It was the same Gypsy nonsense his father used to rave about. The same mind games that had driven him from his home. No wonder his father turned to drugs. It was enough to drive anyone insane.

He flung the shovel and board under a leaning tree and kicked a pile of dead leaves over them. The others might steal them, but it couldn't be helped. The police would be looking for the board and shovel. Walking cross-country would be dangerous enough as it was.

Heavy footsteps crackled up behind him. "Why are you doing this?" Melchi sounded almost as frustrated as he was. Almost. "Don't you see how much you're hurting Mari?"

Jazz swung around and spoke between clenched teeth. "I'm not going to fight you. Go ahead. Hit me if that makes you feel big, but I'm not going to hit you back."

"Is that what you think?" Melchi's eyes went wide. "You think I want to fight you?"

"Then why are you here? Why not just let me go my way in peace?"

"Because I . . . care."

"Whatever." Jazz pushed past the giant and clomped back through the trees. They could have the shovel. They could have the whole stinking treasure for all he cared. He was sick of the whole thing. Everything his grandfather touched had been cursed.

Mari was back on the road, crying into Hailey's shoulder. Hailey flashed Jazz a look that could have killed a grisly bear at ten paces. As if everything were *his* fault.

Whatever . . .

He turned and headed up the road. He hadn't gone more than twenty yards when he heard more footsteps coming up behind him. "What now?" He turned to see the three of them following him. "Am I walking wrong? Am I breaking another secret rule?"

Mari shrank against Hailey's side. Melchi just scowled. "We have to take to the woods before we get to the highway. If anyone were to see us on the road, they might call the police."

We? What did he mean *we?* Jazz's steps faltered. "Where are *you* going? I thought you were taking the limo."

"I told you it's not safe." Hailey's voice was almost a snarl. "Once they trace me to the limo, they'll have every patrolman in the state looking for it."

"But you're . . ." He looked back and forth between Hailey and Melchi. Something wasn't right. "They're not looking for you. Just me and Mari."

"After what happened in the woods?" Hailey stared at him like he was an idiot. "Of course they're after me. They're after all of us."

"But . . . so you're walking too? I thought . . ." Jazz had to look away.

He *was* an idiot.

He wouldn't blame Mari if she never spoke to him again. He took a deep breath and let it out slowly. "I thought you didn't want to be caught with *me.* That you were going away in the limo and . . . were leaving me here to . . ." His voice faded to a whisper.

"That's crazy." Hailey glared at him. "Why would we do that? That's the craziest thing I've ever heard."

Melchi turned to Mari and spoke in a tender voice. "I told you it was a misunderstanding. See? It didn't have anything to do with you. He thought *we* didn't want *him.*" He looked up at Jazz. "I'm sorry. I was wrong to be angry and I ask your forgiveness. I should have asked more clarifying questions."

"Don't mention it." Jazz choked out the words and waited for them to catch up.

Mari still clung to Hailey, but at least she wasn't crying. Her face flushed and she looked away when she noticed him staring. He'd been a jerk. A total and absolute jerk. They would have been better off without him.

They walked in silence for what seemed like hours before they finally heard the sound of traffic ahead. Melchi nodded and led them into the tangled undergrowth of the trees to their right. It was rough going. Several times they had to stop and double back to get around thickets of poison ivy. Melchi pulled out a huge knife and used it to hack a trail through the obstructing vines.

Jazz stumbled behind him in exhausted silence. Melchi was the undisputed leader and protector now. Mari hadn't mentioned the *Jaazaniah the Warrior* bit since they'd joined up with him. It had always been ridiculous, but now with the giant here, it was completely absurd. Even she had to acknowledge that.

They followed the road for over an hour before they finally came to a large trailer set back in the trees.

"What do we do when we get to town?" Jazz whispered as they circled around the cluttered backyard. He was a filthy, sweaty mess. People would take one look at him and know something was wrong—even if they hadn't seen the news bulletins.

"We'll have to get a new car." Melchi shot a wary look at the dark windows of the house.

"Won't the police be watching the rental agencies?"

"We'll have to buy one. Renting requires too much paperwork."

"Are you serious?" Jazz studied Melchi's expression. "You're going to abandon your limo and *buy* a car?"

Melchi nodded. "A used car from a normal Gadzé citizen. Preferably a big one with dark tinted windows. We must get new clothes as well. If pictures of you and Mari are on the television, they'll be searching for us in every state we pass through."

Jazz stared at Melchi. "And you can afford that? To buy a car *and* clothes?"

"Yes." The big man's face flushed, and he looked down at the ground.

What had just happened? Jazz studied Melchi's expression out of the corner of his eye. He was lying! Jazz fought to keep a straight face as everything suddenly clicked into place. That was it! He'd finally discovered the chink in Melchi's sterling-plated armor. Melchi and Hailey were thieves! That's why they were so eager to ditch the limo. They were wanted by the police. It all fit: the limo, the combat training, meeting out in the middle of the swamp . . . everything!

Why hadn't he seen it before? Just when he was about to inherit an enormous fortune from his grandfather, a couple of thieves suddenly turn up and offer to help. Two new best friends ready to rescue him from the clutches of his mysterious enemy, ready to risk their lives to help a perfect stranger find his inheritance. How unbelievably selfless of them.

He turned the evidence over in his mind as they walked past another trailer and a couple of dilapidated houses. Mari was the only thing that didn't fit. Was she working with them? She didn't seem to be. But the whole Gypsy Standing thing was too big a coincidence. Or was it? Maybe Melchi and Hailey had been a part of his grandfather's cult. Maybe that's where they'd found out about the treasure in the first place.

They passed behind a boarded up building that might once have been a fifties-style diner. Just beyond the diner, Jazz noticed a long cinderblock building with a neon *Vacancy* sign. The roar of window AC units made the heat even more unbearable.

"So . . ." Jazz kept his voice casual. "How are we going to do this? I could go with you to find a car to buy, while the girls crash here at this motel. It's not the nicest place I've ever seen, but at least it will give them a chance to get cleaned up. We'll be a lot less conspicuous if there are only two of us walking through town."

Melchi nodded and studied the motel. He was working on an excuse. Jazz could see it in his eyes. There was no way he was going to let Jazz accompany him on his little car-jacking mission. The harder Jazz pushed to go with him, the more likely he'd be to spring for a motel room.

Finally Melchi sighed and turned back to Jazz. "Please understand, I would enjoy your company, and I really don't want to leave you behind, but with your picture on the televisions, I think it would be too dangerous. Perhaps you and Mari . . . would be willing to wait here at the hotel?"

Jazz sighed and looked down at the ground to keep his face from giving him away. He had a decent enough poker face, but it was hard not to celebrate when you'd just been dealt four aces. Maybe he was pushing his luck, but he might as well go for five. "I'd rather go with you." He glanced back at Mari and Hailey. "I'm not sure Mari would go for sharing a room—not with me anyway."

"Of course not!" The big man looked genuinely embarrassed. "We would get two rooms obviously. And it won't be long. Just enough time to bathe and change clothes. She'll feel much better after a bath. You both will."

Jazz nodded reluctantly. Melchi hadn't even flinched about the motel rooms. Was it possible he really *was* planning to buy a car? Jazz looked up and tried to penetrate the mask of innocent goodwill pasted thick across the giant's face. No . . . The guy was trying way too hard. He was definitely a thief—and not a petty thief either. This guy was a pro.

"Okay, I'll get the rooms while you get us a car." Jazz turned and started angling toward the corner of the motel.

"Here's some money." Melchi reached into his pocket and pulled out a couple of bills. He handed them to Jazz and turned to wait for the girls. "Mari, would you mind staying here with Jazz while Hailey and I try to find another car? We should be back in less than an hour. Is this okay?"

Mari shot Jazz a questioning look.

He gave her what he hoped was a reassuring smile. "It's fine with me too. More than fine." He glanced down at the bills in his hand and his pulse quickened. They were hundreds! The guy had handed him two hundred dollars cash and was going to walk away. Just like that. Talk about a confidence scam. It was textbook perfect.

"If anything happens, we'll meet somewhere in these woods." Melchi swept his hand to indicate the region behind him. "An hour hike in should do it. Don't come out of hiding for anyone but Hailey or me."

"Okay, we'll see you in an hour." Jazz turned to face the motel. *Come on guys, get the hint. Let's go already.*

"Be careful." Hailey gave Mari a hug and then followed Melchi toward the road.

Jazz waited until Melchi and Hailey had disappeared around the corner of the motel before turning to Mari. "Sorry about what happened before. I totally overreacted."

"I understand now. Hailey explained it to me. She said you thought we didn't love you."

Jazz nodded. "That's why I was so mad. I didn't want to have to leave you."

Mari's face lit with a shy smile. "That's what she said, only I didn't want to believe her."

"Why not?"

"It seemed . . . more than I deserved." Another shy smile.

If this was an act, she deserved an Academy Award. He couldn't leave her. It wouldn't be right. "Mari, I've got to tell you something you're not going to like. Something about Melchi and Hailey."

"Okay . . ."

"I know you're excited to find more people like . . . us, but they're not what they seem. They're in the business of . . . taking things that don't belong to them. I think they're after your grandfather's inheritance."

She laughed and looked up into his eyes, as though waiting for the punch line.

"I'm not joking. They're professional thieves. Or con artists, something like that. Melchi gave me two hundred dollars to keep me from going with him to find a car. Don't you see what this means?"

"It means he likes you. He thinks you're a great prophet of the Standing."

"No!" Jazz started walking toward the motel. "It means we can't trust him. People don't just give money to strangers and walk off. He's doing it to win our confidence. He trusts me and gives me something so I'll trust him and give him something later. It's called being a con artist. It's just a different name for being a thief."

"But he's not . . . any of those things. He would never hurt us. We're his family. He said so himself."

"Don't you see? That just proves what I'm saying. We've only known him a day, and he's already calling us family? Don't you think that's a little bit odd?"

"But we *are* family. The enemy has killed so many Standing. There aren't many of us left."

Jazz clomped through the brush. He wanted to believe her, but the guy had handed him two hundred dollars. He said they'd driven all the way out from California—on the offhand chance he might be able to help a total stranger. It didn't add up. As much as he'd like to live in her fairy-tale world, that just wasn't the way reality worked.

"Look . . . They say they want to take us back to California, right? But I just can't do it. My grandfather left something for me, and I can't let someone else find it first."

"But they won't. Purodad wouldn't let them."

"Are you willing to take that chance? What if they *did* find it? What if the treasure contained some super-secret prophecy message? What if it helped them track down more of your . . . *our* people?"

"Melchi said we'd come back soon—"

"But what if something more important comes up? What if he had someone else to help and couldn't bring us back? Are you willing to trust your life to someone you've only known for a day?"

"Of course." She sounded hesitant, almost apologetic.

"I'm not. I know it's dangerous, but I need to keep searching— right now, while the trail is still fresh. And I'd like you to come with me. Can you trust me on this? Can you put as much faith in me as you put in Melchi?"

"But we already told him we'd go."

"Okay, fine. I'm not trying to pressure you." Jazz headed for the motel at a fast walk. He could hear Mari trotting along behind him, but he refused to slow down. She'd made her choice. He was making his.

"Melchi said he wanted us to wait for him in a motel room. I take it you're not going to be comfortable with that?"

"Inside?" Mari's voice rose to a panicked squeal. "He wanted us to hide *inside?*"

Jazz nodded.

"But he's a Standing. He couldn't have meant . . . not inside!"

"He gave us money for the room." Jazz pulled the money out of his pocket and held it in front of her face. "Awfully generous for a stranger, don't you think?"

"But it's . . . not allowed."

"I know. Funny, isn't it? You sure you don't want to come with me?"

She stared at the money for a long time and then looked up at him with glistening eyes. "We already gave him our word."

"Fine with me. You can hide back here if you want." He pointed to indicate a shadowy clump of trees directly behind the building. "But I'm taking a shower."

Jazz turned and walked around to the front of the building. She was still standing there as he turned the corner, watching him with the pitiful look of an abandoned puppy.

He swore to himself and marched to the front door of the office. The cramped room was piled halfway to the ceiling with mounds of papers.

"Can I help you?" An old man in a stained white shirt looked up at him from behind a cluttered counter. The flickering light of an old tube television reflected off his pale leathery skin.

"Thanks. Could I use your phone? My car broke down a few miles back, and I need to call a cab."

ᴄᴏ 24 ᴏᴍ

Mariutza

MARI'S BREATH STORMED IN her ears, filling her head with the blackness of the dark and pounding road. The Badness had taken Jaazaniah! She pushed herself harder, forced her wore-out legs to greater and greater speeds. She had to save him. Couldn't let him get out of range.

Straining ahead with her last breath of strength, she reached out with the *dikh* sight. Down the highway, through the trees, through the last fading rays of the setting sun, she searched the ether for the tiniest speck of the prophet's presence. He was out there somewhere. She had to push harder, run faster, search wider.

A hum cut through the roar hammering inside her ears. A red haze, shimmering against a tear-distorted highway. Mari leaped off the road and plunged into the forest leaves. The hum grew louder. It was some kind of transport. A dusty red pick-up with lights shining out from the roof of the cab. She dove behind a bank of weeds and rolled onto her back to listen, but her wind was too loud. She held her breath in two-second gulps, reaching out with the sight as the car past her by. They weren't going to stop. Probably weren't even hunting for her.

She turned the sight back to Jaazaniah again, but he was gone. Springing to her feet, she ran out onto the road. They were out of range. That was all. They'd carted him off so quick it only felt like he'd disappeared. She eased back into a run and searched the road ahead of her. Jaazaniah was school educated. He'd think of a way to slow them down. She'd catch up on them soon.

Another hum sounded from behind. Mari veered off the road and ran back into the woods. A river of trees ran through her head. Worry pinched at her mind like a pot of boiling crawdads. Fear. Dread. It flowed through her brain. Getting stronger. Closer!

Holy One, hide us—

A piercing shriek swallowed up the roar of the car. Mari ducked behind a tree as a loud voice shouted inside her head.

Melchi?

She peeked out from the tree and answered him back. Melchi was running across the road. Behind him was a black car with dark-colored windows. Blue smoke hung like swirling ghosts in the air. It smelled like sulfur and burning rubber.

"Mari!" He called out and crashed through the saplings to reach her. "What happened? Why did you leave the motel?" He plodded suddenly to a stop. "Where's Jazz?" He looked around the trees this way and that. "Mari?"

Her throat tightened and suddenly she was shaking. "It took him," she sobbed. "The Badness got him while I was hiding. I tried to follow but I—"

"Let's go!" Melchi grabbed her by the wrist and pulled her through the trees. Running out onto the road, he opened the back door of the black car and eased her inside.

"What happened?" Hailey called out over the growling engine. "Where's Jazz?"

Mari leaned forward in her seat and pointed up the road. "I was hiding in the woods behind the motel, and all of a sudden . . . he just started moving. Real fast, like he was riding in a car."

The car leaped forward, pressing Mari back against the seat. "I don't know what happened." She pulled herself up to lean over the front seats. "One second he was in the motel, and the next he was moving. Quick as a bunny. I thought I heard a car, but by the time I got to the road it was gone-away."

She gripped the seats tighter as the trees on both sides of the road sped past in a blur. The car was so fast. They were sure to catch him now. They were moving faster than eyes could see.

"Did you feel anything before that?" Melchi turned in his seat to face her. "Fear? Surprise? The presence of a Mulo?"

"I don't think so. He just started moving. I was trying not to pay attention. He said he . . ." Mari shook her head and looked back out the window.

"What?" Melchi's urgent voice. "What did he say?"

"He said he was to be . . . marimé. That he would wash himself with a shower inside the building. It would have been wrong for me to intrude."

Melchi nodded. "But what did you feel when he started moving? Was he afraid? In pain maybe? You must have felt something."

"Nothing." Mari shook her head. "That's what made me so afraid. I felt nothing at all. Just his presence trailing further and further away."

Melchi closed his eyes and faced the front of the car. He was searching. She reached out as well, searching for the tiniest flicker of life in the darkness stretching out all around her.

But it was no use. He had completely disappeared. She slumped forward, burying her face in her arms. They were going so fast. Why couldn't she feel him?

JOHN B. OLSON

"Maybe the Mulo didn't have anything to do with this," Hailey called back from the front seat. "What if Jazz figured out where the treasure was? He might have gone off to look for it on his own."

"Without telling anyone?" Melchi shook his head. "It doesn't make sense. He didn't have a car. If he'd waited for us, we would have been able to help him."

"He didn't know that," Hailey said. "Remember? He wanted to keep looking, but we said it was too dangerous."

"Because we were out of clues. If he'd come up with another idea, we would have listened—as long as it wasn't too danger- ous."

Mari thought back to the conversation she'd had with him right before he went inside. "Hailey might be right. Jaazaniah told me he wanted to keep hunting for his inheritance. He wanted me to come with him, but I—"

Melchi shook his head. "We *told* him we would help. I don't think he would have gone off without us. How would he have got- ten a car?"

Sudden anger flared inside Mari's brain. Jaazaniah was safe. He had to be! She gritted her teeth as a fountain of fury bubbled up inside her. She didn't need Melchi's help. She would search for Jaazaniah on her own!

"Mulo!" Melchi's voice cut through the growing rage. "Coming fast!"

Mari squeezed her eyes shut and tried to fight through the inferno burning inside her brain. She must calm herself, clear her mind . . .

But it was too late. The fire had already taken hold.

Please . . . Help me . . .

The flames in her head died down with a sizzling hiss.

Please . . .

She was a campfire beneath a stream of fresh cold water. She focused her mind, trying to take captive the fiery thoughts raging within. Stomping out each fresh worry before it could flare back to life.

Careful not to lose her focus, she opened her eyes slowly. Hailey was still driving. Her eyes wide and her face pale. Her lips fluttered with a stream of silent prayers.

"Where are they?" Mari whispered.

"Straight ahead." Melchi's voice was cold as winter. He leaned forward in his seat, staring out the front window with hard, penetrating eyes. "Less than two miles away. I don't feel Jazz yet, but that doesn't mean anything. There are too many voices to sift through. He could easily be buried in the noise."

Mari prayed fervently as the car penetrated further into the deepening gloom. The road made a left curve up ahead of them. She bit her lip as she recognized the trees near the turn. They were close to her swamp. Had the Badness carried Jaazaniah away or had he come on his own accord?

"Turn off the headlights," Melchi whispered as the car reached the bend. "Slow down. Be ready to turn around and run if we're discovered."

Hailey pushed a button and everything went dark. Mari's chest clenched into a fist around her heart. How could Hailey see? They were still moving so fast. They would run into a tree!

"Shhh . . . It's okay." Melchi's soothing voice sounded by her car. "We're going to be fine. Keep on praying."

The road ahead of them grew brighter and brighter as they coasted around the curve. The forest took on a pulsing glow. Finally they saw the cause. On the side of the road, just over a mile away, eight sets of flashing blue lights lit the night. The whole forest was aglow.

"Off the road!" Melchi hissed.

Mari leaned forward, as Hailey stopped the car on the side of the road. Bobbing lights were everywhere. The forest was lit up like lightning bugs.

She reached out with the sight, and her head filled once again with the angry roar. Jaazaniah was in *that*? How could anyone stand against such power?

"What do we do now?" Hailey peered into the darkness. "We can't get anywhere near that."

Mari breathed another quick prayer. "They've got Jaazaniah. We don't have a choice."

She turned to Melchi. He sat there for a long time, staring straight ahead. Finally he nodded and his eyes snapped back into focus.

"Mari and I will go in alone. If he's still alive, we'll find him."

Jazz

SUCH A JERK!

Jazz slammed his fist into his leg. What was *wrong* with him? He was a cowardly, low-life jerk!

The taxi driver's eyes wandered to him in the rearview mirror, but Jazz turned and looked out the window. The city lights were sliding past in a blur of streaking stars. They'd be at the hotel soon. If he was going tell the driver to turn around, now would be the time to do it. He couldn't leave Mari in the hands of those thieves. They'd eat her alive. She was too innocent and trusting for her own good. What would they do to her when they found out he'd escaped?

He leaned forward in his seat and checked the meter. $68.00. He'd have more than enough money to go back, but how would he explain the missing money to Melchi? It would be close to $140.00. They would kill him.

"How far are we from the hotel?" The city seemed to hold its breath at the sound of his voice. Something was out there. He could feel it rumbling in his bones. This wasn't some Gypsy parlor trick. There weren't any Gypsies around now. Just him and the driver.

"Just a few minutes. Why?" The driver looked up at the mirror, piercing him with dark rheumy eyes. "You wanna go someplace else maybe first?" A lecherous grin. "I can hook you up."

"No, I'm fine. The hotel is good." Jazz's stomach turned suddenly to ice. Was the driver one of them?

A dank whisper brushed across his mind. He looked out into the flickering streets. An oily haze seemed to permeate the darkness. Sleazy and filthy, he could feel it reaching out to him, grasping at him with a thousand probing tentacles.

"Stop right here! Over there near the light. Anywhere is fine. I need to walk."

"Hotel's only a couple more blocks."

"Right here!"

The car pulled over and jerked to a stop. Jazz tossed a hundred dollar bill over the seat and threw open the door. The thick air closed around him, enveloping him in a dark, suffocating blanket as the cab pulled out into the street and drove away.

He had to get to a phone and call the motel. The old man at the desk would give Mari a message. He'd have to when he heard what it was.

Jazz searched up and down the street before breaking into a slow limping jog. A series of convulsive shivers shuddered down his spine. It hadn't been the taxi driver. Something was in the city. Something big. He could feel it buzzing in his brain.

The hotel lights streaked and jolted in his eyes as he ran. He'd call the motel first and then Hollis. She'd give him a ride. Once she learned Mari was in danger, she wouldn't have a choice.

He stuttered to a stop at the hotel entrance and flung open the door. Good! The desk clerk from before was still at the desk. He flashed her a smile and marched across the lobby, ignoring the surprised looks of the other guests.

"I need to use your phone. It's an emergency," he announced from halfway across the room. "Someone's life could be in danger."

The attendant's eyes went wide as she looked him up and down. He probably looked like a refugee from a war zone. Might as well use it to his advantage.

"I need to use your phone, ma'am." He clipped his words with military-style efficiency and reached over the counter.

"Of course." She pulled out a phone and set it on the counter, watching as he dialed information and asked to be connected to the desk of the motel.

"Maison Motel." A woman's tired voice sounded over the line.

"Hi, this is Jazz Rechabson. I need you to listen very carefully. You're not in any danger, but innocent lives are at stake." He paused to give her a chance to object. Not a word. "There's an agent hiding at the edge of the woods behind your motel. I need you to go out there and deliver a message for me. Tell her to stay right there. I'll be right back as soon as I can."

"Who is this? Is this some sort of a joke?"

"No, ma'am. It's not a joke. This is Jazz Rechabson. Just tell her I'll be there as soon as I can. Jazz Rechabson." He hung up the phone and looked up at the attendant. "Could you call up to room 341 for me? That's Hollis Duke. Room 341."

The girl typed something into the computer and shook her head. "I'm sorry. Miss Duke checked out last night. Is there anything else?"

Jazz swore under his breath and fished in his pocket for her cell number. He pulled out the crumpled slip of paper and smoothed it out on the counter. "Just one more phone call." He dialed the number and paced the length of the cord while it rang.

"Hello?" Hollis's wary voice.

"Hollis, this is Jazz. I'm calling from the Ritz-Carlton. Where are you?"

"You don't sound like Jazz. How do I know it's you?"

"What are you talking about? Who else would I be?"

There was a long pause. He could hear her breathing into the phone. She sounded like she'd been running.

"Look, it's me. You still have my guitar, and I want it back. I need—"

"What was written on the piece of paper you showed me?"

"What piece of paper? You're talking about the will?"

"The other one. What was in the letter? Who was it from?"

"A guy named Melchi. The letter said something else—a foreign name I can't remember, but he goes by Melchi. Melchi and Hailey. Now what's going on?"

"People have been following me. Ever since I got back from Butte La Rose. I saw them in the parking garage. They had guns."

"What? Slow down. Are they still there?"

"This isn't funny any more. I can't do this. I don't know what this is about, and I don't want to. I just want out. Tell them to leave me alone, and I'll get on the first plane out of town. I promise. I won't tell anyone. I couldn't if I wanted to. I don't know anything to tell."

"Hollis, calm down. Everything will be fine. Where are you?"

"Just leave me alone. Tell them I just want to be left alone."
A strangled sob sounded over the phone.

"Hollis, listen to me. They don't care about you. They're looking for me. Okay?"

A muffled breath.

"As long as you have my guitar, they'll keep following you. I need you to find a way to lose them and meet me with the guitar. Someplace safe. Okay? And bring your car keys. If you let me borrow your car, I'll drive it far away from here, and they'll leave you alone. I promise."

"What's my car have to do with it? It's just a cheap rental."

"Mari's in trouble. I need a car to get her away from some bad people. Okay? We won't go anywhere near you. I promise."

"What happened? Is she okay?" She was considering it. Jazz could hear it in her voice.

"I think Melchi and Hailey are thieves. She's with them right now. I need a car to get her away from them. I'll take it back to the rental place after all this is over. I swear."

"I don't care about the car. You're sure Mari's okay?"

"I don't know." Jazz swallowed to clear the tightness building in his throat. "I need to go back for her. Do you think you can lose your friends?"

"I think I already have. I've been watching for them all night, and I haven't seen anyone at all."

"Where are you? Did you check into another hotel?"

There was a long pause. "Meet me at Jackson Square in a half hour. I'll bring my keys and your guitar, and then that's it. No more calling, okay? If they catch you, you have to tell them I didn't have anything to do with anything. I have no idea what this is about. Okay? Promise me."

"Okay, I promise. I'll be there in half an hour."

The receiver went dead. "Hello?" Jazz waited several seconds before returning it to its cradle. When he looked up, the desk attendant was watching him. He could see a dozen questions forming on her lips.

"Thanks for the phone." He turned and fled back through the lobby. "I totally appreciate it."

The scrape of footsteps tingled down his spine as he pushed through the door and stepped out into the night. He stopped and searched the silent street, but it was deserted. He was just imagining things. All the cloak and dagger stuff was finally starting to get to him.

He set off for the park at a quick walk. If it was the place he was thinking of, thirty minutes gave him more than enough time. It was only eight or nine blocks away.

A soft, almost metallic scrape sounded behind him. He spun and searched the gloaming shadows. A chill shuddered through his frame. Nobody. The sidewalk was completely empty. He turned and walked faster, rolling his steps from heel to toe to muffle his steps.

Taking a left onto Bourbon, he jogged out into the middle of the narrow street, pushing his way deeper and deeper into the gloom. Dark balconies pressed down on him from all sides, shredding the light into blobs of shifting, twisting shadow. The air was thick and claustrophobic. It caught in his throat and pooled in his lungs. Suddenly he couldn't breathe.

"Mr. Rechabson?" A deep voice sounded right behind him.

Jazz's heart lurched in his chest. He turned to stare into the muzzle of an enormous handgun.

A dark figure eased into the light, holding a shiny badge out in front of him like a shield.

"Daniel Groves, FBI. Put your hands on your head and kneel down on the ground. You and I need to have a little talk."

৩ 25 ৩

Mariutza

MARI PLUNGED THROUGH THE darkness, dodging and weaving in and out through the trees. The Badness hung like muddy waters on the thick night air. Putrid and choking, clawing into the recesses of her soul. She leaped a shadowy bramble and flung out with the *dikh* sight, but the roar was deafening. So many voices . . . so much power! How were they to find him with so much rackety fuss?

A beam of light swept through the trees. Mari dove for cover and rolled beneath a clump of brambly limbs as the light swept toward her, slowed, and finally came to a rest on the thicket she hid under.

The eyes of the forest pressed in on her. Raw hatred beat down, tearing through the last shreds of her frantic prayers. She was too weak, wretched. A pridesome, wailful sinner playing the harlot with the road. Mari held her breath, waiting for a hailstorm of bullets to rip the life from her body. It had spotted her dead-on. What was it waiting on?

The beam lifted and drifted past. Footsteps tramped off to the right. Three or four shimulo. How did they get so close? She hadn't felt them at all.

The footsteps faded into the distance. Mari breathed in and out, trying to purge the poisons from her system. This was foolishness, simple and true. She couldn't feel Jaazaniah anywhere. She was going to get Melchi killed.

She gathered her feet under her, but a hand clamped around her arm. She turned and peeped into the darkness. She could just make out the outline of Melchi's features. He stared off to the left. Something was out there.

A blob of shadow drifting through the trees.

Mari reached out with the sight, but the Badness was so thickety-thick she almost gagged. She jerked back and ground her forehead into the dirt. It was inside her head. Filthy. Black. Putrid. Pushing down her throat, expanding to fill her lungs. She was going to burst.

Holy One, shield us! She gasped and tried to find her breath. *Please, make it go away.*

Finally, after what seemed an eternity, the sickness began to subside. Mari looked back at Melchi, but he was still staring. How could anyone stand against such power? It was beyond imagining. The entire swamp buzzed with the force of its presence. And there were others too. Soldiers and policemen and strange men shouting into radio devices.

A crash of dead leaves sounded off to the right. Mari pressed herself to the ground and froze. A roar came from straight ahead. It was getting louder. The *thumpas* were coming back! They were flying fast and low over the trees, sweeping the forest with powerful lights.

Melchi tapped her arm and shook his head, slow-like. Mari raised a hand to stop him and then searched the area one last time. Three flashlights swept through the trees about fifty yards to their right. Two more were coming from up ahead. They were heading straight for them.

She and Melchi could take to the trees, but the helicopters would see them. If they moved to the left, they might run into the lurkers.

She sighed and jerked her thumb over her shoulder. Then, popping onto her feet, she zigzagged back through the overgrown forest, running at a low crouch. When they'd gone about a mile, she leaped over an enormous fallen tree and ducked down to press her back against its trunk.

A thud sounded to her right, and suddenly Melchi was beside her. "There are too many of them," he whispered between breaths. "We need to circle around . . . Search from the other side."

Mari shook her head and tried to quiet her racing thoughts. "I don't think he's here."

"You can't know that. There are too many mulo. Their voices may be drowning him out."

"If they brought him here, why are they still searching?" Mari turned and peeped over the fallen tree. The helicopters were moving in a slow circle, playing their searchlights back and forth through the trees. "This feels like normal searching. If he'd escaped, they'd be stirred up like cuckoo bees."

"But you said Jazz was taken in this direction."

"He was moving this way, but what if he left on his own accord? He could have been looking for his inheritance."

"You think he figured out the Ruth passage?"

"Or maybe he figured out the trick with the shovel and board. He could be there right now." She did a quick scan of the area and rose to her feet. Then she was running, with Melchi crashing and clomping close behind. They leaped and dodged and ducked their way back to the open road. Their car was a silent shadow in the distance. Nothing seemed to be moving. The whole clearing was hold-your-breath quiet.

Melchi stepped ahead of her, waving his arms wildly as he inched toward the car. He tapped lightly on the window before flinging open the doors. Mari slid into the back seat as he climbed into the front.

"Where's Jazz?" A shadow rose up from the seat and settled behind the steering wheel. Hailey. "Is he . . . didn't you find him?"

"We need to get out of here." Melchi said in a hoarse whisper. "No headlights."

Hailey started the car and pulled it around in a quick U-turn. "What happened? Did they see you?"

"Not yet." Mari leaned over the two front seats. "We don't think Jazz is here. He's probably hunting his inheritance."

Hailey glanced over at Melchi.

"It makes sense," he said after a pause. "They're searching the woods, but they seem tired, like they've been at it all day. If Jazz had escaped, there'd be a lot more energy."

"So if Jazz isn't here, where is he?"

"I think he might be back at the big black car," Mari said. "It's the right direction, and he might have needed the shovel and board."

"Or he could have come back here." Hailey guided the car around the dark curve. "If he's searching for the treasure, he might have gone back to the swamp on his own. Maybe they sensed his presence and are still trying to catch him."

A pain pierced Mari's chest. She hadn't thought of that. What if Jaazaniah was hiding out in the woods while the Badness was closing in all around him? He wouldn't be able to shield himself for long—especially if he was staying in one place. "Maybe we should go back. If he's there . . ."

"I think you were right the first time." Melchi looked back over the seat. "If Jazz was there, we would have felt him. I say we go back to the limo and check to see if the shovel is still there."

Mari wasn't so sure. To be wrong now . . . it was unthinkable. They had to find him fast. Every heartbeat was precious. They might not have many left.

"Think it's safe to turn the lights on?" Hailey's voice made Mari jump. "If we're going to try to catch up with Jazz, we have to move."

Mari turned and looked out the back window. "Purodad always said, 'When in doubt take the bold path. We can only know what the good Lord has given us to know. The rest is up to Him.'"

A click sounded in front of her and the road lit up with blinding light. Mari slumped back in her seat as the car leaped forward with a throaty purr. Vague trees raced past them in a blur of ghostly motion. Bold steps . . . What if she was chasing after fear instead of faith? If Jaazaniah had gone back to find the shovel, why hadn't she felt him while she was running on the road? If he wasn't back at the swamp, why was the Badness searching so hard?

The further they went, the more the ache in her chest grew. Jaazaniah wouldn't have gone without telling them. He would have at least said good-bye.

But her hand was on the plow now. She couldn't look back until she'd gotten to the end of the row. The car slowed and turned onto a narrow dirt road. They bounced and shimmied and swerved down the narrow lane, plowing through the darkness with their lights. A distant sparkle grew to the size of their old black car. It stood off to the wayside, silent and still as the grave. Everything looked just the same as when they'd left it.

Mari jumped out of the car as it rolled to a grinding stop. Running out into the woods, she felt her way to the spot she'd seen Jaazaniah hide the shovel. She dropped onto her knees and felt through the fallen leaves. It wasn't there! Jaazaniah had come back for it. He wasn't at the swamp after all!

A metallic squawk sounded from the cars. A beam of light swept through the trees. Melchi and Hailey were carrying a hand torch.

"Over here!" Mari called out. "Jaazaniah came back and got them."

The beam hit Mari in the face, filling her eyes with bubbles of streaking light. She raised a hand to her eyes and turned away. As she sat there blinking at the ground, a white bar caught her eye. The handle of the shovel?

Her heart seized up as she stumbled over to the base of a bent dark tree. She dug through the leaves with numb fingers, uncovering both the shovel and the round board. Had Jaazaniah moved them? Why would he have done that? But hadn't he hidden them at the base of the other tree?

"What did you find?" Melchi jogged up behind her and shined the light down on the handle of the shovel. "I thought you said he'd taken them."

"Maybe he moved them?" Mari climbed onto her feet and stepped back, looking back and forth between the two trees. "Didn't he hide them over there?"

Melchi ran the hand torch up and down the first tree and then swung it back to the second one. "I don't know. They both look the same to me. Are you sure?"

She studied the two trees and shrugged. "I went right to the other one. I couldn't even see it. But I . . . don't know. Maybe."

"Look at this!" Hailey stooped down to pick up the partially covered shovel. "See?" She held the handle up to the light. "It's the Ruth clue! Jazz is going where his grandfather went. It's so obvious. I can't believe we didn't think of it before."

"Think of what?" Melchi traced the length of the shovel with his light, but Hailey grabbed his hand and pointed the beam back at the handle.

"See the price tag? It says R&M. That's got to be the name of the hardware store."

"I don't understand," Melchi said. "Why do we care about the hardware store?"

"Because we know Jazz's grandfather went there. Remember the Ruth clue? It's the only place we know his grandfather went. I bet Jazz is at the hardware store right now."

R&M. $24.68. Mari studied the tiny white tag and shook her head. "Purodad said there are thousands of cities and every one of them is filled to bursting with stores. How will Jaazaniah find the right one?"

"Not called R&M, there aren't. Not close by." Hailey pulled a strange flat box from her pocket and opened it up. Bright blue light shined out from the inside of the lid. It was a tiny hand torch.

She poked the light with her finger and lifted it to the side of her face to shine inside her ear. "Hey Boggs, this is Hailey," she spoke the words aloud and turned to face the cars. "Yeah, we found him, but then we kind of lost him again. We think he went to a hardware store—somewhere to the west of New Orleans. It's called R&M—or at least those are its initials. Could you look it up and tell us how to find it?"

Mari turned to Melchi. He didn't even seem to be paying attention. He was peeling the price tag off the handle as if Hailey's behavior was perfectly normal. "What's she doing?" she hissed. "Who's she talking to?"

"It's okay. It's just Boggs. She's a friend of ours. She won't tell anyone else."

"Boggs?" Mari looked out into the darkness. Hailey was still talking, but she could barely see her. Apparently she'd turned her torch off.

Melchi stood up and flashed his light over at Hailey. Mari angled to the side to see around her. Nobody else was there.

Melchi started laughing. "It's a cell phone. It's like a telephone with no wires. Hailey is talking to our friend back in California."

Was he joking her? She could feel the blood flowing into her face. She knew about telephones, but this was impossible. How could Hailey talk to someone who wasn't there?

Hailey turned suddenly and walked back to where they were standing. "You're not going to believe this! The hardware store is two blocks from where we bought the car."

"You already know this?" Mari breathed. "How is it possible?" She looked over at Melchi, but he was carrying the shovel back to the car.

She stood rooted in place as the halo of light bobbed further away from her. It was all so easy. Too easy. Had she made the wrong choice? Where was her faith?

"Are you coming?" Melchi's voice broke through the thoughts clogging up her head. "We must hurry if we want to catch up with Jazz. It's getting late."

Mari took a deep breath and let it out slowly. "I'm coming, but . . ." She shook her head and climbed inside. It wasn't her place to question. She wasn't called to understand. Only to stand.

And having done everything to stand, to stand firm.

Jazz

JAZZ LACED HIS FINGERS over his head and sank onto his knees. The gun stared him right in the face. He could feel it trembling with the man's pent-up tension.

"Don't shoot," he finally managed to stammer. "I . . . I haven't done anything wrong. I've never touched a weapon in my life."

"Face down on the ground!" the man barked. "Nice and slow. Hands out where I can see them."

Jazz crumpled onto the warm asphalt, stretching out his arms and legs.

Hoarse breathing sounded above his head as a rough hand patted him down. The guy sounded nervous. Jumpy. One false move and he'd never even hear the bang.

"Look, I know you're just doing your job"—Jazz grasped at the first straw he could think of—"but whoever you work for isn't on the level. I don't know what you think I've done, but I haven't done anything wrong. I swear. Someone high up in your organization is after something I inherited. If you take me to jail, I'll be dead in five minutes."

"Keep your hands above your head and roll over," the agent growled. "Flat on your back. You so much as hiccough, and I blow your head off. Got that?"

"You're not listening—"

"Do. You. Understand?"

"Yes. I understand." Jazz rolled onto his back and stared up into the muzzle of the gun.

The man reached in with one hand and patted him down in quick staccato bursts. Jazz gritted his teeth and focused on not moving. After the man had poked and prodded more tender spots than Jazz even knew he had, he started going through Jazz's pockets.

"Look, I want to find out what's going on as much as you do. I'll tell you everything. We can help each other, okay?"

The man turned out his pockets and kept on searching.

"I'm just a middle-school-drop-out musician. I've skipped town a couple of times when I didn't have enough money to pay rent, but that's it. That's all I've done wrong. It doesn't amount to more than a couple hundred dollars. Since when does the FBI send out attack helicopters for guys like me? I'm nobody."

The guy patted him down again. An invitation for him to keep talking?

"This is all I know, okay? It started when I passed out at the Hookah Club where I was performing. Right in the middle of a song. Bam. I was out like someone drugged me. They sent me home early, but when I got back to my apartment, somebody had searched through all of my stuff. I don't know what they were looking for, but I got a strange will in the mail. You know. A last will and testament from my grandfather—which I thought was kind of strange, because my father told me my grandfather died when I was a boy. Anyway, I'm freaking out in my room, when I see a bunch of men in black cloaks climbing up the outside wall. I know what it sounds like, but it's the gospel truth. Why would I make something like that up?" He looked up and waited for the agent to say something. Why wasn't he talking? Did he believe him or not?

"I jumped out the window and managed to get away. Okay? There was this rich girl I'd met at the club and she had my guitar . . ." He paused to explain, but the guy glared at him. "Anyway, long story short, I talked her into taking me in. Then the next morning, after we opened up my mail and discovered my grandfather's will, she took me to the police station. I'm in the office, reporting what happened, when all of a sudden this guy in a suit walks in and starts yelling at everyone to arrest me. I freak out and just start running—"

"What did the man look like?"

Jazz flinched at the anger in his voice. "Which man? The police officer or the guy in the suit?"

"The guy in the suit. What did he look like?"

"I don't know. Dark hair, dark eyes. Too young to be the boss. He had a nose on him like—"

"What about the agent who brought you into the station? What did he look like?"

"What agent? I went to the police station of my own free will. Which is another thing. Why would I go to the police if I had done something wrong? The rich girl drove me there. She can back up my story. Why would I have gone to the police?"

"According to the reports, you were brought in for questioning by Agent Scott Mallet. There was a whole station full of witnesses. You sure you don't want to change your story?"

"That's a lie!" Jazz started to sit up, but the gun stabbed into his face, pinning him back against the asphalt. "I went to the police on my own accord. The rich girl drove me there. Her name is Hollis Duke. You can ask her yourself. I'm supposed to meet her at the park right now. That's where I was going before you . . . caught me."

"So you're saying the FBI's official report is a lie?" The agent's voice was incredulous. "I've got a whole station full of witnesses that say different."

"Ask them yourself!" Jazz came dangerously close to shouting. "Can't all of them be dirty. There was a white-haired police officer. He'll tell you. I came in with Hollis—a pretty blonde girl—"

"Shut up! I've heard enough." He pulled a phone from his pocket and flipped it open. Keeping the gun leveled at Jazz, he punched a few buttons with his trigger finger.

"Come on!" Jazz shouted. "The girl's only a few minutes away. She'll be leaving town in the morning. You don't want to—"

The agent pressed the gun against Jazz's forehead and raised the phone to his ear. "Hello, Katie, this is Groves. I need you to do me a favor . . . Tell Chevalier I've got Jaazaniah Rechabson, and I'm bringing him in."

∽ 26 ∾

Mariutza

MARI LEANED HER HEAD back on the padded seat. The car was moving so fast it made her dizzy. Everything was moving fast. The path had so many turns and twists, she barely had time to think. She needed to slow down and pray. If only Purodad hadn't—

She pressed her hands to her eyes. *No ifs.* Looking back made for crooked rows. She forced herself to sit up straight and tried to clear her head. They were in a town now. Houses were running past the car windows, like dogs on a hunt.

"I know I'm being stupid, but tell me again how your friend can see all the way out here from California?"

"She didn't see the real hardware store. Just a picture." Hailey turned the car right onto another road. "She has this thing called the Internet. It's like a giant book with information about every store in the country. That's how she knows it's here."

"And you're not stupid." Melchi turned in his seat. "This is a lot to take in all at once. You're doing remarkably well."

"I don't *feel* remarkably well. What if he's not there? What if he went to the swamp after all?"

"Then we'll keep looking for him." Melchi's voice was steady and low, a promise she could count on. "But even if he's not here, it doesn't mean he went to the swamp. He might be following a clue we don't even know about yet. There are a lot more—"

"This is it!" Hailey turned the car onto a large square road that ended at a building with huge glassed-in windows lined up in a row across the front. A sign like a big red torch said *R&M Hardware*.

Hailey stopped the car and Mari jumped out. She ran across the road to the front of the store where a man in a blue and red shirt was jangling a loop of metal strips hanging out of what looked like a solid glass door.

"Sorry, but we're closed," the man said without turning around. "Hours are 10 a.m. to 9 p.m., Monday through Friday, Saturday 9 to 5:30."

"Hello, I—" Mari bobbed out a quick curtsey. "Did you . . . Did a man named Jaazaniah come here tonight? He's looking to find out where his grandfather went three nights ago. It's very important."

"Sorry." The man turned to look at Mari and his eyes went wide. He stared at her for a long time—like he was looking at a mulani. "What's that you said again?"

"Did a man named Jaazaniah come here tonight? He's wearing a ragged brown shirt and has a very beautiful face and kind eyes. He's trying to find out where his grandfather went, and we thought he might have come here."

"Nope. Haven't seen anybody like that. Not tonight." The man turned suddenly toward the road. Melchi and Hailey were walking across the pavement carrying the shovel and board.

The man stepped back a half step. "Sorry, we're closed. We'll be open tomorrow morning at ten."

"We're with her." Melchi nodded at Mari. "We just need to ask you a few questions."

"I already told her—" The man's eyes locked on Hailey. His face contorted into a scowl. "Where'd you get that? It doesn't belong to you."

"What, the board?" Hailey stepped forward and held out the round piece of wood. "What do you know about it? Do you remember who you sold it to?"

The man looked up at Melchi and inched closer to the door.

"It's all right," Melchi soothed. "We're friends. The man you sold this board to was murdered, and the killers are after his grandson. We're trying to help him."

The man's eyes narrowed. He aimed a quick look at Mari and then looked back up at Melchi. "You work for the police?"

"No, we're just friends. Mari is the old man's granddaughter. His name was Jonah Rechabson. He was a very special man."

"He was a great prophet," Mari said. "And his grandson, Jaazaniah, is a great prophet too. We need very much to find him."

"A prophet, eh?" The man's voice rang with derision, but he seemed a bit more relaxed. "What makes you say that?"

"My grandfather was a healer and an interpreter of dreams. The Lord spoke to him in many special ways." She stepped slowly toward the man and put a hand on his arm. "Did you know him when he was alive?"

"You say you're his granddaughter? You don't look like him."

Mari's throat tightened. Her eyes were beginning to sting. "He called me granddaughter, but I wasn't blood. He took me in and cared after me when I was a little baby. Jaazaniah is his blood. I'm just . . ." She looked down, blinking back the stinging tears.

"He came here Friday night." The man's voice was soft now. "He bought a shovel, a storage bin, a tube of caulk, and some duct tape."

"Was the storage bin made of blue plastic?" Hailey asked.

The man nodded. "He was nervous. Kinda excited. Wanted to make sure the bin would be watertight. Kept saying he was burying a treasure and he didn't want it to get wet."

"What about the board?" Hailey held it out again for him to see. "Did he buy it here too?"

"Hold your horses. I'm getting to that." He glared at Hailey and turned back to Mari, his smile apologetic. "When I was young, I was in the construction business. You wouldn't know it to see me now, but I was strong as an ox. Muscles out to here." He held a rounded hand four full inches from his biceps. "Problem was, my muscles were a lot stronger than my backbone. Doctors said I had three compressed disks. One of them was so flat, it was pinching off my spinal cord, choking it down to half the size. Pain shooting down both legs. I could barely walk. Needed help just to get out of a chair." The old man paused to look at Mari with a shy half smile. "You know what's coming next, don't you, girl?"

Mari returned the smile. She'd heard millions of stories, but she never tired of hearing them. They were her grandfather's legacy. Living monuments to his love.

"I was scheduled for surgery August twenty-first. It has to get pretty bad for an insurance company to admit something's wrong. You know that, don't you?"

Mari nodded. She didn't know what an insurance company was, but Miss Caralee always said it wasn't a lie if only one answer was called for.

"Well, your grandfather, after he paid for his stuff, he tells me my back is sore and asks if it was okay if he prayed for me. I said it was, and he just launches into it—out loud, with other

customers standing in line behind him. Didn't even close his
eyes." He turned and looked at Melchi and Hailey. "Three seconds
after he starts, my back starts getting real hot—not a bad kind
of hot, but a good kind, like having BENGAY slathered on real
thick. And then, when he stops talking, the heat fades away. And
then nothing. No pain at all. Not even a twinge.

"I'm so surprised, I start bending over and standing up
straight and hopping up and down. The other customers look at
me like I'm crazy. One of them gets mad, and I tell him the line's
closed and send them all to Jessie-Lynne at the other register.
Then I sit down with Jonah and we talk for a long time. That's
when he tells me about this board. Wouldn't say what he needed
it for, but I got the idea it was real important to him. When he
gave me the measurements, his eyes got all teared-up and he had
to catch his breath a spell before starting over and saying everything again."

"Did he say anything about writing on it or covering it with
mud?" Hailey asked.

"Just that it had to be wider than his shoulders. That's all he
would say."

Mari nodded solemnly. She had been right all along. Purodad
left it as a guide to dig the hole. But where did the mud come
from? That's the bone that stuck in her craw. "Do you know where
he went after you gave him the board?"

The man looked at her a long time and then let out a sigh.
"He needed a ride into the city, so I took off early and drove him
there myself."

"Where?" Mari stepped closer. "Where did he go? Did he say
what he needed to do there?"

"No, but he took the stuff he bought with him. Plus he had a
big cloth bag filled with something heavy. I didn't ask him what
was in it, but I could tell it was important to him. He held it all

clutched up close to his chest whenever he sat down—like he was loving on a baby."

"So where did you drop him off?" Melchi moved to stand behind Mari. "Do you remember the address?"

"Tricou Road—about half a block from St. Jardin. He didn't say why he needed to go, so I didn't ask."

"Thank you." Melchi took the man's hand in his huge paw. "This helps a lot. We really appreciate it."

"You're welcome, I guess." The man freed his hand and stared at Mari again. His hand came up and reached toward her hair, then jerked back down. "Your name is Mariutza, isn't it?"

Mari's heart froze in her chest. She managed a faltering nod.

"Mariutza, I'm pleased to meet you." He reached out and took her by the hand. "Your grandfather was quite a man. I thought it strange at the time, but he said if I should ever meet you in person, I should be sure and tell you something." He squeezed her hand and lowered his eyes. "It's not an easy thing to say."

"What?" Tears filled Mari's eyes. She already knew what it was. He'd said it himself right before he died. "It's okay. I can bear it. What did he say?"

"He told me to be sure and tell you he loved you—more than life itself. He said he would always love you. Even to the end of the age."

Jazz

JAZZ PAUSED BEHIND A clump of trees at the edge of the dimly lit park. He could just make out Hollis sitting on a bench beside a dark hedge. She checked her watch and looked impatiently around the park. She was going to freak out when she saw Groves's gun. He had to think of something to calm her down. Some kind of diversion. Maybe the agent would be willing to—

"Move." Groves's jabbed the gun into his backbone, shoving him through the trees.

Hollis turned and her eyes went wide. She leaped onto her feet and started to run.

"FBI!" Groves shouted. "Don't make me shoot!"

Hollis shuddered to a stop and jerked her hands into the air. Groves grabbed a handful of Jazz's shirt and thrust him forward. The gun was pointed at Hollis now. She was tottering on her feet, gasping like an asthmatic fish on dry land.

Jazz tried to catch her eye. "Sorry, Hollis. I tried to—"

"Shut up! No talking unless I ask a question. Got it?" The agent gave Jazz's shirt a shake. "Got it?"

"Got it!" Jazz looked back helplessly at Hollis. *Sorry.* He mouthed the word, but she wasn't paying attention. Her eyes were locked on the gun.

"Okay, Miss. I'm going to ask you a few questions, and I want you to answer immediately. Understood?"

Her head waggled up and down.

"Understood?" he lifted the gun to her face.

"Yes, sir." The words broke through a tide of gasping sobs.

"Good. The first question's an easy one. What's your name?"

"H-Hollis Duke."

"See, Hollis? That wasn't so bad." Groves lowered the gun until it was pointing at her feet. "Just tell the truth, and you can be on your way in no time. Okay?"

Hollis nodded vigorously.

"Good. So what did you do Saturday morning?"

"Saturday morning?" She looked at Jazz.

"Don't look at him." Groves yanked Jazz around to point him away from the girl. "I want you to tell me in your own words what you did Saturday. Don't lie to me. I'll know if you're lying."

"I was at the Ritz-Carlton. He said a bunch of men in black hoods ransacked his apartment and attacked him. He was bleeding, but he was afraid to go to the hospital. What was I supposed to do? I couldn't just leave him."

"It's okay. You didn't do anything wrong. I just need you to tell me the truth. What happened next?"

"He had this letter. It was supposed to be his grandfather's will. I thought he was trying to con me."

"So you threw him out?"

"I should have, but I wasn't sure if it was a con or not. And it was kind of, I don't know . . . exciting. He convinced me to take him to the police station. Everything was fine at first. There was this nice policeman named Mr. Cedric who took us to his desk and started asking Jazz questions, but then this angry guy in a department-store suit came up and started yelling. Everybody started fighting each other, and Jazz crawled under a desk and vanished. They kept me at the police station all afternoon asking me questions. Like they blamed me for what happened. I told them I didn't know him, but they didn't believe me. They kept asking me the same questions over and over. I'd probably still be there if I hadn't threatened them with my father's lawyers."

There was a long silence. Jazz turned and watched Groves out of the corner of his eye. He was just standing there, mumbling to himself. He looked furious.

"And where were you the night before? Between 11 p.m. and 2 a.m.?"

"Nowhere. Just hanging out at some clubs with my friend. He can tell you." She nodded at Jazz. "We were at the Hookah Club most of that time. He was playing. He's—"

"Listen to me! Both of you!" Groves swung Jazz around to face him. "In about ten minutes this place is going to be crawling with federal agents. I can help you, but I need you to trust me. Okay?"

Jazz was too stunned to react. Did Groves believe their story, or was this some kind of a trap?

"Your choice, but if you value your life you'd better follow me." Groves took something out of his pocket and tossed it into the hedge. Then, holstering his gun, he turned and started jogging across the park.

Jazz exchanged glances with Hollis and then started running. He caught up with Groves at the edge of the park. Hollis was only a few yards behind. Her breath was coming in short, mewling gasps. If they had to run more than a few blocks, she wasn't going to make it. Where was he taking them anyway?

"This way!" Groves cut down a dark narrow street and slowed to a quick walk. At the end of the block he raised a hand before stopping and peering carefully around the corner. "Okay. We gotta move." He turned to the left and started running again.

The wail of distant sirens drifted through the city. They seemed to be coming from behind them. Jazz shot Hollis an encouraging look and took off after Groves. They zigzagged up one block and down another in what seemed to be a random pattern until Jazz noticed they were coming up on the backside of the Ritz-Carlton. Just when he thought they were going to lose Hollis for good, Groves stopped at a white minivan and pulled out a set of keys. "Get in." He frowned. "Where's the girl?"

"She's coming." Jazz pulled back on the door and climbed inside. "I saw her at the last turn. She was only half a block behind us."

Groves climbed behind the wheel and flipped a switch between the seats. An urgent voice sounded through a burst of static. More voices. They were looking for Groves. The agent started the engine and the van lurched forward.

"Wait!" Jazz poked his head through the door. Hollis was hobbling up the sidewalk at a slow, limping jog. "I see her." He leaned out the door and waved. The sirens were getting louder. One of them was coming their way.

Hollis jogged over to the van and collapsed onto the floor in front of the seats. "Go!" Jazz yanked on the door as Groves gunned the engine. They shot forward onto the street and took a hard right at the next intersection.

Hollis climbed over an infant car seat and strapped herself in next to the window as the van sped down one street after another. Finally, after what seemed an eternity of furious driving, Groves switched off the radio and pulled over to the side of the road. Jazz looked out the window and tried to get his bearings. They were in one of the residential neighborhoods, but he had no idea which one.

"Okay . . ." Groves swiveled in his seat to face them. "We need to talk. What do you know about the killings in the woods?"

"Nothing," Jazz said.

Groves shot him a look.

"Seriously! Nothing!" Jazz looked to Hollis for corroboration. "I was playing at the Hookah Club. You can ask Hollis!"

"If you don't know anything, how do you know when it happened?"

The question was a low growl. Clearly this guy wasn't liking what he was hearing. But Groves would think he was crazy if he started squawking about visions. Or worse, he'd think he was lying. "I know a girl who was there when it happened," he finally said. "Her name is Mariutza. She lived with my grandfather out in the swamps—in some sort of a Gypsy wagon." He took a breath and waited for Groves to interject, but the agent just nodded for him to continue. "She says my grandfather was hunted down and shot by ten men in black cloaks. They formed a circle around him and shot him in some kind of cultic ritual. There was a flash of bright light and thunder. She didn't know what caused it, but apparently it killed them where they stood. They were all dead in the morning when she went back to look."

Groves's face lit up like a Christmas tree. "So were there ten men in all, or were there nine men plus your grandfather?"

Jazz didn't hesitate. "Eleven men total. Ten hooded men plus my grandfather."

"You're sure? How do you know she didn't miscount?"

"I just know, okay? She didn't miscount. There were ten men—evenly spaced in a circle."

"Okay . . . I'm trusting you on this." Groves swung back around and started up the car. "But if you're wrong, I'm taking you in. Don't pass Go. Don't collect two hundred dollars." He pulled the car out onto the road and sped through the quiet neighborhood.

"I'm not lying." Jazz leaned forward in his seat. "Where are you taking us? I'm telling the truth!"

"Just a quick stop to check out your story." Groves turned right onto a main road. "If everything checks out, we may have a few decisions to make." He took a left at the next intersection. He seemed to be heading for the highway.

"We can't go back to the swamp," Jazz said. "They'll be looking for us there."

"We're not going to the swamp. We're going to visit a widow I happen to know about. Seems her husband died of a heart attack about the same time your grandfather was getting shot up in the swamp."

"So?"

"So something's not right. You say there were ten hooded men, but our team leader says there were nine. I want to know why."

Jazz looked over at Hollis and answered her puzzled look with a shrug. He didn't have a clue what the agent was talking about, but at least the man was questioning his superiors. With any luck this widow would add even more fuel to the doubt smoldering in his mind.

"I don't know if this will help," Jazz said, "but something has been bothering me. Mari and I were on the run through the city when a bunch of helicopters flew overhead. She took off running and they started shooting at her. She didn't have a weapon or anything. Is that standard procedure? To gun down unarmed girls in the streets?"

Groves kept on driving. Jazz couldn't tell for sure, but the agent's expression seemed to darken. Maybe potshots in the dark weren't such a good idea. He'd gotten lucky on that one. One false step, though, and Groves might change his mind and take them both in.

Maybe silence really was golden.

They finally stopped in a working-class neighborhood on the outskirts of the city. Groves pulled a long-handled black flashlight out from under the seat and aimed it at the front door. The street number was 237. Apparently it was the right place, because he switched off the light and climbed out of the car.

Jazz started to reach for the door and then pulled back. "What do you want us to do?"

"You're coming with me. Both of you." Groves rolled the passenger door to the side and helped them out. "You're not to speak unless spoken to, understand?"

Jazz nodded. From the back of the house he could hear a dog barking nonstop.

"Remember, this woman just lost her husband. No matter what she says, her husband was a public servant who fell in the line of duty. You're to be respectful and courteous."

"He was an FBI agent?" Jazz followed Groves through a small overgrown front yard to a cement slab porch.

"A City of New Orleans police officer," Groves whispered before punching the doorbell next to the door.

Footsteps sounded inside and the porch light turned on.

A woman's wary voice called through the door, "Who is it?"

"My name is Daniel Groves, and I'm with the FBI." He held a badge up to the peephole and then flipped it over to show a photo I.D. "I have a few questions about your husband, if you don't mind. It will only take a few minutes."

Two locks snapped open and a safety chain rattled before the door swung open to reveal a middle-aged woman with graying fly-away hair. "Thank you for coming. Things have been so hectic; the house is a wreck, but . . ." She stepped back to usher them into a small, formal living room. Dog toys were scattered over the scuffed hardwood floor.

"I'm sorry it's so late, but . . . you were expecting us?" Groves followed the woman over to a floral print sofa and sat down. Jazz and Hollis seated themselves in the armchairs across the room.

"Would you like something to drink?" The woman stepped toward the door and turned suddenly around. "I'm sorry. What was it you asked?"

"It sounded like you were expecting us?" Groves smiled pleasantly.

"Yes, of course!" The woman's smile seemed a little forced. "But we're all busy these days. You can't be expected to drop everything and come running. Not with all those terrorists . . ." Her voice trailed off and her expression clouded. "Oh, yes, drinks. Is iced tea alright?" She turned and bustled from the room before they could answer. Jazz looked over at Groves as the sounds of opening cabinets and clanking ice came from the next room. Groves touched a finger to the corner of his mouth and lifted his lips into a smile.

Jazz nodded. *Respectful and courteous*—even though their hostess seemed to be playing with a broken string.

When the woman finally returned with their drinks, she appeared a little less harried. "Now then," she said as she handed the last glass to Jazz, "what did you want to know?"

Groves's voice was smooth as glass. "Well, first of all, why did you call the FBI?"

The woman crossed the room and perched on the corner of the sofa to face him. "It was Jeff. I know he sometimes seemed all rough and tumble like the other men, but inside he was just as sweet and sensitive and caring as a man could be—until a couple of weeks ago. Then, all of a sudden, he just changed. I barely knew him. He started staying out all night, drinking and swearing and getting in fights . . . He wasn't himself at all. And the way he looked at me. It was like some terrible identical twin had switched places with him. I didn't know him at all."

"And you started noticing this two weeks ago?"

"There wasn't any *started* to it. It was immediate. One night he was Jeff going off to work the night shift. The next morning he just . . . wasn't."

Groves nodded. "Did you ever hear him talk about someone named Marie Paris Glapion?"

The woman sucked in her breath. A hand fluttered to her chest. "You think he was . . . seeing another woman?"

"No, nothing like that. She's just a suspect in a case I've been working on. Have you ever heard the name?"

"I don't think so."

"Okay." Groves seemed to check something off his mental checklist. "So when did you call the FBI?"

"That's the part I was getting to. One night I woke up about two in the morning and Jeff wasn't there. I told myself he'd come back soon and tried to go back to sleep, but about two hours later the dog started barking, and I heard Jeff sneaking into the bathroom. I was worried so I got up to check on him, but when I opened the bathroom door, I saw him standing over the sink, all covered in blood. He said there'd been an accident in front of the house, that a deer had gotten hit by a car, but his clothes were torn, and he had scratches all over his face and arms. It couldn't have come from a dead deer. That's when I called your office. The very next morning, as soon as he left for work."

"And when was that?"

Groves's voice was almost a whisper. Jazz turned to study the man and frowned. Groves looked like he was going to be sick.

"Seven days ago. Just four days before he died." She caught at the bottom corner of her blouse with both hands and started folding it into tight pleats. "What happened to Jeff . . . it wasn't a heart attack, was it, Mr. Groves? His strange behavior, and the blood and all that. That was the real reason he died, wasn't it?"

"I don't know, Mrs. Calder. But I'm going to find out." He nodded at Jazz and rose to his feet. "Thanks for the iced tea. I really appreciate you taking the time."

"Thank you for coming. If there's anything more I can do to help, just let me know." Her hands were shaking as she took Groves's glass.

"I've got it." Jazz took Hollis's glass and followed Mrs. Calder into the kitchen. The barking in the backyard started up the second he reached the counter. He set the glasses by the sink and glanced out the window. A black Labrador was running back and forth along the fence, barking and snarling like a rabid pit bull.

"That's Riley." Mrs. Calder's voice sounded behind him. "He's been like that since Jeff died. He misses him terribly."

"Yes, ma'am." Jazz started to turn away, but something in the shadows caught his eye. "Is there a light in the backyard?"

"Tried that, but it doesn't do any good." She walked across the room and flipped a switch, flooding the backyard with light.

For a second everything seemed normal enough. The backyard was scarred by dog runs and holes, but other than that, it was just a normal backyard. Then he noticed the back corner . . .

It was the doghouse from his dreams.

ᥱᦅ 27 ᥐᥕ

Mariutza

THE CITY LIGHTS FLASHED like a lightning storm. Hundreds of angry voices buzzed in Mari's head. The car was moving faster now. The closer they got to the city, the more insistent the voices grew. She could feel them shooting through her body, red hot sparks of malice and spite and rage. Bitterness rose up inside her like the morning tide. Jaazaniah had betrayed her. He'd abandoned her, left her for dead just like her mother.

She clutched at her chest, ran a finger down the shiny strip of numbness that was her scar. She was marimé—rejected, despised, unclean. The voices mocked her. They knew the blackness of her heart and sent dark thoughts to plague her day and night.

"Shield yourselves!" The voice was almost washed away by the roar. "Mulo are coming up fast!"

Mulo? Mari blinked her eyes and tried to focus on what Jaazaniah was saying. No, not Jaazaniah. Melchi. Jaazaniah had run off and left her. He'd told Hollis he didn't like her. She should have expected it. Why did she have to be so stupid?

"Mari!" The voice was yelling at her, but she hadn't done anything wrong. It wasn't her fault. The voices were the ones who'd said it.

"Mari! Shield yourself. Now! Clear your mind. Do you hear me?"

"Yes . . . sir?" Mari closed her eyes and searched for what to say. *Holy One, we thank Thee* . . . The words came back in a rush. She clasped them to her heart, repeating them over and over, crying out to the Lord from deep inside her soul.

"It's the police!" Hailey called out. "They're right behind us. What do I do?"

"Pull over, quick!" Melchi opened the window and the roar of rushing wind filled her ears. He was tugging on the shovel. Trying to pull the handle inside the car.

Mari turned in her seat. Flashing blue lights lit up the road behind them. A whole line of flashing cars, they were coming up fast.

Their car jerked to the side, tipping Mari off balance. The road rattled and bounced beneath them. They were slowing down, coming to a stop. A loud wail pounded against Mari's ears as the flashing blue lights roared past them.

"Keep praying!" Melchi hissed. "If they stop, we're dead."

Mari fought down a wave of panic. The voices hammered against her senses like a violent, raging sea. One breach in her wall and they would crush the life out of her. She shut her eyes and focused on her Maker, letting the rhythm of her prayers fill her mind. The Holy One would protect her. She had nothing to fear. His promises were a guarantee.

The storm gradually receded, leaving her feeling weak and hollow inside. When the voices finally subsided to a distant murmur, she opened her eyes and looked around. Melchi and Hailey were both slumped forward in their seats. They weren't moving.

"Are you okay?" She reached over the seat and touched their arms. "Hailey? Melchi?"

Hailey sighed and looked back at Mari with a weary smile. "That was close."

Melchi nodded and looked up. "I tried to count, but I couldn't separate them. How many do you think there were?"

"I don't know," Mari said. "They were too strong. I didn't know the Badness could be so powerful."

"They aren't normal mulos." Melchi looked over at Hailey. "They were something else. Something far worse. As soon as there's a break in the traffic, I think we should lay low for a while. For all we know, they could be on their way to Tricou Road. We can't risk letting them get so close. If they hadn't been in such a hurry, they would have found us."

"But what about Jaazaniah?" Mari fought to keep her voice steady. "What if he's the hurry they were rushing off to?"

"There are too many of them. We won't be of help to anyone if they catch us."

"We have to at least try!" Mari turned to Hailey. "Please. What if they're going someplace else? We're supposed to go to Tricou Road. You heard the man at the store."

Hailey didn't say anything for a long time. Finally she sighed and shook her head. "I think Melchi is right. There's no guarantee Jazz will even be there. It might be a wild goose chase."

"But Purodad left me a message. That means he expected me to go to the store. And he'll expect me to go to Tricou Road lickety-click. He wouldn't send me there for no reason."

"But the man said there wasn't anything there."

She had to make them understand. For Purodad. For Jazz. She had to stand firm. "There *has* to be something. Something only a Standing could see. Purodad never did anything without a reason. He wouldn't leave a message that went to nowhere. We have to follow it."

Hailey looked over at Melchi. "What do you think?"

"Please." Mari made the blinking eyes at Melchi. Purodad always gave in to the blinking eyes.

"Okay . . ." He didn't sound so sure. "But we're not going anywhere close to those mulo. If they're on Tricou Road, we leave town and don't come back—not until things have had a chance to cool down. Okay?"

Mari nodded. "The shimulo won't be at Tricou Road. They don't even know about it. Purodad would have made sure of that."

Hailey moved a lever, and the car started rolling forward. Mari looked out the window and lost herself in the endless flow of buildings and lights. So many houses. How would she ever recognize the right one? Or maybe it wasn't a house. It could be a tree with a hollow or maybe a stand of one of Purodad's favorite flowers. He loved pipeworts and pigeonwings, but could he hide an inheritance in a flower? She didn't even know what it was.

The car turned down road after road after road. Twice Hailey had to stop and talk to her hand torch to find out where to turn, but finally she found the right street.

"Okay, this is it." Hailey drove slowly down a dark road surrounded on both sides by the smallest houses they'd seen so far. "Let me know if you see something. We should be about two blocks from the intersection."

"Go slower!" Mari slid from one side of the car to the other to look out at the trees and houses rushing by. There was an old tree in front of one house, but it didn't look particularly familiar. Several houses had flowers—some of them were huge—but she didn't recognize any of them. How could city plants be so different from swamp plants?

The car stopped in front of a row of white-painted boards. "Did you see something?" She looked up at Hailey when the rumble of the engine died to nothing.

"We're here," Hailey said. "This is where the guy dropped off your grandfather."

Melchi got out of the car and held the door open for Mari. The boards next to the path were old and some of the paint was peeling off, but they didn't look anything like the diddlecar or Miss Caralee's shack. Still . . .

She turned in a slow circle to survey the area. "Maybe we'll see it if we walk a spell. It could be hiding from our eyes."

"Maybe." Melchi gripped the shovel like a staff and walked down the path, looking from side to side at the houses. Were there city folk hiding inside of them? What would they do if some of the city folk came out?

They hadn't walked more than two-score yards when she heard the voices. "Someone's coming. What do we do?" She searched the sides of the path for a hiding place. There were bushes to the right, but they were too close to the house.

"It's okay," Hailey spoke in a soft voice. "It's just someone walking a dog. Melchi, lose the shovel or you'll scare them."

Melchi tossed the shovel into some tall grass and stepped in front of the women. Mari could feel his tension deep inside her throat. "What do we do? What if they talk to us?"

"Just act natural. We're not doing anything wrong. We're just going for a walk."

Mari took a deep breath and tried to imitate the casual way Hailey swung her feet and arms, but she couldn't get it right. The folks would know she wasn't from the city. They'd be able to smell her fear.

"Hi," Hailey called out as the city folks got closer. It was a man and a woman with a big dog tied to a rope.

"Hey." It was the woman who answered. The man just nodded and stared. He was looking at Mari's clothes. He knew!

Mari moved closer to Melchi and tried to catch his eye, but he wasn't looking. The city folks were behind them now. What if they told the police?

Finally, after they'd walked another couple score yards, Mari found her voice. "They know. My clothes gave me away. They know I'm not from the city!"

"It's okay." Hailey started laughing. "Relax. We're not doing anything wrong. If they thought anything at all, they were thinking how pretty you are. I know the guy was. I could see it in his eyes."

He thought she was . . . Mari's face burned so hot, she could feel the fire prickling at her skin. "I should wait in the car. I'm not right for this. I'm only causing trouble."

"You're doing fine," Hailey said. "There's a store up here at the corner. Let's check it out."

Mari followed Melchi and Hailey across the road. The building they were walking to didn't look like the hardware store at all. The door faced the coming together of the two streets, but aside from that, it didn't look any different from the other houses.

She hung back as they walked right up to the building and started reading the signs on the door.

A blob of movement caught her eye. She stared into the shadows at the base of a big building. One of the city folks was sleeping in the shelter of the doorway. He was wrapped in a black blanket. Was he one of the Standing? She reached out with the sight. There was a flicker of something, but it didn't feel like a Standing. It didn't feel like anything at all.

"Hello." A slurred voice came from the shadows.

"Hello." Mari bobbed in a shallow curtsey. "My name is Mariutza. How are you?"

"Wilmer Salley." The shadow scooted forward to reveal a man's bearded face. "My name is Wilmer Salley. Who are you?"

Wilmer Salley! Mari gasped. It was the name from the will! She stepped forward and curtseyed again. "I am Mariutza." She fought to keep the trembles from her voice. "Do you know my grandfather?"

Footsteps sounded behind her. The man shrank into the shadows as Hailey and Melchi appeared at Mari's side.

"It's okay, Wilmer. Don't be scared," she whispered. "This is Hailey and Melchi. They're my friends."

The man huddled beneath the dark blanket. She could barely see the light glinting in his eyes. Mari made her voice soft and warm like Miss Caralee during story time. "My grandfather was Jonadab Rechabson. He came here just a few days ago. Did you see him?"

The eyes moved up and down.

"He had a blue plastic box. Did my grandfather tell you where he hid it?"

The man inched forward into the light. His head was shaking and he had a big smile on his face. "Grandfather bought a letter from the store. I wrote my name on it, and he gave me ten dollars."

"He bought a letter from the store?" Hailey crouched down and eased forward. "Did you see what he did with the letter?"

The man nodded even more vigorously. "He bought a letter from the store and I got to sign my name on it. Mr. Don put three stamps on it and mailed it as a letter. I got a chicka-salley and a orange Coke. And at the morning I got more chicka-salley, but you can't drink orange Coke in the morning. No, no . . . It's not good at the morning."

"Was my grandfather carrying a blue plastic box? Or a shovel?"

The old man shook his head. "Just a chicka-salley sandwich and a orange Coke. He didn't have nothing else."

They asked him question after question, but he didn't seem to know anything about the blue box or the shovel or even the round board. Frustration pinched at Mari's mind. Why would Purodad come all the way to the city to write a letter? It didn't make sense.

"One more question." Mari sat down on the door step next to the man and unhooked a gold coin from her necklace. "If you think real hard, I'll give you a gold coin to buy lots of orange Cokes. Okay?"

The man nodded and reached for the coin.

"Try to remember first." Mari held it out to the light so he could see it. "Do you know where my grandfather went after he mailed the letter? Did he say where he was going?"

The man screwed his face into a contorted frown and nodded furiously.

"Where was he going? What did he say?"

"He said Mr. Don was going to mail his letter."

"And that's all? Did he say where he was going after he mailed the letter?"

"It was running right late. I reckon he was going off to bed."

Hailey sighed and looked over at Mari. She didn't say it out loud, but Mari knew she was right.

They'd hit another dead end.

❦ 28 ❧

Jazz

JAZZ STARED OUT INTO the backyard, trying to make sense of what he was seeing. Had there been a connection between his grandfather and the police? It didn't make sense. If his grandfather was working with the police, why were they trying to kill Mari?

"Thanks, Mrs. Calder." Groves's voice carried into the kitchen. "We appreciate you taking the time to talk to us. I know this has been a terrible ordeal for you and your family. I'm sorry for your loss."

Jazz turned and walked back to the living room where Hollis and Groves were standing with Mrs. Calder at the door.

"I'm just happy I could help." The woman was looking up at Groves with a pinched little smile. "I was beginning to think the department didn't believe me."

Groves opened the door and stepped out onto the porch. "No, ma'am. We're taking your story very seriously. I'm handling the case, so if you think of anything else, call me directly. Don't talk to anyone else." He handed her a white card with a blue seal and followed Hollis out onto the front porch.

"Mrs. Calder?" Jazz turned in the doorway. "Did you or your husband know a man named Jonah Rechabson?"

323

A hand closed like a vise around Jazz's upper arm. He tried to keep his face composed as he was dragged out onto the porch.

"Jonah Rechabson, you say?" The woman's features gathered into a squinty frown. "That's a new one on me. I'm not so good with faces, but I never forget a name."

"A crazy old Gypsy gentleman who lived out in the swamps? Did your husband ever mention someone like that?"

"I'm sorry, but we have to go." Groves pulled Jazz toward the porch steps. "Thank you, Mrs. Calder. Let me know if you think of anything else."

"Okay, I will," the woman called from the doorway. "And I've never heard of any old men living out in the swamps, Gypsy or otherwise."

"Thanks, Mrs. Calder." Jazz turned to wave, but he was jerked around and shoved toward the minivan. He barely managed to stay on his feet as Groves dragged him to the car and flung open the door.

"What was that?" Groves spat out the words. "What did you think you were doing back there?"

"I saw something . . . in the backyard. I just wanted to find out—"

"I told you not to say anything." Groves slammed the door behind Hollis and circled around the van to climb behind the wheel. "Once you plant an idea on a witness, you'll never know whether you can believe them or not."

"Okay, sorry . . . I made a mistake." Jazz leaned forward on his seat. "But you heard her. The police are hiding something. I wouldn't be surprised if they're working with the guys who killed my grandfather."

Groves murmured something unintelligible and started the car.

"Wait!" Jazz started to grab Groves's arm and then thought better of it. "Just a minute. At least hear me out. I saw something really strange in the Calders' backyard."

Groves turned impatiently in his seat. "I'm waiting."

"Okay . . ." Jazz swallowed. If he told him the whole story, he'd think he was crazy. But what choice did he have? "First of all, I want to point out that I've already proved my case. I have a whole room full of witnesses who can tell you I couldn't have been involved in the murders and a completely different set of witnesses who'll tell you that I went to the police station on my own without any FBI escorts. Okay?"

"There's going to be a point to this?"

"I just want to point out that I haven't done anything wrong. What I'm about to tell you isn't some lame attempt to clear my name, because I've already done that, right? It's going to sound completely insane, and you're probably going to think I'm crazy. I'm taking a big risk in telling you this. The only reason I'm doing it is because it's true. And it might help clear everything up."

Hollis turned to Jazz, a warning in her eyes. She shook her head slightly. The message was clear: she didn't think he should tell Groves. But she didn't know about the doghouse. He couldn't let Groves drive away without at least trying.

"Go on . . ." Groves's expression was guarded, but he was still listening. That was something. Not a lot, mind you. But Jazz would take what he could get.

"I know this is going to sound crazy, but remember Hollis saying I passed out at the club? What she didn't tell you is that I had a weird dream while I was out. I was being chased through the swamps by ten cloaked men. They surrounded me—or I should probably say the person's whose eyes I was seeing through—and fired their guns at me. I saw the same bright light Mari described and everything." He paused to gauge Groves's reaction. He wasn't

shutting Jazz down. That was the main thing. The agent didn't
have to believe. All Jazz had to do was pique his curiosity.

"I've had other dreams . . . visions too. The weirdest one was
seeing the same faceless person digging a hole next to a doghouse
in the corner of a fenced-in yard. You can ask Hollis. I've seen that
one twice. And just now, while I was in the Calders' kitchen, I saw
the same identical doghouse from my vision . . . in the Calders'
backyard. Even the dug-up spots on the ground were the same."

Groves sat frowning for several seconds. "That's it? That's
your big story?"

"I know it's crazy. I'm not asking you to believe it. I don't even
believe it myself, but what if there's something buried in their
backyard? What if it's the treasure my grandfather talked about
in his will?"

Groves smiled and shook his head. "I don't think so. Just
because you hid something in the Calders' backyard, it isn't going
to clear your name."

"Okay." Jazz nodded. "I can go with that. Let's say I did, for
whatever reason, know you were going to catch me and bring me
here to the Calders' house. And let's say I buried something here
that I thought would clear my name. Aren't you at least curious
what it is? Wouldn't it give you some sort of insight into what
I thought was going on?"

Groves's eyes drifted to the floor. He was playing with it.
Considering . . . All he had to do was set the hook and reel him in.

"Of course, you could always check the yard later. But then
you'd never know whether it was there all along or whether someone else planted it there after . . . hearing my story." Jazz kicked
himself internally. So much for setting the hook. He could come
up with better than that. He had to think. What would intrigue
Groves the most?

"Okay . . . Let's say I'm playing along." Groves eyed him

suspiciously. "When did these visions start? Did you do something or meet someone different that might have brought them on?"

"What?" Jazz studied Groves's expression. "You actually believe the visions are real?"

"Have you ever met someone named Marie Paris Glapion?"

"You asked Mrs. Calder about her. Who is she?"

"Have you ever met her?"

"I don't know. Maybe. The name's not familiar, but I meet a lot of people. Who is she?"

Groves shook his head. "So what are you suggesting? Do you want me to ask Mrs. Calder for permission to dig up her backyard or do you want to do it without her knowledge?"

"You're serious?" Jazz waited for the break in expression that would give Groves away. "You believe me about the visions?"

"I never said that." Groves turned and opened the door of the van. "But what the heck? I don't have anywhere I need to be. You?"

Jazz rolled the door open and stepped back out into the warm night air. The dog had finally stopped barking. Maybe Mrs. Calder let it inside?

"This is convenient."

Jazz turned. Groves was on the sidewalk, behind the van. He was staring at the corner of the weed-choked yard. "Amazingly convenient, don't you think?" He reached down and pulled something from the weeds. It looked just like his grandfather's shovel!

"No way!" Jazz dodged around Hollis and took the shovel away from Groves. "No way!" It had the same blade, the same white handle . . .

Things were getting freakier by the second.

"What's the matter?" Groves spoke in a whisper. "This what you used to bury your thing in the backyard?"

"This morning we found a shovel that looked just like this!" Jazz turned it over in his hands. "It was in my grandfather's swamp. But it couldn't be the same one. The other one was newer. It had a price tag right here." He touched a spot on the handle. He couldn't be sure, but the spot felt a little sticky.

Groves was staring at him like he was an idiot. "Finished?" He yanked the shovel out of Jazz's hands and marched back along the side of the Calders' house. The backyard was dark now. The dog was still quiet.

Jazz caught up to the agent and spoke in a low whisper. "Why don't we just knock on the door and tell her what we're going to do? She won't mind. The whole yard's been torn up by the dog."

Groves tossed the shovel over the fence. "You going to tell her about your psychic powers?"

"Whatever." Jazz stood back as Groves jumped up and threw a leg over the fence.

"What am *I* supposed to do?" Hollis's whisper sounded behind Jazz. "I'm not climbing any fences."

"Wait for us back at the van," Groves hissed from the top of the fence. "If Mrs. Calder comes out, tell her we're out searching for clues." He jumped down and landed with a thud on the other side of the fence.

Hollis leaned close to Jazz and whispered in his ear. "Is this for real? What are you doing?"

"Remember the mind-reading thing with Hailey? I think the visions are the same kind of thing. Something's buried by that doghouse, and I'm going to find out what it is." He jumped up and swung himself over the fence in a single, fluid motion. Why couldn't he move like that when Mari was around?

He jumped down and crept toward the doghouse. Groves was standing beside it with the shovel.

"You're right about the holes," the agent whispered. "Where are we supposed to dig?"

Jazz grabbed the shovel and backed slowly away from the doghouse. He moved up and down and back and forth until the angles matched the images in his head. Then, stomping the shovel into the ground, he brought up a scoop of loose earth and tossed it to the side. Talk about déjà vu . . .

The feeling was so intense it gave him the chills.

He kept digging until the hole was almost two feet deep. The dirt was loose, but it was still hard work. He jabbed the shovel into the ground and arched his back. A street sign glowed eerily in the moonlight over the back of the fence. St. Jardin and N. Miro St. The block was only one lot deep? Why did that make him feel so queasy? Goose bumps tingled up his arms and neck. The shadows in the yard seemed to be moving.

A harsh whisper sounded at his side. "What's wrong? Why'd you stop?"

"This is harder than it looks." He tossed a spade full of dirt and jabbed the shovel at the ground. The blade scraped across something flat. He jabbed the shovel at it again. It sounded like . . .

Plastic.

Jazz dropped to his knees and cleared away the dirt with both hands. It was a big plastic box. He couldn't tell in the dark, but the top looked almost blue! He dug his fingers around the edges and pulled the box out of the ground.

"Don't open it. Not yet!" Groves reached for the box, but Jazz snatched it away. "Jazz, this is important. If you want me to testify that you didn't slip something into that box, I have to be the one to open it."

"Okay, but do it quick." Jazz set the box on the ground. As he scooted back from it, he saw something swirling in the shadows to his left. Something was moving. He could feel the motion in his head. It was getting closer.

"Not here!" Jazz lunged for the box and picked it up. "In the van. Something's coming." He carried the box to the fence and motioned furiously for Groves to follow.

Groves picked up the shovel and started filling in the hole.

"Leave it!" Jazz hissed. "Whatever it is, it's getting closer. Come on! We've got to go!"

"What?" The agent trotted up with the shovel.

"We've got to get out of here. I . . . heard someone coming." He grabbed the shovel and pushed Groves toward the fence. "Come on. I'll hand you the box when you're up!"

The agent looked back at the yard and then clambered up the fence. Once he was at the top, he turned and reached down for the box. Jazz handed it up to him and then tossed the shovel over the top.

A loud metallic clatter split the night. Loud barks sounded from inside the house.

Jazz scampered up the fence and jumped. Hitting the ground running, he took off after Groves, who was already racing for the van.

"Wait!" Jazz hissed, but Groves was too far ahead. If he took off with the treasure Jazz was going to—

A huge billowing figure stepped out of the shadows—right in the path of the fleeing agent.

Groves reached across his body, pulled out his gun . . .

But he was too slow. The figure struck out in a blur of motion. There was a sickening *thunk*, and the agent's body crumpled to the ground.

Jazz skidded to a stop, his eyes glued to the approaching shadow. It had the box! He stumbled backwards as the dark figure stepped forward into the moonlight.

It was Melchi.

IV

So much the rather thou, celestial Light,
Shine inward, and the mind through all her powers
Irradiate; there plant eyes, all mist from thence
Purge and disperse, that I may see and tell
Of things invisible to mortal sight.

—John Milton
Paradise Lost

ᑡᓆ 29 ᓂᑎ

Mariutza

MARI POUNDED DOWN THE deserted street. The whole area was awash with emotion. She could feel it swirling in the darkness, filling her mind with terror and shock and relief. It was Jaazaniah. It had to be. His presence sparkled like Hollis's cold boiling drink. But something was wrong. He was in trouble. He and Melchi were both in trouble.

She bounded across a dark intersection and angled toward the source of the noise. There they were. Two dark figures huddled over a shadow on the ground.

"Jaazaniah!" She ran to him.

The prophet jumped to his feet and turned to her with open arms. She looked up into his beautiful eyes and the strength drained like water from her limbs. She plodded to a stop in front of him, wilting under the intensity of his gaze. Warmth surged through her body and pounded into her brain. Her chest tightened until her heart felt like it was going to explode. This was wrong. He was the prophet. He'd told Hollis he didn't like her. He'd run away from her at the motel.

"I am . . . very happy to see you safe." She looked down at the ground as warmth blossomed in her cheeks. He was staring at her. The weight of his eyes beat down on her like a summer storm.

"I found it." His whisper sent a chill tingling up her spine.

"What?" She looked at his empty hands. Why didn't he ever say what he meant?

Then she saw the body. A tall man stretched out on the ground at Jaazaniah's feet. "What . . . a shimulo?" She sought the prophet's dark eyes.

"I don't think so. He's an FBI agent, but I think he's a friend."

"I am sorry." Melchi spoke behind her, his voice thick with grief. "He had a gun and his presence was—"

"It's okay," the prophet said. "You did the right thing, but he's going to be really mad when he wakes up."

Melchi turned back to Mari. "We must go now. The man isn't himself a mulo, but he's been tainted by their presence. They're getting closer. We mustn't let them get their hands on the treasure."

"The treasure?" Mari noticed the box in Melchi's hands. "This is . . ." She looked to Jaazaniah. "You found it? Where? How did you know we were here? Did you go to the hardware store?"

"Long story." Jaazaniah grinned. "Hollis is waiting in a minivan across the street. Where's Hailey?"

"Still talking to Wilmer Salley. I left her there when I felt . . ."

An angry howl shivered across the base of Mari's neck. She and Melchi swung around at the same time. It came from the city.

Melchi turned to her. "How far? I'm guessing three, maybe five miles?"

Mari shook her head. Tendrils of hunger brushed her awareness, slithering deeper and deeper into her mind. It was getting stronger. "There's more than one, and they're moving fast!" She looked back at Jaazaniah. "We must go. The mulani know we're here."

"Hollis is waiting in this guy's minivan. We could borrow his keys—"

"We have a car." Melchi jogged out onto the street and turned back to wave them on. "But Hailey won't be able to shield herself while she's driving. We must find a place to hide."

"But what about Hollis?" Jaazaniah turned and started walking in the wrong direction.

"She's safer where she is." Mari grabbed him by the arm and pulled him across the street. "The mulani have our scent. They'll be blind to all else but Standing." She searched up the street. Melchi and Hailey were already a block ahead of them. They needed to run faster.

She reached out with the *dikh* sight. Jaazaniah's presence was too strong. The mulani would be able to track him for miles. "Pray the shielding prayer," she whispered. "Just like you did in Hollis's car."

"I already told you. I can't. I don't know how."

"You've done it before. The shimulo were right on top of us, and they couldn't break through."

"I didn't do anything. I just fell asleep. Which is a lot easier when I'm not running."

Another howl rose up inside her. The buzzing voices were getting closer. She could hear the wail of the blue lights in the distance. "Faster," she gasped. "They're here!"

They pounded up the street and cut through a stand of tall trees. Running across a burned-out field, they followed Melchi and Hailey toward a dark line of enormous buildings. The night air was heavy with the voices of a thousand tortured souls. Malice and bitterness; hatred and greed. She could feel it sucking the life from her with every step.

"We can't go in there! Don't you feel it?"

Melchi shook his head. "We don't have a choice." He plunged into the shadows and cut between two crumbling pillars. Jaazaniah followed at her side. His emotions rang out like a clarion call.

They had to find a place to hide. He needed to be still, to close out the world and quiet his soul.

They ran through a courtyard of glaring orange-tinted lights and turned left onto a dark avenue. They cut left and right and left through the buildings, losing themselves in a jungle of concrete, dust, and steel.

"This way!" Melchi turned suddenly and led them toward a flight of crumbling steps.

"What are you doing?" Mari hissed as Melchi ran up the steps and reached for the handle of a bent metal door. "Not inside!"

"It's okay. It's open." Melchi yanked on the door and ducked into the darkness beyond.

"No!" Mari cringed away from the door. "You can't. Mustn't . . ."

"Mari, what's wrong?" Hailey appeared at Mari's side. An arm slid around her shoulders and eased her forward.

"We can't . . ." Mari ducked under Hailey's arm and backed away from the door. "It's wrong. Forbidden. Worse than death!"

"It's against her religion to go inside a building." Jaazaniah's voice sounded from the darkness behind her. "Something about the Standing."

"It'll just be for a few minutes." Hailey looked at Jaazaniah and shrugged. "It's not like we're going to live here."

"But it's wrong! Surely you know this?" Mari looked up at Melchi peering out through the door. "Going inside even for a second, it is forbidden to Standing."

"I didn't know . . ." Melchi stepped out and closed the door behind him. "My training . . ." He looked like he was going to be sick.

"This is where you thought to hide?" Mari flung the question at Melchi. "This is why you brought us to these buildings?"

He nodded and hung his head. "Father, forgive me. I didn't know. I—"

"There's no time. The shimulo will be upon us soon." Mari stepped forward and took the box from Melchi. "We must protect the treasure. Hailey, you can shield yourself while running?"

Hailey nodded.

Mari handed her the box and pointed off to her left. "Take the treasure and go that way. Circle around the shimulo and return to your car. If we don't join you in ten minutes, take the treasure and get as far away from the city as possible."

Melchi stepped toward Hailey. "Shall I go with her?"

"No." Mari pointed to the right. "Take Jaazaniah and circle around that way. He can't run and shield himself at the same time. When you're halfway to the car, stop and pray. Make sure you're both shielded before you meet Hailey at the car."

"And what are you going to do?" Jaazaniah asked.

"I'm going to make sure the shimulo don't follow Hailey." Mari turned and jogged down the steps. At the bottom she stopped. While Hailey carried the box around one side of the building, and Melchi ran with Jaazaniah around the other, Mari gathered a handful of rocks.

When her friends were gone, she reached out and searched the darkness for them. Hailey was an almost undetectable ripple in a sea of raging voices. Jaazaniah, on the other hand, rang out as clear as a whippoorwill call. It wasn't fear or anger or fatigue that filled the air this time. It was worry.

Mari's eyes widened. Worry . . . for her?

She broke into a run and headed straight for the advancing shimulo. They were already among the buildings. Bursts of rage and lust, of unbridled self-indulgence were breaking out like fires all around them. They moved to the right, converging on Jaazaniah's position.

Mari pulled a jagged piece of glass from her pocket and slashed it across her forearm.

No!

She flung her pain out into the night. She must be more careful. Couldn't let the shimulo find her.

She focused on the fear, let it build. If they got their hands on her treasure, the world would be lost! She imagined an ancient scroll, filled with the prophecies and wisdom of her people. They were going to kill her. She could see them tearing Jaazaniah the prophet to shreds with their teeth. Anger and terror and fear.

She skidded around a corner and raced across a littered courtyard. A bright light clung to the side of one of the buildings. She flipped a rock into her hand and let it fly. The courtyard dimmed with the crash of breaking glass. *Yes!* They could be broken! She let her excitement bleed out into the ether. If she could just get rid of the lights, the shimulo wouldn't be able to find her.

The scroll would be safe. She'd be able to find a safe place in the swamps and study it at her leisure. The ancient powers would be hers and hers alone!

A knife-edged pain stabbed into Mari's brain. Hatred, suspicion . . . They were sifting her thoughts like wheat flour. Nothing could stop them. Prayer was useless now. They were already inside . . .

A deep rumbling growl rattled through the surrounding buildings. Power swirled around her. The Badness. There was no turning back now. She reached deep into her reserves and forced herself to even greater speed. Breaking out onto a dark road, she turned and fled from the choking presence. Pounding footsteps sounded behind her. They were getting closer. She couldn't hold out much longer.

She ducked into a narrow chasm between two dark buildings. Two swan-necked lights filled the alley with orange-tinted light. She launched a rock at the first light, but it burst against the encasing glass. A maddening growl rattled through her brain.

It was too late.

They were already here. She wasn't strong enough to stand.

In a last frantic act of desperation, she reached back with her last rock and flung it with all her might. It whirred through the air and smashed into the globe, raining shards of broken glass down onto her head.

But the alley was still too bright. She backed deeper into the gloom as the buzzing in her brain rose to a maddening pitch. An enormous black shadow blotted out the entrance to the alley. The shadow darkened and flickered like a sputtering flame. Mari stood, transfixed. It was a hooded man. No, two hooded men. Three, five, nine . . .

Holy One, help me. Please!

She closed her eyes and struggled against the power battering her mind. Her muscles burned, her head felt like it was going to explode. A scream tore through her body. The sound of something ripping, the hiss of rushing air. She stumbled backward and sprawled on the ground. An old bottle lay by her arm. She grabbed it, pushed to her feet, and ran as a deafening roar shuddered through her brain.

Running toward the second light, she flung the bottle at it with her last remaining strength. The crash of smashing glass rang like sweet music, and the alley plunged into darkness. Mari kept running, reaching out in front of her with groping hands.

Smack!

She slammed into a wall and crumpled to the ground. A triumphant roar echoed in her brain, drowning out all other thoughts. The Badness had her. She was theirs. No power in heaven or earth could save her now. The scrape of gloating footsteps sounded behind her as she felt her way along the back of the wall—

—and felt her heart freeze.

The alley was a dead end.

She was trapped.

◡◦ 30 ◦◡

Jazz

A SILENT SCREAM RIPPED through Jazz's senses, knocking him off his feet. He skidded across the concrete and rolled onto his face.

"Mari?" Gasping to catch his breath, he pushed himself onto his knees, but a blast of exultation knocked him back down. He rolled over and over, clawing at his skin as a firestorm of rage washed through his body. Hunger, malice, unquenchable need . . . it seared into his senses, burned like acid through his veins.

They'd found Mari. She was in trouble. Gritting his teeth against the pain, he climbed to his feet and leaned into the blast.

The slap of footsteps sounded behind him. A hand clamped around his wrist. "There's nothing we can do!" Melchi's voice pierced the tumult. "We must follow Mari's plan. We need to protect the treasure."

"The plan's not working!" Jazz tried to shake Melchi off, but an arm circled his chest. "She needs help. We've got to at least try!"

"Calm yourself. They'll hear you!" Melchi hissed. "You must pray. Now!"

"So what are you saying? You want to just leave her?" He swung around and wrenched free of Melchi's grasp.

"We must stick to the plan. She sacrificed herself to save your life. I'm not letting you throw that away."

"Sacrificed?" Jazz's mind went numb. He turned and reached out toward the blast, straining with all his senses. "Where is she? She was there a minute ago."

"She's gone." Melchi's voice broke. Jazz noticed for the first time the tears streaming down his face.

"No!" Jazz backed away. "It's a trick. She's just trying to fool them. She did it before at the river."

"Jazz, you must calm yourself." Melchi stepped toward him slowly. "Did Mari teach you the shielding prayer?"

"Leave me alone!" He jerked away and started running. She was back at the car. She'd said she'd meet them back at the car. She was probably worried about them. Wondering what was taking them so long.

The street lights starred and blurred in his eyes as he ran back through the howling apartments. Footsteps echoed all around him. Gasping sobs raged in his ears, but still he kept running. Across the parking lot, through the trees, down the blearing darkness of the empty street. Mari would be there. She had to be. Any second he would feel the warmth of her presence. The warmth and innocence. The infuriatingly naïve trust.

"Right here." Melchi's voice sounded close to his ear. "The black car."

Something moved in the car just ahead of them. Jazz's heart leaped in his chest. She was there! He'd known it all along. He ran to the front door and threw it open.

Hailey looked up at him with a scowl. "Why aren't you shielding yourself? I could feel you all the way across the field."

"Where's Mari?" He yanked on the back door and searched inside. Mari wasn't there. Had she gone to the minivan instead? He turned to check, but Melchi blocked his way. "I've got to check the minivan. Mari might have seen Hollis. Gone to help her."

Melchi shook his head slowly.

"I've got to at least check." He pushed his way past the giant, but Melchi swung him back around and shoved him into the car.

"*I'll* check. And as soon as I get back, we must go." The door clicked shut and Melchi was gone.

Jazz leaned over the seat and grabbed Hailey's shoulder. "It's a trick. She's done it before. She pretended to drown in the river and disappeared. We have to wait for her. Okay?"

Hailey didn't answer.

"Okay?"

Her shoulders drooped and her head slumped forward.

"No . . . She's okay. She does this all the time. You've got to believe me."

The front door opened and Melchi slid into the passenger seat. "The minivan was gone. Nobody's there." His voice was flat, emotionless. "We must go now. The mulo are getting close."

"No!" Jazz grabbed Hailey's arm. "Just a few more minutes. She'll be right here."

"Jazz . . ." Melchi sounded angry. "You must control your emotions or the mulo will kill us all. Is that what you want?"

"But she'll be here in a few minutes! You're the one calling me a prophet. Why can't you just listen to me?"

"Shhh . . . Calm down! You must shield yourself—"

A blast of anger erupted in Jazz's head. "I don't pray, okay? I don't believe in the Standing, and I don't believe in your stupid God!"

A jolt passed through Jazz's body. So much for their supposed control. They couldn't control their feelings any better than he could. They just didn't care. Didn't care about Mari or him or anyone but themselves and their stupid religion. Since when was not caring supposed to be a virtue?

The car rumbled to life and started rolling forward.

"I said wait!" Jazz threw open the door and jumped out of the car. His feet skidded across the pavement as he clung to the swinging door. "She's coming. I feel her! Stop! I can't hold on any more."

The car jerked to a stop, slamming Jazz into the door.

"Get inside." Melchi's urgent voice. "The mulo are tracking us. They're getting closer."

"Just a little bit longer. Please." He gripped the door and prepared for another slide.

A low rumbling growl shook the stillness of the night. Jazz could feel it rattling the pavement beneath his feet. Wave after wave of mind-jamming rage. It was too late to run. It was already too strong. Whatever it was, it was upon them now. There was no hope of escape.

Jazz shut his eyes and hugged the door to his chest. Melchi and Hailey couldn't leave her. He wouldn't let them. He couldn't face the darkness by himself.

A gasp sounded inside the car. The slap of running feet. Jazz opened his eyes as the other door squawked open. "Get in the car!" Hailey cried out.

Mari? His body went suddenly limp as her face appeared in the open doorway. Mari pulled him through the door as the car shot forward. They fell back onto the seat in a tangle of arms and flailing legs. Anger exploded all around them. Red hot tendrils of pain lashing against his mind. They were reaching for him, trying to burrow into his brain.

He closed his eyes and crushed Mari against him, burying his face in the luxuriant thickness of her hair. The smell of sunshine and swampland filled his senses. Sweetness and kindness and beauty and light. His lips found the smooth skin of her neck, the soft curve of her jaw line, the infinite depths of her lips.

Mari pulled away with a gasp. "Jaazaniah?" Her eyes blazed like twin suns. In shock? Outrage? He couldn't tell. All he could do was stare and try to drink her in.

"Are you okay?" Melchi's voice sounded above the hammering roar. "We thought they—"

The car squealed around a turn, throwing them forward. Jazz braced an arm against the front seat and held Mari tighter. She twisted around to kneel on the floor, but she didn't pull away. Was that a smile on her lips? Was she okay with . . . him?

"I lured them into an alley and broke all the lights," she said between breaths. "The mulani's senses are very dull. I mind-screamed the false pain and prayed the shielding like Purodad taught me. I don't know if it fooled them, but they couldn't navigate the darkness without my presence to guide them. It took a while, but I was able to climb up a pipe on the side of a wall."

"I told them it was a trick, but they didn't believe me." Jazz leaned in close and whispered. "I wouldn't let them leave you. I couldn't . . ."

A shy smile touched Mari's lips. Her eyes seemed to glow. What was wrong with her? He was the prophet! But she couldn't help herself. The sight of his face sent bubbles of sparkling light cascading through her entire being.

"I . . ." He forced his eyes away from hers and took a deep breath. This wasn't the time. The car rattled and bucked beneath them. Its engine was a high-pitched roar. "Let's get you buckled into a seat belt." He helped her off the floor and pulled the seat belt around her.

"Thank you." She turned toward him.

Jazz sat transfixed. Her eyes filled his mind completely. He felt like all the air had been sucked out of the car. He couldn't breathe, couldn't respond, couldn't do anything but sit there gawking like . . . a caught fish?

The car lurched to the side, sending Jazz sprawling across Mari's lap. He pulled himself up as they squealed around a hairpin curve. Jazz glared at Melchi. "What's going on? Are they following us?"

"Helicopters! They're tracking by feel. We've got to get you out of range."

"Range of what?" Jazz sat up and looked from Mari to Melchi and back again. "This is crazy. We can't outrun a helicopter."

"Jazz, you must calm yourself." Melchi's voice was smooth and soft as velvet. "Focus on my words. You're safe and secure in the middle of a huge forest. Imagine the smell of the leaves—"

"This is crazy!" Jazz scooted forward. "Have you forgotten about the box? We should open it now while we still have a chance."

"He's right." Mari leaned forward. "It could help us."

"The only thing that will help is for Jazz to calm down," Melchi called back over the seat. "Once the helicopters zero in on us—"

"It's *my* inheritance." Jazz reached over the seat. "Give me the box and I'll calm down. Screaming about helicopters isn't making things any better."

Melchi sighed and handed the blue box back across the seat. Jazz hefted it in his hands. It wasn't heavy enough for gold. There weren't any clinks or rattles.

"Much better." Melchi's voice was back to soft and velvety. "Relax and focus on the box . . ."

A spark of irritation kindled in Jazz's chest, but he thrust it aside. The top edge of the box was sealed with a thick layer of duct tape. He found the end and started unwrapping it, rolling the loose tape into a big sticky ball. When he'd finally got to the end of the tape, he tried to pry the lid off the box, but it was stuck. It seemed to be sealed with a thick, elastic glue.

A chill tickled at the base of Jazz's neck. He could feel a faint buzzing in his brain. They were getting closer. He had to hurry.

Digging his fingers into the glue, he pulled up on the corner of the lid with all his might. The lid buckled and then pealed off with a pop.

It was . . . a book?

A shriek sounded in his ears. Mari reached into the box and pulled the book out. "You found it! Purodad's Bible! I thought it was gone forever!" She hugged the book to her chest, and turned to Jazz with shimmering eyes. "Thank you. Thank you so very much."

"That can't be all." Jazz searched the inside of the box. There had to be another clue. Some kind of hidden message. "Wait! Look up the Ruth verse. That's where it will be. A message written next to the verse."

"What?" The smile on Mari's face faded.

"The Ruth verse. That's where we'll find the next clue. Ruth 1:16. Look it up!"

Mari opened the Bible and thumbed through the pages. "It's here! Purodad's handwriting. He left us a note!"

"Read it." Jazz reached for the book, but Mari held it fast. Tears streamed down her face as she stared, wide-eyed, at the page. "What's it say? Read it out loud!"

Mari was silent several seconds and then wiped an arm across her eyes. She took a deep breath and started reading: "I love you, Mari. You're the best granddaughter an old man could ever have. And Jaazaniah. I couldn't be any more proud of you. I've always loved you, and I always will—even to the end of the age."

Mari wiped her eyes again and looked over at Jazz with a trembling smile.

"That's all?" He took the book from her and read the message himself. The tiny handwritten message was all there was. "That can't be it. There has to be something else." He searched the next page and the page after that. They were all clean.

"I think, maybe . . ." Mari's voice was soft as a little girl's. "This was his last best gift. He wanted us to know he loved us."

"No." Jazz slammed the book shut. "Something's wrong. If I hadn't seen the doghouse in a vision, I never would have known to dig in the backyard. We must have skipped a step. There's still another clue. Think! What are we missing? Where else did he go? That's where we'll find the next clue."

"He went to a corner grocery store in the city, but—" Mari gasped and her eyes went suddenly wide.

"What?" Jazz looked down at the scarred cover of the Bible. "Did you find something? What is it?"

"I know what it means!" She grabbed the book out of his hands and waved it in his face. "The verse in Ruth—*where you go, I will go*—he was talking about the Bible, not the city!"

"What?"

"We're supposed to go where he went—in his Bible. See?" She pointed to a discolored band running through the pages of the closed book. "The part of the Bible Purodad read the most!"

Jazz gasped out loud. The pages at the center of the band were so crinkled and worn they left a gap.

Mari held the book out spine downward and let it fall open. It plopped open to the center of the dirty band. Jeremiah 35. The pages were so worn and stained, some of the ink had been rubbed away.

There weren't any handwritten notes, but a name in the text caught his eye. *Jaazaniah—the son of Jeremiah!* Jeremiah was his father's name. And further down there was Jonadab—his grand-father!

He backed up and scanned the passage.

> *Then I took Jaazaniah the son of Jeremiah, the son of Habaziniah, and his brethren, and all his sons, and the whole house of the Rechabites; and I brought them into the house of the* LORD *. . . and I set before the sons of the house of the Rechabites pots full of wine, and cups, and I said unto them, Drink ye wine. But they said, We will drink no wine: for Jonadab the son of Rechab our father commanded us, saying, Ye shall drink no wine, neither ye, nor your sons for ever: Neither shall ye build house, nor sow seed, nor plant vineyard, nor have any: but all your days ye shall dwell in tents; that ye may live many days in the land where ye be strangers.*

"See?" Mari jabbed a finger at the passage. "They're just like us. They're not supposed to live in houses or plant gardens or drink wine. And look down here." She ran her finger down the page and started reading out loud. "'And Jeremiah said unto the house of the Rechabites, Thus saith the LORD of hosts, the God of Israel; Because ye have obeyed the commandment of Jonadab your father, and kept all his precepts, and done according unto all that he hath commanded you: Therefore thus saith the LORD of hosts, the God of Israel; Jonadab the son of Rechab shall not want a man to stand before me for ever.'"

"What's that supposed to mean—*stand before me for ever?*" Jazz looked back to the top of the passage.

"He's talking about us—the Standing. This is why we're the Standing!"

"But what does it mean? Are we supposed to—"

The windshield lit up with blinding white light. A pulsing roar descended on them as silent laughter screamed in his head.

The enemy had found them.

∽ 31 ∾

Mariutza

A BRIGHT LIGHT SWOOPED down out of the night sky, lighting up the front window. Clanging explosions shuddered through the car. *Pop pop pop!* The seat next to Mari's leg erupted in a cloud of shredded foam. Dust particles hung in the air, obscuring her vision as the windshield exploded in a hailstorm of flying glass.

A loud shriek, and Mari was thrown against the front seat.

"Hold on!"

Hailey's shout came too late. Before Mari could grab hold of anything, the car spun around and jolted over bumpy ground, slamming her into the door. The light was behind them now. Jazz reached across the seat and dragged Mari down. He was lying on top of her, wrapping his arms around her waist.

"No!" She struggled and tried to sit up. "I need to get—"

Crash! The back window shattered, covering them with green-tinted jewels.

"Let me up. Purodad's Bible. We must save it!" Mari squirmed out from under Jazz and reached out for the book bumping and sliding across the floor.

"It's too late! We're not going to lose them!"

"Then *help* me!" She grabbed the book and shoved it into the plastic box. "Where's the lid? We have to protect it."

A metallic smack rang in Mari's ears. Hailey screamed and the car jerked to the right. There was a split-second of weightlessness and then a loud crash as the car hit the ground and threw them against their seat belts.

"You okay?" Melchi was shouting. "Where were you hit?"

"I'm fine!" Hailey's voice was almost drowned out by the rattling of the tires. The car swerved and tilted at an alarming angle. Tall grass whipping past the right window. Finally it leveled off with a groan and shot forward in a zigzagging pattern that threw Mari first to one side and then the other.

"Here's the top!" Jaazaniah pulled the plastic lid out from beneath the seat. "What are you doing?"

"We can't let them take it." Mari took the lid and pressed it onto the box. "We need to stop. One of us has to hide it in the woods."

"They're *shooting* at us!" Jazz shouted. "We can't just stop. It's a—"

A metallic smack rang out behind them. Jazz grabbed Mari's arm and dragged her back down onto the seat.

She twisted onto her side and thrust the box into Jazz's hands. "As soon as the light leaves us, throw it out of the car. The front pages are filled with birthdays and names—information about other Standing. We mustn't let the list go over to the Badness."

"Watch out!" Melchi's shout blasted into Mari's brain, leaving her reeling with the force of his presence. She pulled away from Jaazaniah and leaned over the front seat. A wall of flashing blue lights stood across the road ahead.

Mari turned and looked out the back window. More flashing lights. There were four cars behind them. They couldn't escape. At least . . .

Not in the car.

"Stop! Take to the woods!"

A high-pitched squeal rang out, throwing her forward against her seat belt. The car swerved suddenly to the right. They hurtled through the air and bounced into the ceiling before crunching into a tree with a bone-jarring smack.

"Everybody run!" Melchi threw the door open. "Shield yourselves and run. I'll try to slow them down."

"No! We stay together!" Jazz shoved open his door as a bright light swept across the car. A volley of explosions crashed down all around them.

Mari jabbed at her seat belt buckle, but it wouldn't let loose. She yanked on it, pulled, tried to squirm free of its tightening grip. A hailstorm of bullets hit the car. She wasn't going to make it.

The door beside her suddenly flew open and Jazz reached around her. He jabbed at the belt and it went magically slack. Grabbing her around the waist, he pulled her from the car as a line of explosions smacked across the roof. A crash sounded by her ear. Shards of glass pelted her face and neck.

"Where's the Bible? We can't leave it!" Twisting free of Jaazaniah's grip, she lunged for the car, but he grabbed her from behind and dragged her back under the trees.

"Cut it out! The Bible's safe." He pulled her deeper into the forest. "We've got to get out of here."

"You're sure?" Mari backpedaled and managed to regain her feet. She turned and searched his face in the shifting green-tinted light.

"Trust me!"

Crashing footsteps sounded behind them. Mari spun around and dropped into a crouch, but it was Melchi. He was carrying Hailey. Her leg was hurt. She could feel her pain leaking into the night.

"Help her!" Melchi pushed Hailey into Jazz's arms. "I'll hold them off."

"No!" Hailey clung to Melchi, but he grabbed her by the forearms and pushed her back.

"I'll be fine!" He cupped her face in his hand and then turned back to face the road. A cluster of sweeping torch lights were bobbing toward them.

Shimulo.

A hungry growl rumbled up Mari's spine. A blast of rage hit her in the face. Wave after wave of overwhelming power.

Melchi charged the approaching lights, shouting out his defiance.

Hailey lunged after him, but Jazz pulled her back. He twisted her around and lifted her off her feet. He was running with her, struggling to hold on as she twisted and turned and screamed.

Mari caught up with them, tried to grab Hailey's flailing fists. "It's okay. Melchi has the training. The Holy One will help him stand."

"Tell that to your grandfather! And my parents and Melchi's parents and the Standing in Nazi Germany!"

Mari gritted her teeth and kept on running. It was the shimulo. She couldn't let them shake her faith. Wouldn't.

Jaazaniah staggered and went down hard, slamming Hailey into the ground.

"I'm okay. Help Jazz." Hailey shook Mari off and climbed to her feet as a volley of gunshots rang out behind them.

A wave of searing pain crashed through the trees, filling Mari's mind with blinding light. *Melchi!* A sob wracked her body as his presence dimmed and finally winked out.

Tears filled her eyes. She couldn't see. Couldn't breathe.

A high-pitched shriek sounded in her ears. An arm wrapped around her, pulling her to her feet. More shrieks. Hands pushed her forward. She stumbled to the side and clutched at Hailey's trembling form. Still the hands poked and prodded them along.

"Come *on!*" Jaazaniah's voice. "They're getting closer. We've got to move!"

Mari grabbed Hailey and broke into a shambling run. Through the darkness, in and out through the trees. *Holy One, help us. Holy One, please . . .* She had to quiet her heart. She couldn't let her weakness get them killed. She wouldn't. She prayed out loud, repeating the words over and over as she ran deeper into the choking night.

Great moans and hiccupping sobs sounded in her ear. Mari reached out tentatively with her mind and tried to find Hailey's presence against the buzzing roar of the enemy. She was doing it. Even through the pain, she was still shielding herself. Jaazaniah's presence, however, burned at her side like a bonfire, sending out grief and fear helter-skelter.

"Jaazaniah," she gasped. "Please listen to me. You have to shield yourself. Trust yourself to the Lord's protection."

"Hailey's right." Jaazaniah's voice was an angry snarl. "It didn't help Melchi or your grandfather. Why should it be any different for us?"

"We don't know all His plans." She groped for the right words. "It's better for us when we're with Him. No matter what happens in the end."

"Better for Melchi? How? I don't think—"

A beam of light swept across their path. Mari pulled Hailey to the right and charged ahead. A branch slashed across her face. Tangled vines pulled at her feet. Jaazaniah's emotions rang out like an alarm. She had to make him listen. He'd done it before; why did he refuse to do it now? Did he want the enemy to know where they were?

Trees all around her burst into sudden light. Gunshots rang out behind them. Mari pulled Hailey to the left. The lights were getting brighter. She had to—

An explosion slammed into Mari's back, sending her spinning into the ground. Searing pain filled her chest. Her hands clutched at it. Sticky warmth seeped through her fingers. She looked down . . .

There was a huge, jagged hole beneath her hand.

"Mari!" Jaazaniah's voice croaked in her ears. Two shadows were leaning over her. Jaazaniah's terrified face.

"Mari, hold on! Oh, God, there has to be something. Please!"

"Jaazaniah!" Mari could barely whisper. All her air seemed to be leaking from the hole. "Jaazaniah, please. Listen to me!"

His beautiful eyes drifted closer. Tears dripped onto her upturned face. The roaring in her ears, the pain, everything seemed to be receding. She was too dizzy. She had to make him understand.

"Jaazaniah, you must leave me. Keep the Bible safe. Promise me."

A groan sounded above her. The shadows were trembling. Was that a nod?

Jaazaniah staggered onto his feet and a light swept across his beautiful face. Then he was running. Drifting like a ghost between the trees.

"Jaazaniah?" She called out to him, but her voice was a faint whisper. He was gone. Vanished. Just like at the motel.

Only this time he wasn't coming back.

❦ 32 ❦

Jazz

"YOU MURDERERS WANT TO kill me?" Jazz screamed his rage into the beating roar of the circling helicopters. "Come and get me!"

A dancing beam of light swept past him, lighting up the mossy trees.

"That's right. Over here!" Jazz turned and started running, leaping and bounding through the dense vegetation. "Come on! This way!" He slammed into a tree trunk, spun around, kept on running. Further from Mari and Hailey. That's all he needed. Just a little bit further and then he could rest.

A blast of rage sent him crashing into the ground. Scorching flames licked at his skin, coiled around his chest, forced their way into his mouth, his ears, his nose. Where was his hateful God now? Mari had trusted Him!

Something twisted deep inside him and an exultant cry rang in his brain. He was theirs now. He'd always been theirs, since before the beginning of time. His heart leaped in recognition. This was what he was. What he was always meant to be. It was his destiny!

He drew in a long, ragged breath. Fiery tendrils snaked their way into his lungs, crisscrossing and branching, filling his chest, his throat, his brain. Hunger and anger and fear. He could feel it taking hold of him. It was his birthright. His father's legacy. It burned deeper and deeper into his soul. The sting of his father's hatred. The thud of his father's fists as he landed blow after blow after blow.

The sound of a breaking twig jolted through him. Jazz tensed as soft footsteps padded up behind him. A feral growl rumbled in the darkness. Surges of power crackled in the air. He held his breath as the footsteps crept closer and closer. If he moved they would kill him. If he didn't move—

Rolling onto his hands and knees, he scrambled through the undergrowth. Anger erupted all around him. Invisible thorns sliced at his skin. He lunged to his feet and ran. Pushing through trees, twisting and turning and weaving through the branches, he plunged deeper and deeper into the cloying darkness.

The ground melted beneath his feet, and he plunged face first into a pool of boggy water. Sputtering and gasping to catch his breath, he splashed onto his feet and slogged through the sucking mud. A crash sounded behind him. Pounding footsteps, rattling leaves. He had to go faster. He strained forward, churning through the mud like a runaway locomotive.

Finally he reached solid ground and staggered up a reedy bank. Dark branches slashed across his face. Panting breath rasped in his ears. He forced himself to greater and greater speeds. Twisting and turning, dodging this way and that through shadowy trees. Thudding footsteps sounded behind him. They were gaining on him. He vaulted a dark thicket, ducked beneath a canopy of spreading limbs.

A lupine howl sliced through the forest, freezing the blood in his veins. A dark answering presence rose up inside him. He could feel it expanding, stealing away his control.

He was the creature. It had been inside him all along.

A crash sounded to his right. Another to his left. They were spreading out, surrounding him. He had to go faster. They were going to kill him. Just like they had killed—

No! She was still alive. She had to be.

God, why did You have to let—

The darkness rang like a snapped guitar string as a bullet ripped past his ear.

He stumbled and almost went down. He couldn't do it anymore. His legs burned with exhaustion. They were going to kill him. The long fight was finally over. He ducked around one last tree and plodded out into a moonlit clearing.

Just ahead of him, backlit by an enormous pink-orange moon, an old oak tree rose up from a mound like a grasping twisted hand.

The image hit Jazz like a wrecking ball. He dropped to his knees, reached out with tingling arms toward the moon as a million wildfires raged inside his brain.

It was the vision from his dream! Everything was exactly the same. He hadn't been looking through his grandfather's eyes. He'd been looking at . . . this.

A ragged hiss escaped his lips. He was deflating, collapsing in on himself. All this time . . . he thought he'd been running away. But it was never away. He'd always been running . . . *to.*

To this. This moment. This place.

This destiny.

The last shreds of white-knuckled resistance ripped open and slowly sloughed away. He couldn't deny it anymore. He'd been brought here by something outside himself. Something wild and unimaginably powerful. Something . . . no, not something. Some One.

He stared up at the moon as the last few days clicked into place. The doghouse, his grandfather's will, *a man to stand before me for ever . . .* everything suddenly made sense. Mari had tried to tell him, but he hadn't listened. Hadn't wanted to believe. His grandfather was a prophet. A real, honest-to-God, honey-and-locust-fed prophet. His inheritance had never been in a box. It had never been lost.

He'd received it the second his grandfather died.

The night froze around him. Perfect, absolute silence rang in his ears. Every branch, every leaf, every crater dotting the moon's scarred surface stood out in perfect sharp-edged clarity.

And that's when it came to him: He'd had other visions. And in one of them . . .

Mari wore a sparkling green dress!

The night sky spun around him and locked into place with an audible click. His skin tingled with living fire. He was changing, morphing into something completely new. The transformation burned through him in a blaze of heart-wrenching ecstasy.

"Yes!" He threw back his head and howled into the surrounding darkness. "*YES!*"

He staggered to his feet and turned to face his pursuers. He was invincible, unstoppable. Nothing could stand in his way!

A man-shaped shadow flickered against the sizzling darkness. It stepped forward into the clearing, growing darker and darker as the dim moonlight sputtered and distorted around it.

A low growl rattled through his bones.

Jazz swung around. Three more figures advanced across the clearing behind him. Two more on his right, even more on his left. He was surrounded.

He turned, watching, waiting, counting . . . Yes! There were ten hooded figures, shrouded in fluttering black cloaks. All evenly spaced around him in a closing circle.

The tallest stepped forward, raised a gun, and pointed it at Jazz's heart.

A spasm shook Jazz's frame. He gasped for breath, letting the laughter flow. *It was true!* The realization washed through him, filling him with a sense of fiery power. *It was all true!* They couldn't hurt him. He was finally safe.

An explosion sounded. The shock of searing pain. Another explosion. Another.

And then silence.

Jazz collapsed onto his face as a blinding light filled the clearing. He lifted his head, squinted against the light as dozens of blazing figures hit the ground with earth-shattering force. They surrounded him. A blinding wall of impenetrable light.

The ground shuddered as they charged outward in every direction. Agonized screams filled the air. Hatred and fear splattered against his mind like bugs against a windshield. White-hot flames blasted through him, burning the encroaching emotions away.

Then, as suddenly as they had appeared, the lights were gone. Darkness crashed down on him, leaving him light-headed. Confused. He picked himself up off the ground and brushed off his clothes.

What had happened? Where were the cloaked men?

He patted his chest and checked his hands. No pain, no blood . . . He was fine. Had he been dreaming?

He staggered across the clearing and stopped. An inky shadow lay sprawled across the ground, its gloved hand clutching a glinting shadow. It was a gun.

Jazz backed away and turned. Another body . . . and another. It wasn't a dream. The whole clearing was ringed with black shadows, hollow and still as death.

"Mari!" He shouted her name and broke into a run. "Mari, hold on!" He plunged into the shadowy forest, plowing through the branches, splashing through the water, running blindly in and out through the trees. "Mari!"

A spurt of orange flame lit the darkness ahead of him with a reverberating explosion, but Jazz kept on running.

"Mari!" He made for a glowing patch of trees. Two helicopters were circling overhead, lighting the area with powerful spotlights. "I'm counting on you! Don't let me down now!"

Something moved within the halo of light. It was Hailey. It had to be. She wouldn't have left Mari—not even if . . .

He dodged around a tree and plunged into the column of light. Hailey was leaning over Mari, pressing blood-covered hands against her chest.

A volley of gunshots sounded above him. Burning pain stabbed into his back, his shoulder, his head . . . The pain burned brighter and brighter until it became a blinding white light. The ground tilted beneath his feet. Down became up and up became down as a high-pitched whine rent the air behind him. The forest shook in a deafening blast. Waves of heat and smoke pelted his back. The trees around him lit up with flickering orange light.

Jazz dropped to his knees and leaned over Mari as Hailey stared, open-mouthed, at the conflagration behind him. "Mari?" He cupped her face between his hands. "Mari, please. Talk to me. I don't know what I'm supposed to do."

Mari's eyes flickered open and her face went suddenly tight. Her lips moved, but he couldn't make out what she was saying. His name? Did she recognize him?

"Mari, what am I supposed to do? I don't know anything."

Her lips moved again.

"What?" He leaned over her, pressed his ear to her lips.

"Pray." The word floated to him, softer than a whisper. He might have even imagined it.

Jazz looked down at her, but her eyes were closed. She didn't seem to be breathing. "God?" He spoke the name tentatively. "This really sucks. *I* suck!" He flung the words out into the smoke-filled blackness. "You chose the wrong guy. I don't have a clue what I'm doing. I don't know anything. I just want Mari to be better, and I know You can do it." He took a deep breath and tried to think of what else there was to say. "So what are You waiting for? I'm supposed to say please or amen or something? What's it going to take? If You have to kill me to make it happen, I'm okay with that, but please . . . *do* something."

His voice choked off as tears filled his eyes. His throat burned like fire. He could feel the warmth spreading into his chest, down his arms, into his hands. They sizzled like frying bacon as he pressed them against Mari's cheek and shoulder. He could feel the warmth flowing into her. Wave after wave of rippling power.

Something was happening. Did Mari just stir?

"Mari? Wake up. You're freaking me out. I did what you said. What's supposed to happen now?"

Her lips parted in a breathy gasp. Sudden color flowed into her cheeks. Her eyes fluttered open and a broad smile lit her face.

"You're . . . okay? That was it?" Suddenly Jazz was laughing. Mari's arms closed around him, pulling him into a giddy embrace. A high-pitched squeal rang in his ears. Hailey was hugging them too.

It really happened! He'd prayed and God had answered. It was as simple as that. Mari was going to be okay!

∽ 33 ∾

Mariutza

MARI STIFLED A GASP as Jaazaniah and Hailey piled on top of her. Something was wrong. Her chest still pained her. How was that possible? Jaazaniah had prayed a healing. She'd felt the warmth flowing into her, the innards knitting together inside her body. But why hadn't the wound healed? Had he lost faith partway through the healing? It didn't make any sense. The Lord had done all the work. How could a person mess up the Lord's healing?

"Think you can walk?" Jaazaniah's voice sounded against the crackle of a distant fire. "We've got to find Melchi."

An arm slipped around her shoulders. His lips were inches from her cheek. She gritted her teeth to keep from crying out as he lifted her onto her feet. Something was horrifically wrong. The wound was still bleeding. She could feel it oozing into her shirt.

Jaazaniah pulled her arm over his shoulder and slid an arm around her waist. The side of his face glowed with an eerie yellow light.

"What happened?" She looked out onto a scene from a nightmare. Twisted metal wreckage lay burning among the splintered

remains of a dozen leaning trees. It was . . . the helicopters? No
. . . It couldn't be.

"I think they tried to shoot me." Jaazaniah spoke in a soft
voice. "It's . . . kind of hard to explain." He led them in a wide
circle around the crash sites. The flames from the wrecks painted
the trees with wild flickering shadows.

"Where are the soldiers?" Hailey's voice sounded right behind
her. "They should be swarming the place—especially after the
crashes."

Jaazaniah shrugged. "The leaders are dead. I think the
others . . . ran away maybe?"

"What?" Mari reached out with the sight, pushing deeper and
deeper through the trees. Nothing. Not even a tingle. "How?" She
looked up at Jaazaniah. "What happened? How could they . . . be
gone? They were shimulo—the eternally undying."

"I don't know." Jaazaniah shook his head as if in a daze. "They
came after me, but something happened. I think maybe my inheritance isn't what we thought it was. My grandfather was a prophet.
A real, live prophet."

"That's what I've been telling—"

"No. It's more than that. All those visions . . . I wasn't seeing
through his eyes at all. It wasn't him digging by the doghouse.
It was me. And it wasn't him being surrounded by ten cloaked
men either. What I saw just happened. The tree and the moon,
everything. My visions aren't from the past, Mari. They're from
the future. And I'd be willing to bet he had them too. That's how
he had a painting of me, how he knew when to send the will. He
knew where to bury the Bible—because he saw me digging there.
Just like I saw myself digging there. That's my inheritance."

"As a Standing," Mari whispered. "*Jonadab the son of Rechab
shall not want a man to stand before me for ever.*" Purodad had seen
into the future. Hundreds of memories suddenly made sense. He'd

known she'd find Jaazaniah. He'd known what would happen. *You're no granddaughter of mine! No relation at all.* His words came back to her in a rush. He hadn't been angry at her. He'd wanted her to know it was okay! That she and Jaazaniah could . . .

"Are you all right?" The tenderness in Jaazaniah's voice brought a flood of warmth to Mari's cheeks. "Mari?"

She blinked and looked up into his blurry face. "Purodad knew . . . He knew I'd . . ." A new thought washed the others away. "The muddy board!"

"What?"

"He did it to save my life! I thought it was supposed to be a guide, but he'd covered it with mud to match the bottom of the hole. That's why the Badness didn't see me. He knew I'd hide under it!"

"Whoa. Slow down. What hole?"

"Don't you see? He knew all this would happen. He knew—"

A car engine rumbled to life in the distance. She reached toward it with her mind, but the night was completely still. Too still—like something was hiding. A blackness of silence against the hazy darkness of space.

"I think I feel—"

"Shhh . . ." Jaazaniah held up a hand. They crept forward, pausing to listen at every step. The trees ahead were pulsing. A flashing blue light filtered its way through the thinning trees.

Jaazaniah angled to the right, picking his way through the deepest shadows. A lone car with a flashing blue light was stopped by the side of the road. A huge dark shadow shifted in front of its headlights.

Hailey gasped and ran out into the clearing. "Melchi! Are you okay? What's wrong?"

Melchi's deep voice rang out. "Stay back! It's a trap!"

Sudden joy flooded through Mari. He was alive! Melchi was alive!

A shadow rose up behind Hailey. "FBI!" A man leveled a gun at the back of Hailey's head. "Put your hands on top of your head!"

"Don't!" Melchi called out. "She's not armed. She's a scientist. She's never hurt anyone in her life!"

"Don't do it, Groves!" Jaazaniah gripped Mari and tugged her toward the clearing. Mari stared at him. What was he *doing?* He'd just given away their advantage of surprise.

The man grabbed Hailey and swung her around to face them. "Come on out!" He held the gun to Hailey's head. "Give yourself up and things will go easier on you."

"Put the gun down." Jaazaniah's voice rang like steel. He led Mari out into the light and squared off in front of the agent. "We didn't do anything wrong."

"Sure you didn't. This is all just a conspiracy, right?"

Hailey gasped as the man pushed her forward. Mari tensed.

"You guys are the good guys. That's why you shot down the helicopters."

Jaazaniah let Mari go and stepped toward the man. "I know what this looks like, but when you run your lab tests you'll see then none of us have fired any weapons. We—"

"Hands in the air where I can see them!"

Jaazaniah's hands remained by his side. He took another step forward. Another.

What was happening? Did he want to get himself killed? Mari circled around to the left. She had to do something before—

"Hands in the air now, or I shoot!"

Jaazaniah laughed. Laughed! In the face of the gun! "I wouldn't do that if I were you. The guys in the helicopters shot me and look what it got them."

The man pushed Hailey onto her knees and leveled the gun at Jaazaniah's face. "What happened to the helicopters, Jazz? What'd you do?"

"I didn't do anything. As far as I can tell, it was an act of God."

Mari's heart leaped at Jazz's words, but Groves just sneered. "That what you're planning to tell the judge?"

"I'm just telling you what happened. They shot me in the back, and God didn't like it. Just like He didn't like it when ten of your people tried to kill me in the swamp. And when ten more of your people shot my grandfather."

The muscles in the agent man's jaw bulged. Mari edged slowly around the man as he sighted down his gun. He was going to shoot. She could feel his tension in her bones.

"Go ahead and shoot if you want." Jaazaniah laughed again— like the whole thing was a funny story. Didn't he have eyes? The man was serious.

Mari edged further to the left. If she could get a few feet closer . . .

"Don't do it, Mari." Jaazaniah's voice froze her where she stood. "He's not one of them. I think God might be giving him a second chance." He took another step forward.

"Don't!" The gun inched higher to point at Jazz's chest. "I don't want to shoot you, but I will!"

Jaazaniah took another step. "Maybe so, but it won't do any good, and it may do you a whole lot of bad. I don't know why, but God's got our backs tonight. I think it may be because we're the last of our kind. Have you ever heard of the Standing? Is that why your department has been trying to kill us? Because you think we pose some kind of threat?" He took another step.

The man dropped down onto one knee and raised the gun.

Something in Mari snapped. It was the kneeling kata. She'd practiced it a thousand times! Faster than thought, she was flying through the air, up and over his arm, wrenching it to the side.

The gun went off with a deafening explosion. She snatched it from his hand and rolled across the ground to come up with it in her own hand, pointing at the agent's chest.

The man's eyes went wide. He raised his hands into the air and looked back and forth between Mari and Jaazaniah, a heap of fear in his eyes.

"She just saved your life." Jaazaniah stepped toward the man and raised him onto his feet. "Do you believe us now? We haven't done anything wrong, and we don't mean you any harm."

The man didn't move.

"Give him his gun, Mari. He won't try that again."

Mari didn't lower the weapon. She studied Jaazaniah's face. "Are you sure?" The agent man was tense as a spring. He would pounce any second.

"I'm positive. I haven't seen you in green yet, and green is my favorite color."

"What?" Mari lowered the gun. He sounded just like Purodad—neither one of them made a lick of sense. Flipping the gun in her hand, she stepped slowly toward the agent.

Jaazaniah nodded in answer to her questioning look. She handed the gun butt-first to the agent and cringed as the man pointed it at her face.

"You're still bleeding." Jaazaniah turned his back on the man and examined the wound below her shoulder. "Why didn't you say something? Was it for him?" He lifted a hand to her face and placed the other one on her shoulder. "God's doing this for your benefit, Groves. Mari's been in a lot of pain for this. I hope you're paying attention."

Mari sighed as warmth radiated out from his hands. Her eyes drifted shut even as she felt the mending. And the hands that held her with such tenderness. What had happened to Jaazaniah? He was suddenly so confident. So . . . confusing. Just like Purodad. He even sounded like Purodad.

The agent gasped and uttered a harsh-sounding word. Something heavy thudded to the ground.

The warmth gradually receded, and she opened her eyes. Jaazaniah was beaming at her. She didn't need to look at her shoulder to know that she'd been fully healed. "Thank you," she breathed. "Thank you for everything."

Jaazaniah turned to Groves and started laughing. "Isn't that the coolest thing you've ever seen? I still can't believe it's real!"

Groves sputtered like a candle wick drowning in the wax.

Mari pressed a hand to her chest while Jazz and the agent released Melchi from the chain binding him to the front of the car. Her traveling blouse wasn't bloody anymore, but there was still a ragged tear. She took a deep breath and reached two fingers inside the hole. *Yes! Thank You, Jesus!*

The healing had left her a scar—another Standing stone to remember Him by, a monument to His mercy and love and power.

"Hey, you okay?" Jaazaniah waded through twin beams of light to stand only a few inches away from her. His eyes burned into hers with an intensity that took her breath away. "Does it still hurt? We could pray some more."

"No, it's perfect." She lifted her eyes to his and sighed. "More than I ever could have hoped for."

Jazz stared at her for a long time, then finally broke the silence. "You were amazing. Like some kind of comic book hero. How did you do that?"

"How did I do what?" Mari ran a finger across the fresh scar on her shoulder. "You prayed the healing."

"No, taking Groves's gun away. It was like you were flying."

"It was the training. Purodad called it the kneeling kata. He made me practice it all—" A new thought exploded into her mind. Helicopter evasion, night vision training, breaching a perimeter guard . . . Purodad had seen her future. He'd known what would happen all along.

And trained her for every assault.

"Mari, what's wrong? Are you okay?"

"Purodad saw it. He made me practice it over and over and over again. I've been practicing all my life."

"What? Taking Groves's gun away?"

Mari nodded. "And everything else. The police officers in the alley, you and Hailey with the four soldiers, a man who grabbed me and tried to kiss me. He knew about all of it. That's what the training was for."

"You mean . . ." Jazz shook his head. "All those years of training. They were all . . . for this?"

"Oh no . . ." A lifetime of memories flooded into her mind. Suddenly she couldn't breathe. Her stomach was filled to the brim with the heavy nets.

"Are you okay?" Jazz put an arm around her and pulled her forward to lean against his broad chest. "What's wrong?"

All those years of training . . . She pressed her face into his chest and clung to him, sifting through the kata as the strong beat of his heart pounded in her ears.

"Mari?"

"There were hundreds of kata. Hundreds and hundreds: the six-man kata, the two-sword kata, the two-cars-and-four-guns kata . . . I've only used six. Out of hundreds!"

"It's okay. Purodad was looking out for you. You'll be fine."

"You don't understand." Mari leaned back and looked up into his eyes. "Jaazaniah, some of the kata . . . There was a whole set of dragon kata! *Dragons!* That's impossible, right? Night timey stories, that's all they are, right? The dragon kata are for tanks or jeeps or helicopters . . . There aren't any real dragons?"

Jazz shrugged and pulled her back into his arms. "A few days ago I would have said all *this* was impossible. Now . . ." He stroked her hair and let out a windy sigh. "I just don't know."

༄ 34 ༄

Jazz

JAZZ CLOMPED AFTER MARI as she glided between the trees with the grace of a forest nymph. A single, sustained note hung on the still night air, giving voice to the mad joy bubbling up inside him. High E-flat. What were they? Crickets? Tree frogs? The whole forest was rocking out. It made him want to throw back his head and sing at the top of his lungs. To run crashing through the woods, to dance and leap and crush her to his heart. For the first time in the history of his petty, self-serving life, he was finally alive!

Mari paused by a bank of trees and turned to Jazz with a shy smile. Moonlight flashed in shining eyes, etching her exquisite features in silver light. He stood there, transfixed. She was so beautiful. So absolutely, heart-breakingly beautiful. What could he say to someone like her? There weren't enough words in the universe, but he had to say something. He was staring like an idiot.

Her eyes fell away from his with the flutter of thick lashes. She leaned forward, framing a question with her lips. Jazz's heart strained against his chest, pulling him closer and closer with every beat. What was it she wanted to tell him? He leaned closer. He had to catch every drop of music that fell from her lips.

"Why are you stopping?" Groves's voice grated, discordant against the music. "If you're trying to find another bog to wade through, my shoes are already ruined."

Jazz squinted into the agent's flashlight and stepped toward the wall of trees. The guy was incredible. He'd seen what happened to the helicopters, but he was still waving that stupid gun around.

"The clearing's on the other side of these trees." Jazz held a branch back for Mari and plunged after her through a tunnel of rustling needles. The clearing stretched in front of them like a surreal clock. Ten black shadows dotted the edges, twisted and contorted into grotesque alien numerals.

"That's the tree I saw in my visions," Jazz whispered to Mari and pointed to the gnarled old oak. "The moon was right behind it when I got here. I took one look at it and realized what was happening. I hadn't seen Purodad's death. I'd seen mine."

Mari nodded and stared at the grotesque shadows dotting the field. Tears pooled in her eyes and then spilled over onto her cheeks.

"I'm sorry. I . . ."

She shook her head and looked up at him, determination hardening her eyes. "When the shimulo fell . . . what happened to them? Did their spirits turn on you and attack?"

"I don't understand. What do you mean attack?" Jazz glanced back at the clearing. Groves was moving among the bodies, shining his light from corpse to rigid corpse. "They just fell over and the voices were suddenly gone."

She nodded and stared up at him with wide eyes. Her lips were trembling.

"What? Do we need to get out of here? What's wrong?"

"Nothing's wrong. It's just . . . Purodad saw it. This is one of the bedtime stories he used to tell me."

"What stories? What are you—"

"They're all dead!" Groves's shout stabbed Jazz in the back. He turned and squinted into the light. Groves was kneeling beside one of the bodies. His gun was pointing straight at Jazz's chest.

"That's what I told you." Jazz stepped toward the kneeling agent. "There was a swarm of bright lights, and they just fell over backward."

"What is it? Some kind of virus? You know I have to take you in. If you're innocent, then everything will be fine, but if you're lying—"

Jazz took another step toward the agent. "The police are trying to kill us. Who knows how many others are in on this. You can shoot me if you want, but we're not going with you."

"Sorry, but I don't have a choice. My boss would kill me if I let you go. I'd lose my job." Groves rose to his feet and, still covering Jazz with the gun, edged around to the next body, and crouched down beside it.

"We didn't do anything wrong." Jazz stepped toward the agent, hands outstretched. "You don't have any evidence, and you know it."

"Evidence?" Groves swept the light around the clearing. "We have a whole field full of evidence. Even if you weren't responsible, you were a witness. I can't—" The light fixed on one of the bodies. Groves jumped up and ran over to the still form. He pulled back the cloak and let out a volley of oaths before running to the next body and the next.

"What's going on? What'd you find?" Jazz ran over to where the agent stood. He was staring at the lead figure, the one who had shot Jazz first.

Groves didn't say anything for a long time. He just stood there, shining his light on the man's frozen face. Jazz peered more closely.

It was the man in the suit.

"This guy"—Jazz finally found his voice—"he was at the police station. He's the one that yelled for everyone to arrest me."

Groves just stared. "His name was Jean Chevalier. He was the leader of the special task force I was assigned to. Four of the other men were agents on my team. I don't know how deep this goes, but it doesn't look good. These death robes aren't exactly agency issue."

Jazz stared down at the dead man's contorted features. "That's why we can't go to the police. Who knows how many others are involved? They'd be able to kill us any time they wanted."

"Okay, point taken." Groves sighed and stared down at his feet. "There's going to be an investigation. We'll have a million questions. You can't just disappear. I have to be able to contact you."

"Fine, we'll stay in touch. But right now I have to go . . ." He turned his back on Groves and walked over to the edge of the field to Mari. Her eyes were filled with questions as he took her by the hand and led her back into the dark vastness of the forest.

They waded through a shallow bog and climbed up the far bank. High E-flat. The woods chirruped all around them, belting out their joyous song as the moon filled the night with beams of bright magic.

Jazz took a deep breath and slid an arm around Mari's waist. She tensed but didn't pull away. His arm felt so right around her. He pulled her closer until her head was leaning against his chest. "You never told me the name of the story," he whispered. "Does it have a happy ending?"

"I think it's the story of"—her cheeks dimpled—"Jaazaniah and the Princess."

Jazz couldn't help it. His heart was so full, it spilled out in laughter. When he finally managed to catch his breath, he turned to her. "I take it I played the part of Jaazaniah. Who's the princess?"

Mari's smile faded. "I'm not sure." Her voice was suddenly grave. "It could be Hailey, but I think maybe it's Hollis. She's rich and beautiful, and she certainly acts like a princess . . ."

Her eyes drew him toward her, stealing the air from his lungs. He leaned forward, took a deep breath to keep from passing out, and then plunged heart and soul into the kiss he'd longed to give her since that first morning they'd met.

The night music swelled around them, buoying them up in its warm embrace. Moonlight puddled on their skin, ran down their cheeks to flow together into an infinite, inseparable stream.

Jazz finally pulled away and stared into Mari's radiant eyes.

A slow smile spread itself across her face. "I think maybe I was wrong."

"About the princess?"

She gave a slight nod, and her gaze drifted to the ground.

He cupped her chin gently in his hands and raised her eyes to his. "Think maybe she's somewhere close by?"

Her words brushed, sweet as a whisper, across his lips.

"Close as breathing, and never going away."

Epilogue

MARI TENSED AS A scorching torrent shrieked past her ears, whipping her wet hair into a frenzy. The wind pounded against her head, burning into her scalp like the noonday sun. It was too hot, too chaotic, too mind-numbingly loud.

"Please, no more!" She lunged forward in her seat, but strong hands pulled her back. "Make it stop. The Badness could come, and I'd never sense a thing!"

The roar of the wind machine snapped off. Comforting arms draped around her from behind. "Shhh . . . It's okay." Hollis's lilting voice.

"The mulo are gone." Hailey circled around the chair and dropped to a crouch in front of Mari. "Jazz said we're safe here. Don't you think we can trust him?"

"But all these machines and showers and contraptious whatnots. They're all so loud. How do you keep to your heads in all the fuss?"

Hailey looked down at the hot wind machine clasped like a gun in her hand. "You mean the blow-dryer?"

Mari nodded. "I don't mean to be ungrateful. I like being on the inside. I really do. But it's all so jumbly and distractful. I know the sons of Rechab went inside the house of the Lord, but the story didn't say anything about music-makers and blowing hot air in their ears."

"It's okay, sweetie. We don't need the blow-dryer." Hollis took the machine from Hailey and snapped it into the wall. "Your hair's perfect just the way it is."

"I know. It's disgusting." Hailey pulled a brush from the counter and sank it into Mari's stubborn curls. "There's enough here for all three of us. It's so not fair."

"I tried to tell you. Wash-soap makes it wild as stickers." Mari started to stand up, but Hailey eased her back down into the seat. "It'll be the good side of a week before it tames back down to jungle. Miss Caralee was right. She was going to saw it off at the roots and start over with a new crop, but she didn't want to dull her scissors."

Hollis made a strangled squeaking noise that set Hailey to the giggles. They attacked her hair from both sides with round brushes and long-toothed clamps. But they didn't stop there. After they were finished with her hair, they went to work on her face, brushing paint around her eyes and covering her lips with all kinds of sweet-smelling wax. But she knew it wouldn't do any good. She could take hot-water showers and go inside fancy hotels all she liked, but she was still just a swamp girl inside. All the paint in the world couldn't cover over the truth.

And Jaazaniah was a prophet of the Standing. He paid money for shopping and sang city music to life with his electrical guitar. Wherever he went, people left off what they were doing and gawped. Beautiful city women with their clacky-clack shoes and glory bright crowns of golden hair. He pretended not to notice, but she could see the smile behind his eyes. He was electricity and music and flame. The city wildness raged inside his heart. Its calamitous magic flowed joyful and free through his veins.

Even when he looked the fire into her eyes, even when he petted her hands with fingertips soft and warm as liquid wax, she knew the city wildness would never be tamed. He was a prophet, filled with the dook magic of old. And she was a simple swamp girl. Destined before time to be swept away by the glory of his passing train.

Yes, he said he loved her. But he was a prophet. He loved the whole world!

"Sweety?" Hollis's distorted features filled her eyes. "What's wrong? Tell me you're not still worried about tonight."

Mari shook her head and reached a hand to her face, but Hailey batted it away and dabbed at her eyes with a fluff of soft paper.

"It's okay. It's just dinner," Hailey cooed. "Melchi already checked out the restaurant. We'll be in a private room with two back doors. It'll be fine."

"And if you're worried about Jazz, you can cut that out right now." Hollis reached in and dabbed at her eyes with another tiny brush. "You've got to trust me on this. One look at this dress, and he'll melt through the floorboards. He's already so far gone it's disgusting."

"But he's a prophet of the Standing. I'm just a—"

"I don't care if he's Moses or Ghandi or Prince William himself . . . He's still a man. And no man on earth could know you for five minutes without falling madly and hopelessly—"

A clank sounded from the other room. The rumble of men's voices.

"He's here!" Mari clutched her hands to her chest. "What do I do? We haven't gone over the forks yet. I can't go inside a restaurant. I haven't finished the training!"

"Calm down. It's okay." Hollis took Mari by the hands and raised her out of the chair. "Believe me. Jazz isn't going to be looking at your forks."

"But I don't know what to do. He'll—"

"Shhh . . . It's okay. Now close your eyes."

"Close my eyes? Why?"

"For the grand unveiling." Hailey helped her out of the silky loose shirt they'd draped around her shoulders and lifted a hand to her face. "Close them tight. No peeking."

Mari closed her eyes and allowed them to guide her across the stonework floor.

"Hailey?" Melchi's voice sounded low and muffled through the door. "Our reservations are for seven o'clock. Are you about ready?"

"Just about." Pleasured excitement bubbled in Hailey's singsong voice. "Just a few more seconds."

They turned her toward the light. Unseen hands patted her hair and tugged at the fabric of her dress.

"Okay, open your eyes."

Mari squinted into the mirror. The dress shimmered and sparkled like the sun on windy waters. So beautiful . . . And her hair! It was perfect! Almost as good as city hair. "How'd you do it?" she gasped. "We scrubbed my hair with wash-soap. How'd you make it behave?"

"You like?" Hollis took Mari by the arms and angled her from side to side. "It's called conditioner. Stick with me, girl, and I'll teach you all kinds of city magic."

Mari stared at the gawping reflection. It was like looking into a dream. Painted lips, colored eyes . . . She looked just like a city person. Even better. She'd never seen a dress with so many sparkles. What would Jaazaniah think when he saw her? Would he think it was too much?

"I can call the restaurant if you need more time." Melchi's apologetic voice. "Groves says he can wait. His meeting with internal affairs was put off until tomorrow."

Hailey turned to Mari. "You okay? We can go over table etiquette again if you want, but I promise you'll be fine."

Mari swallowed and turned to face the door. Her arms and throat were exposed for all the world to see. She could already feel the warmth rising to her face.

"Okay, we're ready." Hailey turned a smile on Mari and then, with an encouraging nod, swung open the door.

Jaazaniah was standing between Melchi and Special Agent Groves. He turned toward the door and his eyes went wide.

A wall of roiling emotion hit Mari full in the face, choking off her breath. She staggered forward, leaning into the churning maelstrom. He thought she looked nice. Better than nice!

She stopped before him and looked up into his beautiful face as his feelings washed all around her.

He wanted to take her in his arms, to hold her, to crush his face tight against hers. Emerald light sparkling in jeweled eyes. So beautiful. So amazingly, impossibly beautiful . . .

And then, just as suddenly as they began, the feelings stopped.

Jaazaniah's mouth dropped open, and his face seemed to collapse in on itself. A look of stunned realization spread across his features. Apprehension. Disbelief. Disappointment.

He backed slowly away from her, looking her up and down. Rivers of deep sorrow splashed against her mind, the bitterness of crushing loss. His thoughts whispered through her. She'd be hurt. She'd never forgive him, but he had to tell her. There wasn't any other way. It was for her own good.

Mari nodded and looked down at the floor. He knew. He'd seen into her thoughts and couldn't let her feelings for him continue. He was a high prophet of the Standing. She should have known better. His love was prophet love. Not special man-and-woman love. She should have known from the start. "Don't worry about my feelings. I'm fine. Say what it is you have to say."

"I'm sorry." His voice was ragged and torn. He didn't want to hurt her, but it was for her own good. It was for everybody's good. "But we can't do it. We can't go to the restaurant tonight."

"Why?" Melchi moved to the door and snapped a metal latch across its edge. "Do you feel something? I thought you said we were safe."

"We were." Jaazaniah's eyes rested on Mari. "Until now. We probably still are. But Groves says he can't be sure. The task force was ultra-hush-hush. Nobody even knows who was part of it. For all we know there could be a hundred more agents out there. The longer we stay here in the city, the more likely they'll eventually track us down."

Melchi shot a look at Hailey and closed his eyes. He was searching with the *dikh* sight, but Mari knew he wouldn't see anything. Jazz had been looking at *her.* She was the reason he didn't want to go to the city restaurant.

He was disappointed with her.

"I'm sorry." Jaazaniah turned, but he couldn't look Mari in the eyes. "I didn't want it to be like this. I wanted tonight to be special, but now . . . it's not safe. We need to pack up our stuff and leave. Tonight. The further we get from New Orleans, the better I'll feel."

Jazz's face distorted and shimmered in Mari's eyes. Suddenly she couldn't breathe. "I understand." She choked out the words. "You must be free to fight the battle. I'll change into traveling clothes and wrap Purodad's Bible."

"Mari!" He started toward her, but she made the curtsey and fled the room. She closed the door to her retreat quietly and then flung herself onto the cloudy-soft bed. They'd said it was hers to sleep on. All to herself alone. They were supposed to go to a city restaurant and eat salads with special forks and sugared milk as cold as the winter rains, but Jaazaniah was disappointed. He didn't want to go with her at all.

She pulled Purodad's Bible from the wall-table and hugged it to her chest. The others were racing around now. She could hear them hollering orders and packing things away in big boxes. She should be helping them. The strain in their voices was thick as stew.

But here she was, Little Miss Slug-a-bed. Too up in her britches to say the sorrys and help with the chores. Miss Caralee would have brought out the switch limb.

She opened the weathered old tome and flipped through its whispery pages. Purodad's warm, flowing hand leaped from the pages. His comforting presence surrounded her, soothing and caressing, brushing the jaggy hurtfuls from her heart. Turning to the front of the book, she opened it to the family notices section and read the inscription Jaazaniah had written there after the burial services in the swamp.

Friday, May 13. Jonadab Rechabson and Caralee Boogeos were taken but not defeated. They stand now before Jesus forever.

She wiped a hand across her eyes and looked up at the names of those who had stood before. Jeremiah Rechabson—born Friday, November 13. Hollis Rechabson . . .

Hollis? Mari searched up and down the page. It was Purodad's handwriting, but it looked all new and clean-like. What did it mean? Hollis wasn't a Standing name. Was it another secret clue?

Mari examined the handwritten inscription. Hollis Rechabson, born April 29 . . . *2018?* That couldn't be right.

A knock sounded at the door. "Mari? Are you okay?" Jaazaniah's gentle voice. "Can I come in?"

Mari stared at the dated inscriptions covering the page. *2015, 2016, 2017* . . . They were all from the future. The whole page was from the future.

"Mari? What's wrong?" Jaazaniah pounded on the door. He was worried now. If she didn't say something soon, he'd break the door to tiny pieces.

"I'm fine. Everything is fine. You can come in. I just—"

The door swung open and Jaazaniah swept into the room. He took one look at her and stopped dead in his tracks. Suddenly he looked confused.

"Mari, I know you're upset. You and the girls went to a lot of trouble getting ready for tonight. I was looking forward to it too, I really was, but I can explain. When I saw your dress—"

"You don't like it." Mari looked down at the Bible.

"No, it's not that. I just—"

"It's a city dress for city people. I tried to tell Hailey and Hollis, but they wouldn't listen."

"Mari, you look fabulous. Better than fabulous. I love the dress, and I . . . love you. How could you think otherwise?"

"You were disappointed. I could feel it."

"Of course I was disappointed. But not with you. It's . . . Mari, I've seen the dress before. In my visions. It was my one last vision of the future, and in it we were both alive. So I knew until I saw the dress in real life, we were safe. It was the one get-out-of-jail-free card I had left. That's why I haven't been worried about the enemy, because I hadn't seen the dress yet. But now that the dress has come out, all bets are off. Anything can happen."

"That's why you were sad? You're afraid of the danger? I thought you were disappointed."

"Of course I was disappointed. I'm still disappointed. I had to tell the most beautiful woman I've ever known I couldn't go out with her—after she'd spent all afternoon preparing for our first date. Do you have any idea how *not me* that was?"

Mari shook her head. He was talking prophet talk again. She wasn't meant to understand.

"Mari, I love you. You've got to believe that. I'm Jaazaniah the Prophet, and you're my princess, but if we're going to live happily ever after, I've got to do what it takes to keep you safe."

Happily ever after? The smiles broke out all over Mari's face. It was man-woman love he was talking about! She looked down at the Bible, let her eyes drift across Purodad's beautiful hand.

It was too much to hope for. Too much happy even for a dream.

Then she saw the words—written boldly across the top of the page. *Birth announcements.* Sucking in her breath, she turned to the page before—the page of marriages—and scanned the list of names and dates. There it was: Jaazaniah Rechabson and Mariutza Glapion.

She and Jaazaniah would be married in less than a year!

"Mari?" Jaazaniah crossed the room and knelt down beside her. "Mari, what's wrong? You're shaking like a leaf."

"Yes! The answer is yes!" Mari slid from the bed and flung her arms around his neck.

Strong arms closed around her, pulling her into the stormy warmth of his embrace. Gentle fingers stroked shivers through her hair. She sighed and looked up into that beautiful face. The face she would spend a lifetime savoring.

Amazement and wonder. Happily-ever-after love.

Jaazaniah shook his head wondrous slow and looked the wild magic into her eyes. "I'm sorry . . . what was the question?"

"You'll see." Mari laughed and reached behind her to snap the Bible shut. "Probably more than once."

Acknowledgments

I MAY HAVE BEEN the hand that penned these words, but behind me and working through me is a body of self-sacrificing, loving, encouraging friends who gave up much to make this book happen. I'd like to thank:

Ari and Peter—The eyes who light my world and fill me with joy.

Rick Acker—The backbone who held me upright when I was about to fall.

Karen Ball, Julie Gwinn, and Steve Laube—The ears who listen and the smiles who never cease to delight.

Sylvia and Mike Turpin—The memories and experiences of all it means to be Gypsy.

Tosca Lee and Carl Olsen—The brains who shone light on the dark gray matters of my story.

Peter Sleeper, Michael Platt, Julian Farnam, and Craig Coengsten—The mouths who speak wisdom and comfort into my life.

Mom, Dad, Kathy, and Bill—The corpus collosa who understand what corpus collosum means.

Lynne Thompson—The tendons and ligaments who helped join the body together.

Ken Jensen—The strong right hand who tutored me in bu-speak.

Katie Vorreiter, Jim Rubart, Katie Cushman, and Jenn Doucette—The winks and nods of encouragement.

The Criswells, Englers, Halls, Roscoes, Scharffs, Syeva Breus, and Robinette—The knees who hold me up in prayer.

Anette Acker, Lori Arthur, Jan Collins, Tasra Dawson, Catherine Felt, Ellen Graebe, Donna Fujimoto, Judith Guerino, Nancy Hird, Margaret Horwitz, Kim Lavoie, Sibley Law, Manuel Magana, Candy Campbell, Jennifer Rempel, Barbara Smith, Jennifer Vallier, Cheri Williams, and John Zelaski—The SCUM-spattered feet upon whom I stand, and having done everything, stand firm.

Without all of you, this hand can do nothing.